PHILISTIA

GRANT ALLEN

Philistia

Grant Allen

© 1st World Library, 2007
PO Box 2211
Fairfield, IA 52556
www.1stworldlibrary.com
First Edition

LCCN: 2007901792

Softcover ISBN: 978-1-4218-4260-8
Hardcover ISBN: 978-1-4218-4162-5
eBook ISBN: 978-1-4218-4358-2

Purchase *"Philistia"*
as a traditional bound book at:
www.1stWorldLibrary.com/purchase.asp?ISBN=978-1-4218-4260-8

1st World Library is a literary, educational organization
dedicated to:

- Creating a free internet library of downloadable ebooks

- Hosting writing competitions and offering book
publishing scholarships.

Interested in more 1st World Library books?
contact: literacy@1stworldlibrary.com
Check us out at: www.1stworldlibrary.com

1st World Library Literary Society

Giving Back to the World

"If you want to work on the core problem, it's early school literacy."

- James Barksdale, former CEO of Netscape

"No skill is more crucial to the future of a child, or to a democratic and prosperous society, than literacy."

- Los Angeles Times

Literacy... means far more than learning how to read and write... The aim is to transmit... knowledge and promote social participation."

- UNESCO

"Literacy is not a luxury, it is a right and a responsibility. If our world is to meet the challenges of the twenty-first century we must harness the energy and creativity of all our citizens."

- President Bill Clinton

"Parents should be encouraged to read to their children, and teachers should be equipped with all available techniques for teaching literacy, so the varying needs and capacities of individual kids can be taken into account."

- Hugh Mackay

CONTENTS

CHAPTER I

CHILDREN OF LIGHT

It was Sunday evening, and on Sundays Max Schurz, the chief of the London Socialists, always held his weekly receptions. That night his cosmopolitan refugee friends were all at liberty; his French disciples could pour in from the little lanes and courts in Soho, where, since the Commune, they had plied their peaceful trades as engravers, picture-framers, artists'-colourmen, models, pointers, and so forth—for most of them were hangers-on in one way or another of the artistic world; his German adherents could stroll round, pipe in mouth, from their printing-houses, their ham-and-beef shops, or their naturalists' chambers, where they stuffed birds or set up exotic butterflies in little cabinets—for most of them were more or less literary or scientific in their pursuits; and his few English sympathisers, chiefly dissatisfied philosophical Radicals of the upper classes, could drop in casually for a chat and a smoke, on their way home from the churches to which they had been dutifully escorting their un-emancipated wives and sisters. Max Schurz kept open house for all on Sunday evenings, and there was not a drawing-room in London better filled than his with the very advanced and not undistinguished set who alone had the much-prized entree of his exclusive salon.

The salon itself did not form any component part of Max Schurz's own private residence in any way. The great Socialist, the man whose mandates shook the thrones of Russia and Austria, whose movements spread terror in Paris and Berlin, whose dictates were even obeyed in Kerry and in Chicago, occupied for his own use two small rooms at the top of a shabby composite tenement in a doubtful district of Marylebone. The little parlour where he carried on his trade of a microscope-lens grinder would not have sufficed to hold one-tenth of the eager half-washed crowd that pressed itself enthusiastically upon him every Sunday. But a large room on the ground floor of the tenement, opening towards the main street, was used during the week by one of his French refugee friends as a dancing-saloon; and in this room on every Sunday evening the uncrowned king of the proletariate Socialists was permitted to hold his royal levees. Thither all that was best and truest in the socially rebellions classes domiciled in London used to make its way; and there men calmly talked over the ultimate chances of social revolutions which would have made the hair of respectable Philistine Marylebone stand stiffly on end, had it only known the rank political heresies that were quietly hatching in its unconscious midst.

While Max Schurz's hall was rapidly filling with the polyglot crowd of democratic solidarists, Ernest Le Breton and his brother were waiting in the chilly little drawing-room at Epsilon Terrrace, Bayswater, for the expected arrival of Harry Oswald. Ernest had promised to introduce Oswald to Max Schurz's reception; and it was now past eight o'clock, getting rather a late hour for those simple-minded, early-rising Communists. 'I'm afraid, Herbert,' said Ernest to his brother, 'he forgets that Max is a working-man who has to be at his trade again punctually by seven o'clock to-morrow. He thinks he's going out to a regular society At Home, where ten o'clock's considered just the beginning of the evening. Max won't at all like his turning up so late; it smells of non-productivity.'

'If Herr Schurz wants to convert the world,' Herbert answered chillily, rolling himself a tiny cigarette, 'he must convince the unproductive as well as the proletariate before he can set things fairly on the roll for better arrangement. The proletariate's all very well in its way, no doubt, but the unproductive happen to hold the key of the situation. One convert like you or me is worth a thousand ignorant East-end labourers, with nothing but their hands and their votes to count upon.'

'But you are not a convert, Herbert.'

'I didn't say I was. I'm a critic. There's no necessity to throw oneself open-armed into the embrace of either party. The wise man can wait and watch the progress of the game, backing the winner for the time being at all the critical moments, and hedging if necessary when the chances turn momentarily against the favourite. There's a ring at the bell: that's Oswald; let's go down to the door to meet him.'

Ernest ran down the stairs rapidly, as was his wont; Herbert followed in a more leisurely fashion, still rolling the cigarette between his delicate finger and thumb. 'Goodness gracious, Oswald!' Ernest exclaimed as his friend stepped in, 'why, you've actually come in evening dress! A white tie and all! What on earth will Max say? He'll be perfectly scandalised at such a shocking and unprecedented outrage. This will never do; you must dissemble somehow or other.'

Oswald laughed. 'I had no idea,' he said, 'Herr Schurz was such a truculent sans-culotte as that comes to. As it was an evening reception I thought, of course, one ought to turn up in evening clothes.'

'Evening clothes! My dear fellow, how on earth do you suppose a set of poor Leicester Square outlaws are going to get themselves correctly set up in black broadcloth coats and trousers? They might wash their white ties themselves, to be sure; they mostly do their own washing, I believe, in their own basins.' ('And not much at that either,' put in Herbert, paren-thetically.) 'But as to evening clothes, why, they'd as soon think of arraying themselves for dinner in full court dress as of putting on an obscurantist swallow-tail. It's the badge of a class, a distinct aristocratic outrage; we must alter it at once, I assure you, Oswald.'

'At any rate,' said Oswald laughing, 'I've had the pleasure of finding myself accused for the first time in the course of my existence of being aristocratic. It's quite worth while going to Max Schurz's once in one's life, if it were only for the sake of that single new sensation.'

'Well, my dear fellow, we must rectify you, anyhow, before you go. Let me see; luckily you've got your dust-coat on, and you needn't take that off; it'll do splendidly to hide your coat and waistcoat. I'll lend you a blue tie, which will at once transform your upper man entirely. But you show the cloven hoof below; the trousers will surely betray you. They're absolutely inadmissible under any circumstances whatsoever, as the Court Circular says, and you must positively wear a coloured pair of Herbert's instead of them. Run upstairs quickly, there's a good fellow, and get rid of the mark of the Beast as fast as you can.'

Oswald did as he was told without demur, and in about a minute more presented himself again, with the mark of the Beast certainly most effectually obliterated, at least so far as outer appearance went. His blue tie, light dust-coat, and borrowed grey trousers, made up an ensemble much more like an omnibus conductor out for a holiday than a gentleman of the period in correct evening dress. 'Now mind,' Ernest said seriously, as he opened the door, 'whatever you do, Oswald, if you stew to death for it—and Schurz's rooms are often very close and hot, I can assure you—don't for heaven's sake go and unbutton your dust-coat. If you do they'll see at once you're a wolf in sheep's clothing, and I shouldn't be at all surprised if they were to turn and rend you. At least, I'm sure Max would be very much annoyed with me for unsocially introducing a plutocratic traitor into the bosom of the fold.'

They walked along briskly in the direction of Marylebone, and stopped at last at a dull, yellow-washed house, which bore on its door a very dingy brass plate, inscribed in red letters, 'M. et Mdlle. Tirard. Salon de Danse.' Ernest opened the door without ringing, and turned down the passage towards the salon. 'Remember,' he said, turning to Harry Oswald by way of a last warning, with his hand on the inner door-handle, 'coute que coute, my dear fellow, don't on any account open your dust-coat. No anti-social opinions; and please bear in mind that Max is, in his own way, a potentate.'

The big hall, badly lighted by a few contribution candles (for the whole colony subscribed to the best of its ability for the support of the weekly entertainment), was all alive with eager figures and the mingled busy hum of earnest conversation. A few chairs ranged round the wall were mostly occupied by Mdlle. Tirard and the other ladies of the Socialist party; but the mass of the guests were men, and they were almost all smoking, in utter indifference to the scanty presence of the fair sex. Not that they were intentionally rude or boorish; that they never were; except where an emperor or an aristocrat is concerned, there is no being on earth more courteous, kindly, and considerate for the feelings of others than your exiled Socialist. He has suffered much himself in his own time, and so miseris succurrere discit. Emperors he mentally classes with cobras, tarantulas, and scorpions, as outside the pale of human-itarian sympathies altogether; but, with this slight political exception, he is the broadest and tenderest and most catholic in his feelings of all living breathing creatures. However, the ladies of his party have all been brought up from their child-hood onward in a mingled atmosphere of smoke and demo-cracy; so that he no more thinks of abstaining from tobacco in their presence than he thinks of commiserating the poor fish for being so dreadfully wet, or the unfortunate mole for his unpleasantly slimy diet of live earthworms.

'Herr Schurz,' said Ernest, singling out the great leader in the gloom immediately, 'I've brought my brother Herbert here, whom you know already, to see you, as well as another Oxford friend of mind, Mr. Harry Oswald, Fellow and Lecturer of Oriel. He's almost one of us at heart, I'm happy to say, and at any rate I'm sure you'll be glad to make his acquaintance.'

The little spare wizened-up grey man, in the threadbare brown velveteen jacket, who stood in the middle of the hall, caught

Ernest's hand warmly, and held it for a moment fettered in his iron grip. There was an honesty in that grip and in those hazy blue-spectacled eyes that nobody could for a second misunderstand. If an emperor had been introduced to Max Schurz he might have felt a little abashed one minute at the old Socialist's royal disdain, but he could not have failed to say to himself as he looked at him from head to foot, 'Here, at least, is a true man.' So Harry Oswald felt, as the spare grey thinker took his hand in his, and grasped it firmly with a kindly pressure, but less friendly than that with which he had greeted his known admirer, Ernest Le Breton. As for Herbert, he merely bowed to him politely from a little distance; and Herbert, who had picked up at once with a Polish exile in a corner, returned the bow frigidly without coming up to the host himself at all for a moment's welcome.

'I'm always pleased to meet friends of the cause from Oxford,' Herr Schurz said, in almost perfect English. 'We want recruits most of all among the thinking classes. If we are ever to make headway against the banded monopolies—against the place-holders, the land-grabbers, the labour-taxers, the robbers of the poor—we must first secure the perfect undivided confidence of the brain-workers, the thinkers, and the writers. At present everything is against us; we are but a little leaven, trying vainly in our helpless fashion to leaven the whole lump. The capitalist journals carry off all the writing talent in the world; they are timid, as capital must always be; they tremble for their tens of thousands a year, and their vast circulations among the proper-tied classes. We cannot get at the heart of the people, save by the Archimedean lever of the thinking world. For that reason, my dear Le Breton, I am always glad to muster here your Oxford neophytes.'

'And yet, Herr Schurz,' said Ernest gently, 'you know we must not after all despair. Look at the history of your own people! When the cause of Jehovah seemed most hopeless, there were still seven thousand left in Israel who had not bowed the knee to Baal. We are gaining strength every day, while they are losing it.'

Grant Allen

'Ah yes, my friend. I know that too,' the old man answered, with a solemn shake of the head; 'but the wheels move slowly, they move slowly—very surely, but oh, so slowly. You are young, friend Ernest, and I am growing old. You look forward to the future with hope; I look back to the past with regret: so many years gone, so little, so very little done. It will come, it will come as surely as the next glacial period, but I shall not live to see it. I stand like Moses on Pisgah; I see the promised land before me; I look down upon the equally allotted viney-ards, and the glebe flowing with milk and honey in the distance; but I shall not lead you into it; I shall not even lead you against the Canaanites; another than I must lead you in. But I am an old man, Mr. Oswald, an old man now, and I am talking all about myself—an anti-social trick we have inherited from our fathers. What is your friend's special line at Oxford, did you say, Ernest?'

'Oswald is a mathematician, sir,' said Ernest, 'perhaps the greatest mathematician among the younger men in the whole University.'

'Ah! that is well. We want exact science. We want clear and definite thinking. Biologists and physicists and mathemati-cians, those are our best recruits, you may depend upon it. We need logic, not mere gas. Our French friends and our Irish friends—I have nothing in the world to say against them; they are useful men, ardent men, full of fire, full of enthusiasm, ready to do and dare anything—but they lack ballast. You can't take the kingdom of heaven by storm. The social revolution is not to be accomplished by violence, it is not even to be carried by the most vivid eloquence; the victory will be in the end to the clearest brain and the subtlest intellect. The orthodox political economists are clever sophists; they mask and confuse the truth very speciously; we must have keen eyes and sharp noses to spy out and scent out their tortuous fallacies. I'm glad you're a mathematician, Mr. Oswald. And so you have thought on social problems?'

'I have read "Gold and the Proletariate,"' Oswald answered

modestly, 'and I learned much from it, and thought more. I won't say you have quite converted me, Herr Schurz, but you have given me plenty of food for future reflection.'

'That is well, said the old man, passing one skinny brown hand gently up and down over the other. 'That is well. There's no hurry. Don't make up your mind too fast. Don't jump at conclusions. It's intellectual dishonesty to do that. Wait till you have convinced yourself. Spell out your problems slowly; they are not easy ones; try to see how the present complex system works; try to probe its inequalities and injustices; try to compare it with the ideal commonwealth: and you'll find the light in the end, you'll find the light.'

As he spoke, Herbert Le Breton lounged up quietly from his farther corner towards the little group. 'Ah, your brother, Ernest!' said Max Schurz, drawing himself up a little more stiffly; 'he has found the light already, I believe, but he neglects it; still he is not with us, and he that is not with us is against us. You hold aloof always, Mr. Herbert, is it not so?'

'Well, not quite aloof, Herr Schurz, I'm certain, but not on your side exactly either. I like to look on and hold the balance evenly, not to throw my own weight too lightly into either stale. The objective attitude of the mere spectator is after all the right one for an impartial philosopher to take up.'

'Ah, Mr. Herbert, this philosophy of your Oxford contemplative Radicals is only another name for a kind of social selfishness, I fancy,' said the old man solemnly. 'It seems to me your head is with us, but your heart, your heart is elsewhere.'

Herbert Le Breton played a moment quietly with the Roman aureus of Domitian on his watch-chain; then he said slowly in his clear cold voice, 'There may be something in that, no doubt, Herr Schurz, for each of us has his own game to play, and while the world remains unreformed, he must play it on his own gambit to a great extent, without reference to the independent game of others. We all agree that the board is too full of counters, and as each counter is not responsible for its own presence and position on the board, having been put there without previous consultation by the players, we must each do the best we can for ourselves in our own fashion. My sympathies, as you say, are on your side, but perhaps my interests lie the other way, and after all, till you start your millennium, we must all rattle along as well as we can in the box together, jarring against one another in our old ugly round of competition, and supply and demand, and survival of the fittest, and mutual accommodation, and all the rest of it, to the end of the chapter. Every man for himself and God for us all, you know. You have the logic, to be sure, Herr Schurz, but the monopolists have the law and the money.'

'Ah, yes,' said the old Socialist grimly; 'Demas, Demas; he and his silver mine; you remember your Bunyan, don't you? Well, all faiths and systems have their Demases. The cares of this world and the deceitfulness of riches. He's bursar of his college, isn't he, Ernest? I thought so. "He had the bag, and bare what was put therein." A dangerous office, isn't it, Mr. Oswald? A very dangerous office. You can't touch pitch or property without being defiled.'

'You at least, sir, said Ernest, reverentially, 'have kept yourself unspotted from the world.'

The old man sighed, and turned for a moment to speak in French to a tall, big-bearded new-comer who advanced to meet him. 'Impossible!' he said quickly; 'I am truly distressed to hear it. It is very imprudent, very unnecessary.'

'What is the news?' asked Ernest, also in French.

The new-comer answered him with a marked South Russian accent. 'There has been another attempt on the life of Alexander Nicolaiovitch.'

'You don't mean to say so!' cried Ernest in surprise.

'Yes, I do,' replied the Russian, 'and it has nearly succeeded too.'

'An attempt on whom?' asked Oswald, who was new to the peculiar vocabulary of the Socialists, and not particularly accustomed to following spoken French.

'On Alexander Nicolaiovitch,' answered the red-bearded stranger.

'Not the Czar?' Oswald inquired of Ernest.

'Yes, the one whom you call Czar,' said the stranger, quickly, in tolerable English. The confusion of tongues seemed to be treated as a small matter at Max Schurz's receptions, for everybody appeared to speak all languages at once, in the true spirit of solidarity, as though Babel had never been.

Oswald did not attempt to conceal a slight gesture of horror. The tall Russian looked down upon him commiseratingly. 'He is of the Few?' he asked of Ernest, that being the slang of the initiated for a member of the aristocratic and capitalist oligarchy.

'Not exactly,' Ernest answered with a smile; 'but he has not entirely learned the way we here regard these penal measures. His sympathies are one-sided as to Alexander, no doubt. He thinks merely of the hunted, wretched life the man bears about with him, and he forgets poor bleeding, groaning, downtrodden, long-suffering Russia. It is the common way of Englishmen. They do not realise Siberia and Poland and the Third Section, and all the rest of it; they think only of Alexander as of the benevolent despot who freed the serf and befriended the Bulgarian. They never remember that they have all the freedom and privileges themselves which you poor Russians ask for in vain; they do not bear in mind that he has only to sign his name to a constitution, a very little constitution, and he might walk abroad as light-hearted in St. Petersburg to-morrow as you and I walk in Regent Street to-day. We are mostly lopsided, we English, but you must bear with us in our obliquity; we have had freedom ourselves so long that we hardly know how to make due allowance for those unfortunate folks who are still in search of it.'

'If you had an Alexander yourselves for half a day,' the Russian said fiercely, turning to Oswald, 'you would soon see the difference. You would forget your virtuous indignation against Nihilist assassins in the white heat of your anger against unendurable tyranny. You had a King Charles in England once—the mere shadow of a Russian Czar—and you were not so very ceremonious with him, you order-loving English, after all.'

'It is a foolish thing, Borodinsky,' said Max Schurz, looking up from the long telegram the other had handed him, 'and I told Toroloff as much a fortnight ago, when he spoke to me about the matter. You can do no good by these constant attacks, and you only rouse the minds of the oligarchy against you by your importunity. Bloodshed will avail us nothing; the world cannot be regenerated by a baptism like that. Every peasant won over, every student enrolled, every mother engaged to feed her little ones on the gospel of Socialism together with her own milk, is worth a thousand times more to us and to the people than a dead Czar. If your friends had really blown him up, what then? You would have had another Czar, and another Third Section, and another reign of terror, and another raid and massacre; and we should have lost twenty good men from our poor little side for ever. We must not waste the salt of the earth in that reckless fashion. Besides, I don't like this dynamite. It's a bad argument, it smacks too much of the old royal and repressive method. You know the motto Louis Quatorze used to cast on his bronze cannon—"Ultima ratio regum." Well, we Socialists ought to be able to find better logic for our opponents than that, oughtn't we?'

'But in Russia,' cried the bearded man hotly, 'in poor stricken-down groaning Russia, what other argument have they left us? Are we to be hunted to death without real law or trial, tortured into sham confessions, deluded with mock pardons, arraigned before hypocritical tribunals, ensnared by all the chicanery, and lying, and treachery, and ferreting of the false bureaucracy, with its spies, and its bloodhounds, and its knout-bearing police-agents; and then are we not to make war the only way we can—open war, mind you, with fair declaration, and due formalities, and proper warning beforehand—against the irresponsible autocrat and his wire-pulled office-puppets who kill us off mercilessly? You are too hard upon us, Herr Schurz; even you yourself have no sympathy at all for unhappy Russia.'

The old man looked up at him tenderly and regretfully. 'My poor Borodinsky,' he said in a gentle tremulous voice, 'I have indeed sympathy and pity in abundance for you. I do not blame you; you will have enough and to spare to do that, even here in free England; I would not say a harsh word against you or your terrible methods for all the world. You have been hard-driven, and you stand at bay like tigers. But I think you are going to work the wrong way, not using your energies to the best possible advantage for the proletariate. What we have really got to do is to gain over every man, woman, and child of the working-classes individually, and to array on our side all the learning and intellect and economical science of the thinking classes individually; and then we can present such a grand united front to the banded monopolists that for very shame they will not dare to gainsay us. Indeed, if it comes to that, we can leave them quietly alone, till for pure hunger they will come and beg our assistance. When we have enticed away all the workmen from their masters to our co-operative factories, the masters may keep their rusty empty mills and looms and engines to themselves as long as they like, but they must come to us in the end, and ask us to give them the bread they used to refuse us. For my part, I would kill no man and rob no man; but I would let no man kill or rob another either.'

'And how about Alexander Nicolaiovitch, then?' persisted the Russian, eagerly. 'Has he killed none in his loathsome prisons and in his Siberian quicksilver mines? Has he robbed none of their own hardly got earnings by his poisoned vodki and his autocratically imposed taxes and imposts? Who gave him an absolute hereditary right to put us to death, to throw us in prison, to take our money from us against our will and without our leave, to treat us as if we existed, body and soul, and wives and children, only as chattels for the greater glory of his own orthodox imperial majesty? If we may justly slay the highway robber who meets us, arms in hand, in the outskirts of the city, and demands of us our money or our life, may we not justly slay Alexander Nicolaiovitch, who comes to our homes in the person of his tax-gatherers to take the bread out of our children's mouths and to help himself to whatever he chooses by the divine right of his Romanoff heirship? I tell you, Herr Max, we may blamelessly lie in wait for him wherever we find him, and whoso says us nay is siding with the wolf against the lambs, with the robber and the slayer against the honest representative of right and justice.'

'I never met a Nihilist before,' said Oswald to Ernest, in a half-undertone,' and it never struck me to think what they might have to say for themselves from their own side of the question.'

'That's one of the uses of coming here to Herr Schurz's,' Ernest answered quickly. 'You may not agree with all you hear, but at least you learn to see others as they see themselves; whereas if you mix always in English society, and read only English papers, you will see them only as we English see them.'

'But just fancy,' Oswald went on, as they both stood back a little to make way for others who wished for interviews with the great man, 'just fancy that this Borodinsky, or whatever his name may be, has himself very likely helped in dynamite plots, or manufactured nitro-glycerine cartridges to blow up the Czar; and yet we stand here talking with him as coolly as if he were an ordinary respectable innocent Englishman.'

'What of that?' Ernest answered, smiling. 'Didn't we meet Prince Strelinoffsky at Oriel last term, and didn't we talk with him too, as if he was an honest, hard-working, bread-earning Christian? and yet we knew he was a member of the St.

Petersburg office clique, and at the bottom of half the trouble in Poland for the last ten years or so. Grant even that Borodinsky is quite wrong in his way of dealing with noxious autocrats, and yet which do you think is the worst criminal of the two—he with his little honest glazier's shop in a back slum of Paddington, or Strelinoffsky with his jewelled fingers calmly signing accursed warrants to send childing Polish women to die of cold and hunger and ill-treatment on the way to Siberia?'

'Well, really, Le Breton, you know I'm a passably good Radical, but you're positively just one stage too Radical even for me.'

'Come here oftener,' answered Ernest; 'and perhaps you'll begin to think a little differently about some things.'

An hour later in the evening Max Schurz found Ernest alone in a quiet corner. 'One moment, my dear Le Breton,' he said; 'you know I always like to find out all about people's political antecedents; it helps one to fathom the potentialities of their characters. From what social stratum, now, do we get your clever friend, Mr. Oswald?'

'His father's a petty tradesman in a country town in Devonshire, I believe,' Ernest answered; 'and he himself is a good general democrat, without any very pronounced socialistic colouring.'

'A petty tradesman! Hum, I thought so. He has rather the mental bearing and equipment of a man from the petite bourgeoisie. I have been talking to him, and drawing him out. Clever, very, and with good instincts, but not wholly and entirely sound. A fibre wrong somewhere, socially speaking, a false note suspected in his ideas of life; too much acquiescence in the thing that is, and too little faith or enthusiasm for the thing that ought to be. But we shall make something of him yet. He has read "Gold" and understands it. That is already a beginning. Bring him again. I shall always be glad to see

Grant Allen

him here.'

'I will,' said Ernest, 'and I believe the more you know him, Herr Max, the better you will like him.'

'And what did you think of the sons of the prophets?' asked Herbert Le Breton of Oswald as they left the salon at the close of the reception.

'Frankly speaking,' answered Oswald, looking half aside at Ernest, 'I didn't quite care for all of them—the Nihilists and Communards took my breath away at first; but as to Max Schurz himself I think there can be only one opinion possible about him.'

'And that is—?'

'That he's a magnificent old man, with a genuine apostolic inspiration. I don't care twopence whether he is right or wrong, but he's a perfectly splendid old fellow, as honest and transparent as the day's long. He believes in it all, and would give his life for it freely, if he thought he could forward the cause a single inch by doing it.'

'You're quite right,' said Herbert calmly. 'He's an Elijah thrown blankly upon these prosaic latter days; and what's more, his gospel's all true; but it doesn't matter a sou to you or me, for it will never come about in our time, no nor for a century after. "Post nos millennium." So what on earth's the good of our troubling our poor overworked heads about it?'

'He's the only really great man I ever knew,' said Ernest enthusiastically, 'and I consider that his friendship's the one thing in my life that has been really and truly worth living for. If a pessimist were to ask me what was the use of human existence, I should give him a card of introduction to go to Max Schurz's.'

'Excuse my interrupting your rhapsody, Ernest,' Herbert put

in blandly, 'but will you have your own trousers tonight, Oswald, or will you wear mine back to your lodgings now, and I'll send one of the servants round with yours for them in the morning?'

'Thanks,' said Harry Oswald, slapping the sides of the unopened dust-coat; 'I think I'll go home as I am at present, and I'll recover the marks of the Beast again to-morrow. You see, I didn't betray my evening waistcoat after all, now did I?'

And they parted at the corner, each of them going his own way in his own mood and manner.

CHAPTER II

THE COASTS OF THE GENTILES

The decayed and disfranchised borough of Calcombe Pomeroy, or Calcombe-on-the-Sea, is one of the prettiest and quietest little out-of-the-way watering-places in the whole smiling southern slope of the county of Devon. Thank heaven, the Great Western Railway, when planning its organised devastations along the beautiful rural region of the South Hams, left poor little Calcombe out in the cold; and the consequence is that those few people who still love to linger in the uncontaminated rustic England of our wiser forefathers can here find a beach unspoiled by goat-carriages or black-faced minstrels, a tiny parade uninvaded by stucco terraces or German brass bands, and an ancient stone pier off which swimmers may take a header direct, in the early morning, before the sumptuary edicts of his worship the Mayor compel them to resort to the use of bathing-machines and the decent covering of an approved costume, between the hours of eight and eight. A board beside the mouth of the harbour, signed by a Secretary of State to his late Majesty King William the Fourth, still announces to a heedless world the tolls to be paid for entry by the ships that never arrive; and a superannuated official in a wooden leg and a gold cap-band retains the honourable sinecure of a harbour-mastership, with a hypothetical salary nominally payable from the non-existent fees and port dues. The little river Cale, at the bottom of whose combe the wee town nestles snugly, has cut itself a deep valley in the soft sandstone hills; and the gap in the cliffs formed by its mouth gives room for the few hundred yards of level on which the antiquated little parade is warmly ensconced. On either hand tall bluffs of brilliant red marl raise their honeycombed faces fronting the sea; and in the distance the sheeny grey rocks of the harder Devonian promontories gleam like watered satin in the slant rays of the afternoon sun. Altogether a very sleepy little old-world place is Calcombe Pomeroy, specially reserved by the overruling chance of the universe to be a summer retreat for quiet, peace-loving, old-world people.

The Londoner who escapes for a while from the great teeming human ant-hill, with its dark foggy lanes and solid firmament of hanging smoke, to draw in a little unadulterated atmosphere at Calcombe Pomeroy, finds himself landed by the Plymouth slow train at Calcombe Road Station, twelve miles by cross-country highway from his final destination. The little grey box, described in the time-tables as a commodious omnibus, which takes him on for the rest of his journey, crawls slowly up the first six miles to the summit of the intervening range at the Cross Foxes Inn, and jolts swiftly down the other six miles, with red hot drag creaking and groaning lugubriously, till it seems to topple over sheer into the sea at the clambering High Street of the old borough. As you turn to descend the seaward slope at the Cross Foxes, you appear to leave modern industrial England and the nineteenth century well behind you on the north, and you go down into a little isolated primaeval dale, cut off from all the outer world by the high ridge that girds it round on every side, and turned only on the southern front towards the open Channel and the backing sun. Half-way down the steep cobble-paved High Street, just after you pass the big dull russet church, a small shop on the left-hand side bears a signboard with the painted legend, 'Oswald, Family Grocer and Provision Dealer.' In the front bay window of that red-brick house, built out just over the shop, Harry Oswald, Fellow and Lecturer of Oriel College, Oxford, kept his big oak writing-desk; and at that desk he might be seen reading or writing on most mornings during the long vacation, after the end of his three weeks' stay at a London West-end lodging-house, from which he had paid his first visit to Max Schurz's

Sunday evening receptions.

'Two pounds of best black tea, good quality—yours is generally atrocious, Mrs. Oswald—that's the next thing on the list,' said poor trembling, shaky Miss Luttrell, the Squire's sister, a palsied old lady with a quavering, querulous, rasping voice. 'Two pounds of best black tea, and mind you don't send it all dust, as you usually do. No good tea to be got nowadays, since they took the duties off and ruined the country. And I see a tall young man lounging about the place sometimes, and never touching his hat to me as he ought to do. Young people have no manners in these times, Mrs. Oswald, as they used to have when you and I were young. Your son, I suppose, come home from sea or something? He's in the fish-curing line, isn't he, I think I've heard you say?'

'I don't rightly know who 'ee may mean, Miss Luttrell,' replied the mother proudly, 'by a young man lounging about the place; but my son's at home from Oxford at present for his vacations, and he isn't in the fish-curing line at all, ma'am, but he's a Fellow of his college, as I've told 'ee more than once already; but you're getting old, I see, Miss Luttrell, and your memory isn't just what it had used to be, dost know.'

'Oh, at Oxford, is he?' Miss Luttrell chimed on vacantly, wagging her wrinkled old head in solemn deprecation of tke evil omen. She knew it as well as Mrs. Oswald herself did, having heard the fact at least a thousand times before; but she made it a matter of principle never to encourage these upstart pretensions on the part of the lower orders, and just to keep them rigorously at their proper level she always made a feint of forgetting any steps in advance which they might have been bold enough to take, without humbly obtaining her previous permission, out of their original and natural obscurity. 'Fellow of his college is he, really? Fellow of a college! Dear me, how completely Oxford is going to the dogs. Admitting all kinds of odd people into the University, I understand. Why, my second brother—the Archdeacon, you know—was a Fellow of Magdalen for some time in his younger days. You surprise me, quite. Fellow of a college! You're perfectly sure he isn't a National schoolmaster at Oxford instead, and that you and his father haven't got the two things mixed up together in your heads, Mrs. Oswald?'

'No, ma'am, we'in perfectly sure of it, and we haven't got the things mixed up in our heads at all, no more nor you have, Miss Luttrell. He was a scholar of Trinity first, and now he's got a Fellowship at Oriel. You must mind hearing all about it at the time, only you're getting so forgetful like now, with years and such like.' Mrs. Oswald knew there was nothing that annoyed the old lady so much as any allusion to her increasing age or infirmities, and she took her revenge out of her in that simple retributive fashion.

'A scholar of Trinity, was he? Ah, yes, patronage will do a great deal in these days, for certain. The Rector took a wonderful interest in your boy, I think, Mrs. Oswald. He went to Plymouth Grammar School, I remember now, with a nomination no doubt; and there, I dare say, he attracted some attention, being a decent, hard-working lad, and got sent to Oxford with a sizarship, or something of the sort; there are all kinds of arrangements like that at the Universities, I believe, to encourage poor young men of respectable character. They become missionaries or ushers in the end, and often get very good salaries, considering everything, I'm told.'

'There you're wrong, again, ma'am,' put in Mrs. Oswald, stoutly. 'My husband, he sent Harry to Plymouth School at our own expense; and after that he got an exhibition from the school, and an open scholarship, I think they call it, at the college; and he's been no more beholden to patronage, ma'am, than your brother the Archdeacon was, nor for the matter o' that not so much neither; for I've a'ways understood the old Squire sent him first to the Charterhouse, and afterwards he got a living through Lord Modbury's influence, as the Squire voted regular with the Modbury people for the borough and county. But George was always independent, Miss Luttrell, and beholden to neither Luttrells nor Modburies, and that I tell 'ee to your face, ma'am, and no shame of it either.'

'Well, well, Mrs. Oswald,' said the old lady, shaking her head more violently than ever at this direct discomfiture, 'I don't want to argue with you about the matter. I dare say your son's a very worthy young man, and has worked his way up into a position he wasn't intended for by Providence. But it's no business of mine, thank heaven, it's no business of mine, for I'm not responsible for all the vagaries of all the tradespeople on my brother's estate, nor don't want to be. There's Mrs. Figgins, now, the baker's wife; her daughter has just chosen to get married to a bank clerk in London; and I said to her this morning, "Well, Mrs. Figgins, so you've let your Polly go and pick up with some young fellow from town that you've never seen before, haven't you? And that's the way of all you people. You marry your girls to bank clerks without a reference, for the sake of getting 'em off your hands, and what's the consequence? They rob their employers to keep up a pretty household for their wives, as if they were fine ladies; and then at last the thing's discovered, there comes a smash, they run away to America, and you have your daughters and their children thrown back again penniless upon your hands." That's what I said to her, Mrs. Oswald. And how's YOUR daughter, by the way—Jemima I think you call her; how's she, eh, tell me?'

'I beg your pardon, Miss Luttrell, but her name's not Jemima; it's Edith.'

'Oh, Edith, is it? Well to be sure! The grand names girls have dangling about with them nowadays! My name's plain Catherine, and it's good enough for me, thank goodness. But these young ladies of the new style must be Ediths and Eleanors and Ophelias, and all that heathenish kind of thing, as if they were princesses of the blood or play-actresses, instead of being good Christian Susans and Janes and Betties, like their grandmothers were before them. And Miss Edith, now, what is SHE doing?'

'She's doing nothing in particular at this moment, Miss

Luttrell, leastways not so far as I know of; but she's going up to Oxford part of this term on a visit to her brother.'

'Going up to Oxford, my good woman! Why, heaven bless the girl, she'd much better stop at home and learn her catechism. She should try to do her duty in that station of life to which it has pleased Providence to call her, instead of running after young gentlemen above her own rank and place in society at Oxford. Tell her so from me, Mrs. Oswald, and mind you don't send the tea dusty. Two pounds of your best, if you please, as soon as you can send it. Good-morning.' And Miss Luttrell, having discovered the absolute truth of the shocking rumour which had reached her about Edith's projected visit, the confirmation of which was the sole object of her colloquy, wagged her way out of the shop again successfully, and was duly assisted by the page-boy into her shambling little palsied donkey-chair.

'That was all the old cat came about, you warr'nt you,' muttered Mr. Oswald himself from behind his biscuit-boxes. 'Must have heard it from the Rector's wife, and wanted to find out if it was true, to go and tell Mrs. Walters o' such a bit o' turble presumptiousness.'

Meanwhile, in the little study with the bow-window over the shop, Harry and Edie Oswald were busily discussing the necessary preparations for Edie's long-promised visit to the University.

'I hope you've got everything nice in the way of dress, you know, Edie,' said Harry. 'You'll want a decent dinner dress, of course, for you'll be asked out to dine at least once or twice; and I want you to have everything exceedingly proper and pretty.'

'I think I've got all I need in that way, Harry; I've my dark poplin, cut square in the bodice, for one dinner dress, and my high black silk to fall back upon for another. Worn open in front, with a lace handkerchief and a locket, it does really very

　　　　　　　　　Grant Allen

nicely. Then I've got three afternoon dresses, the grey you gave me, the sage-greeny aesthetic one, and the peacock-blue with the satin box-pleats. It's a charming dress, the peacock-blue; it looks as if it might have stepped straight out of a genuine Titian. It came home from Miss Wells's this morning. Wait five minutes, like a dear boy, and I'll run and put it on and let you see me in it.'

'That's a good girl, do. I'm so anxious you should have all your clothes the exact pink of perfection, Popsy. Though I'm afraid I'm a very poor critic in that matter—if you were only a problem in space of four dimensions, now! Yet, after all, every man or woman is more of a problem than anything in x square plus y square you can possibly set yourself.'

Edie ran lightly up into her own room, and soon reappeared clad resplendent in the new peacock-blue dress, with hat and parasol to match, and a little creamy lamb's-wool scarf thrown with artful carelessness around her pretty neck and shoulders. Harry looked at her with unfeigned admiration. Indeed, you would not easily find many lighter or more fairly-like little girls than Edie Oswald, even in the beautiful half-Celtic South Hams of Devon. In figure she was rather small than short, for though she was but a wee thing, her form was so exactly and delicately modelled that she might have looked tall if she stood alone at a little distance. She never walked, but seemed to dance about from place to place, so buoyant and light, that Harry doubted whether in her case gravitation could really vary as the square of the distance—it seemed, in fact, to be almost diminished in the proportions of the cube. Her hair and eyes—such big bright eyes!—were dark; but her complexion was scarcely brunette, and the colour in her cheeks was rich and peach-like, after the true Devonian type. She was dimpled whenever she smiled, and she smiled often; her full lips giving a peculiar ripe look to her laughing mouth that suited admirably with her light and delicate style of beauty. Perhaps some people might have thought them too full; certainly they irresistibly suggested to a critical eye the distinct notion of kissability. As she stood there, faintly blushing, waiting to be admired by her brother, in her neatly fitting dainty blue dress, her lips half parted, and her arms held carelessly at her side, she looked about as much like a fairy picture as it is given to mere human flesh and blood to look.

'It's delicious, Edie,' said Harry, surveying her from, head to foot with a smile of satisfaction which made her blush deepen; 'it's simply delicious. Where on earth did you get the idea of it?'

'Well, it's partly the present style,' said Edie; 'but I took the notion of the bodice partly too from that Vandyck, you know, in the Palazzo Bossi at Genoa.'

'I remember, I remember,' Harry answered, contemplating her with an admiring eye. 'Now just turn round and show me how it sits behind, Edie. You recollect Theophile Gautier says the one great advantage which a beautiful woman possesses over a beautiful statue is this, that while a man has to walk round the beautiful statue in order to see it from every side, he can ask the beautiful woman to turn herself round and let him see her, without requiring to take that trouble.'

'Theophile Gautier was a horrid man, and if anybody but my brother quoted such a thing as that to me I should be very angry with him indeed.'

'Theophile Gautier was quite as horrid as you consider him to be, and if you were anybody but my sister it isn't probable I should have quoted him to you. But if there is any statue on earth prettier or more graceful than you are in that dress at this moment, Edie, then the Venus of Milo ought immediately to be pulverised to ultimate atoms for a rank artistic impostor.'

'Thank you, Harry, for the compliment. What pretty things you must be capable of saying to somebody else's sister, when you're so polite and courtly to your own.'

'On the contrary, Popsy, when it comes to somebody else's

sister I'm much too nervous and funky to say anything of the kind. But you must at least do Gautier the justice to observe that if I had described a circle round you, instead of allowing you to revolve once on your own axis, I shouldn't have been able to get the gloss on the satin in the sunlight as I do now that you turn the panniers toward the window. That, you must admit, is a very important aesthetic consideration.'

'Oh, of course it's essentially a sunshiny dress,' said Edie, smiling. 'It's meant to be worn out of doors, on a fine after-noon, when the light is falling slantwise, you know, just as it does now through the low window. That's the light painters always choose for doing satin in.'

'It's certainly very pretty,' Harry went on, musing; 'but I'm afraid Le Breton would say it was a serious piece of economic hubris.'

'Piece of what?' asked Edie quickly.

'Piece of hubris—an economical outrage, don't you see; a gross anti-social and individualist demonstration. Hubris, you know, is Greek for insolence; at least, not quite insolence, but a sort of pride and overweening rebelliousness against the gods, the kind of arrogance that brings Nemesis after it, you understand. It was hubris in Agamemnon and Xerxes to go swelling about and ruffling themselves like turkey-cocks, because they were great conquerors and all that sort of thing; and it was their Nemesis to get murdered by Clytemnestra, or jolly well beaten by the Athenians at Salamis. Well, Le Breton always uses the word for anything that he thinks socially wrong—and he thinks a good many things socially wrong, I can tell you—anything that partakes of the nature of a class distinction, or a mere vulgar ostentation of wealth, or a useless waste of good, serviceable, labour-gotten material. He would call it hubris to have silver spoons when electroplate would do just as well; or to keep a valet for your own personal attendant, making one man into the mere bodily appanage of another; or to buy anything you didn't really need, causing somebody else to do work for you which might otherwise have been avoided.'

'Which Mr. Le Breton—the elder or the younger one?'

'Oh, the younger—Ernest. As for Herbert, the Fellow of St. Aldate's, he's not troubled with any such scruples; he takes the world as he finds it.'

'They've both gone in for their degrees, haven't they?'

'Yes, Herbert has got a fellowship; Ernest's up in residence still looking about for one.'

'It's Ernest that would think my dress a piece of what-you-may-call-it?'

'Yes, Ernest.'

'Then I'm sure I shan't like him. I should insist upon every woman's natural right to wear the dress or hat or bonnet that suits her complexion best.'

'You can't tell, Edie, till you've met him. He's a very good fellow; and of one thing I'm certain, whatever he thinks right he does, and sticks to it.'

'But do YOU think, Harry, I oughtn't to wear a new peacock-blue camel-hair dress on my first visit up to Oxford?'

'Well, Edie dear, I don't quite know what my own opinions are exactly upon that matter. I'm not an economist, you see, I'm a man of science. When I look at you, standing there so pretty in that pretty dress, I feel inclined to say to myself, "Every woman ought to do her best to make herself look as beautiful as she can for the common delectation of all humanity." Your beauty, a Greek would have said, is a gift from the gods to us all, and we ought all gratefully to make the most of it. I'm sure *I* do.'

Grant Allen

'Thank you, Harry, again. You're in your politest humour this afternoon.'

'But then, on the other hand, I know if Le Breton were here he'd soon argue me over to the other side. He has the enthusiasm of humanity so strong upon him that you can't help agreeing with him as long as he's talking to you.'

'Then if he were here you'd probably make me put away the peacock-blue, for fear of hubris and Nemesis and so forth, and go up to Oxford a perfect fright in my shabby old Indian tussore!'

'I don't know that I should do that, even then, Edie. In the first place, nothing on earth could make you look a perfect fright, or anything like one, Popsy dear; and in the second place, I don't know that I'm Socialist enough myself ever to have the courage of my opinions as Le Breton has. Certainly, I should never attempt to force them unwillingly upon others. You must remember, Edie, it's one thing for Le Breton to be so communistic as all that comes to, and quite another thing for you and me. Le Breton's father was a general and a knight, you see; and people will never forget that his mother's Lady Le Breton still, whatever he does. He may do what he likes in the way of social eccentricities, and the world will only say he's such a very strange advanced young fellow. But if I were to take you up to Oxford badly dressed, or out of the fashion, or looking peculiar in any way, the world wouldn't put it down to our political beliefs, but would say we were mere country tradespeople by birth, and didn't know any better. That makes a lot of difference, you know.'

'You're quite right, Harry; and yet, do you know, I think there must be something, too, in sticking to one's own opinions, like Mr. Le Breton. I should stick to mine, I'm sure, and wear whatever dress I liked, in spite of anybody. It's a sweet thing, really, isn't it?' And she turned herself round, craning over her shoulder to look at the effect, in a vain attempt to assume an objective attitude towards her own back.

'I'm glad I'm going to Oxford at last, Harry,' she said, after a short pause. 'I HAVE so longed to go all these years while you were an undergraduate; and I'm dying to have got there, now the chance has really come at last, after all. I shall glory in the place, I'm certain; and it'll be so nice to make the acquaintance of all your clever friends.'

'Well, Edie,' said her brother, smiling gently at the light, joyous, tremulous little figure, 'I think I've done right in putting it off till now. It's just as well you haven't gone up to Oxford till after your trip on the Continent with me. That three months in Paris, and Switzerland, and Venice, and Florence, did you a lot of good, you see; improved you, and gave you tone, and supplied you with things to talk about.'

'Why, you oughtn't to think I needed any improvement at all, sir,' Edie answered, pouting; 'and as to talking, I'm not aware I had ever any dearth of subjects for conversation even before I went on the Continent. There are things enough to be said about heaven and earth in England, surely, without one having to hurry through France and Italy, like Cook's excursionists, just to hunt up something fresh to chatter about. It's my belief that a person who can't find anything new to say about the every-day world around her won't discover much suggestive matter for conversation in a Continental Bradshaw. It's like that feeble watery lady I met at the table d'hote at Geneva. From something she said I gathered she'd been in India, and I asked her how she liked it. "Oh," she said, "it's very hot." I told her I had heard so before. Presently she said something casually about having been in Brazil. I asked her what sort of place Brazil was. "Oh." she said, "it's dreadfully hot." I told her I'd heard that too. By-and-by she began to talk again about Barbadoes. "What did you think of the West Indies?" I said. "Oh," said she, "they're terribly hot, really." I told her I had gathered as much from previous travellers. And that was positively all in the end I ever got out of her, for all her travels.'

'My dear Edie, I've always admitted that you were simply perfect,' Harry said, glancing at her with visible admiration, 'and I don't think anything on earth could possibly improve you—except perhaps a judicious course of differential and integral calculus, which might possibly serve to tone down slightly your exuberant and excessive vitality. Still, you know, from the point of view of society, which is a force we have always to reckon with—a constant, in fact, that we may call Pi—there can be no doubt in the world that to have been on the Continent is a differentiating factor in one's social position. It doesn't matter in the least what your own private evaluation of Pi may be; if you don't happen to know the particular things and places that Pi knows, Pi's evaluation of you will be approximately a minimum, of that you may be certain.'

'Well, for my part, I don't care twopence about Pi as you call it,' said Edie, tossing her pretty little head contemptuously; 'but I'm very glad indeed to have been on the Continent for my own sake, because of the pictures, and palaces, and mountains, and waterfalls we've seen, and not because of Pi's opinion of me for having seen them. I would have been the same person really whether I'd seen them or not; but I'm so much the richer myself for that view from the top of the Col de Balme, and for that Murillo—oh, do you remember the flood of light on that Murillo?—in the far corner of that delicious gallery at Bologna. Why, mother darling, what on earth has been vexing you?'

'Nothing at all, Edie dear; leastways, that is, nothing to speak of,' said her mother, coming up from the shop hot and flurried from her desperate encounter with the redoubtable Miss Luttrell.

'Oh, I know just what it is, darling,' cried the girl, putting her arm around her mother's waist caressingly, and drawing her down to kiss her face half a dozen times over in her outburst of sympathy. 'That horrid old Miss Catherine has been here again, I'm sure, for I saw her going out of the shop just now, and she's been saying something or other spiteful, as she always does, to vex my dearie. What did she say to you to-day, now do tell us, duckie mother?'

'Well, there,' said Mrs. Oswald, half laughing and half crying, 'I can't tell 'ee exactly what she did say, but it was just the kind of thing that she mostly does, impudent like, just to hurt a body's feelings. She said you'd better not go to Oxford, Edie, but stop at home and learn your catechism.'

'You might have pointed out to her, mother dear,' said the young man, smoothing her hair softly with his hand, and kissing her forehead, 'that in the most advanced intellectual centres the Church catechism is perhaps no longer regarded as the absolute ultimatum of the highest and deepest economical wisdom.'

'Bless your heart, Harry, what'd be the good of talking that way to the likes of she? She wouldn't understand a single word of what you were driving at. It must be all plain sailing with her, without it's in the way of spite, and then she sees her chance to tack round the hardest corner with half a wind in her sails only, as soon as look at it. Her sharpness goes all off toward ill-nature, that it do. Why, she said you'd got on at Oxford by good patronage!'

'There, you see, Edie,' cried Harry demonstratively, 'that's an infinitesimal fraction of Pi; that's a minute decimal of this great, sneering, ugly aggregate "society" that we have to deal with whether we will or no, and that rends us and grinds us to powder if only it can once get in the thin end of a chance. Take shaky bitter old Miss Catherine for your unit, multiply her to the nth, and there you see the irreducible power we have to fight against. All one's political economy is very well in its way; but the practical master of the situation is Pi, sitting autocratically in many-headed judgment on our poor solitary little individualities, and crushing us irretrievably with the dead weight of its inexorable cumulative nothingness. And to think that that quivering old mass of perambulating jealousy— that living incarnation of envy, hatred, malice, and all uncharitableness—should be able to make you uncomfortable for a single moment, mother darling, with her petty, dribbling, doddering venom, why, it's simply unendurable.'

'There now, Harry,' said Mrs. Oswald, relenting, 'you mustn't be too hard, neither, on poor old Miss Catherine. She's a bit soured, you see, by disappointments and one thing and another. She doesn't mean it, really, but it's just her nature. Folks can't be blamed for their nature, now, can they?'

'It occurs to me,' said Harry quietly, 'that vipers only sting because it's their nature; and Dr. Watts has made a similar observation with regard to the growling and fighting of bears and lions. But I'm not aware that anybody has yet proposed to get up a Society for the protection of those much-misunderstood creatures, on the ground that they are not really responsible for their own inherited dispositions. Mr. William Sikes had a nature (no doubt congenital) which impelled him to beat his wife—I'm not sure that she was even his wife at all, now I come to think of it, but that's a mere detail—and to kick his familiar acquaintances casually about the head. We, on the other hand, have natures which impel us, when we catch Mr. William Sikes indulging in these innate idiosyncrasies by way of recreation, to clap him promptly into prison, and even, under certain aggravating conditions, to cause him to be hanged by the neck till he be dead. This may be a regrettable incident of our own peculiar dispositions, mother dear, but it has at least the same justification as Mr. Sikes's or the bears' and lions', that 'tis our nature to. And I feel pretty much the same way about old Miss Luttrell.'

'Well, there,' said his mother, kissing him gently, 'you're a bad rebellious boy to be calling names, like a chatter-mag, and I won't listen to you any longer. How pretty Edie do look in her new dress, to be sure, Harry. I'll warr'nt there won't be a prettier girl in Oxford next week than what she is; no, nor a better one and a sweeter one neither.'

Harry put his arms round both their waists at once, with an affectionate pressure; and they went down to their old-fashioned tea together in the little parlour behind the shop, looking out over the garden, and the beach, and the great cliffs beyond on either hand, to the very farthest edge of the distant clear-cut blue horizon.

Grant Allen

CHAPTER III

MAGDALEN QUAD

The Reverend Arthur Collingham Berkeley, curate of St. Fredegond's, lounged lazily in his own neatly padded wicker-work easy-chair, opposite the large lattice-paned windows of his pretty little first-floor rooms in the front quad of Magdalen.

'There's a great deal to be said, Le Breton, in favour of October term,' he observed, in his soft, musical voice, as he gazed pensively across the central grass-plot to the crimson drapery of the Founder's Tower. 'Just look at that magnificent Virginia creeper over there, now; just look at the way the red on it melts imperceptibly into Tyrian purple and cloth of gold! Isn't that in itself argument enough to fling at Hartmann's head, if he ventured to come here sprinkling about his heresies, with his affected little spray-shooter, in the midst of a drowsy Oxford autumn? The Cardinal never saw Virginia creeper, I suppose; a man of his taste wouldn't have been guilty of committing such a gross practical anachronism as that, any more than he would have smoked a cigarette before tobacco was invented; but if only he could have seen the October effect on that tower yonder, he'd have acknowledged that his own hat and robe were positively nowhere in the running, for colour, wouldn't he?'

'Well,' answered Herbert, putting down the Venetian glass goblet he had been examining closely with due care into its niche in the over-mantel, 'I've no doubt Wolsey had too much historical sense ever to step entirely out of his own century, like my brother Ernest, for instance; but I've never heard his opinion on the subject of colour-harmonies, and I should suspect it of having been distinctly tinged with nascent symptoms of renaissance vulgarity. This is a lovely bit of Venetian, really, Berkeley. How the dickens do you manage to pick up all these pretty things, I wonder? Why can't I afford them, now?'

'What a question for the endowed and established to put to a poor starving devil of a curate like me!' said Berkeley lightly. 'You, an incarnate sinecure and vested interest, a creature revelling in an unearned income of fabulous Oriental magnificence—I dare say, putting one thing with another, fully as much as five hundred a year—to ask me, the unbeneficed and insignificant, with my wretched pittance of eighty pounds per annum and my three pass-men a term for classical mods, how I scrape together the few miserable, hoarded ha'pence which I grudgingly invest in my pots and pipkins! I save them from my dinner, Mr. Bursar—I save them. If the Church only recognised modest merit as it ought to do!—if the bishops only listened with due attention to the sound and scholarly exegesis of my Sunday evening discourses at St. Fredegond's!—then, indeed, I might be disposed to regard things through a more satisfied medium —the medium of a nice, fat, juicy country living. But for you, Le Breton—you, sir, a pluralist and a sanguisorb of the deepest dye—to reproach me with my Franciscan poverty—oh, it's too cruel!'

'I'm an abuse, I know,' Herbert answered, smiling and waving his hand gracefully. 'I at once admit it. Abuses exist, unhappily; and while they continue do so, isn't it better they should envisage themselves as me than as some other and probably less deserving fellow?'

'No, it's not, decidedly. I should much prefer that one of them envisaged itself as me.'

'Ah, of course. From your own strictly subjective point of view that's very natural. I also look at the question abstractly from the side of the empirical ego, and correctly deduce a corresponding conclusion. Only then, you see, the terms of the minor premiss are luckily reversed.'

'Well, my dear fellow,' said the curate, 'the fact about the tea-things is this. You eat up your income, devour your substance in riotous living; I prefer to feast my eyes and ears to my grosser senses. You dine at high table, and fare sumptuously every day; I take a commons of cold beef for lunch, and have tea off an egg and roll in my own rooms at seven. You drink St. Emilion or still hock; I drink water from the well or the cup that cheers but not obfuscates. The difference goes to pay for the crockery. Do likewise, and with your untold wealth you might play Aunt Sally at Oriental blue, and take cock-shots with a boot-jack at hawthorn-pattern vases.'

'At any rate, Berkeley, you always manage to get your money's worth of amusement out of your money.'

'Of course, because I lay myself out to do it. Buy a bottle of champagne, drink it off, and there you have to show for your total permanent investment on the transaction the memory of a noisy evening and a headache the next morning. Buy a flute, or a book of poems, or a little picture, or a Palissy platter, and you have something to turn to with delight and admiration for half a lifetime.'

'Ah, but it isn't everybody who can isolate himself so utterly from the workaday world and live so completely in his own little paradise of art as you can, my dear fellow. Non omnia possumus omnes. You seem to be always up in the aesthetic clouds, with your own music automatically laid on, and no need of cherubim or seraphim to chant continually for your gratification. Play me something of your own on your flute now, like a good fellow.'

'No, I won't; because the spirit doesn't move me. It's treachery to the divine gift to play when you don't want to. Besides, what's the use of playing before YOU when you're not the dean of a musical cathedral? David was wiser; he played only before Saul, who had of course all the livings in his own gift, no doubt. I've got a new thing running in my head this very minute that you shall hear though, all the same, as soon as I've hammered it into shape—a sort of villanette in music, a little whiff of country freshness, suggested by the new ethereal acquisition, little Miss Butterfly. Have you seen Miss Butterfly yet?'

'Not by that name, at any rate. Who is she?'

'Oh, the name's my own invention. Mademoiselle Volauvent, I mean—the little bit of whirligig thistledown from Devonshire, Oswald's sister, you know, of Oriel.'

'Ah, that one! Yes; just caught a glimpse of her in the High on Thursday. Very pretty, certainly, and as airy as a humming-bird.'

'That's her! She's coming here to lunch this morning. If you're a good boy, and will promise not to say anything naughty, you may stop and meet her. She's a nice little thing, but rather timid at seeing so many fresh faces. You mustn't frighten her by discussing the Absolute and the Unconditioned, or bore her by talking about Aristotle's Politics, or the revolutions in Corcyra. For you know, my dear Le Breton, if you HAVE a fault, it is that you're such a consummate and irrepressible prig; now aren't you really?'

'I'm hardly a fair judge on that subject, I suppose, Berkeley; but if YOU have a rudimentary glimmering of a virtue, it is that you're such a deliciously frank and yet considerate critic. I'll pocket your rudeness though, and eat your lunch, in spite of it. Is Miss Butterfly, as you call her, as stand-off as her brother?'

'Not at all. She's accueillante to the last degree.'

Grant Allen

'Very restricted, I suppose—a country girl of the first water? Horizon absolutely bounded by the high hedges of her native parish?'

'Oh dear no! Anything but that. She's like her brother, naturally quick and adaptive.'

'Oswald's an excellent fellow in his way,' said Herbert, button-holing his own waistcoat; 'but he's spoilt by two bad traits. In the first place, he's so dreadfully conscious of the fact that he has risen from a lower position; and then, again, he's so engrossingly and pervadingly mathematical. X square seems to have seized upon him bodily, and to have wormed its fatal way into his very marrow.'

'Ah, you must remember, he's true to his first love. Culture came to him first, while yet he abode in Philistia, under the playful disguise of a conic section. He scaled his way out of Gath by means of a treatise on elementary trigonometry, and evaded Askelon on the wings of an undulatory theory of light. It is different with us, you know, who have emerged from the land of darkness by the regular classical and literary highway. We feed upon Rabelais and Burton; he flits carelessly from flower to flower of the theory of Quantics. If he were an idealist painter, like Rossetti, he would paint great allegorical pictures for us, representing an asymptotic curve appearing to him in a dream, and introducing that blushing maiden, Hyperbola, to his affectionate consideration.'

As Berkeley spoke, a rap sounded on the oak, and Ernest Le Breton entered the room.

'What, you here, Herbert?' he said with a shade of displeasure in his tone. 'Are you, too, of the bidden?'

'Berkeley has asked me to stop and lunch with him, if that's what you mean.'

'We shall be quite a party,' said Ernest, seating himself, and looking abstractedly round the room. 'Why, Berkeley,' as his eye fell upon the Venetian vase, 'you've positively got some more gew-gaws here. This one's new, isn't it? Eh!'

'Yes. I picked it up for a song, this long, at a stranded village in the Apennines. Literally for a song, for it cost me just what I got from Fradelli for that last little piece of mine. It's very pretty, isn't it?'

'Very; exquisite, really; the blending of the tones is so perfect. I wish I knew what to think about these things. I can't make up my mind about them. Sometimes I think it's all right to make them and buy them; sometimes I think it's all wrong.'

'Oh, if that's your difficulty,' said Berkeley, pulling his white tie straight at the tiny round looking-glass, 'I can easily reassure you. Do you think a hundred and eighty pounds a year an excessive sum for one person to spend upon his own entire living?'

'It doesn't seem so, as expenses go amongst US,' said Ernest, seriously, 'though I dare say it would look like shocking extravagance to a working man with a wife and family.'

'Very well, that's the very outside I ever spend upon myself in any one year, for the excellent reason that it's all I ever get to spend in any way. Now, why shouldn't I spend it on the things that please me best and are joys for ever, instead of on the things that disappear at once and perish in the using?'

'Ah, but that's not the whole question,' Ernest answered, looking at the curate fixedly. 'What right have you and I to spend so much when others are wanting for bread? And what right have you or I to make other people work at producing these useless trinkets for our sole selfish gratification?'

'Well now, Le Breton,' said the parson, assuming a more serious tone, 'you know you're a reasonable creature, so I don't mind discussing this question with you. You've got an ethical foundation to your nature, and you want to see things done on decent grounds of distributive justice. There I am one with you. But you've also got an aesthetic side to your nature, which makes you worth arguing with upon the matter. I won't argue with your vulgar materialised socialist, who would break up the frieze of the Parthenon for road metal, or pull down Giotto's frescoes because they represent scenes in the fabulous lives of saints and martyrs. You know what a work of art is when you see it; and therefore you're worth arguing with, which your vulgar Continental socialist really isn't. The one cogent argument for him is the whiff of grape-shot.'

'I recognise,' said Ernest, 'that the works of art, of poetry, or of music, which we possess are a grand inheritance from the past; and I would do all I could to preserve them intact for those that come after us.'

'I'm sure you would. No restoration or tinkering in you, I'm certain. Well, then, would you give anything for a world which hadn't got this aesthetic side to its corporate existence? Would you give anything for a world which didn't care at all for painting, sculpture, music, poetry? I wouldn't. I don't want such a world. I won't countenance such a world. I'll do nothing to further or advance such a world. It's utterly repugnant to me, and I banish it, as Themistocles banished the Athenians.'

'But consider,' said Ernest, 'we live in a world where men and women are actually starving. How can we reconcile to our consciences the spending of one penny on one useless thing when others are dying of sheer want, and cold, and nakedness? That's the great question that's always oppressing my poor dissatisfied conscience.'

'So it does everybody's—except Herbert's: he explains it all on biological grounds as the beautiful discriminative action of natural selection. Simple, but not consolatory. Still, look at the other side of the question. Suppose you and everybody else were to give up all superfluities, and confine all your energies to the unlimited production of bare necessaries. Suppose you occupy every acre of land with your corn-fields, or your piggeries; and sweep away all the parks, and woods, and heaths, and moorlands in England. Suppose you keep on letting your population multiply as fast as it chooses—and it WILL multiply, you know, in that ugly, reckless, anti-Malthusian fashion of its own—till every rood of ground maintains its man, and only just maintains him; and what will you have got then?'

'A dead level of abject pauperism,' put in Herbert blandly; 'a reductio ad absurdum of all your visionary Schurzian philosophy, my dear Ernest. Look at it another way, now, and just consider. Which really and truly matters most to you and me, a great work of art or a highly respectable horny-handed son of toil, whose acquaintance we have never had the pleasure of personally making? Suppose you read in the Times that the respectable horny-handed one has fallen off a scaffolding and broken his neck; and that the Dresden Madonna has been burnt by an unexpected accident; which of the two items of intelligence affects you the most acutely? My dear fellow, you may push your humanitarian enthusiasm as far as ever you like; but in your heart of hearts you know as well as I do that you'll deeply regret the loss of the Madonna, and you'll never think again about the fate of the respectable horny-handed, his wife or children.'

Ernest's answer, if he had any to make, was effectually nipped in the bud by the entrance of the scout, who came in to announce Mr. and Miss Oswald and Mrs. Martindale. Edie wore the grey dress, her brother's present, and flitted into the room after her joyous fashion, full of her first fresh delight at the cloistered quad of Magdalen.

'What a delicious college, Mr. Berkeley!' she said, holding out her hand to him brightly. 'Good-morning, Mr. Le Breton; this is your brother, I know by the likeness. I thought New College very beautiful, but nothing I've seen is quite as beautiful as Magdalen. What a privilege to live always in such a place! And

Grant Allen

what an exquisite view from your window here!'

'Yes,' said Berkeley, moving a few music-books from the seat in the window-sill; 'come and sit by it, Miss Oswald. Mrs. Martindale, won't you put your shawl down? How's the Professor to-day? So sorry he couldn't come.'

'Ah, he had to go to sit on one of his Boards,' said the old lady, seating herself. 'But you know I'm quite accustomed to going out without him.'

Arthur Berkeley knew as much; indeed, being a person of minute strategical intellect, he had purposely looked out a day on which the Professor had to attend a meeting of the delegates of something or other, so as to secure Mrs. Martindale's services without the supplementary drawback of that prodigious bore. Not that he was particularly anxious for Mrs. Martindale's own society, which was of the most strictly negative character; but he didn't wish Edie to be the one lady in a party of four men, and he invited the Professor's wife as an excellent neutral figure-head, to keep her in countenance. Ladies were scarcer then in Oxford than they are nowadays. The married fellow was still a tentative problematical experiment in those years, and the invasion of the Parks by young couples had hardly yet begun in earnest. So female society was still at a considerable local premium, and Berkeley was glad enough to secure even colourless old Mrs. Martindale to square his party at any price.

'And how do you like Oxford, Miss Oswald?' asked Ernest, making his way towards the window.

'My dear Le Breton, what a question to put to her!' said Berkeley, smiling. 'As if Oxford were a place to be appraised offhand, on three days' acquaintance. You remind me of the American who went to look at Niagara, and made an approving note in his memorandum book to say that he found it really a very elegant cataract.'

'Oh, but you MUST form some opinion of it at least, at first sight,' cried Edie; 'you can't help having an impression of a place from the first moment, even if you haven't a judgment on it, can you now? I think it really surpasses my expectations, Mr. Le Breton, which is always a pleasant surprise. Venice fell below them; Florence just came up to them; but Oxford, I think, really surpasses them.'

'We have three beautiful towns in Britain,' Berkeley said. ('As if he were a Welsh Triad,' suggested Herbert Le Breton, parenthetically.) 'Torquay, Oxford, Edinburgh. Torquay is all nature, spoilt by what I won't call art; Oxford is all art, superimposed on a swamp that I won't call nature; Edinburgh is both nature and art, working pretty harmoniously together, to make up a unique and exquisite picture.'

'Just like Naples, Venice, and Heidelberg,' said Edie, half to herself; but Berkeley caught at the words quickly as she said them. 'Yes,' he answered; 'a very good parallel, only Oxford has a trifle more nature about it than Venice. The lagoon, without the palaces, would be simply hideous; the Oseney flats, without the colleges, would be nothing worse than merely dull.'

'We owe a great deal,' said Ernest, gazing out towards the quadrangle, 'to the forgotten mass of labouring humanity who piled all those blocks of shapeless stone into beautiful forms for us who come after to admire and worship. I often wonder, when I sit here in Berkeley's window-seat, and look across the quad to the carved pinnacles on the Founder's Tower there, whether any of us can ever hope to leave behind to our successors any legacy at all comparable to the one left us by those nameless old mediaeval masons. It's a very saddening thought that we for whom all these beautiful things have been put together—we whom labouring humanity has pampered and petted from our cradles upward, feeding us on its whitest bread, and toiling for us with all its weary sinews—that we probably will never do anything at all for it and for the world in return, but will simply eat our way through life aimlessly, and die forgotten in the end like the beasts that perish. It ought to make us, as a class, terribly ashamed of our own utter and abject inutility.'

Edie looked at him with a sort of hushed surprise; she was accustomed to hear Harry talk radical talk enough after his own fashion, but radicalism of this particular pensive tinge she was not accustomed to. It interested her, and made her wonder what sort of man Mr. Le Breton might really be.

'Well, you know, Mr. Le Breton,' said old Mrs. Martindale, complacently, 'we must remember that Providence has wisely ordained that we shouldn't all of us be masons or carpenters. Some of us are clergymen, now, and look what a useful, valuable life a clergyman's is, after all, isn't it, Mr. Berkeley?' Berkeley smiled a faint smile of amusement, but said nothing. 'Others are squires and landed gentry; and I'm sure the landed gentry are very desirable in keeping up the tone of the country districts, and setting a pattern of virtue and refinement to their poorer neighbours. What would the country villages be, for example, if it weren't for the centres of culture afforded by the rectory and the hall, eh, Miss Oswald.' Edith thought of quavering old Miss Catherine Luttrell gossiping with the rector's wife, and held her peace. 'You may depend upon it Providence has ordained these distinctions of classes for its own wise purposes, and we needn't trouble our heads at all about trying to alter them.'

'I've always observed,' said Harry Oswald, 'that Providence is supposed to have ordained the existing order for the time being, whatever it may be, but not the order that is at that exact moment endeavouring to supplant it. If I were to visit Central Africa, I should confidently expect to be told by the rain-doctors that Providence had ordained the absolute power of the chief, and the custom of massacring his wives and slaves at his open grave side. I believe in Russia it's usually allowed that Providence has placed the orthodox Czar at the head of the nation, and that any attempt to obtain a constitution from him is simply flat rebellion and flying in the face of

Providence. In England we had a King John once, and we extracted a constitution out of him and sundry other kings by main force; and here, it's acquiescence in the present limited aristocratic government that makes up obedience to the Providential arrangement of things apparently. But how about America? eh, Mrs. Martindale? Did Providence ordain that George Washington was to rebel against his most sacred majesty King George III., or did it not? And did it ordain that George Washington was to knock his most sacred majesty's troops into a cocked hat, or did it not? And did it ordain that Abraham Lincoln was to free the slaves, or did it not? What I want to know is this: can it be said that Providence has ordained every class distinction in the whole world, from Dahomey to San Francisco? And has it ordained every Government, past and present, from the Chinese Empire to the French Convention? Did it ordain, for example, the revolution of '89? That's the question I should like to have answered.'

'Dear me, Mr. Oswald,' said the old lady meekly, taken aback by Harry's voluble vehemence: 'I suppose Providence permits some things and ordains others.'

'And does it permit American democracy or ordain it?' asked the merciless Harry.

'Don't you see, Mrs. Martindale,' put in Berkeley, coming gently to her rescue, 'your principle amounts in effect to saying that whatever is, is right.'

'Exactly,' said the old lady, forgetting at once all about Dahomey or the Convention, and coming back mentally to her squires and rectors. 'The existing order is wisely arranged by Providence, and we mustn't try to set ourselves up against it.'

'But if whatever is, is right,' Edie said, laughing, 'then Mr. Le Breton's socialism must be right too, you see, because it exists in him no doubt for some wise purpose of Providence; and if he and those who think with him can succeed in changing

Grant Allen

things generally according to their own pattern, then the new system that they introduce will be the one that Providence has shown by the result to be the favoured one.'

'In short,' said Ernest, musingly, 'Mrs. Martindale's principle sanctifies success. It's the old theory of "treason never prospers —what's the reason? Because whene'er it prospers 'tis not treason." If we could only introduce a socialist republic, then it would be the reactionaries who would be setting themselves up against constituted authority, and so flying in the face of Providence.'

'Fancy lecturing a recalcitrant archbishop and a remonstrant ci-devant duchess,' cried Berkeley, lightly, 'upon the moral guilt and religious sinfulness of rebellion against the constituted authority of a communist phalanstery. It would be simply charming. I can imagine myself composing a dignified exhortation to deliver to his grace, entirely compiled out of his own printed pastorals, on the duty of submission and the danger of harbouring an insubordinate spirit. Do make me chaplain-in-ordinary to your house of correction for irreclaimable aristocrats, Le Breton, as soon as you once get your coming socialist republic fairly under way.'

'Luncheon is on the table, sir,' said the scout, breaking in unceremoniously upon their discussion.

If Arthur Berkeley lunched by himself upon a solitary commons of cold beef, he certainly did not treat his friends and guests in corresponding fashion. His little entertainment was of the daintiest and airiest character, so airy that, as Edie herself observed afterwards to Harry, it took away all the sense of meat and drink altogether, and left one only a pleased consciousness of full artistic gratification. Even Ernest, though he had his scruples about the aspic jelly, might eat the famous Magdalen chicken cutlets, his brother said, 'with a distinct feeling of exalted gratitude to the arduous culinary evolution of collective humanity.'

'Consider,' said Herbert, balancing neatly a little pyramid of whip cream and apricot jam upon his fork, 'consider what ages of slow endeavour must have gone to the development of such a complex mixture as this, Ernest, and thank your stars that you were born in this nineteenth century of Soyer and Francatelli, instead of being condemned to devour a Homeric feast with the unsophisticated aid of your own five fingers.'

'But do tell me, Mr. Le Breton,' asked Edie, with one of her pretty smiles, 'what will this socialist republic of yours be like when it actually comes about? I'm dying to know all about it.'

'Really, Miss Oswald,' Ernest answered, in a half-embarrassed tone, 'I don't quite know how to reply to such a very wide and indefinite question. I haven't got any cut-and-dried constitutional scheme of my own for reorganising the whole system of society, any distinct panacea to cure all the ills that collective flesh is heir to. I leave the details of the future order to your brother Harry. The thing that troubles me is not so much how to reform the world at large as how to shape one's own individual course aright in the actual midst of it. As a single unit of the whole, I want rather guidance for my private conduct than a scheme for redressing the universal dislocation of things in general. It seems to me, every man's first duty is to see that he himself is in the right attitude towards society, and afterwards he may proceed to enquire whether society is in the right attitude towards him and all its other members. But if we were all to begin by redressing ourselves, there would be nothing left to redress, I imagine, when we turned to attack the second half of our problem. The great difficulty I myself experience is this, that *I* can't discover any adequate social justification for my own personal existence. But I really oughtn't to bore other people with my private embarrassments upon that head.'

'You see,' said Herbert Le Breton, carelessly, 'my brother represents the ethical element in the socialist movement, Miss Oswald, while Harry represents the political element. Each is valuable in its way; but Oswald's is the more practical. You can

Grant Allen

move great masses into demanding their rights; you can't so easily move them into cordially recognising their duties. Hammer, hammer, hammer at the most obvious abuses; that's the way all the political victories are finally won. If I were a radical at all, I should go with you, Oswald. But happily I'm not one; I prefer the calm philosophic attitude of perfectly objective neutrality.'

'And if I were a radical,' said Berkeley, with a tinge of sadness in his voice as he poured himself out a glass of hock, 'I should go with Le Breton. But unfortunately I'm not one, Miss Oswald, I'm only a parson.'

CHAPTER IV

A LITTLE MUSIC

After lunch, Herbert Le Breton went off for his afternoon ride—a grave social misdemeanour, Ernest thought it—and Arthur Berkeley took Edie round to show her about the college and the shady gardens. Ernest would have liked to walk with her himself, for there was something in her that began to interest him somewhat; and besides, she was so pretty, and so graceful, and so sympathetic: but he felt he must not take her away from her host for the time being, who had a sort of proprietary right in the pleasing duty of acting as showman to her over his own college. So he dropped behind with Harry Oswald and old Mrs. Martindale, and endeavoured to simulate a polite interest in the old lady's scraps of conversation upon the heads of houses, their wives and families.

'This is Addison's Walk, Miss Oswald,' said Berkeley, taking her through the gate into the wooded path beside the Cherwell; 'so called because the ingenious Mr. Addison is said to have specially patronised it. As he was an undergraduate of this college, and a singularly lazy person, it's very probable that he really did so; every other undergraduate certainly does, for it's the nearest walk an idle man can get without ever taking the trouble to go outside the grounds of Magdalen.'

'The ingenious Mr. Addison was quite right then,' Edie answered, smiling; 'for he couldn't have chosen a lovelier place on earth to stroll in. How exquisite it looks just now, with the mellow light falling down upon the path through this beautiful autumnal foliage! It's just a natural cathedral aisle, with a lot of pale straw-coloured glass in the painted windows, like that splendid one we went to see the other day at Merton Chapel.'

'Yes, there are certainly tones in that window I never saw in any other,' Berkeley said, 'and the walk to-day is very much the same in its delicate colouring. You're fond of colour, I should think, Miss Oswald, from what you say.'

'Oh, nobody could help being struck by the autumn colouring of the Thames valley, I should fancy,' said Edie, blushing. 'We noticed it all the way up as we came in the train from Reading, a perfect glow of crimson and orange at Pangbourne, Goring, Mapledurham, and Nuneham. I always thought the Dart in October the loveliest blaze of warm reds and yellows I had ever seen anywhere in nature, but the Thames valley beats it hollow, as Harry says. This walk to-day is just one's ideal picture of Milton's Vallombrosa.'

'Ah, yes, I always look forward to the first days of October term,' said Berkeley, slowly, 'as one of the greatest and purest treats in the whole round workaday twelvemonth. When the creeper on the Founder's Tower first begins to redden and crimson in the autumn, I could sit all day long by my open window, and just look at that glorious sight alone instead of having my dinner. But I'm very fond of these walks in full summer time too. I often stop up alone all through the long (being tied to my curacy here permanently, you know), and then I have the run of the place entirely to myself. Sometimes I take my flute out, and sit under the shade here and compose some of my little pieces.'

'I can easily understand that they were composed here,' said Edie quickly. 'They've caught exactly the flavour of the place—especially your exquisite little Penseroso.'

'Ah, you know my music, then, Miss Oswald?'

'Oh yes, Harry always brings me home all your pieces whenever he comes back at the end of term. I can play every one of them without the notes. But the Penseroso is my special favourite.'

'It's mine, too. I'm so glad you like it. But I'm working away at a little thing now which you shall hear as soon as I've finished it; something lighter and daintier than anything else I've ever attempted. I shall call it the Butterfly Canzonet.'

'Why don't you publish your music under your own name, Mr. Berkeley?'

'Oh, because it would never do. I'm a parson now, and I must keep up the dignity of the cloth by fighting shy of any aesthetic heterodoxies. It would be professional suicide for me to be suspected of artistic leanings. All very well in an archdeacon, you know, to cultivate his tastes for chants and anthems, but for a simple curate!—and secular songs too!—why, it would be sheer contumacy. His chances of a living would shrink at once to what your brother would call a vanishing quantity.'

'Well, you can't imagine how much I admire your songs and airs, Mr. Berkeley. I was so pleased when you invited us, to think I was going to lunch with a real composer. There's no music I love so much as yours.'

'I'm very glad to hear it, Miss Oswald, I assure you. But I'm only a beginner and a trifler yet. Some day I mean to produce something that will be worth listening to. Only, do you remember what some French novelist once said?—"A poet's sweetest poem is always the one he has never been able to compose." I often think that's true of music, too. Away up in the higher stories of one's brain somewhere, there's a tune floating about, or rather a whole oratorio full of them, that one can never catch and fix upon ruled paper. The idea's there, such a beautiful and vague idea, so familiar to one, but so utterly unrealisable on any known instrument—a sort of musical Ariel, flitting before one and tantalising one for ever, but never allowing one to come up with it and see its real features. I'm always dissatisfied with what I've actually written, and longing to crystallise into a score the imaginary airs I can never catch. Except in this last piece of mine; that's the only thing I've ever done that thoroughly and completely pleases me. Come and see me next week, and I'll play it over to you.'

They walked all round the meadows, and back again beside the arches of the beautiful bridge, and then returned to Berkeley's rooms once more for a cup of afternoon tea, and an air or two of Berkeley's own composing. Edie enjoyed the walk and the talk immensely; she enjoyed the music even more. In a way, it was all so new to her. For though she had always seen much of Harry, and though Harry, who was the kindest and proudest of brothers, had always instinctively kept her up to his own level of thought and conversation, still, she wasn't used to seeing so many intelligent and educated young men together, and the novelty of their society was delightfully exhilarating to her eager little mind. To a bright girl of nineteen, wherever she may come from, the atmosphere of Oxford has a wonderfully cheering and stimulating effect; to a country tradesman's daughter from a tiny west-country village it is like a little paradise on earth with a ceaseless round of intensely enjoyable breakfasts, luncheons, dinners, and water-parties.

Ernest, for his part, was not so well pleased. He wanted to have a little conversation with Oswald's sister; and he was compelled by politeness to give her up in favour of Arthur Berkeley. However, he made up for it when he returned, and monopolised the pretty little visitor himself for almost the entire tea-hour.

As soon as they had gone, Arthur Berkeley sported his oak, and sat down by himself in his comfortable crimson-covered basket chair. 'I won't let anybody come and disturb me this evening,' he said to himself moodily. 'I won't let any of these noisy Magdalen men come with their racket and riot to cut off the memory of that bright little dream. No desecration after she has gone. Little Miss Butterfly! What a pretty, airy, dainty, delicate little morsel it is! How she flits, and sips, and natters about every possible subject, just touching the tip of it so gracefully with her tiny white fingers, and blushing so unfeignedly when she thinks she's paid you a compliment, or you've paid her one. How she blushed when she said she liked my music! How she blushed when I said she had a splendid ear for minute discrimination! Somehow, if I were a falling-in-love sort of fellow, I half fancy I could manage to fall in love with her on the spot. Or rather, if I were a good analytical psychologist, perhaps I ought more correctly to say I AM in love with her already.'

He sat down idly at the piano and played a few bars softly to himself—a beautiful, airy sort of melody, as it shaped itself vaguely in his head at the moment, with a little of the new wine of first love running like a trill through the midst of its fast-flowing quavers and dainty undulations. 'That will do,' he said to himself approvingly. 'That will do very well; that's little Miss Butterfly. Here she flits, flits, flits, flickers, sip, sip, sip, at her honeyed flowers; twirl away, whirl away, off in the sunshine—there you go, Miss Butterfly, eddying and circling with your painted mate. Flirt, flirt, flirt, coquetting and curvetting, in your pretty rhythmical aerial quadrille. Down again, down to the hare-bell on the hill side; sip at it, sip at it, sip at it, sweet little honey-drops, clear little honey-drops, bright little honey-drops; oh, for a song to be set to the melody! Tra-la-la, tro-lo-lo, up again, Butterfly. Little silk handkerchief, little lace neckerchief, fluttering, fluttering! Feathery wings of her, bright little eyes of her, flit, flit, flicker! Now, she blushes, blushes, blushes; deep crimson; oh, what a colour! Paint it, painter! Now she speaks. Oh, what laughter! Silvery, silvery, treble, treble, treble; trill away, trill away, silvery treble. Musical, beautiful; beautiful, musical; little Miss Butterfly—fly—fly—fly away!' And he brought his fingers down upon the gamut at last, with a hasty, flickering touch that seemed really as delicate as Edie's own.

'I can never get words for it in English,' he said again, half speaking with his parted lips; 'it's too dactylic in rhythm for

English verse to go to it. Beranger might have written a lilt for it, as far as mere syllables go, but Beranger to write about Miss Butterfly!—pho, no Frenchman could possibly catch it. Swinburne could fit the metres, I dare say, but he couldn't fit the feeling. It shall be a song without words, unless I write some Italian lines for it myself. Animula, blandula vagula— that's the sort of ring for it, but Latin's mostly too heavy. Io, Hymen, Hymenae, Io; Io, Hymen, Hymenae! What's that? A wedding song of Catullus—absit omen. I must be in love with her indeed.' He got up from the piano, and paced quickly and feverishly up and down the room.

'And yet,' he went on, 'if only I weren't bound down so by this unprofitable trade of parson! A curate on eighty pounds a year, and a few pupils! The presumptuousness of the man in venturing to think of falling in love, as if he were actually one of the beneficed clergy! What are deacons coming to, I wonder! And yet, hath not a deacon eyes; hath not a deacon hands, organs, dimensions, senses, affections, passions? If you prick us, do we not bleed? If you tickle us, do we not laugh? And if you show us a little Miss Butterfly, beautiful to the finger-ends, do we not fall in love with her at least as unaffectedly as if we were canons residentiary or rural deans? Fancy little Miss Butterfly a rural deaness! the notion's too ridiculous. Fly away, little Miss Butterfly; fly away, sweet little frolicsome, laugh-some creature. I won't try to tie you down to a man in a black clerical coat with a very distant hypothetical reversionary prospect of a dull and dingy country parsonage. Flit elsewhere, little Miss Butterfly, flit elsewhere, and find yourself a gayer, gaudier-coloured mate!'

He sat down again, and strummed a few more bars of his half-composed, half-extemporised melody. Then he leant back on the music-stool, and said gently to himself once more: 'Still, if it were possible, how happy I should try to make her! Bright little Miss Butterfly, I would try never to let a cold cloud pass chillily over your sunshiny head! I would live for you, and work for you, and write songs for your sake, all full of you, you, you, and so all full of life and grace and thrilling music.

What's my life good for, to me or to the world? "A clergyman's life is such a useful one," that amiable old conventionality gurgled out this morning; what's the good of mine, as it stands now, to its owner or to anybody else, I should like to know, except the dear old Progenitor? A mere bit of cracked blue china, a fanciful air from a comic opera, masquerading in black and white as a piece of sacred music! What good am I to anyone on earth but the Progenitor (God bless him!), and when he's gone, dear old fellow, what on earth shall I have left to live for. A selfish blank, that's all. But with HER, ah, how different! With her to live for and to cherish, with an object to set before oneself as worth one's consideration, what mightn't I do at last? Make her happy—after all, that's the great thing. Make her fond of my music, that music that floats and evades me now, but would harden into scores as if by magic with her to help one to spell it out—I know it would, at last, I know it would. Ah, well, perhaps some day I may be able; perhaps some day the dream will realise itself; till then, work, work, work; let me try to work towards making it possible, a living or a livelihood, no matter which. But not a breath of it to you meanwhile, Miss Butterfly; flit about freely and joyously while you may; I would not spoil your untrammelled flight for worlds by trying to tether it too soon around the fixed centre of my own poor doubtful diaconal destinies.'

At the same moment while Arthur Berkeley was thus garrulously conversing with his heated fancy, Harry and Edie Oswald were strolling lazily down the High, to Edie's lodgings.

'Well, what do you think now of Berkeley and Le Breton, Edie?' asked her brother. 'Which of them do you like the best?'

'I like them both immensely, Harry; I really can't choose between them. When Mr. Berkeley plays, he almost makes me fall in love with him; and when Mr. Le Breton talks, he almost makes me transfer my affections to him instead... But Mr. Berkeley plays divinely... And Mr. Le Breton talks beautifully... You know, I've never seen such clever men before—except you, of course, Harry dear, for you're cleverer and nicer than

Grant Allen

anybody. Oh, do let me look at those lovely silks over there?'
And she danced across the road before he could answer her,
like a tripping sylph in a painter's dreamland.

'Mr. Le Breton's very nice,' she went on, after she had duly
examined and classified the silks, 'but I don't exactly understand what it is he's got on his conscience.'

'Nothing whatsoever, except the fact of his own existence,'
Harry answered with a laugh. 'He has conscientious scruples
against the existence of idle people in the community—do-
nothings and eat-alls—and therefore he has conscientious
scruples against himself for not immediately committing
suicide. I believe, if he did exactly what he thought was
abstractly right, he'd go away and cut his own throat incontinently for an unprofitable, unproductive, useless citizen.'

'Oh, dear, I hope he'll do nothing of the sort,' cried Edie
hastily. 'I think I shall really ask him not to for my sake, if not
for anybody else's.'

'He'd be very much flattered indeed by your interposition on
his behalf, no doubt, Popsy; but I'm afraid it wouldn't produce
much effect upon his ultimate decision.'

'Tell me, Harry, is Mr. Berkeley High Church?'

'Oh dear no, I shouldn't say so. I don't suppose he ever gave
the subject a single moment's consideration.'

'But St. Fredegond's is very High Church, I'm told.'

'Ah, yes; but Berkeley's curate of St. Fredegond's, not in virtue
of his theology—I never heard he'd got any to speak of—but
in virtue of his musical talents. He went into the Church, I
suppose, on purely aesthetic grounds. He liked a musical
service, and it seemed natural to him to take part in one, just
as it seemed natural to a mediaeval Italian with artistic tendencies to paint Madonnas and St. Sebastians. There's nothing

more in his clerical coat than that, I fancy, Edie. He probably never thought twice about it on theological grounds.'

'Oh, but that's very wrong of him, Harry. I don't mean having no particular theological beliefs, of course; one expects that nowadays; but going into the Church without them.'

'Well, you see, Edie, you mustn't judge Berkeley in quite the same way as you'd judge other people. In his mind, the aesthetic side is always uppermost; the logical side is comparatively in abeyance. Questions of creed, questions of philosophical belief, questions of science don't interest him at all; he looks at all of them from the point of view of the impression alone. What he sees in the Church is not a body of dogmas, like the High Churchmen, nor a set of opinions, like the Low Churchmen, but a close corporation of educated and cultivated gentlemen, charged with the duty of caring for a number of beautiful mediaeval architectural monuments, and of carrying on a set of grand and impressive musical or oral services. To him, a cathedral is a magnificent historical heritage; a sermon is a sort of ingenious literary exercise; and a hymn is a capital vehicle for very solemn emotional music. That's all; and we can hardly blame him for not seeing these things as we should see them.'

'Well, Harry, I don't know. I like them both immensely. Mr. Berkeley's very nice, but perhaps I like Mr. Le Breton the best of the two.'

Grant Allen

CHAPTER V

ASKELON VILLA, GATH

Number, 28, Epsilon Terrace, Bayswater, was one of the very smallest houses that a person with any pretensions to move in that Society which habitually spells itself with a capital initial could ever possibly have dreamt of condescending to inhabit. Indeed, if Dame Eleanor, relict of the late Sir Owen Le Breton, Knight, had consulted merely the length of her purse and the interests of her personal comfort, she would doubtless have found for the same rental a far more convenient and roomy cottage in Upper Clapton or Stoke Newington. But Lady Le Breton was a thoroughly and conscientiously religious woman, who in all things consulted first and foremost the esoteric interests of her ingrained creed. It was a prime article of this cherished social faith that nobody with any shadow of personal self-respect could endure to live under any other postal letter than W. or S.W. Better not to be at all than to drag out a miserable existence in the painful obscurity of N. or S.E. Happily for people situated like Lady Le Breton, the metropolitan house-contractor (it would be gross flattery to describe him as a builder) has divined, with his usual practical sagacity, the necessity for supplying this felt want for eligible family residences at once comparatively cheap and relatively fashionable. By driving little culs-de-sac and re-entrant alleys at the back of his larger rows of shoddy mansions, he is enabled to run up a smaller terrace, or crescent, or place, as the case may be, composed of tiny shallow cottages with the narrowest possible frontage, and the tallest possible elevation, which will yet entitle their occupiers to feel themselves within the sacred pale of social salvation, in the blest security of the mystic W. Narrowest, shallowest, and tallest of these marginal Society residences is the little block of blank-faced, stucco-fronted, porticoed rabbit-hutches, which blazons itself forth in the Court Guide under the imposing designation of Epsilon Terrace, Bayswater.

The interior of No. 28 in this eminently respectable back alley was quite of a piece, it must be confessed, with the vacant Philistinism of its naked exterior. 'Mother has really an immense amount of taste,' Herbert Le Breton used to say, blandly, 'and all of it of the most atrocious description; she picked it up, I believe, when my poor father was quartered at Lahore, a station absolutely fatal to the aesthetic faculties; and she will never get rid of it again as long as she lives.' Indeed, when once Lady Le Breton got anything whatsoever into her head, it was not easy for anybody else to get it out again; you might much more readily expect to draw one of her double teeth than to eliminate one of her pet opinions. Not that she was a stupid or a near-sighted woman—the mother of clever sons never is—but she was a perfectly immovable rock of social and political orthodoxy. The three Le Breton boys—for there was a third at home—would gladly have reformed the terrors of that awful drawing-room if they had dared; but they knew it was as much as their places were worth, Herbert said, to attempt a remonstrance, and they wisely left it alone, and said nothing.

Of course the house was not vulgarly furnished, at least in the conventional sense of the word; Lady Le Breton was far too rigid in her social orthodoxy to have admitted into her rooms anything that savoured of what she considered bad form, according to her lights. It was only vulgar with the underlying vulgarity of mere tasteless fashionable uniformity. There was nothing in it that any well-bred footman could object to; nothing that anybody with one grain of genuine originality could possibly tolerate. The little occasional chairs and tables set casually about the room were of the strictest neglige

Grant Allen

Belgravian type, a sort of studied protest against the formal stiffness of the ordinary unused middle-class drawing-room. The portrait of the late Sir Owen in the wee library, presented by his brother-officers, was painted by that distinguished R. A., Sir Francis Thomson, a light of the middle of this century; and an excellent work of art it was too, in its own solemn academic kind. The dining-room, tiny as it was, possessed that inevitable Canaletti without which no gentleman's dining-room in England is ever considered to be complete. Everything spoke at once the stereotyped Society style of a dozen years ago (before Mr. Morris had reformed the outer aspect of the West End), entirely free from anything so startling or indecorous as a gleam of spontaneity in the possessor's mind. To be sure, it was very far indeed from the centre round-table and brilliant-flowered-table-cover style of the utter unregenerate Philistine household; but it was further still from the simple natural taste acd graceful fancy of Edie Oswald's cosy little back parlour behind the village grocer's shop at Calcombe-Pomeroy.

The portrait and the Canaletti were relics of Lady Le Breton's best days, when Sir Owen was alive, and the boys were still in their first babyhood. Sir Owen was an Indian officer of the old school, a simple-minded, gentle, brave man, very religious after his own fashion, and an excellent soldier, with the true Anglo-Indian faculty for administration and organisation. It was partly from him, no doubt, that the boys inherited their marked intelligence; and it was wholly from him, beyond any doubt at all, that Ernest and his younger brother Ronald inherited their moral or religious sincerity—for that was an element in which poor formally orthodox Lady Le Breton was wholly deficient. The good General had been brought up in the strictest doctrines of the Clapham sect; he had gone to India young, as a cadet from Haileybury; and he had applied his intellect all his life long rather to the arduous task of extending 'the blessings of British rule' to Sikhs and Ghoorkas, than to those abstract ethical or theological questions which agitated the souls of a later generation. If a new district had to be assimilated in settlement to the established model of the British raj, if a tribe of hill-savages had to be conciliated by gentler means than rifles or bayonets, if a difficult bit of diplomatic duty had to be performed on the debateable frontiers, Sir Owen Le Breton was always the person chosen to undertake it. An earnest, honest, God-fearing man he remained to the end, impressed by a profound sense of duty as he understood it, and a firm conviction that his true business in life consisted in serving his Queen and country, and in bringing more and more of the native populations within the pale of the Company's empire, and the future evangelisation that was ultimately to follow. But during the great upheaval of the Mutiny, he fell at the head of his own unrevolted regiment in one of the hottest battles of that terrible time, and my Lady Le Breton found herself left alone with three young children, on little more than the scanty pension of a general officer's widow on the late Company's establishment.

Happily, enough remained to bring up the boys, with the aid of their terminable annuities (which fell in on their attaining their majority), in decent respect for the feelings and demands of exacting Society; and as the two elder were decidedly clever boys, they managed to get scholarships at Oxford, which enabled them to tide over the dangerous intermediate period as far as their degree. Herbert then stepped at once into a fellowship and sundry other good things of like sort; and Ernest was even now trying to follow in his brother's steps, in this particular. Only the youngest boy, Ronald, still remained quite unprovided for. Ronald was a tall, pale, gentle, weakly, enthusiastic young fellow of nineteen, with so marked a predisposition to lung disease that it had not been thought well to let him run the chance of over-reading himself; and so he had to be content with remaining at home in the uncongenial atmosphere of Epsilon Terrace, instead of joining his two elder brothers at the university. Uncongenial, because Ronald alone followed Sir Owen in the religious half of his nature, and found the 'worldliness' and conventionality of his unflinching mother a serious bar to his enjoyment of home society.

'Ronald,' said my lady, at the breakfast-table on the very morning of Arthur Berkeley's little luncheon party, 'here's a letter for you from Mackenzie and Anderson. No doubt your Aunt Sarah's will has been recovered and proved at last, and I hope it'll turn out satisfactory, as we wish it.'

'For my part, I really almost hope it won't, mother,' said Ronald, turning it over; 'for I don't want to be compelled to profit by Ernest's excessive generosity. He's too good to me, just because he thinks me the weaker vessel; but though we must bear one another's burdens, you know, we should each bear his own cross as well, shouldn't we, mother?'

'Well, it can't be much in any case,' said his mother, a little testily, 'whoever gets it. Open the envelope at once, my boy, and don't stand looking at it like a goose in that abstracted way.'

'Oh, mother, she was my father's only sister, and I'm not in such a hurry to find out how she has disposed of her mere perishing worldly goods,' answered Ronald, gravely. 'It seems to me a terrible thing that before poor dear good Aunt Sarah is cold in her grave almost, we should be speculating and conjecturing as to what she has done with her poor little trifle of earthly riches.'

'It's always usual to read the will immediately after the funeral,' said Lady Le Breton, firmly, to whom the ordinary usage of society formed an absolutely unanswerable argument; 'and how you, Ronald, who haven't even the common decency to wear a bit of crape around your arm for her—a thing that Ernest himself, with all his nonsensical theories, consents to do—can talk in that absurd way about what's quite right and proper to be done, I for my part, really can't imagine.'

'Ah, but you know, mother, I object to wearing crape on the ground that it isn't allowable for us to sorrow as them that have no hope: and I'm sure I'm paying no disrespect to dear Aunt Sarah's memory in this matter, for she was always the first herself, you remember, to wish that I should follow the dictates of my own conscience.'

'I remember she always upheld you in acts of opposition to your own mother, Ronald,' Lady Le Breton said coldly, 'and I suppose you're going to do honour to her religious precepts now by not opening that letter when your mother tells you to do so. In MY Bible, sir, I find a place for the Fourth Commandment.'

Ronald looked at her gently and unreprovingly; but though a quiet smile played involuntarily around the corners of his mouth, he resisted the natural inclination to correct her mistake, and to suggest blandly that she probably alluded to the fifth. He knew he must turn his left cheek also—a Christian virtue which he had abundant opportunities of practising in that household; and he felt that to score off his mother for such a verbal mistake as the one she had just made would not be in keeping with the spirit of the commandment to which, no doubt, she meant to refer him. So without another word he opened the envelope and glanced rapidly at the contents of the letter it enclosed.

'They've found the second will,' he said, after a moment, with a rather husky voice, 'and they're taking steps to get it confirmed, whatever that may be.'

'Broad Scotch for getting probate, I believe,' said Lady Le Breton, in a slight tone of irony; for to her mind any departure from the laws or language she was herself accustomed to use, assumed at once the guise of a rank and offensive provincialism. 'Your poor Aunt WOULD go and marry a Scotchman, and he a Scotch business man too; so of course we must expect to put up with all kinds of ridiculous technicalities and Edinburgh jargon accordingly. All law's bad enough in the way of odd words, but commend me to Scotch law for utter and meaningless incomprehensibility. Well, and what does the second will say, Ronald?'

'There, mother,' cried Ronald, flinging the letter down hurriedly with a burst of tears. 'Read it yourself, if you will, for I can't. Poor dear Aunt Sarah, and dear, good unselfish Ernest!

Grant Allen

It makes me cry even to think of them.'

Lady Le Breton took the paper up from the table without a word and read it carefully through. 'I am very glad to hear it,' she said, 'very glad indeed to hear it. "And in order to guard against any misinterpretation of my reasons for making this disposition of my property," your Aunt says, "I wish to put it on record that I had previously drawn up another will, bequeathing my effects to be divided between my two nephews Ernest and Ronald Le Breton equally; that I communicated the contents of that will"—a horrid Scotticism—"to my nephew Ernest; and that at his express desire I have now revoked it, and drawn up this present testament, leaving the share intended for him to his brother Ronald." Why, she never even mentions dear Herbert!'

'She knew that Herbert had provided for himself,' Ronald answered, raising his head from his hands, 'while Ernest and I were unprovided for. But Ernest said he could fight the world for himself, while I couldn't; and that unearned wealth ought only to be accepted in trust for those who were incapacitated by nature or misfortune from earning their own bread. I don't always quite agree with all Ernest's theories any more than you do, but we must both admit that at least he always conscientiously acts up to them himself, mother, mustn't we?'

'It's a very extraordinary thing,' Lady Le Breton went on, 'that Aunt Sarah invariably encouraged both you boys in all your absurdities and Quixotisms. She was Quixotic herself at heart, that's the truth of it, just like your poor dear father. I remember once, when we were quartered at Meean Meer in the Punjaub, poor dear Sir Owen nearly got into disgrace with the colonel—he was only a sub. in those days—because he wanted to go trying to convert his syces, which was a most imprudent thing to do, and directly opposed to the Company's orders. Aunt Sarah was just the same. Herbert's the only one of you three who has never given me one moment's anxiety, and of course poor Herbert must be passed over in absolute silence. However, I'm very glad she's left the money to you, Ronald, as you need it the most, and Mackenzie and Anderson say it'll come to about a hundred and sixty a year.'

'One can do a great deal of good with that much money,' said Ronald meditatively. 'I mean, after arranging with you, mother, for the expenses of my maintenance at home, which of course I shall do, as soon as the pension ceases, and after meeting one's own necessary expenditure in the way of clothing and so forth. It's more than any one Christian man ought to spend upon himself, I'm sure.'

'It's not at all too much for a young man in your position in society, Ronald; but there—I know you'll want to spend half of it on indiscriminate charity. However, there'll be time enough to talk about that when you've actually got it, thank goodness.'

Ronald murmured a few words softly to himself, of which Lady Le Breton only caught the last echo—'laid them down at the apostles' feet; and distribution was made unto every man according as he had need.'

'Just like Ernest's communistic notions,' she murmured in return, half audibly. 'I do declare, between them both, a plain woman hardly knows whether she's standing on her head or on her heels. I live in daily fear that one or other of them will be taken up by the police, for being implicated in some dynamite plot or other, to blow up the Queen or destroy the Houses of Parliament.' Ronald smiled again, gently, but answered nothing. 'There's another letter for you there, though, with the Exmoor coronet upon it. Why don't you open it? I hope it's an invitation for you to go down and stop at Dunbude for a week or two. Nothing on earth would do you so much good as to get away for a while from your ranters and canters, and mix occasionally in a little decent and rational society.'

Ronald took up the second letter with a sigh. He feared as much himself, and had doleful visions of a painful fortnight to be spent in a big country house, where the conversation would be all concerning the slaughter of pheasants and the torture of foxes, which his soul loathed to listen to. 'It's from Lady Hilda,' he said, glancing through it, 'and it ISN'T an invitation after all.' He could hardly keep down a faint tone of gratification as he discovered this reprieve. 'Here's what she says:—

'"DEAR MR. LE BRETON,—Mamma wishes me to write and tell you that Lynmouth's tutor, Mr. Walsh, is going to leave us at Christmas, and she thinks it just possible that one of your two brothers at Oxford might like to come down to Dunbude and give us their kind aid in taking charge of Lynmouth. He's a dreadful pickle, as you know; but we are very anxious to get somebody to look after him in whom mamma can have perfect confidence. We don't know your brothers' addresses or we would have written to them direct about it. Perhaps you will kindly let them hear this suggestion; and if they think the matter worth while, we might afterwards arrange details as to business and so forth. With kind regards to Lady Le Breton, believe me,

'"Yours very sincerely,

'"HILDA TREGELLIS."'

'My dear Ronald,' said Lady Le Breton, much more warmly than before, 'this is really quite providential. Are they at Dunbude now?'

'No, mother. She writes from Wilton Place. They're up in town for Lord Exmoor's gout, I know. I heard they were on Sunday.'

'Then I shall go and see Lady Exmoor this very morning about it. It's exactly the right place for Ernest. A little good society will get rid of all his nonsensical notions in a month or two. He's lived too exclusively among his radical set at Oxford. And then it'll be such a capital thing for him to be in the house continually with Hilda; she's a girl of such excellent tone. I fancy—I'm not quite sure, but I fancy—that Ernest has a decided taste for the company of people, and even of young girls, who are not in Society. He's so fond of that young man Oswald, who Herbert tells me is positively the son of a grocer—yes, I'm sure he said a grocer!—and it seems, from what Herbert writes me, that this Oswald has brought a sister of his up this term from behind the counter, on purpose to set her cap at Ernest. Now you boys have, unfortunately, no sisters, and therefore you haven't seen as much of girls of a good stamp—not daily and domestically I mean—as is desirable for you, from the point of view of Society. But if Ernest can only be induced to take this tutorship at the Exmoors', he'll have an opportunity of meeting daily with a really nice girl, like Hilda; and though of course it isn't likely that Hilda would take a fancy to her brother's tutor—the Exmoors are such VERY conservative people in matters of rank and wealth and family and so forth—quite un-Christianly so, I consider—yet it can't fail to improve Ernest's tone a great deal, and raise his standard of female society generally. It's really a very distressing thought to me, Ronald, that all my boys, except dear Herbert, should show such a marked preference for low and vulgar companionship. It seems to me, you both positively prefer as far as possible the society of your natural inferiors. There's Ernest must go and take up with the friendship of that snuffy old German Socialist glass-cutter; while you are always running after your Plymouth Brethren and your Bible Christians, and your other ignorant fanatical people, instead of going with me respectably to St. Alphege's to hear the dear Archdeacon! It's very discouraging to a mother, really, very discouraging.'

CHAPTER VI

DOWN THE RIVER

'Berkeley couldn't come to-day, Le Breton: it's Thursday, of course: I forgot about it altogether,' Oswald said, on the barge at Salter's. 'You know he pays a mysterious flying visit to town every Thursday afternoon—to see an imprisoned lady-love, I always tell him.'

'It's very late in the season for taking ladies on the water, Miss Oswald,' said Ernest, putting his oar into the rowlock, and secretly congratulating himself on the deliverance; 'but better go now than not see Iffley church and Nuneham woods at all. You ought to have come up in summer term, and let us have the pleasure of showing you over the place when it was in its full leafy glory. May's decidedly the time to see Oxford to the greatest advantage.'

'So Harry tells me, and he wanted me to come up then, but it wasn't convenient for them at home to spare me just at that moment, so I was obliged to put it off till late in the autumn. I have to help my mother a good deal in the house, you know, and I can't always go dancing about the world whenever I should like to. Which string must I pull, Harry, to make her turn into the middle of the river? She always seems to twist round the exact way I don't want her to.'

'Right, right, hard right,' cried Harry irom the bow—they were in a tub pair bound down the river for Iffley. 'Keep to the

Oxfordshire shore as far as the willows; then cross over to the Berkshire. Le Breton'll tell you when and where to change sides; he knows the river as well as I do.'

'That'll do splendidly for the present,' Ernest said, looking ahead over his shoulder. 'Mind the flags there; don't go too near the corner. You certainly ought to see these meadows in early spring, when the fritillaries are all out over the spongy places, Miss Oswald. Has your brother ever sent you any of the fritillaries?'

'What? snake-heads? Oh, boxes full of them. They're lovely flowers, but not lovelier than our own Devonshire daffodils. You should see a Devonshire water-meadow in April! Why don't you come down some time to Calcombe Pomeroy? It's the dearest little peaceful seaside corner in all England.'

Harry bit his lip, for he was not over-fond of bringing people down to spy out his domestic sanctities; but Ernest answered cordially, 'I should like it above everything in the world, Miss Oswald. If you will let me, I certainly shall as soon as possible. Mind, quick, get out of the way of that practising eight, or we shall foul her! Left, as hard as you can! That'll do. The cox was getting as red as a salamander, till he saw it was a lady steering. When coxes catch a man fouling them, their language is apt to be highly unparliamentary.—Yes, I shall try to get away to Calcombe as soon as ever I can manage to leave Oxford. It wouldn't surprise me if I were to run down and spend Christmas there.'

'You'd find it as dull as ditch-water at Christmas, Le Breton,' said Harry. 'Much better wait till next summer.'

'I'm sure I don't think so, Harry dear,' Edie interrupted, with that tell-tale blush of hers. 'If Mr. Le Breton wants to come then, I believe he'd really find it quite delightful. Of course he wouldn't expect theatres, or dances, or anything like that, in a country village; and we're dreadfully busy just about Christmas day itself, sending out orders, and all that sort of

Grant Allen

thing,'—Harry bit his lip again:—'but if you don't mind a very quiet place and a very quiet time, Mr. Le Breton, I don't think myself our cliffs ever look grander, or our sea more impressive, than in stormy winter weather.'

'I wish to goodness she wasn't so transparently candid and guileless,' thought Harry to himself. 'I never CAN teach her duly to respect the prejudices of Pi. Not that it matters twopence to Le Breton, of course: but if she talks that way to any of the other men here, they'll be laughing in every common-room in Oxford over my Christmas raisins and pounds of sugar—commonplace cynics that they are. I must tell her about it the moment we get home again, and adjure her by all that's holy not to repeat the indiscretion.'

'A penny for your thoughts, Harry,' cried Edie, seeing by his look that she had somehow vexed him. 'What are you thinking of?'

'Thinking that all Oxford men are horrid cynics,' said Harry, boldly shaming the devil.

'Why are they?' Edie asked.

'I suppose because it's an inexpensive substitute for wit or intellect,' Harry answered. 'Indeed, I'm a bit of a cynic myself, I believe, for the same reason and on strictly economical principles. It saves one the trouble of having any intelligible or original opinion of one's own upon any subject.'

Below Iffley Lock they landed for half an hour, in order to give Edie time for a pencil sketch of the famous old Norman church-tower, with its quaint variations on the dog-tooth ornament, and its ancient cross and mouldering yew-tree behind. Harry sat below in the boat, propped on the cushions, reading the last number of the 'Nineteenth Century;' Ernest and Edie took their seat upon the bank above, and had a first chance of an unbroken tete-a-tete.

'How delicious to live in Oxford always!' said Edie, sketching in the first outline of the great round arches. 'I would give anything to have the opportunity of settling here for life. Some day I shall make Harry set up house, and bring me up here as his housekeeper:—I mean,' she added with a blush, thinking of Harry's warning look just before, 'as soon as they can spare me from home.' She purposely avoided saying 'when they retire from business,' the first phrase that sprang naturally to her simple little lips. 'Let me see, Mr. Le Breton; you haven't got any permanent appointment here yourself, have you?'

'Oh no,' Ernest answered: 'no appointment of any sort at all, Miss Oswald. I'm loitering up casually on the look-out for a fellowship. I've been in for two or three already, but haven't got them.'

'Why didn't you?' asked Edie, with a look of candid surprise.

'I suppose I wasn't clever enough,' Ernest answered simply. 'Not so clever, I mean, as the men who actually got them.'

'Oh, but you MUST be,' Edie replied confidently; 'and a great deal cleverer, too, I'm sure. I know you must, because Harry told me you were one of the very cleverest men in the whole 'Varsity. And besides, I see you are, myself. And Harry says most of the men who get fellowships are really great donkeys.'

'Harry must have been talking in one of those cynical moods he told us about,' said Ernest, laughing. 'At any rate, the examiners didn't feel satisfied with my papers, and I've never got a fellowship yet. Perhaps they thought my political economy just a trifle too advanced for them.'

'You may depend upon it, that's it,' said Edie, jumping at the conclusion with the easy omniscience of a girl of nineteen. 'Next time, make your political economy a little more moderate, you know, without any sacrifice of principle, just to suit them. What fellowship are you going in for now?'

Grant Allen

'Pembroke, in November.'

'Oh, I do hope you'll get it.'

'Thank you very much. So do I. It would be very nice to have one.'

'But of course it won't matter so much to you as it did to Harry. Your family are such very great people, aren't they?'

Ernest smiled a broad smile at her delicious simplicity. 'If by very great people you mean rich,' he said, 'we couldn't very well be poorer—for people of our sort, I mean. My mother lives almost entirely on her pension; and we boys have only been able to come up to Oxford, just as Harry was, by the aid of our scholarships. If we hadn't saved in our first two years, while we had our government allowances, we shouldn't have been able to stop up for our degrees at all. So if I don't get a fellowship I shall have to take to school-mastering or something of the sort, for a livelihood. Indeed, this at Pembroke will be my very last chance, for I can't hold on much longer.'

'And if you got a fellowship you could never marry, could you?' asked Edie, going on with her work.

'Not, while I held it, certainly. But I wouldn't hold it long. I regard it only as a makeshift for a time. Unhappily, I don't know how to earn my own bread by the labour of my hands, as I think we ought all to do in a well-constituted society; so unless I choose to starve (about the rightfulness of which I don't feel quite certain), I MUST manage somehow to get over the interval. But as soon as I could I would try to find some useful work to do, in which I could repay society the debt I owe it for my bringing up. You see, I've been fed and educated by a Government grant, which of course came out of the taxes—your people have had to help, whether they would or not, in paying for my board and lodging—and I feel that I owe it as a duty to the world to look out some employment in which I could really repay it for the cost of my maintenance.'

'How funnily you do look at everything, Mr. Le Breton,' said Edie. 'It would never have struck me to think of a pension from the army in that light. And yet of course it's the right light; only we don't most of us take the trouble to go to the bottom of things, as you do. But what will you do if you don't get the fellowship?'

'In that case, I've just heard from my mother that she would like me to take a tutorship at Lord Exmoor's,' Ernest answered. 'Lynmouth, their eldest son, was my junior at school by six or seven years, and now he's going to prepare for Christ Church. I don't quite know whether it's a right place for me to accept or not; but I shall ask Max Schurz about it, if I don't get Pembroke. I always take Herr Max's advice in all questions of conscience, for I'm quite sure whatever he approves of is the thing one ought to do for the greatest good of humanity.'

'Harry told me about Herr Schurz,' Edie said, filling in the details of the doorway. 'He thinks him a very earnest, self-convinced, good old man, but a terrible revolutionist. For my part, I believe I rather like revolutionists, provided, of course, they don't cut off people's heads. Harry made me read Carlyle, and I positively fell in love with Camille Desmoulins; only I don't really think he ought to have approved of QUITE so much guillotining, do you? But why shouldn't you take the tutorship at the Exmoors'?'

'Oh, because it isn't a very useful work in the world to prepare a young hereditary loafer like Lynmouth for going to Christ Church. Lynmouth will be just like his father when he grows up—an amiable wholesale partridge-slayer; and I don't see that the world at large will be any the better or the worse off for his being able to grope his way somehow through two plays of Sophocles and the first six books of Euclid. If only one were a shoemaker now! What a delightful thing to sit down at the end of a day and say to oneself, "I have made two pairs of good, honest boots for a fellow-mortal this week, and now I deserve to have my supper!" Still, it'll be better, anyway, than doing nothing at all, and living off my mother.'

'If you went to Dunbude, when would you go?'

'After the Christmas vacation, I suppose, from what Lady Hilda says.'

'Lady Hilda? Oh, so there's a sister, is there?'

'Yes. A very pretty girl, about twenty, I should say, and rather clever too, I believe. My mother knows them a little.'

Poor little Edie! What made her heart jump so at the mere mention of Lady Hilda? and what made the last few strokes at the top of the broken yew-tree look so very weak and shaky? How absurd of herself, she thought, to feel so much moved at hearing that there was another girl in the world whom Ernest might possibly fall in love with! And yet she had never even seen Ernest only ten days ago! Lady Hilda! What a grand name, to be sure, and what a grand person she must be. And then Ernest himself belonged by birth to the same class! For in poor little Edie's mind, innocent as she was of the nice distinctions of the peerage, Lady So-and-So was Lady So-and-So still, whoever she might be, from the wife of a premier marquis to the wife of the latest created knight bachelor. To her, Lady Hilda Tregellis and Lady Le Breton were both 'ladies of title'; and the difference between their positions, which seemed so immense to Ernest, seemed nothing at all to the merry little country girl who sat sketching beside him. After all, how could she ever have even vaguely fancied that such a young man as Ernest, in spite of all his socialistic whims, would ever dream of caring for a girl of the people like her? No doubt he would go to the Exmoors', fall naturally in love with Lady Hilda, and marry decorously in what Edie considered his own proper sphere of life! She went on with the finishing touches of her little picture in silence, and folded it up into the tiny portfolio at last with a half-uttered sigh. So her poor wee castle in the air was knocked down before she had begun to build it up in any real seriousness, and she turned to join Harry in the boat almost without speaking.

'I hope you'll get the Pembroke fellowship,' she said again, a little later, as they rowed onward down the river to Nuneham. 'But in any case, Mr. Le Breton, you mustn't forget you've half promised to come and look us up at Calcombe Pomeroy in the Christmas vacation.'

Ernest smiled, and nodded acquiescence.

Meanwhile, on that same Thursday afternoon, Arthur Berkeley had gone up from Oxford by the fast train to Paddington, as was his weekly wont, and had dived quickly down one of the small lanes that open out from the left-hand side of Praed Street. He walked along it for a little way, humming an air to himself as he went, and then stopped at last in front of a small, decent brick house, with a clean muslin blind across the window (clean muslin forms a notable object in most London back streets), and a printed card hanging from the central pane, bearing the inscription, 'G. Berkeley, Working Shoemaker.—The Trade supplied with Ready-closed Uppers.' At the window a beaming face was watching for his appearance, and Arthur said to himself as he saw it through the curtain, 'The dear old Progenitor's looking better again this week, God bless him!' In a moment he had opened the door, and greeted his father in the old boyish fashion, with an honest kiss on either cheek. They had kissed one another so whenever they met from Arthur's childhood upward; and the Oxford curate had never felt himself grown too much of a man to keep up a habit which seemed to him by far the most sacred thing in his whole existence.

'Well, father dear, I needn't ask you how you are to-day,' said Arthur, seating himself comfortably in the second easy-chair of the trim little workshop parlour. 'I can see at once you're a good deal better. Any more pain in the head and eyes, eh, or any trouble about the forehead?'

The old shoemaker passed his hand over his big, bulging brow, bent outward as it is so often in men of his trade by the constant habit of stooping over their work, and said briskly,

'No, Artie, my boy, not a sign of it this week—not a single sign of it. I've been taking a bit of holiday, you see, and it's done me a lot of good, I can tell you;—made me feel another man entirely. I've been playing my violin till the neighbours began to complain of it; and if I hadn't asked them to come and hear me tune up a bit, I really believe they'd have been having me up before the magistrate for a public nuisance.'

'That's right, Daddy dear; I'm always glad when you've been having a little music. It does you more good than anything. And the jelly—I hope you've eaten the jelly?'

'Oh, I've eaten it right enough, Artie, thank your dear heart; and the soup too, dearie. Came by a boy from Walters's every day, addressed to "Berkeley, Esquire, 42 Whalley Street;" and the boy wouldn't leave it the first day, because he thought there must have been a mistake about the address. His contention was that a journeyman shoemaker wasn't an esquire; and my contention was that the "Berkeley" was essential, and the "Esquire" accidental, which was beyond his logic, bless you, Artie; for I've often noticed, my son, that your errand-boy is a naturally illogical and contradictory creature. Now, shoemakers aren't, you know. I've always taken a just pride in the profession, and I've always asserted that it develops logic; it develops logic, Artie, or else why are all cobblers good Liberals, I should like to know? Eh, can you tell me that; with all your Oxford training, sir, can you tell me that?'

'It develops logic beyond the possibility of a doubt. Daddy; and it develops a good kind heart as well,' said Arthur, smiling. 'And it develops musical taste, and literary talent, and a marked predilection for the beautiful in art and nature. In fact, whenever I meet a good man of any sort, anywhere, I always begin now by inquiring which of his immediate ancestors can have been a journeyman shoemaker. Depend upon it, Daddy, there's nothing like leather.'

'There you are, poking fun at your poor old Progenitor again,' said the old cobbler, with a merry twinkle in the corner of his eye. 'If it weren't for the jelly, and the natural affections always engendered by shoemaking, I think I should almost feel inclined to cut you off with a shilling, Artie, my boy—to cut you off with a shilling. Well, Artie, I'm quite convalescent now (don't you call it? I'm afraid of my long shoemaker's words before you, nowadays, you've grown so literary; for I suppose parsons are more literary than even shoemakers). I'm quite convalescent now, and I think, my boy, I must get to work again this week, and have no more of your expensive soups and jellies. If I didn't keep a sharp look-out upon you, Artie, lad, I believe you'd starve yourself outright up there at Oxford to pamper your poor old useless father here with luxuries he's never been accustomed to in his whole life.'

'My dear simple old Progenitor, you don't know how utterly you're mistaken,' cried Arthur, eagerly. 'I believe I'm really the most selfish and unnatural son in all Christendom. I'm positively rolling in wealth up there at Magdalen; I've had my room papered again since you saw it last long vacation; and I live like a prince, absolutely like a Russian prince, upon my present income. I assure you on my solemn word of honour, Father, that I eat meat for lunch—that's my dinner—every day; and an egg for tea as regular as clockwork. I often think when I look around my palatial rooms in college, what a shame it is that I should let you, who are worth ten of me, any day, live any longer in a back street up here in London; and I won't allow it, Daddy, I really won't allow it from this day forth, I'm determined. I've come up especially to speak to you about it this afternoon, for I've made up my mind that this abnormal state of things can't continue.'—'Very good word, abnormal,' murmured his father.—'And I've also made up my mind,' Arthur said, almost firmly, for him, 'that you shall come up and live at Oxford. I can't bear having you so far away from me, now that you're weaker than you used to be, Father dear, and so often ailing.'

The old shoemaker laughed aloud. 'Oh no, Artie, my boy,' he said cheerily, shaking his head with a continuous series of merry chuckles. 'It won't do at all, it won't do, I assure you. I may be a terrible free-thinker and all that kind of thing, as the neighbours say I am—poor bodies, they never read a word of modern criticism in their lives, heaven bless 'em—stragglers from the march of intellect, mere stragglers—but I've too much respect for the cloth to bring a curate of St. Fredegond's into such disgrace as that would mean for you, Artie. You shan't have your career at Oxford spoiled by its being said of you that your father was a working shoemaker. What with the ready-closed uppers, and what with your ten shillings a week, and what with all the presents you give me, and what with the hire of the piano, I'm as comfortable as ever I want to be, growing into a gentleman in my old age, Artie, and I even begin to have my doubts as to whether it's quite consistent in me as a good Radical to continue my own acquaintance with myself—I'm getting to be such a regular idle do-nothing aristocrat! Go to Oxford and mend shoes, indeed, with you living there as a full-fledged parson in your own rooms at Magdalen! No, no, I won't hear of it. I'll come up for a day or two in long vacation, my boy, as I've always done hitherto, and take a room in Holywell, and look in upon you a bit, accidentally, so as not to shame you before the scouts (who are a servile set of flunkeys, incapable of understanding the elevated feelings of a journeyman shoemaker); but I wouldn't dream of going to live in the place, any more than I'd dream of asking to be presented at court on the occasion of my receiving a commission for a pair of evening shoes for the Queen's head footman.'

'Father,' said Arthur, smiling, 'you're absolutely incorrigible. Such a dreadful old rebel against all constituted authority, human and divine, I never did meet in the course of my existence, I believe you're really capable of arguing a point of theology against an archbishop. But I don't want you to come up to Oxford as a shoemaker; I mean you to come up and live with me in rooms of our own, out of college. Whenever I think of you, dear Father—you, who are so infinitely nobler, and better, and truer, and more really a gentleman than any other than I ever knew in my life—whenever I think of you, coming secretly up to Oxford as if you were ashamed of yourself, and visiting your own son by stealth in his rooms in college as if you were a dun coming to ask him for money, instead of the person whom he delights to honour—whenever I think of it, Father, it makes my cheeks burn with shame, and I loathe myself for ever allowing you so to bemean your own frank, true, noble nature. I oughtn't to permit it, Father, I oughtn't to permit it; and I won't permit it any longer.'

'Well, you never would have permitted it, Artie, if I hadn't compelled you; for I've got all the prudence and common sense of the family bottled up here in my own forehead,' said the old man, tapping his bulging brow significantly. 'I don't deny that Oxford may be an excellent school for Greek and Latin, and philosophy, and so forth; but if you want prudence and sagacity and common-sense it's a well-known fact that there's nothing like the practice of making ready-closed uppers, sir, to develop 'em. If I'd taken your advice, my boy, I'd have come up to visit you when you were an undergraduate, and ruined your prospects at the very outset. No, no, Artie, I shall stop here, and stick to my last, my dear boy, stick to my last, to the end of all things.'

'You shall do nothing of the sort, Daddy; that I'm determined upon,' Arthur cried vehemently. 'I'm not going to let you do any more shoemaking. The time has come when you must retire, and devote all your undivided energies to the constant study of modern criticism. Whether you come to Oxford or stop in London, I've made up my mind that you shan't do another stroke of work as long as you live. Look here, dear old Daddy, I'm getting to be a perfect millionaire, I assure you. Do you see this fiver? well, I got that for knocking out that last trashy little song for Fradelli; and it cost me no more trouble to compose it than to sit down and write the score out on a sheet of ruled paper. I'm as rich as Croesus—made a hundred and eighty pounds last year, and expect to make over two hundred this one. Now, if a man with that perfectly prodigious fortune can't afford to keep his own father in comfort and affluence, what an absolute Sybarite and gourmand of a fellow he must be himself.'

'It's a lot of money, certainly, Artie,' said the old shoemaker, turning it over thoughtfully: 'two hundred pounds is a lot of money; but I doubt very much whether it's more than enough to keep you up to the standard of your own society, up there at Oxford. As John Stuart Mill says, these things are all comparative to the standard of comfort of your class. Now, Artie, I believe you have to stint yourself of things that every-body else about you has at Oxford, to keep me in luxuries I was never used to.'

'My dear Dad, it's only of the nature of a repayment,' cried Arthur, earnestly. 'You slaved and sacrificed and denied yourself when I was a boy to send me to school, without which I would never have got to Oxford at all; and you taught me music in your spare hours (when you had any); and I owe everything I have or am or ever will be to your unceasing and indefatigable kindness. So now you've got to take repayment whether you will or not, for I insist upon it. And if you won't come up to Oxford, which perhaps would be an uncongenial place for you in many ways, I'll tell you what I'll do, Daddy; I'll look out for a curacy somewhere in London, and we'll take a little house together, and I'll furnish it nicely, and there we shall live, sir, whatever you say, so not another word about it. And now I want you to listen to the very best thing I've ever composed, and tell me what you think of it.'

He sat down to the little hired cottage piano that occupied the corner of the neat small room, and began to run his deft fingers lightly over the keys. It was the Butterfly fantasia. The father sat back in his red easy-chair, listening with all his ears, first critically, then admiringly, at last enthusiastically. As Arthur's closing notes died away softly towards the end, the old shoemaker's delight could be restrained no longer. 'Artie,' he cried, gloating over it, 'that's music! That's real music! You're quite right, my boy; that's far and away the best thing you've ever written. It's exquisite—so light, so airy, so unearthlike. But, Artie, there's more than that in it. There's soul in it; and I know what it means. You don't deceive your poor old Progenitor in a matter of musical inspiration, I can tell you. I know where you got that fantasia from as well as if I'd seen you getting it. You got it out of your own heart, my boy, out of your own heart. And the thing it says to me as plain as language is just this—you're in love! You're in love, Artie, and there's no good denying it. If any man ever wrote that fantasia without being in love at the time—first love—ecstasy—tremor—tiptoe of expectation—why, then, I tell you, music hasn't got such a thing as a tongue or a meaning in it.'

Arthur looked at him gently and smiled, but said nothing.

'Will you tell me about her, Artie?' asked the old man, caressingly, laying his hand upon his son's arm.

'Not now, Father; not just now, please. Some other time, perhaps, but not now. I hardly know about it myself, yet. It may be something—it may be nothing; but, at any rate, it was peg enough to hang a fantasia upon. You've surprised my little secret, Father, and I dare say it's no real secret at all, but just a passing whiff of fancy. If it ever comes to anything, you shall know first of all the world about it. Now take out your violin, there's a dear old Dad, and give me a tune upon it.'

The father took the precious instrument from its carefully covered case with a sort of loving reverence, and began to play a piece of Arthur's own composition. From the moment the bow touched the chords it was easy enough to see whence the son got his musical instincts. Old George Berkeley was a born musician, and he could make his violin discourse to him with rare power of execution. There they sat, playing and talking at intervals, till nearly eight, when Arthur went out hurriedly to catch the last train to Oxford, and left the old shoemaker once more to his week's solitude. 'Not for much longer,' the curate whispered to himself, as he got into his third-class carriage quickly; 'not for much longer, if I can help it. A curacy in or near London's the only right thing for me to look out for!'

Grant Allen

CHAPTER VII

GHOSTLY COUNSEL

November came, and with it came the Pembroke fellowship examination. Ernest went in manfully, and tried hard to do his best; for somehow, in spite of the immorality of fellowships, he had a sort of floating notion in his head that he would like to get one, because he was beginning to paint himself a little fancy picture of a home that was to be, with a little fairy Edie flitting through it, and brightening it all delightfully with her dainty airy presence. So he even went so far as to mitigate considerably the native truculence of his political economy paper, after Edie's advice—not, of course, by making any suggestion of opinions he did not hold, but by suppressing the too-prominent expression of those he actually believed in. Max Schurz's name was not once mentioned throughout the whole ten or twelve pages of closely written foolscap; 'Gold and the Proletariate' was utterly ignored; and in place of the strong meat served out for men by the apostles of socialism in the Marylebone dancing-saloon, Ernest dished up for his examiner's edification merely such watery milk for babes as he had extracted from the eminently orthodox economical pages of Fawcett, Mill, and Thorold Rogers. He went back to his rooms, satisfied that he had done himself full justice, and anxiously waited for the result to be duly announced on the Saturday morning.

Was it that piece of Latin prose, too obviously modelled upon the Annals of Tacitus, while the senior tutor was a confirmed

Ciceronian, with the Second Philippic constitutionally on the brain? Was it the Greek verse, containing one senarius with a long syllable before the caesura in the fifth foot, as Herbert pointed out to his brother on the very evening when that hideous oversight—say rather crime—had been openly perpetrated in plain black and white on a virgin sheet of innocent paper? Was it some faint ineffaceable savour of the Schurzian economics, peeping through in spite of all disguises, like the garlic in an Italian ragout, from under the sedulous cloak of Ricardo's theory of rent? Was it some flying rumour, extra-official, and unconnected with the examination in any way, to the effect that young Le Breton was a person of very dubious religious, political, and social orthodoxy? Or was it merely that fortunate dispensation of Providence whereby Oxford almost invariably manages to let her best men slip unobserved through her fingers, and so insures a decent crop of them to fill up her share of the passing vacancies in politics, literature, science, and art? Heaven or the Pembroke examiners alone can answer these abstruse and difficult questions; but this much at least is certain, that when Ernest Le Breton went into the Pembroke porter's lodge on the predestined Saturday, he found another name than his placarded upon the notice board, and turned back, sick at heart and disappointed, to his lonely lodgings. There he spent an unhappy hour or two, hewing down what remained of his little aerial castle off-hand; and then he went out for a solitary row upon the upper river, endeavouring to work off his disappointment like a man, with a good hard spell of muscular labour.

Edie had already returned to Calcombe-Pomeroy, so in the evening he went to tell his misfortune to Harry Oswald. Harry was really sorry to hear it, for Ernest was his best friend in Oxford, and he had hoped to have him settled close by. 'You'll stop up and try again for Christ Church in February, won't you, Le Breton?' he asked.

'No,' said Ernest, shaking his head a little gloomily; 'I don't think I will. It's clear I'm not up to the Oxford standard for a fellowship, and I couldn't spend another term in residence

without coming down upon my mother to pay my expenses—
a thing she can't easily afford to do. So I suppose I must fall
back for the present upon the Exmoor tutorship. That'll give
me time to look about me, till I can get something else to do;
and after all, it isn't a bit more immoral than a fellowship,
when one comes to look it fairly in the face. However, I shall
go first and ask Herr Max's opinion upon the matter.'

'I'm going to spend a fortnight in town in the Christmas vac,'
said Oswald, 'and I should like to go with you to Max's again,
if I may.'

Ernest coloured up a little, for he would have liked to invite
Oswald to his mother's house; and yet he felt there were two
reasons why he should not do so; he must himself be
dependent this time upon his mother's hospitality, and he
didn't think Lady Le Breton would be perfectly cordial in her
welcome to Harry Oswald.

In the end, however, it was arranged that Harry should engage
rooms at his former lodgings in London, and that Ernest
should take him once more to call upon the old socialist when
he went to consult him on the question of conscience.

'For my part, Ernest,' said Lady Le Breton to her son, the
morning after his return from Oxford, 'I'm not altogether
sorry you didn't get this Pembroke fellowship. It would have
kept you among the same set you are at present mixing in for
an indefinite period. Of course now you'll accept Lady
Exmoor's kind proposal. I saw her about it the same morning
we got Hilda's letter; and she offers 200L. a year, which, of
course, is mere pocket money, as your board and lodging are
all found for you, so to speak, and you'll have nothing to do
but to dress and amuse yourself.'

'Well, mother, I shall see about it. I'm going to consult Herr
Schurz upon the subject this morning.'

'Herr Schurz!' said Lady Le Breton, in her bitterest tone of irony. 'It appears to me you make that snuffy old German microscope man your father confessor. It's very disagreeable to a mother to find that her sons, instead of taking her advice about what is most material to their own interests, should invariably go to confer with communist refugees and ignorant ranters. Ronald, what is your programme, if you please, for this morning's annoyance?'

Ronald, with the fear of the fifth commandment steadily before his eyes, took no notice of the last word, and answered calmly, 'You know, mother, this is the regular day for the mission-house prayer-meeting.'

'The mission-house prayer-meeting! I know nothing of the sort, I assure you. I don't keep a perfect calendar in my mind of all your meetings and your religious engagements. Then I suppose I must go alone to the Waltons' to see Mr. Walton's water-colours?'

'I'll give up the prayer-meeting, if you wish it,' Ronald answered, with his unvarying meekness. 'Only, I'm afraid I must walk very slowly. My cough's rather bad this morning.'

'No, no,' Ernest put in, 'you mustn't dream of going, Ronald; I couldn't allow you to walk so far on any account. I'll put off my engagement with Oswald, who was going with me to Herr Schurz's, and I'll take you round to the Waltons', mother, whenever you like.'

'Dear me, dear me,' moaned Lady Le Breton, piteously, pretending to wring her hands in lady-like and mitigated despair; 'I can't do anything without its being made the opportunity for a scene, it seems. I shall NOT go to the Waltons'; and I shall leave you both to follow your own particular devices to your heart's content. I'm sorry I proposed anything whatsoever, I'm sure, and I shall take care never to do such an imprudent thing again.' And her ladyship walked in her stateliest and most chilly manner out of the freezing little dining-room.

'It's a great cross, living always with poor mother, Ernest,' said Ronald, his eyes filling with tears as he spoke; 'but we must try to bear with her, you know, for after all she leads a very lonely life herself, because she's so very unsympathetic.' Ernest took the spare white hand in his and smoothed it compassionately. 'My dear, dear Ronald,' he said, 'I know it's hard for you. I must try the best I can to make it a little easier!'

They walked together as far as the mission-house, arm in arm, for though in some things the two young Le Bretons were wide apart as the poles, in others they were fundamentally at one in inmost spirit; and even Ronald, in spite of his occasional little narrow sectarianisms, felt the underlying unity of purpose no less than Ernest. He was one of those enthusiastic ethereal natures which care little for outer forms or ceremonies, and nothing at all for churches and organisations, but love to commune as pure spirit with pure spirit, living every day a life of ecstatic spirituality, and never troubling themselves one whit about theological controversy or established religious constitutions. As long as Ronald Le Breton could read his Greek Testament every morning, and talk face to face in their own tongue with the Paul of First Corinthians or the John of the Epistles, in the solitude of his own bedroom, he was supremely indifferent about the serious question, of free-will and fore-knowledge, or about the important question of apostolical succession, or even about that other burning question of eternal punishment, which was just then setting his own little sect of Apostolic Christian Missioners roundly by the ears. These things seemed to his enthusiastic mind mere fading echoes of an alien language; all that he himself really cared for in religion was the constant sense of essential personal commu-nion with that higher Power which spoke directly to his soul all day long and always; or the equally constant sense of moral exaltation which he drew from the reading of the written Word in its own original language. He had never BECOME an Apostolic Christian; he had grown up to be one, unconsci-ously to himself. 'Your son Ronald's religion, my dear Lady Le Breton,' Archdeacon Luttrell used often to say, 'is, I fear, too purely emotional. He cannot be made to feel sufficiently the necessity for a sound practical grasp of doctrinal Christianity.' To Ronald himself, he might as well have talked about the necessity for a sound practical grasp of doctrinal Buddhism. And if Ronald had really met a devout Buddhist, he would doubtless have found, after half an hour's conversation, that they were at one in everything save the petty matter of dialect and vocabulary.

At Oswald's lodging, Ernest found his friend ready and waiting for him. They went on together to the same street in Marylebone as before, and mounted the stair till they reached Herr Schurz's gloomy little work-room on the third floor. The old apostle was seated at his small table by the half-open window, grinding the edges of a lens to fit the brass mounting at his side; while his daughter Uta, a still good-looking, quiet, broad-faced South German woman, about forty or a little more, sat close by, busily translating a scientific book into English by alternate reading and consultation with her father. Harry saw the title on her page was 'Researches into the Embryology of the Isopodal Crustaceans,' and conceived at once an immense respect for the learning and wisdom of the communist exile's daughter. Herr Schurz hardly stopped a moment from his work—he never allowed his numerous visitors to interfere in any way with his daily duties—but motioned them both to seats on the bare bench beside him, and waited to bear the nature of their particular business. It was an understood thing that no one came to see the Socialist leader on week days except for a good and sufficient reason.

The talk at first was general and desultory; but after a little time Ernest brought conversation round to its proper focus, and placed his case of conscience fairly before his father confessor. Was it allowable for a consistent socialist to accept the place of tutor to the son of a peer and a landowner?

'For my part, Herr Schurz,' Oswald said confidently, 'I don't see any reason on earth, from the point of view of any political economy whatsoever, why Ernest shouldn't take the position. The question isn't how the Exmoors have come by their money, even allowing that private property in land is in itself utterly indefensible; which is a proposition I don't myself feel inclined unreservedly to admit, though I know you and Le Breton do: the real question's this,—since they've got this money into their hands to distribute, and since in any case they will have the distribution of it, isn't it better that some of it should go into Le Breton's pocket than that it should go into any other person's? That's the way I for my part look at the matter.'

'What do you say to that, friend Ernest?' asked the old German, smiling and waiting to see whether Ernest would detect what from their own standpoint he regarded as the ethical fallacy of Harry Oswald's argument.

'Well, to tell you the truth, Herr Schurz,' answered Ernest, in his deliberate, quiet way, 'I don't think I've envisaged the subject to myself from quite the same point of view as Oswald has done. I have rather asked myself whether it was right of a man to accept a function in which he would really be doing nothing worthy for humanity in return for his daily board and lodging. It isn't so much a question who exactly is to get certain sums out of the Exmoors' pockets, which ought no doubt never to have been in them; it's more a question whether a man has any right to live off the collective labour of the world, and do nothing of any good to the world on his own part by way of repayment.'

'That's it, friend Ernest,' cried the old man, with a pleased nod of his big grey head; 'the socialistic Iliad in a nutshell! That's the very root of the question. Don't be deceived by capitalist sophisms. So long as we go on each of us trying to get as much as we can individually out of the world, instead of asking what the world is getting out of us, in return, there will be no revolution and no millennium. We must make sure that we're doing some good ourselves, instead of sponging upon the people perpetually to feed us for nothing. What's the first gospel given to man at the creation in your popular cosmogonies? Why, that in the sweat of his face shall he eat bread, and till the ground from which he was taken. That's the native gospel of the toiling many, always; your doctrines of fair exchange, and honest livelihoods, and free contract, and all the rest of it, are only the artificial gospel of the political economists, and of the bourgeoisie and the aristocrats into whose hands they play—the rascals!'

'Then you think I oughtn't to take the post?' asked Ernest, a little ruefully.

'I don't say that, Le Breton—I don't say that,' said Herr Schurz, more quietly than before, still grinding away at his lens. 'The question's a broad one, and it has many aspects. The best work a man can do is undoubtedly the most useful work—the work that conduces most to the general happiness. But we of the proletariate can't take our choice always: as your English proverb plainly puts it, with your true English bluntness, "beggars mustn't be choosers." We must, each in his place, do the work that's set before us by the privileged classes. It's impossible for us to go nicely discriminating between work that's useful for the community, work that's merely harmless, and work that's positively detrimental. How can we insure it? A man's a printer, say. There's a generally useful trade, in which, on the whole, he labours for the good and enlightenment of the world—for he may print scientific books, good books, useful books; and most printing, on the average, is useful. But how's he to know what sort of thing he's printing? He may be printing "Gold and the Proletariate," or he may be printing obscurantist and retrogressive treatises by the enemies of humanity. Look at my own trade, again. You'd say at first sight, Mr. Oswald, that to make microscopes must be a good thing in the end for the world at large: and so it is, no doubt; but half of them—ay, more than half of them—are thrown away: mere wasted labour, a good workman's time and skill lavished needlessly on some foolish rich man's caprices and amusement. Often enough, now, I make a good instrument—an instrument, with all its fittings, worth fifty or a hundred pounds. That takes a long time to make, and I'm a skilled workman; and the instrument may fall into the hands of a scientific man who'll use it in discovery, in verification, in promoting knowledge, in lessening disease and mitigating human suffering. That's the good side of my trade. But, mark you, now,' and the old man wiped his forehead rapidly with his sleeve, 'it has its bad side too. As often as not, I know, some rich man will buy that machine, that cost me so much time and trouble to make, and will buy a few dozen stock slides with it, and will bring it out once in a moon to show his children or a few idle visitors the scales on a butterfly's wing, or the hairs on the leg of a common flea. Uta sets those things up by the thousand for the dealers to sell to indolent dilettanti. The appetite of the world at large for the common flea is simply insatiable. And it's for that, perhaps, that I'm spoiling my eyesight now, grinding and grinding and grinding at this very lens, and fitting the thing to an accurate fraction of a millimetre, as we always fit these things—we who are careful and honest workmen—to show an idle man's friends the hairs on a flea's fore-leg. If that isn't enough to make a man asha-med of our present wasteful and chaotic organisation, I should think he must be a survival from the preglacial epoch—as, indeed, most of us actually are!'

'But, after all, Herr Schurz,' said Harry, expostulating, 'you get paid for your labour, and the rich man is doing better by encouraging your skill than by encouraging the less useful skill of other workmen.'

'Ah, yes,' cried Herr Schurz, warmly, 'that's the doctrine of the one-eyed economists; that's the capitalist way of looking at it; but it isn't our way—it isn't ours. Is it nothing, think you, that all that toil of mine—of a sensible man's—goes to waste, to gratify the senseless passing whim of a wealthy nobody? Is it nothing that he uselessly monopolises the valuable product of my labour, which in other and abler hands might be bringing forth good fruit for the bettering and furthering of universal humanity? I tell you, Mr. Oswald, half the best books, half the best apparatus, half the best appliances in all Europe, are locked up idle in rich men's cabinets, effecting no good, beget-ting no discoveries, bringing forth no interest, doing nothing but foster the anti-social pride of their wealthy possessors. But that isn't what friend Ernest wants to ask me about to-day. He wants to know about his own course in a difficult case; and instead of answering him, here am I, maundering away, like an old man that I am, into the generalised platitudes of "Gold and the Proletariate." Well, Le Breton, what I should say in your particular instance is this. A man with the fear of right before his eyes may, under existing circumstances, lawfully accept any work that will keep him alive, provided he sees no better and more useful work equally open to him. He may take the job the capitalists impose, if he can get nothing worthier to do elsewhere. Now, if you don't teach this young Tregellis, what alternative have you? Why, to become a master in a school—Eton, perhaps, or Rugby, or Marlborough—and teach other equally useless members of prospective aristocratic society. That being so, I think you ought to do what's best for yourself and your family for the present—for the present—till the time of deliverance comes. You see, there is one member of your family to whom the matter is of immediate importance.'

'Ronald,' said Ernest, interrupting him.

'Yes, Ronald. A good boy; a socialist, too, though he doesn't know it—one of us, born of us, and only apart from us in bare externals. Well, would it be most comfortable for poor Ronald that you should go to these Exmoor people, or that you should take a mastership, get rooms somewhere, and let him live with you? He's not very happy with your mother, you say. Wouldn't he be happier with you? What think you? Charity begins at home, you know: a good proverb—a good, sound, sensible, narrow-minded, practical English proverb!'

'I've thought of that,' Ernest said, 'and I'll ask him about it. Whichever he prefers, then, I'd better decide upon, had I?'

'Do so,' Herr Max answered, with a nod. 'Other things equal, our first duty is to those nearest to us.'

What Herr Max said was law to his disciples, and Ernest went

Grant Allen

his way contented.

'Mr. Oswald seems a very nice young man,' Uta Schurz said, looking up from the microscope slides she had begun to mount at the moment her regular translating work was interrupted by their sudden entry. She had been taking quiet glances at Harry all the while, in her unobtrusive fashion; for Uta had learned always to be personally unobtrusive—'the prophet's donkey,' those irreverent French exiles used to call her—and she had come to the conclusion that he was a decidedly handsome and manly fellow.

'Which do you like best, Uta—Oswald or Le Breton?' asked her father.

'Personally,' Uta answered, 'I should prefer Mr. Oswald. To live always with Mr. Le Breton would be like living with an abstraction. No woman would ever care for him; she might just as well marry Spinoza's Ethics or the Ten Commandments. He's a perfect model of a socialist, and nothing else. Mr. Oswald has some human nature in him as well.'

'There are two kinds of socialists,' said Herr Max, bending once more over his glasses; 'the one kind is always thinking most of its rights; the other kind is always thinking most of its duties. Oswald belongs to the first, Le Breton to the second. I've often observed it so among men of their two sorts. The best socialists never come from the bourgeoisie, nor even from the proletariate; they come from among the voluntarily declasses aristocrats. Your workman or your bourgeois who has risen, and who interests himself in social or political questions, is always thinking, "Why shouldn't I have as many rights and privileges as these other people have?" The aristocrat who descends is always thinking, "Why shouldn't these other people have as many rights and privileges as I have?" The one type begets aggressive self-assertion, the other type begets a certain gentle spirit of self-effacement. You don't often find men of the aristocratic class with any ethical element in them—their hereditary antecedents, their breeding, their environment, are all hostile to it; but when you do find them, mark my words, Uta, they make the truest and most earnest friends of the popular cause of any. Their sympathy and interest in it is all unselfish.'

'And yet,' Uta answered firmly, 'I still prefer Mr. Oswald. And if you care for my opinion, I should say that the aristocrat does all the dreaming, but the bourgeois does all the fighting; and that's the most important thing practically, after all.'

An hour later, Ernest was talking his future plans over with his brother Ronald. Would it be best for Ronald that he should take a mastership, and both should live together, or that he should go for the present to the Exmoors', and leave the question of Ronald's home arrangements still unsettled?

'It's so good of you to think of me in the matter, Ernest,' Ronald said, pressing his hand gently; 'but I don't think I ought to go away from mother before I'm twenty-one. To tell you the truth, Ernest, I hardly flatter myself she'd be really sorry to get rid of me; I'm afraid I'm a dreadful thorn in her side at present; she doesn't understand my ways, and perhaps I don't sympathise enough with hers; but still, if I were to propose to go, I feel sure she'd be very much annoyed, and treat it as a serious act of insubordination on my part. While I'm a minor, at least, I ought to remain with her; the Apostle tells us to obey our parents, in the Lord; and as long as she requires nothing from me that doesn't involve a dereliction of principle I think I must bear with it, though I acknowledge it's a cross, a heavy cross. Thank you so much for thinking of it, dearest Ernest.' And his eyes filled once more with tears as he spoke.

So it was finally arranged that for the present at least Ernest should accept Lady Exmoor's offer, and that as soon as Ronald was twenty-one he should look about for a suitable mastership, in order for the two brothers to go immediately into rooms together. Lady Le Breton was surprised at the decision; but as it was in her favour, she wisely abstained from gratifying her

Grant Allen

natural desire to make some more uncomplimentary references to the snuffy old German socialist. Sufficient unto the day was the triumph thereof; and she had no doubt in her own mind that if once Ernest could be induced to live for a while in really good society the well-known charms and graces of that society must finally tame his rugged breast, and wean him away from his unaccountable devotion to those horrid continental communists.

CHAPTER VIII

IN THE CAMP OF THE PHILISTINES

Dunbude Castle, Lord Exmoor's family seat, stands on the last spurs of the great North Devon uplands, overlooking the steep glen of a little boulder-encumbered stream, and commanding a distant view of the Severn Sea and the dim outlines of the blue Welsh hills beyond it. Behind the house, a castle only by courtesy (on the same principle as that by which every bishop lives in a palace), rises the jagged summit of the Cleave, a great weather-worn granite hill, sculptured on top by wind and rain into those fantastic lichen-covered pillars and tora and logans in which antiquarian fancy used so long to find the visible monuments of Druidical worship. All around, a wide brown waste of heather undulates and tosses wildly to the sky; and on the summit of the rolling moor where it rises and swells in one of its many rounded bosses, the antlered heads and shoulders of the red deer may often be seen etched in bold relief against the clear sky-line to the west, on sunny autumn evenings. But the castle itself and the surrounding grounds are not planned to harmonise with the rough moorland English scenery into whose midst they were unceremoniously pitchforked by the second earl. That distinguished man of taste, a light of the artistic world in his own day, had brought back from his Grand Tour his own ideal of a strictly classical domestic building, formed by impartially compounding a Palladian palace, a Doric temple, and a square redbrick English manor-house. After pulling down the original fourteenth-century castle, he had induced an eminent architect of the time to conspire with him in giving solid and permanent reality to this his awful imagining; and when he had completed it all, from portico to attic, he had extorted even the critical praise of Horace Walpole, who described it in one of his letters as a 'singular triumph of classical taste and architectural ingenuity.' It still remains unrivalled in its kind, the ugliest great country-seat in the county of Devon—some respectable authorities even say in the whole of England.

In front of the house an Italian garden, with balustrades of very doubtful marble, leads down by successive terraces and broad flights of steps to an artificial octagonal pool, formed by carefully destroying the whole natural beauty of the wild and rocky little English glen beneath. To feed it by fitting a conduit, the moss-grown boulders that strew the bed of the torrent above and below have been carefully removed, and the unwilling stream, as it runs into the pool, has been coerced into a long straight channel, bordered on either side by bedded turf, and planed off at measured intervals so as to produce a series of eminently regular and classical cascades. Even Lord Exmoor himself, who was a hunting man, without any pretence to that stupid rubbish about taste, did not care for the hopeless exterior of Dunbude Castle: he frankly admitted that the place was altogether too doosid artificial for the line of country. If they'd only left it alone, he said, in its own native condition, it would have been really pretty; but as they'd doctored it and spoilt it, why, there was nothing on earth to be done but just put up with it and whistle over it. What with the hounds, and the mortgages, and the settlements, and the red deer, and Goodwood, the estate couldn't possibly afford any money for making alterations down in the gardens.

The dog-cart was in waiting at the station to carry Ernest up to the castle; and as he reached the front door, Lady Hilda Tregellis strolled up the broad flight of steps from the garden to meet him. Lady Hilda was tall and decidedly handsome, as Ernest had rightly told Edie, but not pretty, and she was also just twenty. There was a free, careless, bold look in her face, that showed her at once a girl of spirit; indeed, if she had not been born a Tregellis, it was quite clear that she would have been predestined to turn out a strong-minded woman. There was nothing particularly delicate in Lady Hilda's features; they were well-modelled, but neither regular nor cold, nor with that peculiar stamp of artificial breeding which is so often found in the faces of English ladies. On the contrary, she looked like a perfectly self-confident handsome actress, too self-confident to be self-conscious, and accustomed to admiration wherever she turned. As Ernest jumped down from the dog-cart she advanced quickly to shake hands with him, and look him over critically from head to foot like a schoolboy taking stock of a new fellow.

'I'm so glad you've come, Mr. Le Breton,' she said, with an open smile upon her frank face. 'I was dreadfully afraid you wouldn't care for our proposition. Dunbude's the dullest hole in England, and we want somebody here to brighten it up, sadly. Did you ever see such an ugly monstrosity before, anywhere?'

'The country about's lovely,' Ernest answered, 'but the house itself is certainly rather ugly.'

'Ugly! It's hideous. And it's as dull as it's big,' said Hilda vehemently. 'You can't think what a time we have of it here half the year! I'm always longing for the season to come. Papa fills the house here with hunting men and shooting men— people without two ideas in their heads, you know, just like himself; and even THEY go out all day, and leave us women from morning till night to the society of their wives and daughters, who are exactly like them. Mr. Walsh—that's Lynmouth's last tutor—he was a perfect stick, a Cambridge man; Cambridge men always ARE sticks, I believe; you're Oxford, of course, aren't you? I thought so. Still, even Mr. Walsh was a little society, for I assure you, if it hadn't been for him, I should never have seen anybody, to talk to, from year's end to year's end. So when Mr. Walsh was going to leave us, I said to mamma, "Why not ask one of the Mr. Le Bretons?" I wanted to have somebody sensible here, and so I got her to let me write to your brother Ronald about the tutorship. Did he send you the letter? I hope you didn't think it was mine. Mamma dictated it, for I don't write such formal letters as that on my own account, I can tell you. I hate conventionality of any sort. At Dunbude we're all conventional, except me; but I won't be. Come up into the billiard-room, here, and sit down awhile; William will see about your portmanteau and things. Papa's out, of course, and so's Lynmouth; and mamma's somewhere or other, I don't know where; and so there's nobody in particular at home for you to report yourself to. You may as well come in here while I ring for them to get you some lunch ready. Nobody ever gets anything ready beforehand in this house. We lunched ourselves an hour ago.'

Ernest smiled at her volubility, and followed her quickly into the big bare billiard-room. He walked over to the fire and began to warm himself, while Hilda took down a cue and made stray shots in extraordinary angles at impossible cannons, all the time, as she went on talking to him. 'Was it very cold on the way down?' she asked.

'Yes, fairly. I'm not sorry to see the fire again. Why, you're quite an accomplished player.'

'There's nothing else to do at Dunbude, that's why. I practise about half my lifetime. So I wrote to your brother Ronald, as I was telling you, from mamma's dictation; and when I heard you were really coming, I was quite delighted about it. Do you remember, I met you twice last year, once at the Dolburys', and once somewhere else; and I thought you'd be a very good sort of person for Dunbude, you know, and about as much use to Lynmouth as anybody could be, which isn't saying much, of course, for he's a dreadful pickle. I insisted on putting in my letter that he was a dreadful pickle (that's a good stroke off the red; just enough side on), though mamma didn't want me to; because I thought you ought to know about it beforehand. But you remember him at Marlborough, of course; he was only a little fellow then, but still a pickle. He always was and he always will be. He's out shooting, now, with papa; and you'll never get him to settle down to anything, as long as there's a snipe or a plover banging about on the moor anywhere. He's quite incorrigible. Do you play at all? Won't you take a cue till your lunch's ready?'

'No, I don't play,' Ernest answered, half hesitating, 'or at least very little.'

'Oh, then you'll learn here, because you'll find nothing else to do. Do you shoot?'

'Oh no, never. I don't think it right.'

'Ah, yes, I remember. How delightful! Lady Le Breton told me all about it. You've got notions, haven't you? You're a Nihilist or a Fenian or something of that sort, and you don't shoot anything but czars and grand dukes, do you? I believe you want to cut all our heads off and have a red republic. Well, I'm sure that's very refreshing; for down here we're all as dull as sticks together; Tories, every one of us to a man; perfect unanimity; no differences of opinion; all as conventional and proper as the vicar's sermons. Now, to have somebody who wants to cut your head off, in the house, is really delightful. I love originality. Not that I've ever seen anybody original in all my life, for I haven't, but I'm sure it would be delightful if I did. One reads about original people in novels, you know, Dickens and that sort of thing; and I often think I should like to meet some of them (good stroke again; legs, legs, legs, if you please—no, it hasn't legs enough); but here, or for the matter of that, in town either, we never see anybody but the same eternal round of Algies, and Monties, and Berties, and Hughs—all very nice young men, no doubt; exceedingly proper, nothing against them; good shots, capital partners, excellent families, everything on earth that anybody could desire, except a single atom of personal originality. I assure you, if they were all shaken up in a bag together and well mixed, in evening clothes (so as not to tell them apart by the tweeds, you know), their own mothers wouldn't be able to separate them afterwards. But if you don't shoot and don't play billiards, I'm sure I don't know what you'll ever find to do with yourself here at Dunbude.'

'Don't you think,' Ernest said quietly, taking down a, cue, 'one ought to have something better to do with one's time than shooting and playing billiards? In a world where so many labouring people are toiling and slaving in poverty and misery on our behalf, don't you think we should be trying to do something or other in return for universal humanity, to whom we owe so much for our board and lodging and clothing and amusement?'

'Well, now, that's just what I mean,' said Hilda ecstatically, with a neat shot off the cushion against the red and into the middle pocket; 'that's such a delightfully original way of looking at things, you see. We all of us here talk always about the partridges, and the red deer, and the turnips, and the Church, and dear Lady This, and that odious Lady That, and the growing insolence of the farmers, and the shocking insubordination of the lower classes, and the difficulty of getting really good servants, and the dreadful way those horrid Irish are shooting their kind-hearted indulgent landlords; or else we talk—the women especially—about how awfully bored we are. Lawn-tennis, you know, and dinners, and what a bad match Ethel Thingumbob has made. But you talk another kind of slang; I dare say it doesn't mean much; you know you're not working at anything very much more serious than we are; still it's a novelty. When we go to a coursing meeting, we're all on the hounds; but you're on the hare, and that's so delightfully original. I haven't the least doubt that if we were to talk about the Irish, you'd say you thought they ought to shoot their landlords. I remember you shocked mamma by saying something like it at the Dolburys'. Now, of course, it doesn't matter to me a bit which is right; you say the poor tenants are starving, and papa says the poor landlords can't get in their rents, and actually have to give up their hounds, poor fellows; and I don't know which of you is the most to be believed; only, what papa says is just the same thing that everybody says, and what you say has a certain charming freshness and variety about it. It's so funny to be told that one ought really to take the tenants into consideration. Exactly like your brother Ronald's notions about servants!'

'Your lunch is ready in the dining-room, sir,' said a voice at the door.

'Come back here when you've finished, Mr. Le Breton,' Hilda called after him. 'I'll teach you how to make that cannon you missed just now. If you mean to exist at Dunbude at all, it's absolutely necessary for you to learn billiards.'

Ernest turned in to lunch with an uncomfortable misgiving on his mind already that Dunbude was not exactly the right place for such a man as he to live in.

During the afternoon he saw nothing more of the family, save Lady Hilda; and it was not till the party assembled in the drawing-room before dinner that he met Lord and Lady Exmoor and his future pupil. Lynmouth had grown into a tall, handsome, manly-looking boy since Ernest last saw him; but he certainly looked exactly what Hilda had called him—a pickle. A few minutes' introductory conversation sufficed to show Ernest that whatever mind he possessed was wholly given over to horses, dogs, and partridges, and that the post of tutor at Dunbude Castle was not likely to prove a bed of roses.

'Seen the paper, Connemara?' Lord Exmoor asked of one of his guests, as they sat down to dinner. 'I haven't had a moment myself to snatch a look at the "Times" yet this evening; I'm really too busy almost even to read the daily papers. Anything fresh from Ireland?'

'Haven't seen it either,' Lord Connemara answered, glancing towards Lady Hilda. 'Perhaps somebody else has looked at the papers'?'

Nobody answered, so Ernest ventured to remark that the Irish news was rather worse again. Two bailiffs had been murdered near Castlebar.

'That's bad,' Lord Exmoor said, turning towards Ernest. 'I'm afraid there's a deal of distress in the West.'

'A great deal,' Ernest answered; 'positive starvation, I believe, in some parts of County Galway.'

'Well, not quite so bad as that,' Lord Exmoor replied, a little startled. 'I don't think any of the landlords are actually starving yet, though I've no doubt many of them are put to very great straits indeed by their inability to get in their rents.'

Ernest couldn't forbear gently smiling to himself at the misapprehension. 'Oh, I didn't mean the landlords,' he said quickly: 'I meant among the poor people.' As he spoke he was aware that Lady Hilda's eyes were fixed keenly upon him, and that she was immensely delighted at the temerity and originality displayed in the notion of his publicly taking Irish tenants into consideration at her father's table.

'Ah, the poor people,' Lord Exmoor answered with a slight sigh of relief, as who should say that THEIR condition didn't much matter to a philosophic mind. 'Yes, to be sure; I've no doubt some of them are very badly off, poor souls. But then they're such an idle improvident lot. Why don't they emigrate now, I should like to know?'

Ernest reflected silently that the inmates of Dunbude Castle did not exactly set them a model of patient industry; and that Lady Hilda's numerous allusions during the afternoon to the fact that the Dunbude estates were 'mortgaged up to the eyelids' (a condition of affairs to which she always alluded as though it were rather a subject of pride and congratulation than otherwise) did not speak very highly for their provident economy either. But even Ernest Le Breton had a solitary grain of worldly wisdom laid up somewhere in a corner of his brain, and he didn't think it advisable to give them the benefit of his own views upon the subject.

'There's a great deal of rubbish talked in England about Irish affairs, you know, Exmoor,' said Lord Connemara confidently. 'People never understand Ireland, I'm sure, until they've actually lived there. Would you believe it now, the correspondent of one of the London papers was quite indignant the other day because my agent had to evict a man for three years' rent at Ballynamara, and the man unfortunately went and died a week later on the public roadside. We produced medical evidence to show that he had suffered for years from heart disease, and would have died in any case, wherever he had been; but the editor fellow wanted to make political capital out of it, and kicked up quite a fuss about my agent's shocking inhumanity. As if we could possibly help ourselves in the matter! People must get their rents in somehow, mustn't they?'

'People must get their rents in somehow, of course,' Lord Exmoor assented, sympathetically; 'and I know all you men who are unlucky enough to own property in Ireland have a lot of trouble about it nowadays. Upon my word, what with Fenians, and what with Nihilists, and what with Communards, I really don't know what the world is coming to.'

'Most unchristian conduct, I call it,' said Lady Exmoor, who went in for being mildly and decorously religious. 'I really can't understand how people can believe such wicked doctrines as these communistic notions that are coming over people in these latter days.'

'No better than downright robbery,' Lord Connemara answered. 'Shaking the very foundations of society, I think it. All done so recklessly, too, without any care or any consideration.'

Ernest thought of old Max Schurz, with his lifelong economical studies, and wondered when Lord Connemara had found time to turn his own attention from foxes and fishing to economical problems; but, by a perfect miracle, he said nothing.

'You wouldn't believe the straits we're put to, Lady Exmoor,'

Grant Allen

the Irish Earl went on, 'through this horrid no-rent business. Absolute poverty, I assure you—absolute downright poverty. I've had to sell the Maid of Garunda this week, you know, and three others of the best horses in my stable, just to raise money for immediate necessities. Wanted to buy a most interesting missal, quite unique in its way, offered me by Menotti and Cicolari, dirt cheap, for three thousand guineas. It's quite a gem of late miniaturist art—vellum folio, with borders and head-pieces by Giulio Clovio. A marvellous bargain!'

'Giulio Clovio,' said Lord Exmoor, doubtfully. 'Who was he? Never heard of him in my life before.'

'Never heard of Giulio Clovio!' cried Lord Connemara, seizing the opportunity with well-affected surprise. 'You really astonish me. He was a Croatian, I believe, or an Illyrian—I forget which—and he studied at Rome under Giulio Romano. Wonderful draughtsman in the nude, and fine colourist; took hints from Raphael and Michael Angelo.' So much he had picked up from Menotti and Cicolari, and, being a distinguished connoisseur, had made a mental note of the facts at once, for future reproduction upon a fitting occasion. 'Well, this missal was executed for Cardinal Farnese, as a companion volume to the famous Vita Christi in the Towneley collection. You know it, of course, Lady Exmoor?'

'Of course,' Lady Exmoor answered faintly, with a devout hope that Lord Connemara wouldn't question her any further upon the subject; in which case she thought it would probably be the safest guess to say that she had seen it at the British Museum or in the Hamilton Library.

But Lord Connemara luckily didn't care to press his advantage. 'The Towneley volume, you see,' he went on fluently—he was primed to the muzzle with information on that subject—'was given by the Cardinal to the Pope of that time—Paul the Third, wasn't it, Mr. Le Breton?—and so got into the possession of old Christopher Towneley, the antiquary. But this companion folio, it seems, the Cardinal wouldn't let go out of his own possession; and so it's been handed down in his own family (with a bar sinister, of course, Exmoor—you remember the story of Beatrice Malatesta?) to the present time. It's very existence wasn't suspected till Cicolari—wonderfully smart fellow, Cicolari—unearthed it the other day from a descendant of the Malatestas, in a little village in the Campagna. He offered it to me, quite as an act of friendship, for three thousand guineas; indeed, he begged me not to let Menotti know how cheap he was selling it. for fear he might interfere and ask a higher price for it. Well, I naturally couldn't let such a chance slip me—for the credit of the family, it ought to be in the collection—and the consequence was, though I was awfully sorry to part with her, I was absolutely obliged to sell the Maid for pocket-money, Lady Hilda—I assure you, for pocket-money. My tenants won't pay up, and nothing will make them. They've got the cash actually in the bank; but they keep it there, waiting for a set of sentimentalists in the House of Commons to interfere between us, and make them a present of my property. Rolling in money, some of them are, I can tell you. One man, I know as a positive fact, sold a pig last week, and yet pretends he can't pay me. All the fault of these horrid communists that you were speaking of, Lady Exmoor—all the fault of these horrid communists.'

'You're rather a communist yourself, aren't you, Mr. Le Breton?' asked Lady Hilda boldly from across the table. 'I remember you told me something once about cutting the throats of all the landlords.'

Lady Exmoor looked as though a bomb-shell had dropped into the drawing-room. 'My dear Hilda,' she said, 'I'm sure you must have misunderstood Mr. Le Breton. You can't have meant anything so dreadful as that, Mr. Le Breton, can you?'

'Certainly not,' Ernest answered, with a clear conscience. 'Lady Hilda has put her own interpretation upon my casual words. I haven't the least desire to cut anybody's throat, even metaphorically.'

Hilda looked a little disappointed; she had hoped for a good rattling discussion, in which Ernest was to shock the whole table—it does people such a lot of good, you know, to have a nice round shocking; but Ernest was evidently not inclined to show fight for her sole gratification, and so she proceeded to her alternative amusement of getting Lord Connemara to display the full force of his own inanity. This was an easy and unending source of innocent enjoyment to Lady Hilda, enhanced by the fact that she knew her father and mother were anxious to see her Countess of Connemara, and that they would be annoyed by her public exposition of that eligible young man's intense selfishness and empty-headedness.

Altogether, Ernest did not enjoy his first week at the Exmoors'. Nor did he enjoy the second, or the third, or the fourth week much better. The society was profoundly distasteful to him: the world was not his world, nor the talk his talk; and he grew so sick of the perpetual discussion of horses, dogs, pheasants, dances, and lawn tennis, with occasional digressions on Giulio Clovio and the Connemara gallery, that he found even a chat with Lady Hilda (who knew and cared for nothing, but liked to chat with him because he was 'so original') a pleasant relief, by comparison, from the eternal round of Lord Exmoor's anecdotes about famous racers or celebrated actresses. But worst of all he did not like his work; he felt that, useless as he considered it, he was not successfully performing even the useless function he was paid to fulfil. Lynmouth couldn't learn, wouldn't learn, and wasn't going to learn. Ernest might as well have tried to din the necessary three plays of Euripides into the nearest lamp-post. Nobody encouraged him to learn in any way, indeed Lord Exmoor remembered that he himself had scraped through somehow at Christ Church, with the aid of a private tutor and the magic of his title, and he hadn't the least doubt that Lynmouth would scrape through in his turn in like manner. And so, though most young men would have found the Dunbude tutorship the very acme of their wishes—plenty of amusements and nothing to do for them—Ernest Le Breton found it to the last degree irksome and unsatisfactory. Not that he had ever to complain of any unkindliness on the part of the Exmoor family; they were really in their own way very kind-hearted, friendly sort of people—that is to say, towards all members of their own circle; and as they considered Ernest one of themselves, in virtue of their acquaintance with his mother, they really did their best to make him as happy and comfortable as was in their power. But then he was such a very strange young man! 'For what on earth can you do,' as Lord Exmoor justly asked, 'with a young fellow who won't shoot, and who won't fish, and who won't hunt, and who won't even play lansquenet?' Such a case was clearly hopeless. He would have liked to see more of Miss Merivale, little Lady Sybil's governess (for there were three children in the family); but Miss Merivale was a timid, sensitive girl, and she did not often encourage his advances, lest my lady should say she was setting her cap at the tutor. The consequence was that he was necessarily thrown much upon Lady Hilda's society; and as Lady Hilda was laudably eager to instruct him in billiards, lawn tennis, and sketching, he rapidly grew to be quite an adept at those relatively moral and innocuous amusements, under her constant instruction and supervision.

'It seems to me,' said that acute observer, Lord Lynmouth, to his special friend and confidante, the lady's-maid, 'that Hilda makes a doocid sight too free with that fellow Le Breton. Don't you think so, Euphemia?'

'I should hope, my lord,' Euphemia answered demurely, 'that Lady Hilda would know her own place too well to demean herself with such as your lordship's tutor. If I didn't feel sure of that, I should have to mention the matter seriously to my lady.'

Nevertheless, the lady's-maid immediately stored up a mental note on the subject in the lasting tablets of her memory, and did not fail gently to insinuate her views upon the question to Lady Exmoor, as she arranged the pearls in the false plaits for dinner that very evening.

CHAPTER IX

THE WOMEN OF THE LAND

'Mr. Le Breton! Mr. Le Breton! Papa says Lynmouth may go out trout-fishing with him this afternoon. Come up with me to the Clatter. I'm going to sketch there.'

'Very well, Lady Hilda; if you want my criticism, I don't mind if I do. Let me carry your things; it's rather a pull up, even for you, with your box and easel!'

Hilda gave him her sketch-book and colours, and they turned together up the Cleave behind the Castle.

A Clatter is a peculiar Devonshire feature, composed of long loose tumbled granite blocks piled in wild disorder along the narrow summit of a saddle-backed hill. It differs from a tor in being less high and castellated, as well as in its longer and narrower contour. Ernest and Hilda followed the rough path up through the gorse and heather to the top of the ridge, and then scrambled over the grey lichen-covered rooks together to the big logan-stone whose evenly-poised and tilted mass crowned the actual summit. The granite blocks were very high and rather slippery in places, for it was rainy April weather, so that Ernest had to take his companion's hand more than once in his to help her over the tallest boulders. It was a small delicate hand, though Hilda was a tall well-grown woman; ungloved, too, for the sake of the sketching; and Hilda didn't seem by any means unwilling to accept Ernest's proffered help, though if it had been Lord Connemara who was with her instead, she would have scorned assistance, and scaled the great mossy masses by herself like a mountain antelope. Light-footed and lithe of limb was Lady Hilda, as befitted a Devonshire lass accustomed to following the Exmoor stag-hounds across their wild country on her own hunter. Yet she seemed to find a great deal of difficulty in clambering up the Clatter on that particular April morning, and move than once Ernest half fancied to himself that she leaned on his arm longer than was absolutely necessary for support or assistance over the stiffest places.

'Here, by the logan, Mr. Le Breton,' she said, motioning him where to put her camp-stool and papers. 'That's a good point of view for the rocks yonder. You can lie down on the rug and give me the benefit of your advice and assistance.'

'My advice is not worth taking,' said Ernest. 'I'm a regular duffer at painting and sketching. You should ask Lord Connemara. He knows all about art and that sort of thing.'

'Lord Connemara!' echoed Hilda contemptuously. 'He has a lot of pictures in his gallery at home, and he's been told by sensible men what's the right thing for him to say about them; but he knows no more about art, really, than he knows about fiddlesticks.'

'Doesn't he, indeed?' Ernest answered languidly, not feeling any burning desire to discuss Lord Connemara's artistic attainments or deficiencies.

'No, he doesn't,' Hilda went on, rather defiantly, as though Ernest had been Lady Exmoor; 'and most of these people that come here don't either. They have galleries, and they get artists and people who understand about pictures to talk with them, and so they learn what's considered the proper thing to say of each of them. But as to saying anything spontaneous or original of their own about a picture or any other earthly thing—why, you know, Mr. Le Breton, they couldn't possibly

Grant Allen

do it to save their lives.'

'Well, there I should think you do them, as a class, a great injustice,' said Ernest, quietly; 'you're evidently prejudiced against your own people. I should think that if there's any subject on which our old families really do know anything, it's art. Look at their great advantages.'

'Nonsense,' Hilda answered, decisively. 'Fiddlesticks for their advantages. What's the good of advantages without a head on your shoulders, I should like to know. And they haven't got heads on their shoulders, Mr. Le Breton; you know they haven't.'

'Why, surely,' said Ernest, in his simple fashion, looking the question straight in the face as a matter of abstract truth, 'there must be a great deal of ability among peers and peers' sons. All history shows it; and it would be absurd if it weren't so; for the mass of peers have got their peerages by conspicuous abilities of one sort or another, as barristers, or soldiers, or politicians, or diplomatists, and they would naturally hand on their powers to their different descendants.'

'Oh, yes, there are some of them with brains, I suppose,' Hilda answered, as one who makes a great concession. 'There's Herbert Alderney, who's member for somewhere or other— Church Stretton, I think—and makes speeches in the House; he's clever, they say, but such a conceited fellow to talk to. And there's Wilfrid Faunthorp, who writes poems, and gets them printed in the magazines, too, because he knows the editors. And there's Randolph Hastings, who goes in for painting, and has little red and blue daubs at the Grosvenor by special invitation of the director. But somehow they none of them strike me as being really original. Whenever I meet anybody worth talking to anywhere—in a railway train or so on—I feel sure at once he's an ordinary commoner, not even Honourable; and he is invariably, you may depend upon it.'

'That would naturally happen on the average of instances,'

Ernest put in, smiling, 'considering the relative frequency of peers and commoners in this realm of England. Peers, you know, or even Honourables are not common objects of the country, numerically speaking.'

'They are to me, unfortunately,' Hilda replied, looking at him inquiringly. 'I hardly ever meet anybody else, you know, and I'm positively bored to death by them, and that's the truth, really. It's most unlucky, under the circumstances, that I should happen to be the daughter of one peer, and be offered promiscuously as wife to the highest bidder among half a dozen others, if only I would have them. But I won't, Mr. Le Breton, I really won't. I'm not going to marry a fool, just to please my mother. Nothing on earth would induce me to marry Lord Connemara, for example.'

Ernest looked at her and smiled, but said nothing.

Lady Hilda put in a stroke or two more to her pencil outline, and then continued her unsolicited confidences. 'Do you know, Mr. Le Breton,' she went on, 'there's a conspiracy—the usual conspiracy, but still a regular conspiracy I call it— between Papa and Mamma to make me marry that stick of a Connemara. What is there in him, I should like to know, to make any girl admire or love him? And yet half the girls in London would be glad to get him, for all his absurdity. It's monstrous, it's incomprehensible, it's abominable; but it's the fact. For my part, I must say I do like a little originality. And whenever I hear Papa, and Uncle Sussex, and Lord Connemara talking at dinner, it does seem to me too ridiculously absurd that they should each have a separate voice in Parliament, and that you shouldn't even have a fraction of a vote for a county member. What sort of superiority has Lord Connemara over you, I wonder?' And she looked at Ernest again with a search-ing glance, to see whether he was to be moved by such a personal and emphatic way of putting the matter.

Ernest looked back at her curiously in his serious simplicity, and only answered, 'There are a great many queer inequalities and absurdities in all our existing political systems, Lady Hilda.'

Hilda smiled to herself—a quiet smile, half of disappointment, half of complacent feminine superiority. What a stupid fellow he was in some ways, after all! Even that silly Lord Connemara would have guessed what she was driving at, with only a quarter as much encouragement. But Ernest must be too much afraid of the social barrier clearly; so she began again, this time upon a slightly different but equally obvious tack.

'Yes, there are; absurd inequalities really, Mr. Le Breton; very absurd inequalities. You'd get rid of them all, I know. You told me that about cutting all the landlords' heads off, I'm sure, though you said when I spoke about it before Mamma, the night you first came here, that you didn't mean it. I remember it perfectly well, because I recollect thinking at the time the idea was so charmingly and deliciously original.'

'You must be quite mistaken, Lady Hilda,' Ernest answered calmly. 'You misunderstood my meaning. I said I would get rid of landlords—by which I meant to say, get rid of them as landlords, not as individuals. I don't even know that I'd take away the land from them all at once, you know (though I don't think it's justly theirs); I'd deprive them of it tentatively and gradually.'

'Well, I can't see the justice of that, I'm sure,' Hilda answered carelessly. 'Either the land's ours by right, or it isn't ours. If it's ours, you ought to leave it to us for ever; and if it isn't ours, you ought to take it away from us at once, and make it over to the people to whom it properly belongs. Why on earth should you keep them a day longer out of their own?'

Ernest laughed heartily at this vehement and uncompromising sans-culottism. 'You're a vigorous convert, anyhow,' he said, with some amusement; 'I see you've profited by my instruction. You've put the question very plump and straightforward. But in practice it would be better, no doubt, gradually to educate out the landlords, rather than to dispossess them at one blow of what they honestly, though wrongly, imagine to be their own. Let all existing holders keep the land during their own lifetime and their heirs', and resume it for the nation after their lives, allowing for the rights of all children born of marriages between people now living.'

'Not at all,' Hilda answered in a tone of supreme conviction. 'I'm in favour of simply cutting our heads off once for all, and making our families pay all arrears of rent from the very beginning. That or nothing. Put the case another way. Suppose, Mr. Le Breton, there was somebody who had got a grant from a king a long time ago, allowing him to hang any three persons he chose annually. Well, suppose this person and his descendants went on for a great many generations extorting money out of other people by threatening to kill them and letting them off on payment of a ransom. Suppose, too, they always killed three a year, some time or other, pour encourager les autres—just to show that they really meant it. Well, then, if one day the people grew wise enough to inquire into the right of these licensed extortioners to their black mail, would you say, "Don't deprive them of it too unexpectedly. Let them keep it during their own lifetime. Let their children hang three of us annually after them. But let us get rid of this fine old national custom in the third generation." Would that be fair to the people who would be hanged for the sake of old prescription in the interval, do you think?'

Ernest laughed again at the serious sincerity with which ehe was ready to acquiesce in his economical heresies. 'You're quite right,' he said: 'the land is the people's, and there's no reason on earth why they should starve a minute longer in order to let Lord Connemara pay three thousand guineas for spurious copies of early Italian manuscripts. And yet it would be difficult to get most people to see it. I fancy, Lady Hilda, you must really be rather cleverer than most people.'

'I score one,' thought Hilda to herself, 'and whatever happens, whether I marry a peer or a revolutionist, I certainly won't marry a fool.' 'I'm glad you think so,' she went on aloud, 'because I know your opinion's worth having. I should like to be clever, Mr. Le Breton, and I should like to know all about everything, but what chance has one at Dunbude? Do you know, till you came here, I never got any sensible conversation with anybody.' And she sighed gently as she put her head on one side to take a good view of her sketchy little picture. Lady Hilda's profile was certainly very handsome, and she showed it to excellent advantage when she put her head on one side. Ernest looked at her and thought so to himself; and Lady Hilda's quick eye, glancing sideways for a second from the paper, noted immediately that he thought so.

'Mr. Le Breton,' she began again, more confidentially than ever, 'one thing I've quite made up my mind to; I won't be tied for life to a stick like Lord Connemara. In fact, I won't marry a man in that position at all. I shall choose for myself, and marry a man for the worth that's in him, I assure you it's a positive fact, I've been proposed to by no fewer than six assorted Algies and Berties and Monties in a single season; besides which some of them follow me even down here to Dunbude. Papa and mamma are dreadfully angry because I won't have any of them: but I won't. I mean to wait, and marry whoever I choose, as soon as I find a man I can really love and honour.'

She paused and looked hard at Ernest. 'I can't speak much plainer than that,' she thought to herself, 'and really he must be stupider than the Algies and the Monties themselves if he doesn't see I want him to propose to me. I suppose all women would say it's awfully unwomanly of me to lead up to his cards in this way—throwing myself at his head they'd call it; but what does that matter? I WON'T marry a fool, and I WILL marry a man of some originality. That's the only thing in the world worth troubling one's head about. Why on earth doesn't he take my hand, I wonder? What further can he be waiting for?' Lady Hilda was perfectly accustomed to the usual preliminaries of a declaration, and only awaited Ernest's first step to proceed in due order to the second. Strange to say, her heart was actually beating a little by anticipation. It never even occurred to her—the belle of three seasons—that possibly Ernest mightn't wish to marry her. So she sat looking pensively at her picture, and sighed again quietly.

But Ernest, wholly unsuspicious, only answered, 'You will do quite right, Lady Hilda, to marry the man of your own choice, irrespective of wealth or station.'

Hilda glanced up at him curiously, with a half-disdainful smile, and was just on the point of saying, 'But suppose the man of my own choice won't propose to me?' However, as the words rose to her lips, she felt there was a point at which even she should yield to convention: and there were plenty of opportunities still before her, without displaying her whole hand too boldly and immediately. So she merely turned with another sigh, this time a genuine one, to her half-sketched outline. 'I shall bring him round in time,' she said to herself, blushing a little at her unexpected discomfiture. 'I shall bring him round in time; I shall make him propose to me! I don't care if I have to live in a lodging with him, and wash up my own tea-things; I shall marry him; that I'm resolved upon. He's as mad as a March hare about his Communism and his theories and things; but I don't care for that; I could live with him in comfort, and I couldn't live in comfort with the Algies and Monties. In fact, I believe—in a sort of way—I believe I'm almost in love with him. I have a kind of jumpy feeling in my heart when I'm talking with him that I never feel when I'm talking with other young men, even the nicest of them. He's not nice; he's a bear; and yet, somehow, I should like to marry him.'

'Mr. Le Breton,' she said aloud, 'the sun's all wrong for sketching to-day, and besides it's too chilly. I must run about a bit among the rocks.' ('At least I shall take his hand to help me,' she thought, blushing.) 'Come and walk with me? It's no use trying to draw with one's hands freezing.' And she crumpled up the unfinished sketch hastily between her fingers. Ernest jumped up to follow her; and they spent the next hour scrambling up and down the Clatter, and talking on less dangerous subjects than Lady Hilda's matrimonial aspirations.

'Still I shall make him ask me yet,' Lady Hilda thought to herself, as she parted from him to go up and dress for dinner. 'I shall manage to marry him, somehow; or if I don't marry him, at any rate I'll marry somebody like him.' For it was really the principle, not the person, that Lady Hilda specially insisted upon.

CHAPTER X

THE DAUGHTERS OF CANAAN

May, beautiful May, had brought the golden flowers, and the trees in the valley behind the sleepy old town of Calcombe Pomeroy were decking themselves in the first wan green of their early spring foliage. The ragged robins were hanging out, pinky red, from the hedgerows; the cuckoo was calling from the copse beside the mill stream; and the merry wee hedge-warblers were singing lustily from the topmost sprays of hawthorn, with their full throats bursting tremulously in the broad sunshine. And Ernest Le Breton, too, filled with the season, had come down from Dunbude for a fortnight's holiday, on his premised visit to his friend Oswald, or, to say the truth more plainly, to Oswald's pretty little sister Edie. For Ernest had fully made up his mind by this time what it was he had come for, and he took the earliest possible opportunity of taking a walk with Edie alone, through the tiny glen behind the town, where the wee stream tumbles lazily upon the big slow-turning vanes of the overshot mill-wheel.

'Let us sit down a bit on the bank here, Miss Oswald,' he said to his airy little companion, as they reached the old stone bridge that crosses the stream just below the mill-house; 'it's such a lovely day one feels loath to miss any of it, and the scenery here looks so bright and cheerful after the endless brown heather and russet bracken about Dunbude. Not that Exmoor isn't beautiful in its way, too—all Devonshire is beautiful alike for that matter; but then it's more sombre and woody in the north, and much less spring-like than this lovely quiet South Devon country.'

'I'm so glad you like Calcombe,' Edie said, with one of her unfailing blushes at the indirect flattery to herself implied in praise of her native county; 'and you think it prettier than Dunbude, then, do you?'

'Prettier in its own way, yes, though not so grand of course; everything here is on a smaller scale. Dunbude, you know, is almost mountainous.'

'And the Castle?' Edie asked, bringing round the conversation to her own quarter, 'is that very fine? At all like Warwick, or our dear old Arlingford?'

'Oh, it isn't a castle at all, really,' Ernest answered; 'only a very big and ugly house. As architecture it's atrocious, though it's comfortable enough inside for a place of the sort.'

'And the Exmoors, are they nice people? What kind of girl is Lady Hilda, now?' Poor little Edie? she asked the question shyly, but with a certain deep beating in her heart, for she had often canvassed with herself the vague possibility that Ernest might actually fall in love with Lady Hilda. Had he fallen in love with her already, or had he not? She knew she would be able to guess the truth by his voice and manner the moment he answered her. No man can hide that secret from a woman who loves him. Yet it was not without a thrill and a flutter that she asked him, for she thought to herself, what must she seem to him after all the grand people he had been mixing with so lately at Dunbude? Was it possible he could see anything in her, a little country village girl, coming to her fresh from the great ladies of that unknown and vaguely terrible society?

'Lady Hilda!' Ernest answered, laughing—and as he said the words Edie knew in her heart that her question was answered, and blushed once more in her bewitching fashion. 'Lady Hilda! Oh, she's a very queer girl, indeed; she's not at all clever, really, but she has the one virtue of girls of her class—their perfect frankness. She's frank all over—no reserve or reticence at all about her. Whatever she thinks she says, without the slightest idea that you'll see anything to laugh at or to find fault with in it. In matters of knowledge, she's frankly ignorant. In matters of taste, she's frankly barbaric. In matters of religion, she's frankly heathen. And in matters of ethics, she's frankly immoral—or rather extra-moral,' he added, quickly correcting himself for the misleading expression.

'I shouldn't think from your description she can be a very nice person,' Edie said, greatly relieved, and pulling a few tall grasses at her side by way of hiding her interest in the subject. 'She can't be a really nice girl if she's extra-moral, as you call it.'

'Oh, I don't mean she'd cut one's throat or pick one's pocket, you know,' Ernest went on quickly, with a gentle smile. 'She's got a due respect for the ordinary conventional moralities like other people, no doubt; but in her case they're only social prejudices, not genuine ethical principles. I don't suppose she ever seriously asked herself whether anything was right or wrong or not in her whole lifetime. In fact, I'm sure she never did; and if anybody else were to do so, she'd be immensely surprised and delighted at the startling originality and novelty of thought displayed in such a view of the question.'

'But she's very handsome, isn't she?' Edie asked, following up her inquiry with due diligence.

'Handsome? oh, yes, in a bold sort of actress fashion. Very handsome, but not, to me at least, pleasing. I believe most men admire her a great deal; but she lacks a feminine touch dreadfully. She dashes away through everything as if she was hunting; and she DOES hunt too, which I think bad enough in anybody, and horrible in a woman.'

'Then you haven't fallen in love with her, Mr. Le Breton? I half imagined you would, you know, as I'm told she's so very attractive.'

'Fallen in love with HER, Miss Oswald! Fallen in love with Hilda Tregellis! What an absurd notion! Heaven forbid it!'

'Why so, please?'

'Why, in the first place, what would be the use of it? Fancy Lady Exmoor's horror at the bare idea of her son's tutor falling in love with Lady Hilda! I assure you, Miss Oswald, she would evaporate at the very mention of such an unheard-of enormity. A man must be, if not an earl, at least a baronet with five thousand a year, before he dare face the inexpressible indignation of Lady Exmoor with an offer of marriage for Lady Hilda.'

'But people don't always fall in love by tables of precedence,' Edie put in simply. 'It's quite possible, I suppose, for a man who isn't a duke himself to fall in love with a duke's daughter, even though the duke her papa mayn't personally happen to approve of the match. However, you don't seem to think Lady Hilda herself a pleasant girl, even apart from the question of Lady Exmoor's requirements?'

'Miss Oswald,' Ernest said, looking at her suddenly, as she sat half hiding her face with her parasol, and twitching more violently than ever at the tall grasses; 'Miss Oswald, to tell you the truth, I haven't been thinking much about Hilda Tregellis or any of the other girls I've met at Dunbude, and for a very sufficient reason, because I've had my mind too much preoccupied by somebody else elsewhere.'

Edie blushed even more prettily than before, and held her peace, half raising her eyes for a second in an enquiring glance at his, and then dropping them hastily as they met, in modest trepidation. At that moment Ernest had never seen anything so beautiful or so engaging as Edie Oswald.

'Edie,' he said, beginning again more boldly, and taking her little gloved hand almost unresistingly in his; 'Edie, you know my secret. I love you. Can you love me?'

Edie looked up at him shyly, the tears glistening and trembling a little in the corner of her big bright eyes, and for a moment she answered nothing. Then she drew away her hand hastily and said with a sigh, 'Mr. Le Breton, we oughtn't to be talking so. We mustn't. Don't let us. Take me home, please, at once, and don't say anything more about it.' But her heart beat within her bosom with a violence that was not all unpleasing, and her looks half belied her words to Ernest's keen glance even as she spoke them.

'Why not, Edie?' he said, drawing her down again gently by her little hand as she tried to rise hesitatingly. 'Why not? tell me. I've looked into your face, and though I can hardly dare to hope it or believe it, I do believe I read in it that you really might love me.'

'Oh, Mr. Le Breton,' Edie answered, a tear now quivering visibly on either eyelash, 'don't ask me, please don't ask me. I wish you wouldn't. Take me home, won't you?'

Ernest dropped her hand quietly, with a little show of despondency that was hardly quite genuine, for his eyes had already told him better. 'Then you can't love me, Miss Oswald,' he said, looking at her closely. 'I'm sorry for it, very sorry for it; but I'm grieved if I have seemed presumptuous in asking you.'

This time the two tears trickled slowly down Edie's cheek— not very sad tears either—and she answered hurriedly, 'Oh, I don't mean that, Mr. Le Breton, I don't mean that. You misunderstand me, I'm sure you misunderstand me.'

Ernest caught up the trembling little hand again. 'Then you CAN love me, Edie?' he said eagerly, 'you can love me?'

Edie answered never a word, but bowed her head and cried a little, silently. Ernest took the dainty wee gloved hand between his own two hands and pressed it tenderly. He felt in return a faint pressure.

'Then why won't you let me love you, Edie?' he asked, looking at the blushing girl once more.

'Oh, Mr. Le Breton,' Edie said, rising and moving away from the path a little under the shade of the big elm-tree, 'it's very wrong of me to let you talk so. I mustn't think of marrying you, and you mustn't think of marrying me. Consider the difference in our positions.'

'Is that all?' Ernest answered gaily. 'Oh, Edie, if that's all, it isn't a very difficult matter to settle. My position's exactly nothing, for I've got no money and no prospects; and if I ask you to marry me, it must be in the most strictly speculative fashion, with no date and no certainty. The only question is, will you consent to wait for me till I'm able to offer you a home to live in? It's asking you a great deal, I know; and you've made me only too happy and too grateful already; but if you'll wait for me till we can marry, I shall live all my life through to repay you for your sacrifice.'

'But, Mr. Le Breton,' Edie said, turning towards the path and drying her eyes quickly, 'I really don't think you ought to marry me. The difference in station is so great—even Harry would allow the difference in station. Your father was a great man, and a general and a knight, you know; and though my dear father is the best and kindest of men, he isn't anything of that sort, of course.'

A slight shade of pain passed across Ernest's face. 'Edie,' he said, 'please don't talk about that—please don't. My father was a just and good man, whom I loved and honoured deeply; if there's anything good in any of us boys, it comes to us from my dear father. But please don't speak to me about his profession. It's one of the griefs and troubles of my life. He was a soldier, and an Indian soldier too; and if there's anything more certain to me than the principle that all fighting is very wrong and indefensible, it's the principle that our rule in India is utterly unjust and wicked. So instead of being proud of my father's profession, much as I respected him, I'm profoundly ashamed of it; and it has been a great question to me always how far I was justified at all in living upon the pension given me for his Indian services.'

Edie looked at him half surprised and half puzzled. It was to her such an odd and unexpected point of view. But she felt instinctively that Ernest really and deeply meant what he said, and she knew she must not allude to the subject again. 'I beg your pardon,' she said simply, 'if I've put it wrong; yet you know I can't help feeling the great disparity in our two situations.'

'Edie,' said Ernest, looking at her again with all his eyes—'I'm going to call you "Edie" always now, so that's understood between us. Well, I shall tell you exactly how I feel about this matter. From the first moment I saw you I felt drawn towards you, I felt that I couldn't help admiring you and sympathising with you and loving you. If I dared I would have spoken to you that day at Iffley; but I said to myself "She will not care for me; and besides, it would be wrong of me to ask her just yet." I had nothing to live upon, and I oughtn't to ask you to wait for me—you who are so pretty, and sweet and good, and clever—I ought to leave you free to your natural prospect of marrying some better man, who would make you happier than I can ever hope to do. So I tried to put the impulse aside; I waited, saying to myself that if you really cared for me a little bit, you would still care for me when I came to Calcombe Pomeroy. But then my natural selfishness overcame me—you can forgive me for it, Edie; how could I help it when I had once seen you? I began to be afraid some other man would be beforehand with you; and I liked you so much I couldn't bear to think of the chance that you might be taken away from me before I asked you. All day long, as I've been walking alone on those high grey moors at Dunbude, I've been thinking of you; and at last I made up my mind that I MUST come and ask you to be my wife—some time—whenever we could afford to marry. I know I'm asking you to make a great sacrifice for me; it's more than I have any right to ask you; I'm ashamed of myself for asking it; I can only make you a poor man's wife, and how long I may have to wait even for that I can't say; but if you'll only consent to wait for me, Edie, I'll do the best that lies in me to make you as happy and to love you as well as any man on earth could ever do.'

Edie turned her face towards his, and said softly, 'Mr. Le Breton, I will wait for you as long as ever you wish; and I'm so happy, oh so happy.'

There was a pause for a few moments, and then, as they walked homeward down the green glen, Edie said, with something more of her usual archness, 'So after all you haven't fallen in love with Lady Hilda! Do you know, Mr. Le Breton, I rather fancied at Oxford you liked me just a little tiny bit; but when I heard you were going to Dunbude I said to myself, "Ah, now he'll never care for a quiet country girl like me!" And when I knew you were coming down here to Calcombe, straight from all those grand ladies at Dunbude, I felt sure you'd be disenchanted as soon as you saw me, and never think anything more about me.'

'Then you liked me, Edie?' Ernest asked eagerly. 'You wanted me really to come to Calcombe to see you?'

'Of course I did, Mr. Le Breton. I've liked you from the first moment I saw you.'

'I'm so glad,' Ernest went on quickly. 'I believe all real love is love at first sight. I wouldn't care myself to be loved in any other way. And you thought I might fall in love with Lady Hilda?'

'Well, you know, she is sure to be so handsome, and so accomplished, and to have had so many advantages that I have never had. I was afraid I should seem so very simple to you after Lady Hilda.'

'Oh, Edie!' cried Ernest, stopping a moment, and gazing at the little light airy figure. 'I only wish you could know the difference. Coming from Dunbude to Calcombe is like coming from darkness into light. Up there one meets with nobody but essentially vulgar-minded selfish people—people whose whole life is passed in thinking and talking about nothing but dogs, and horses, and partridges, and salmon; racing, and hunting, and billiards, and wines; amusements, amusements, amusements, all of them coarse and most of them cruel, all day long. Their talk is just like the talk of grooms and gamekeepers in a public-house parlour, only a little improved by better English and more money. Will So-and-so win the Derby? What a splendid run we had with the West Somerset on Wednesday! Were you in at the death of that big fox at Coulson's Corner? Ought the new vintages of Madeira to be bottled direct or sent round the Cape like the old ones? Capital burlesque at the Gaiety, but very slow at the Lyceum. Who will go to the Duchess of Dorsetshire's dance on the twentieth:—and so forth for ever. Their own petty round of selfish pleasures from week's end to week's end—no thought of anybody else, no thought of the world at large, no thought even of any higher interest in their own personalities. Their politics are just a selfish calculation of their own prospects— land, Church, capital, privilege. Their religion (when they have any) is just a selfish regard for their own personal future welfare. From the time I went to Dunbude to this day, I've never heard a single word about any higher thought of any sort—I don't mean only about the troubles or the aspirations of other people, but even about books, about science, about art, about natural beauty. They live in a world of amusing oneself and of amusing oneself in vulgar fashions—as a born clown would do if he came suddenly into a large fortune. The women are just as bad as the men, only in a different way— not always even that; for most of them think only of the Four-in-hand Club and the pigeon-shooting at Hurlingham—things to sicken one. Now, I've known selfish people before, but not selfish people utterly without any tincture of culture. I come away from Dunbude, and come down here to Calcombe: and the difference in the atmosphere makes one's very breath come and go freer. And I look at you, Edie, and think of you beside Lady Hilda Tregellis, and I laugh in my heart at the difference that artificial rules have made between you. I wish you knew how immeasurably her superior you are in every way. The fact is, it's a comfort to escape from Dunbude for a while and get down here to feel oneself once more, in the only true sense of the word, in a little good society.'

While these things were happening in the Bourne Close, palsied old Miss Luttrell, mumbling and grumbling inarticulately to herself, was slowly tottering down the steep High Street of Calcombe Pomeroy, on her way to the village grocer's. She shambled in tremulously to Mrs. Oswald's counter, and seating herself on a high stool, as was her wont, laid herself out distinctly for a list of purchases and a good deliberate ill-natured gossip.

'Two pounds of coffee, if you please, Mrs. Oswald,' she began with a quaver; 'coffee, mind, I say, not chicory; your stuff always has the smallest possible amount of flavour in it, it seems to me, for the largest possible amount of quantity; all chicory, all chicory—no decent coffee to be had now in Calcombe Pomeroy. So your son's at home this week, is he? Out of work, I suppose? I saw him lounging about on the beach, idling away his time, yesterday; pity he wasn't at some decent trade, instead of hanging about and doing nothing, as if he was a gentleman. Five pounds of lump sugar, too; good lump sugar, though I expect I shall get nothing but beetroot; it's all beetroot now, my brother tells me; they've ruined the West Indies with their emancipation fads and their differential duties and the Lord knows what—we had estates in the West Indies ourselves, all given up to our negroes nowadays—and now I believe they have to pay the French a bounty or something of the sort to induce them to make sugar out of beetroot, because the negroes won't work without whipping, so I understand; that's what comes in the end of your Radical fal-lal notions. Well, five pounds of lump, and five pounds of moist, though the one's as bad as the other, really. A great pity about your son. I hope he'll get a place again soon. It must be a trial to you to have him so idle!'

'Well, no, ma'am, it's not,' Mrs. Oswald answered, with such self-restraint as she could command. 'It's not much of a trial to his father and me, for we're glad to let him have a little rest after working so hard at Oxford. He works too hard, ma'am, but he gets compensation for it, don't 'ee see, Miss Luttrell, for he's just been made a Fellow of the Royal Society—"for his mathematical eminence," the "Times" says—a Fellow of the Royal Society.'

Even this staggering blow did not completely crush old Miss Luttrell. 'Fellow of the Royal Society,' she muttered feebly through her remaining teeth. 'Must be some mistake some-where, Mrs. Oswald—quite impossible. A very meritorious young man, your son, doubtless; but a National schoolmaster's hardly likely to be made a Fellow of the Royal Society. Oh, I remember you told me he's not a National schoolmaster, but has something to do at one of the Oxford colleges. Yes, yes; I see what it is—Fellow of the Royal Geographical Society. You subscribe a guinea, and get made a Fellow by subscription, just for the sake of writing F.R.G.S. after your name; it gives a young man a look of importance.'

'No, Miss Luttrell, it isn't that; it's THE Royal Society; and if you'll wait a moment, ma'am, I'll fetch you the president's letter, and the diploma, to let you see it.'

'Oh, no occasion to trouble yourself, Mrs. Oswald!' the old lady put in, almost with alacrity, for she had herself seen the announcement of Harry Oswald's election in the 'Times' a few days before. 'No occasion to trouble yourself, I'm sure; I daresay you may be right, and at any rate it's no business of mine, thank heaven. I never want to poke my nose into anybody else's business. Well, talking of Oxford, Mrs. Oswald, there's a very nice young man down here at present; I wonder if you know where he's lodging? I want to ask him to dinner. He's a young Mr. Le Breton—one of the Cheshire Le Bretons, you know. His father was Sir Owen Le Breton, a general in the Indian army—brother officer of Major Standish Luttrell's and very nice people in every way. Lady Le Breton's a great friend of the Archdeacon's, so I should like to show her son some little attention. He's had a very distinguished career at Oxford—your boy may have heard his name, perhaps—and now he's acting as tutor to Lord Lynmouth, the eldest son of Lord Exmoor, you know; Lady Exmoor was a second cousin of my brother's wife; very nice people, all of them. The Le Bretons are a really good family, you see; and the Archdeacon's exceedingly fond of them. So I thought if you could tell me where this young man is lodging—you shop-people pick up all the gossip in the place, always—I'd ask him to dinner to meet the Rector and Colonel Turnbull and my nephew, who would probably be able to offer him a little shooting.'

'There's no partridges about in May, Miss Luttrell,' said Mrs. Oswald, quietly smiling to herself at the fancy picture of Ernest seated in congenial converse with the Rector, Colonel Turnbull, and young Luttrell; 'but as to Mr. Le Breton, I DO happen to know where he's stopping, though it's not often that I know any Calcombe gossip, save and except what you're good enough to tell me when you drop in, ma'am; for Mr. Le Breton's stopping here, in this house, with us, ma'am, this very minute.'

'In this house, Mrs. Oswald!' the old lady cried with a start, wagging her unsteady old head this time in genuine surprise; 'why, I didn't know you let lodgings. I thought you and your daughter were too much of fine ladies for THAT, really. I'm glad to hear it. I'll leave a note for him.'

'No, Miss Luttrell, we don't let lodgings, ma'am, and we don't need to,' Mrs. Oswald answered, proudly. 'Mr. Le Breton's stopping here as my son's guest. They were friends at Oxford together: and now that Mr. Le Breton has got his holiday, like, Harry's asked him down to spend a fortnight at Calcombe Pomeroy. And if you'll leave a note I'll be very happy to give it to him as soon as he comes in, for he's out walking now with Harry and Edith.'

Old Miss Luttrell sat for half a minute in unwonted silence, revolving in her poor puzzled head what line of tactics she ought to adopt under such a very singular and annoying combination of circumstances. Stopping at the village grocer's!—this was really too atrocious! The Le Bretons were all as mad as hatters, that she knew well; all except the mother, who was a sensible person, and quite rational. But old Sir Owen was a man with the most absurd religious fancies—took an interest in the souls of the soldiers; quite right and proper, of course, in a chaplain, but really too ridiculous in a regular field officer. No doubt Ernest Le Breton had taken up some equally extraordinary notions—liberty, equality, fraternity, and a general massacre, probably; and he had picked up Harry Oswald as a suitable companion in his revolutionary schemes and fancies. There was no knowing what stone wall one of those mad Le Bretons might choose to run his head against. Still, the practical difficulty remained—how could she extricate herself from this awkward dilemma in such a way as to cover herself with glory, and inflict another bitter humiliation on poor Mrs. Oswald? If only she had known sooner that Ernest was stopping at the Oswalds, she wouldn't have been so loud in praise of the Le Breton family; she would in that case have dexterously insinuated that Lady Le Breton was only a half-pay officer's widow, living on her pension; and that her boys had got promotion at Oxford as poor scholars, through the Archdeacon's benevolent influence. It was too late now, however, to adopt that line of defence; and she fell back accordingly upon the secondary position afforded her by the chance of taking down Mrs. Oswald's intolerable insolence in another fashion.

'Oh, he's out walking with your daughter, is he?' she said, maliciously. 'Out walking with your daughter, Mrs. Oswald, NOT with your son. I saw her passing down the meadows half an hour ago with a strange young man; and her brother stopped behind near the millpond. A strange young man; yes, I noticed particularly that he looked like a gentleman, and I was quite surprised that you should let her walk out with him in that extraordinary manner. Depend upon it, Mrs. Oswald, when young gentlemen in Mr. Le Breton's position go out walking with young women in your daughter's position, they mean no good by it—they mean no good by it. Take my advice, Mrs. Oswald, and don't permit it. Mr. Le Breton's a very nice young man, and well brought up no doubt—I know his mother's a woman of principle—still, young men will be young men; and if your son goes bringing down his fine Oxford acquaintances to Calcombe Pomeroy, and you and your husband go flinging Miss Jemima—her name's Jemima, I think—at the young men's heads, why, then, of course, you must take the consequences—you must take the consequences!' And with this telling Parthian shot discharged carefully from the shadow of the doorway, accompanied by a running comment of shrugs, nods, and facial distortions, old Miss Luttrell successfully shuffled herself out of the shop, her list unfinished, leaving poor Mrs. Oswald alone and absolutely speechless with indignation. Ernest Le Breton never got a note of invitation from the Squire's sister: but before nightfall all that was visitable in Calcombe Pomeroy had heard at full length of the horrid conspiracy by which those pushing upstart Oswalds had inveigled a son of poor Lady Le Breton's down to stop with them, and were now trying to ruin his prospects by getting him to marry their brazen-faced hussey, Jemima Edith.

When Edie returned from her walk that afternoon, Mrs. Oswald went up into her bedroom to see her daughter. She knew at once from Edie's radiant blushing face and moist eyes what had taken place, and she kissed the pretty shrinking girl tenderly on her forehead. 'Edie darling, I hope you will be happy,' she whispered significantly.

'Then you guess it all, mother dear?' asked Edie, relieved that she need not tell her story in set words.

'Yes, darling,' said the mother, kissing her again. 'And you said "yes."'

Edie coloured once more. 'I said "yes," mother, for I love him dearly.'

'He's a dear fellow,' the mother answered gently; 'and I'm sure he'll do his best to make you happy.'

Later on in the day, Harry came up and knocked at Edie's door. His mother had told him all about it, and so had Ernest. 'Popsy,' he said, kissing her also, 'I congratulate you. I'm so glad about it. Le Breton's the best fellow I know, and I couldn't wish you a better or a kinder husband. You'll have to wait for him, but he's worth waiting for. He's a good fellow and a clever fellow, and an affectionate fellow; and his family are everything that could be desired. It'll be a splendid thing for you to be able to talk in future about "my mother-in law, Lady Le Breton." Depend upon it, Edie dear, that always counts for something in society.'

Edie blushed again, but this time with a certain tinge of shame and disappointment. She had never thought of that herself, and she was hurt that Harry should think and speak of it at such a moment. She felt with a sigh it was unworthy of him and unworthy of the occasion. Truly the iron of Pi and its evaluations had entered deeply into his soul!

CHAPTER XI

CULTURE AND CULTURE

'I wonder, Berkeley,' said Herbert Le Breton, examining a coin curiously, 'what on earth can ever have induced you, with your ideas and feelings, to become a parson!'

'My dear Le Breton, your taste, like good wine, improves with age,' answered Berkeley, coldly. 'There are many reasons, any one of which may easily induce a sensible man to go into the Church. For example, he may feel a disinterested desire to minister to the souls of his poorer neighbours; or he may be first cousin to a bishop; or he may be attracted by an ancient and honourable national institution; or he may possess a marked inclination for albs and chasubles; or he may reflect upon the distinct social advantages of a good living; or he may have nothing else in particular to do; or he may simply desire to rouse the impertinent curiosity of all the indolent quidnuncs of his acquaintance, without the remotest intention of ever gratifying their underbred Paul Pry proclivities.'

Herbert Le Breton winced a little—he felt he had fairly laid himself open to this unmitigated rebuff—but he did not retire immediately from his untenable position. 'I suppose,' he said quietly, 'there are still people who really do take a practical interest in other people's souls—my brother Ronald does for one—but the idea is positively too ridiculous. Whenever I read any argument upon immortality it always seems to me remarkably cogent, if the souls in question were your soul and my soul; but just consider the transparent absurdity of supposing that every Hodge Chawbacon, and every rheumatic old Betty Martin, has got a soul, too, that must go on enduring for all eternity! The notion's absolutely ludicrous. What an infinite monotony of existence for the poor old creatures to endure for ever—being bored by their own inane personalities for a million aeons! It's simply appalling to think of!'

But Berkeley wasn't going to be drawn into a theological discussion—that was a field which he always sedulously and successfully avoided. 'The immortality of the soul,' he said quietly, 'is a Platonic dogma too frequently confounded, even by moderately instructed persons like yourself, Le Breton, with the Church's very different doctrine of the resurrection of the body. Upon this latter subject, my dear fellow, about which you don't seem to be quite clear or perfectly sound in your views, you'll find some excellent remarks in Bishop Pearson on the Creed—a valuable work which I had the pleasure of studying intimately for my ordination examination.'

'Really, Berkeley, you're the most incomprehensible and mysterious person I ever met in my whole lifetime!' said Herbert, dryly. 'I believe you take a positive delight in deceiving and mystifying one. Do you seriously mean to tell me you feel any interest at the present time of day in books written by bishops?'

'A modern bishop,' Berkeley answered calmly, 'is an unpicturesque but otherwise estimable member of a very distinguished ecclesiastical order, who ought not lightly to be brought into ridicule by lewd or lay persons. On that ground, I have always been in favour myself of gradually reforming his hat, his apron, and even his gaiters, which doubtless serve to render him at least conspicuous if not positively absurd in the irreverent eyes of a ribald generation. But as to criticising his literary or theological productions, my dear fellow, that would be conduct eminently unbecoming in a simple curate, and savouring of insubordination even in the person of an elderly archdeacon. I decline, therefore, to discuss the subject, especially

with a layman on whose orthodoxy I have painful doubts.—
Where's Oswald? Is he up yet?'

'No; he's down in Devonshire, my brother Ernest writes me.'

'What, at Dunbude? What's Oswald doing there?'

'Oh dear no; not at Dunbude: the peerage hasn't yet adopted
him—at a place called Calcombe Pomeroy, where it seems he
lives. Ernest has gone down there from Exmoor for a
fortnight's holiday. You remember, Oswald has a pretty
sister—I met her here in your rooms last October, in fact—
and I apprehend she may possibly form a measurable portion
of the local attractions. A pretty face goes a long way with
some people.'

Berkeley drew a deep breath, and looked uneasily out of the
window. This was dangerous news, indeed! What, little Miss
Butterfly, has the boy with the gauze net caught sight of you
already? Will he trap you and imprison you so soon in his little
gilded matrimonial cage, enticing you thereinto with soft
words and, sugared compliments to suit your dainty, delicate
palate? and must I, who have meant to chase you for the chief
ornament of my own small cabinet, be only in time to see you
pinioned and cabined in your white lace veils and other pretty
disguised entanglements, for his special and particular delectation? This must be looked into, Miss Butterfly; this must be
prevented. Off to Calcombe Pomeroy, then, or other parts
unknown, this very next to-morrow; and let us fight out the
possession of little Miss Butterfly with our two gauze nets in
opposition—mine tricked as prettily as I can trick it with tags
and ends of art-allurements and hummed to in a delicate
tune—before this interloping anticipating Le Breton has had
time to secure you absolutely for himself. Too austere for you,
little Miss Butterfly; good in his way, and kindly meaning, but
too austere. Better come and sun yourself in the modest wee
palace of art that I mean to build myself some day in some
green, sunny, sloping valley, where your flittings will not be
rudely disturbed by breath of poverty, nor your pretty feathery

wings ruthlessly clipped with a pair of doctrinaire, ethico-socialistic scissors. To Calcombe, then, to Calcombe—and not a day's delay before I get there. So much of thought, in his own quaint indefinite fashion, flitted like lightning through Arthur Berkeley's perturbed mind, as he stood gazing wistfully for one second out of his pretty latticed creeper-clad window. Then he remembered himself quickly with a short little sigh, and turned to answer Herbert Le Breton's last half-sneering innuendo.

'Something more than a pretty face merely,' he said, surveying Herbert coldly from head to foot; 'a heart too, and a mind, for all her flitting, not wholly unfurnished with good, sensible, solid mahogany English furniture. You may be sure Harry Oswald's sister isn't likely to be wanting in wits, at any rate.'

'Oswald's a curious fellow,' Herbert went on, changing the venue, as he always did when he saw Berkeley was really in earnest; 'he's very clever, certainly, but he can never outlive his bourgeois origin. The smell of tea sticks about him somehow to the end of the chapter. Don't you know, Berkeley, there are some fellows whose clothes seem to have been born with them, they fit so perfectly and impede their movement so little; while there are other fellows whose clothes look at once as if they'd been made for them by a highly respectable but imperfectly successful tailor. That's just what I always think about Harry Oswald in the matter of culture. He's got a great deal of culture, the very best culture, from the very best shop—Oxford, in fact—dressed himself up in the finest suit of clothes from the most fashionable mental tailor; but it doesn't seem to fit him naturally. He moves about in it uneasily, like a man unaccustomed to be clothed by a good workman. He looks in his mental upholstery like a greengrocer in evening dress. Now there's all the difference in the world between that sort of put-on culture and culture in the grain, isn't there? You may train up a grocer's son to read Dante, and to play Mendelssohn's Lieder, and to admire Fra Angelico; but you can't train him up to wear these things lightly and gracefully upon him as you and I do, who come by them naturally. WE are born to the

Grant Allen

sphere; HE rises to it.'

'You think so, Le Breton?' asked the curate with a quiet and suppressed smile, as he thought silently of the placid old shoemaker.

'Think so! my dear fellow, I'm sure of it. I can spot a man of birth from a man of mere exterior polish any day, anywhere. Talk as much nonsense as you like about all men being born free and equal—they're not. They're born with natural inequalities in their very nerve and muscle. When I was an undergraduate, I startled one of the tutors of that time by beginning my English essay once, "All men are by nature born free and unequal." I stick to it still; it's the truth. They say it takes three generations to make a gentleman; nonsense utterly; it takes at least a dozen. You can't work out the common fibre in such a ridiculous hurry. That results as a simple piece of deductive reasoning from all modern theories of heredity and variation.'

'I agree with you in part, Le Breton,' the parson said, eyeing him closely; 'in part but not altogether. What you say about Oswald's very largely true. His culture sits upon him like a suit made to order, not like a skin in which he was born. But don't you think that's due more to the individual man than to the class he happens to belong to? It seems to me there are other men who come from the same class as Oswald, or even from lower classes, but whose culture is just as much ingrained as, say, my dear fellow, yours is. They were born, no doubt, of naturally cultivated parents. And that's how your rule about the dozen generations that go to make a gentleman comes really true. I believe myself it takes a good many generations; but then none of them need have been gentlemen, in the ordinary sense of the word, before him. A gentleman, if I'm to use the expression as implying the good qualities conventionally supposed to be associated with it, a gentleman may be the final outcome and efflorescence of many past generations of quiet, unobtrusive, working-man culture—don't you think so?'

Herbert Le Breton smiled incredulously. 'I don't know that I do, quite,' he answered languidly. 'I confess I attach more importance than you do to the mere question of race and family. A thoroughbred differs from a cart-horse, and a greyhound from a vulgar mongrel, in mind and character as well as in body. Oswald seems to me in all essentials a bourgeois at heart even now.'

'But remember,' Berkeley said, rather warmly for him, 'the bourgeois class in England is just the class which must necessarily find it hardest to throw off the ingrained traces of its early origin. It has intermarried for a long time—long enough to have produced a distinct racial type like those you speak of among dogs and horses—the Philistine type, in fact—and when it tries to emerge, it must necessarily fight hard against the innate Philistinism of which it is conscious in its own constitution. No class has had its inequality with others, its natural inferiority, so constantly and cruelly thrust in its face; certainly the working-man has not. The working-man who makes efforts to improve himself is encouraged; the working-man who rises is taken by the hand; the working-man, whatever he does, is never sneered at. But it's very different with the shopkeeper. Naturally a little prone to servility—that comes from the very necessities of the situation—and laudably anxious to attain the level of those he considers his superiors, he gets laughed at on every hand. Being the next class below society, society is always engaged in trying to keep him out and keep him down. On the other hand, he naturally forms his ideal of what is fine and worth imitating from the example of the class above him; and therefore, considering what that class is, he has unworthy aims and snobbish desires. Either in his own person, or in the persons of his near relations, the wholesale merchant and the manufacturer—all bourgeois alike—he supplies the mass of nouveaux riches who are the pet laughing-stock of all our playwrights, and novelists, and comic papers. So the bourgeois who really knows he has something in him, like Harry Oswald, feels from the beginning painfully conscious of the instability of his position, and of the fact that men like you are cutting

Grant Allen

jokes behind his back about the smell of tea that still clings to him. That's a horrible drag to hold a man back—the sense that he must always be criticised as one of his own class—and that a class with many recognised failings. It makes him self-conscious, and I believe self-consciousness is really at the root of that slight social awkwardness you think you notice in Harry Oswald. A working-man's son need never feel that. I feel sure there are working-men's sons who go through the world as gentlemen mixing with gentlemen, and never give the matter of their birth one moment's serious consideration. Their position never troubles them, and it never need trouble them. Put it to yourself, now, Le Breton. Suppose I were to tell you my father was a working shoemaker, for example, or a working carpenter, you'd never think anything more about it; but if I were to tell you he was a grocer, or a baker, or a confectioner, or an ironmonger, you'd feel a certain indefinable class barrier set up between us two immediately and ever after. Isn't it so, now?'

'Perhaps it is,' Herbert answered dubitatively. 'But as he's probably neither the one nor the other, the hypothesis isn't worth seriously discussing. I must go off now; I've got a lecture at twelve. Good-bye. Don't forget the tickets for Thursday's concert.'

Arthur Berkeley looked after him with a contemptuous smile. 'The outcome of a race himself,' he thought, 'and not the best side of that race either. I was half tempted, in the heat of argument, to blurt out to him the whole truth about the dear gentle old Progenitor; but I'm glad I didn't now. After all, it's no use to cast your pearls before swine. For Herbert's essentially a pig—a selfish self-centred pig; no doubt a very refined and cultivated specimen of pigdom—the best breed; but still a most emphatic and consummate pig for all that. Not the same stuff in him that there is in Ernest—a fibre or two wanting somewhere. But I mustn't praise Ernest—a rival! a rival! It's war to the death between us two now, and no quarter. He's a good fellow, and I like him dearly; but all's fair in love and war; and I must go down to Calcombe to-morrow morning and forestall him immediately. Dear little Miss Butterfly, 'tis for your sake; you shall not be pinched and cramped to suit the Procrustean measure of Ernest Le Breton's communistic fancies. You shall fly free in the open air, and flash your bright silken wings, decked out bravely in scales of many hues, not toned down to too sober and quaker-like a suit of drab and dove-colour. You were meant by nature for the sunshine and the summer; you shall not be worried and chilled and killed with doses of heterodox political economy and controversial ethics. Better even a country rectory (though with a bad Late Perpendicular church), and flowers, and picnics, and lawn-tennis, and village small-talk, and the squire's dinner-parties, than bread and cheese and virtuous poverty in a London lodging with Ernest Le Breton. Romance lives again. The beautiful maiden is about to be devoured by a goggle-eyed monster, labelled on the back "Experimental Socialism"; the red cross knight flies to her aid, and drives away the monster by his magic music. Lance in rest! lyre at side! third class railway ticket in pocket! A Berkeley to the rescue! and there you have it.' And as he spoke, he tilted with his pen at an imaginary dragon supposed to be seated in the crimson rocking-chair by the wainscotted fireplace.

'Yes, I must certainly go down to Calcombe. No use putting it off any longer. I've arranged to go next summer to London, to keep house for the dear old Progenitor; the music is getting asked for, two requests for more this very morning; trade is looking up. I shall throw the curacy business overboard (what chance for modest merit that ISN'T first cousin to a Bishop in the Church as at present constituted?) and take to composing entirely for a livelihood. I wouldn't ask Miss Butterfly before, because I didn't wish to tie her pretty wings prematurely; but a rival! that's quite a different matter. What right has he to go poaching on my preserves, I should like to know, and trying to catch the little gold fish I want to entice for my own private and particular fish-pond! An interloper, to be turned out unmercifully. So off to Calcombe, and that quickly.'

He sat down to his desk, and taking out some sheets of blank music-paper, began writing down the score of a little song at which he had been working. So he continued till lunch-time, and then, turning to the table when the scout called him, took his solitary lunch of bread and butter, with a volume of Petrarch set open before him as he eat. He was lazily Englishing the soft lines of the original into such verse as suited his fastidious ear, when the scout came in suddenly once more, bringing in his hand the mid-day letters. One of them bore the Calcombe postmark. 'Strange,' Berkeley said to himself; 'at the very moment when I was thinking of going there. An invitation perhaps; the age of miracles is not yet past—don't they see spirits in a conjuror's room in Regent Street?—from Oswald, too; by Jove, it must be an invitation.' And he ran his eye down the page rapidly, to see if there was any mention of little Miss Butterfly. Yes; there was her name on the second sheet; what could her brother have to say to him about her?

'We have Ernest Le Breton down here now,' Oswald wrote, 'on a holiday from the Exmoors', and you may be surprised to hear that I shall probably have him sooner or later for a brother-in-law. He has proposed to and been accepted by my sister Edith; and though it is likely, as things stand at present, to be a rather long engagement (for Le Breton has nothing to marry upon), we are all very much pleased about it here at Calcombe. He is just the exact man I should wish my sister to marry; so pleasant and good and clever, and so very well connected. Felicitate us, my dear Berkeley!'

Arthur Berkeley laid the letter down with a quiet sigh, and folded his hands despondently before him. He hadn't seen very much of Edie, yet the disappointment was to him a very bitter one. It had been a pleasant day-dream, truly, and he was both to part with it so unexpectedly. 'Poor little Miss Butterfly,' he said to himself, tenderly and compassionately; 'poor, airy, flitting, bright-eyed little Miss Butterfly. I must give you up, must I, and Ernest Le Breton must take you for better, for worse, must he? La reyne le veult, it seems, and her word is law. I'm afraid he's hardly the man to make you happy, little lady; kind-hearted, well-meaning, but too much in earnest, too much absorbed in his ideas of right for a world where right's impossible, and every man for himself is the wretched sordid rule of existence. He will overshadow and darken your bright little life, I fear me; not intentionally—he couldn't do that—but by his Quixotic fads and fancies; good fads, honest fads, but fads wholly impracticable in this jarring universe of clashing interests, where he who would swim must keep his own head steadily above water, and he who minds his neighbour must sink like lead to the unfathomable bottom. He will sink, I doubt not, poor little Miss Butterfly; he will sink inevitably, and drag you down with him, down, down, down to immeasurable depths of poverty and despair. Oh, my poor little butterfly, I'm sorry for you, and sorry for myself. It was a pretty dream, and I loved it dearly. I had made you a queen in my fancy, and throned you in my heart, and now I have to dethrone you again, me miserable, and have my poor lonely heart bare and queenless!'

The piano was open, and he went over to it instinctively, strumming a few wild bars out of his own head, made up hastily on the spur of the moment. 'No, not dethrone you,' he went on, leaning back on the music-stool, and letting his hand wander aimlessly over the keys; 'not dethrone you; I shall never, never be able to do that. Little Miss Butterfly, your image is stamped there too deep for dethronement, stamped there for ever, indelibly, ineffaceably, not to be washed out by tears or laughter. Ernest Le Breton may take you and keep you; you are his; you have chosen him, and you have chosen in most things not unwisely, for he's a good fellow and true (let me be generous in the hour of disappointment even to the rival, the goggle-eyed impracticable dragon monstrosity), but you are mine, too, for I won't give you up; I can't give you up; I must live for you still, even if you know it not. Little woman, I will work for you and I will watch over you; I will be your earthly Providence; I will try to extricate you from the quagmires into which the well-meaning, short-sighted dragon will infallibly lead you. Dear little bright soul, my heart aches for you; I know the trouble you are bringing upon yourself;

but la reyne le veult, and it is not your humble servitor's business to interfere with your royal pleasure. Still, you are mine, for I am yours; yours, body and soul; what else have I to live for? The dear old Progenitor can't be with us many years longer; and when he is gone there will be nothing left me but to watch over little Miss Butterfly and her Don Quixote of a future husband. A man can't work and slave and compose sonatas for himself alone—the idea's disgusting, piggish, worthy only of Herbert Le Breton; I must do what I can for the little queen, and for her balloon-navigating Utopian Ernest. Thank heaven, no law prevents you from loving in your own heart the one woman whom you have once loved, no matter who may chance to marry her. Go, day-dream, fly, vanish, evaporate; the solid core remains still—my heart, and little Miss Butterfly. I have loved her once, and I shall love her, I shall love her for ever!'

He crumpled the letter up in his fingers, and flung it half angrily into the waste-paper basket, as though it were the embodied day-dream he was mentally apostrophising. It was sermon-day, and he had to write his discourse that very afternoon. A quaint idea seized him. 'Aha,' he said, almost gaily, in his volatile irresponsible fashion, 'I have my text ready; the hour brings it to me unsought; a quip, a quip! I shall preach on the Pool of Bethesda: "While I am coming, another steppeth down before me." The verse seems as if it were made on purpose for me; what a pity nobody else will understand it!' And he smiled quietly at the conceit, as he got the scented sheets of sermon-paper out of his little sandalwood davenport. For Arthur Berkeley was one of those curiously compounded natures which can hardly ever be perfectly serious, and which can enjoy a quaintness or a neat literary allusion even at a moment of the bitterest personal disappointment. He could solace himself for a minute for the loss of Edie by choosing a text for his Sunday's sermon with a prettily-turned epigram on his own position.

CHAPTER XII

THE MORE EXCELLENT WAY

At the very top of the winding footpath cut deeply into the sandstone side of the East Cliff Hill at Hastings, a wooden seat, set a little back from the road, invites the panting climber to rest for five minutes after his steep ascent from the primitive fisher village of Old Hastings, which nestles warmly in the narrow sun-smitten gulley at his feet. On this seat, one bright July morning, Herbert Le Breton lay at half length, basking in the brilliant open sunshine and evidently waiting for somebody whom he expected to arrive by the side path from the All Saints' Valley. Even the old coastguardsman, plodding his daily round over to Ecclesbourne, noticed the obvious expectation implied in his attentive attitude, and ventured to remark, in his cheery familiar fashion, 'She won't be long a-comin' now, sir, you may depend upon it: the gals is sure to be out early of a fine mornin' like this 'ere.' Herbert stuck his double eye-glass gingerly upon the tip of his nose, and surveyed the bluff old sailor through it with a stony British stare of mingled surprise and indignation, which drove the poor man hastily off, with a few muttered observations about some people being so confounded stuck up that they didn't even understand the point of a little good-natured seafarin' banter.

As the coastguardsman disappeared round the corner of the flagstaff, a young girl came suddenly into sight by the jutting edge of sandstone bluff near the High Wickham; and Herbert, jumping up at once from his reclining posture, raised his hat to

Grant Allen

her with stately politeness, and moved forward in his courtly graceful manner to meet her as she approached. 'Well, Selah,' he said, taking her hand a little warmly (judged at least by Herbert Le Breton's usual standard), 'so you've come at last! I've been waiting here for you for fully half an hour. You see, I've come down to Hastings again as I promised, the very first moment I could possibly get away from my pressing duties at Oxford.'

The girl withdrew her hand from his, blushing deeply, but looking into his face with evident pleasure and admiration. She was tall and handsome, with a certain dashing air of queenliness about her, too; and she was dressed in a brave, outspoken sort of finery, which, though cheap enough in its way, was neither common nor wholly wanting in a touch of native good taste and even bold refinement of contrast and harmony. 'It's very kind of you to come, Mr. Walters,' she answered in a firm but delicate voice. 'I'm so sorry I've kept you waiting. I got your letter, and tried to come in time; but father he's been more aggravating than usual, almost, this morning, and kept saying he'd like to know what on earth a young woman could want to go out walking for, instead of stopping at home at her work and minding her Bible like a proper Christian. In HIS time young women usen't to be allowed to go walking except on Sundays, and then only to chapel or Bible class. So I've not been able to get away till this very minute, with all this bundle of tracts, too, to give to the excursionists on the way. Father feels a most incomprehensible interest, somehow, in the future happiness of the Sunday excursionists.'

'I wish he'd feel a little more interest in the present happiness of his own daughter,' Herbert said smiling. 'But it hasn't mattered your keeping me waiting here, Selah. Of course I'd have enjoyed it all far better in your society—I don't think I need tell you that now, dear—but the sunshine, and the sea breeze, and the song of the larks, and the plash of the waves below, and the shouts of the fishermen down there on the beach mending their nets and putting out their smacks, have all been so delightful after our humdrum round of daily life at

Oxford, that I only wanted your presence here to make it all into a perfect paradise.—Why, Selah, how pretty you look in that sweet print! It suits your complexion admirably. I never saw you wear anything before so perfectly becoming.'

Selah drew herself up with the conscious pride of an unaffected pretty girl. 'I'm so glad you think so, Mr. Walters,' she said, playing nervously with the handle of her dark-blue parasol. 'You always say such very flattering things.'

'No, not flattering,' Herbert answered, smiling; 'not flattering, Selah, simply truthful. You always extort the truth from me with your sweet face, Selah. Nobody can look at it and not forget the stupid conventions of ordinary society. But please, dear, don't call me Mr. Walters. Call me Herbert. You always do, you know, when you write to me.'

'But it's so much harder to do it to your face, Mr. Walters,' Selah said, again blushing. 'Every time you go away I say to myself, "I shall call him Herbert as soon as ever he comes back again;" and every time you come back, I feel too much afraid of you, the moment I see you, ever to do it. And yet of course I ought to, you know, for when we're married, why, naturally, then I shall have to learn to call you Herbert, shan't I?'

'You will, I suppose,' Herbert answered, rather chillily: 'but that subject is one upon which we shall be able to form a better opinion when the time comes for actually deciding it. Meanwhile, I want you to call me Herbert, if you please, as a personal favour and a mark of confidence. Suppose I were to go on calling you Miss Briggs all the time! a pretty sort of thing that would be! what inference would you draw as to the depth of my affection? Well, now, Selah, how have these dreadful home authorities of yours been treating you, my dear girl, all the time since I last saw you?'

'Much the same as usual, Mr. Walters—Herbert, I mean,' Selah answered, hastily correcting herself. 'The regular round. Prayers; clean the shop; breakfast, with a chapter; serve in the shop all morning; dinner, with a chapter; serve in the shop all afternoon; tea, with a chapter; prayer meeting in the evening; supper, with a chapter; exhortation; and go to bed, sick of it all, to get up next morning and repeat the entire performance da capo, as they always say in the music to the hymn-books. Occasional relaxations,—Sunday at chapel three times, and Wednesday evening Bible class; mothers' assembly, Dorcas society, missionary meeting, lecture on the Holy Land, dissolving views of Jerusalem, and Primitive Methodist district conference in the Mahanaim Jubilee meeting hall. Salvation privileges every day and all the year round, till I'm ready to drop with it, and begin to wish I'd only been lucky enough to have been born one of those happy benighted little pagans in a heathen land where they don't know the value of the precious Sabbath, and haven't yet been taught to build Primitive Methodist district chapels for crushing the lives out of their sons and daughters!'

Herbert smiled a gentle smile of calm superiority at this vehement outburst of natural irreligion. 'You must certainly be bored to death with it all, Selah,' he said, laughingly. 'What a funny sort of creed it really is, after all, for rational beings! Who on earth could believe that the religion these people use to render your life so absolutely miserable is meant for the same thing as the one that makes my poor dear brother Ronald so perfectly and inexpressibly serene and happy? The formalism of lower natures, like your father's, has turned it into a machine for crushing all the spontaneity out of your existence. What a regime for a high-spirited girl like you to be compelled to live under, Selah!'

'It is, it is!' Selah answered, vehemently. 'I wish you could only see the way father goes on at me all the time about chapel, and so on, Mr. Wal—Herbert, I mean. You wouldn't wonder, if you were to hear him, at my being anxious for the time to come when you can leave Oxford and we can get comfortably married. What between the drudgery of the shop and the drudgery of the chapel my life's positively getting almost worn out of me.'

Herbert took her hand in his, quietly. It was not a very small hand, but it was prettily, though cheaply, gloved, and the plain silver bracelet that encircled the wrist, though simple and inexpensive, was not wanting in rough tastefulness. 'You're a bad philosopher, Selah,' he said, turning with her along the path towards Ecclesbourne; 'you're always anxious to hurry on too fast the lagging wheels of an unknown future. After all, how do you know whether we should be any the happier if we were really and truly married? Don't you know what Swinburne says, in "Dolores"—you've read it in the Poems and Ballads I gave you—

Time turns the old days to derision,
Our loves into corpses or wives,
And marriage and death and division
Make barren our lives?'

'I've read it,' Selah answered, carelessly, 'and I thought it all very pretty. Of course Swinburne always is very pretty: but I'm sure I never try to discover what on earth he means by it. I suppose father would say I don't read him tearfully and prayerfully—at any rate, I'm quite sure I never understand what he's driving at.'

'And yet he's worth understanding,' Herbert answered in his clear musical voice—'well worth understanding, Selah, especially for you, dearest. If, in imitation of obsolete fashions, you wished to read a few verses of some improving volume every night and morning, as a sort of becoming religious exercise in the elements of self-culture, I don't know that I could recommend you a better book to begin upon than the Poems and Ballads. Don't you see the moral of those four lines I've just quoted to you? Why should we wish to change from anything so free and delightful and poetical as lovers into anything so fettered, and commonplace, and prosaic, and BANAL, as wives and husbands? Why should we wish to give up the fanciful paradise of fluttering hope and expectation for the dreary reality of housekeeping and cold mutton on Mondays? Why should we not be satisfied with the real pleasure of the passing moment, without for ever torturing our souls about the imaginary but delusive pleasure of the unrealisable, impossible future?'

'But we MUST get married some time or other, Herbert,' Selah said, turning her big eyes full upon him with a doubtful look of interrogation. 'We can't go on courting in this way for ever and ever, without coming to any definite conclusion. We MUST get married by-and-by, now mustn't we?'

'Je n'en vois pas la necessite, moi,' Herbert answered with just a trace of cynicism in his curling lip. 'I don't see any MUST about it, that is to say, in English, Selah. The fact is, you see, I'm above all things a philosopher; you're a philosopher, too, but only an instinctive one, and I want to make your instinctive philosophy assume a rather more rational and extrinsic shape. Why should we really be in any hurry to go and get married? Do the actual married people of our acquaintance, as a matter of fact, seem so very much more ethereally happy— with their eight children to be washed and dressed and schooled daily, for example—than the lovers, like you and me, who walk arm-in-arm out here in the sunshine, and haven't yet got over their delicious first illusions? Depend upon it, the longer you can keep your illusions the better. You haven't read Aristotle in all probability; but as Aristotle would put it, it isn't the end that is anything in love-making, it's the energy, the active pursuit, the momentary enjoyment of it. I suppose we shall have to get married some day, Selah, though I don't know when; but I confess to you I don't look forward to the day quite so rapturously as you do. Shall we feel more the thrill of possession, do you think, than I feel it now when I hold your hand in mine, so, and catch the beating of your pulse in your veins, even through the fingers of your pretty little glove? Shall we look deeper into one another's eyes and hearts than I look now into the very inmost depths of yours? Shall we drink in more fully the essence of love than when I touch your lips here—one moment, Selah, the gorse is very deep here—now don't be foolish—ah, there, what's the use of philosophising, tell me, by the side of that? Come over here to the bench,

Selah, by the edge of the cliff; look down yonder into Ecclesbourne glen; hear the waves dashing on the shore below, and your own heart beating against your bosom within—and then ask yourself what's the good of living in any moment, in any moment but the present.'

Selah turned her great eyes admiringly upon him once more. 'Oh, Herbert,' she said, looking at him with a clever uneducated girl's unfeigned and undisguised admiration for any cultivated gentleman who takes the trouble to draw out her higher self. 'Oh, Herbert, how can you talk so beautifully to me, and then ask me why it is I'm longing for the day to come when I can be really and truly married to you? Do you think I don't feel the difference between spending my life with such a man as you, and spending it for years and years together with a ranting, canting Primitive Methodist?'

Herbert smiled to himself a quiet, unobtrusive, self-satisfied smile. 'She appreciates me,' he thought silently in his own heart, 'she appreciates me at my true worth; and, after all, that's a great thing. Well, Selah,' he went on aloud, toying unreproved with her pretty little silver bracelet, 'let us be practical. You belong to a business family and you know the necessity for being practical. There's a great deal to be said in favour of my hanging on at Oxford a little longer. I must get a situation somewhere else as soon as possible, in which I can get married; but I can't give up my fellowship without having found something else to do which would enable me to put my wife in the position I should like her to occupy.'

'A very small income would do for me, with you, Herbert,' Selah put in eagerly. 'You see, I've been brought up economically enough, heaven knows, and I could live extremely well on very little.'

'But *I* could not, Selah,' Herbert answered, in his colder tone. 'Pardon me, but I could not. I've been accustomed to a certain amount of comfort, not to say luxury, which I couldn't readily do without. And then, you know, dear,' he added, seeing a certain cloud gathering dimly on Selah's forehead, 'I want to make my wife a real lady.'

Selah looked at him tenderly, and gave the hand she hold in hers a faint pressure. And then Herbert began to talk about the waves, and the cliffs, and the sun, and the great red sails, and to quote Shelley and Swinburne; and the conversation glided off into more ordinary everyday topics.

They sat for a couple of hours together on the edge of the cliff, talking to one another about such and other subjects, till, at last, Selah asked the time, hurriedly, and declared she must go off at once, or father'd be in a tearing passion. Herbert walked back with her through the green lanes in the golden mass of gorse, till he reached the brow of the hill by the fisher village. Then Selah said lightly, 'Not any nearer, Herbert—you see I can say Herbert quite naturally now—the neighbours will go talking about it if they see me standing here with a strange gentleman. Good-bye, good-bye, till Friday.' Herbert held her face up to his in his hands, and kissed her twice over in spite of a faint resistance. Then they each went their own way, Selah to the little green-grocer's shop in a back street of the red-brick fisher village, and Herbert to his big fashionable hotel on the Marine Parade in the noisy stuccoed modern watering place.

'It's an awkward sort of muddle to have got oneself into.' he thought to himself as he walked along the asphalte pavement in front of the sea-wall: 'a most confoundedly awkward fix to have got oneself into with a pretty girl of the lower classes. She's beautiful certainly; that there's no denying; the handsomest woman on the whole I ever remember to have seen at any time anywhere; and when I'm actually by her side—though it's a weakness to confess it—I'm really not quite sure that I'm not positively quite in love with her! She'd make a grand sort of Messalina, without a doubt, a model for a painter, with her frank imperious face, and her splendid voluptuous figure; a Faustina, a Catherine of Russia, an Ann Boleyn—to be fitly painted only by a Rubens or a Gustave Courbet. Yet how I can ever have been such a particular fool as to go and get myself entangled with her I can't imagine. Heredity, heredity; it must run in the family, for certain. There's Ernest has gone and handed himself over bodily to this grocer person somewhere down in Devonshire; and I myself, who perfectly see the folly of his absurd proceeding, have independently put myself into this very similar awkward fix with Selah Briggs here. Selah Briggs, indeed! The very name reeks with commingled dissent, vulgarity, and greengrocery. Her father's deacon of his chapel, and goes out at night when there's no missionary meeting on, to wait at serious dinner parties! Or rather, I suppose he'd desert the most enticing missionary to earn a casual half-crown at even an ungodly champagne-drinking dinner! Then that's the difference between me and Ernest. Ernest's selfish, incurably and radically selfish. Because this Oswald girl happens to take his passing fancy, and to fit in with his impossible Schurzian notions, he'll actually go and marry her. Not only will he have no consideration for mother—who really is a very decent sort of body in her own fashion, if you don't rub her up the wrong way or expect too much from her—but he'll also interfere, without a thought, with MY prospects and my advancement. Now, THAT I call really selfish; and selfishness is a vulgar piggish vice that I thoroughly abominate. I don't deny that I'm a trifle selfish myself, of course, in a refined and cultivated manner—I flatter myself, in fact, that introspective analysis is one of my strong points; and I don't conceal my own failings from my own consciousness with any weak girlish prevarications. But after all, as Hobbes very well showed (though our shallow modern philosophers pretend to laugh at him), selfishness in one form or another is at the very base of all human motives; the difference really is between sympathetic and unsympathetic selfishness—between piggishness and cultivated feelings. Now *I* will NOT give way to the foolish and selfish impulses which would lead me to marry Selah Briggs. I will put a curb upon my inclinations, and do what is really best in the end for all the persons concerned—and for myself especially.'

He strolled down on to the beach, and began throwing pebbles carelessly into the plashing water. 'Yes,' he went on in his internal colloquy, 'I can only account for my incredible stupidity in this matter by supposing that it depends somehow upon some incomprehensible hereditary leaning in the Le Breton family idiosyncrasy. It's awfully unlike me, I will do myself the justice to say, to have got myself into such a silly dilemma all for nothing. It was all very well a few years ago, when I first met Selah. I was an undergraduate in those days, and even if somebody had caught me walking with a young lady of unknown antecedents and doubtful aspirates on the East Cliff at Hastings, it really wouldn't have much mattered. She was beautiful even then—though not so beautiful as now, for she grows handsomer every day; and it was natural enough I should have taken to going harmless walks about the place with her. She attracted me by her social rebelliousness— another family trait, in me passive not active, contemplative not personal; but she certainly attracted me. She attracts me still. A man must have some outlet for the natural and instinctive emotions of our common humanity; and if a mona-stic Oxford community imposes celibacy upon one with mediaeval absurdity—why, Selah Briggs is, for the time being, the only possible sort of outlet. One needn't marry her in the end; but for the moment it is certainly very excellent fooling. Not unsentimental either—for my part I could never care for mere coarse, commonplace, venal wretches. Indeed, when I spoke to her just now about my wishing to make my wife a lady, upon my word, at the time, I almost think I was just then quite in earnest. The idea flitted across my mind vaguely— "Why not send her for a year or two to be polished up at Paris or somewhere, and really marry her afterwards for good and always?" But on second thoughts, it won't hold water. She's magnificent, she's undeniable, she's admirable, but she isn't possible. The name alone's enough to condemn her. Fancy marrying somebody with a Christian name out of the hundred and somethingth psalm! It's too atrocious! I really couldn't inflict her for a moment on poor suffering innocent society.'

He paused awhile, watching the great russet sails of the fishing vessels flapping idly in the breeze as the men raised them to catch the faint breath of wind, and then he thought once more, 'But how to get rid of her, that's the question. Every time I come here now she goes on more and more about the necessity of our getting soon married—and I don't wonder at it either, for she has a perfect purgatory of a life with that snivelling Methodistical father of hers, one may be sure of it. It would be awfully awkward if any Oxford people were to catch me here walking with her on the cliff over yonder—some sniggering fellow of Jesus or Worcester, for example, or, worse than all, some prying young Pecksniff of a third-year undergraduate! Somehow, she seems to fascinate me, and I can't get away from her; but I must really do it and be done with it. It's no use going on this way much longer. I must stop here for a few days more only, and then tell her that I'm called away on important college business, say to Yorkshire or Worcestershire, or somewhere. I needn't tell her in person, face to face: I can write hastily at the last moment to the usual name at the Post Office—to be left till called for. And as a matter of fact I won't go to Yorkshire either—very awkward and undignified, though, these petty prevarications; when a man once begins lowering himself by making love to a girl in an inferior position, he lets himself in for all kinds of disagreeable necessities afterwards;—I shall go to Switzerland. Yes, no place better after the bother of running away like a coward from Selah: in the Alps, one would forget all petty human degradations; I shall go to Switzerland. Of course I won't break off with her altogether—that would be cruel; and I really like her; upon my word, even when she isn't by, up to her own level, I really like her; but I'll let the thing die a natural death of inanition. As they always put it in the newspapers, with their stereotyped phraseology, a gradual coldness shall intervene between us. That'll be the best and only way out of it.

'And if I go to Switzerland, why not ask Oswald of Oriel to go with me? That, I fancy, wouldn't be a bad stroke of social policy. Ernest WILL marry this Oswald girl; unfortunately he's as headstrong as an allegory on the banks of the Nile; and as he's going to drag her inevitably into the family, I may as well put the best possible face upon the disagreeable matter. Let's

Grant Allen

make a virtue of necessity. The father and mother are old: they'll die soon, and be gathered to their fathers (if they had any), and the world will straightway forget all about them. But Oswald will always be there en evidence, and the safest thing to do will be to take him as much as possible into the world, and let the sister rest upon HIS reputation for her place in society. It's quite one thing to say that Ernest has married the daughter of a country grocer down in Devonshire, and quite another thing to say that he has married the sister of Oswald of Oriel, the distinguished mathematician and fellow of the Royal Society. How beautifully that warm brown sail stands out in a curve against the cold grey line of the horizon—a bulging curve just like the swell of Selah's neck, when she throws her head back, so, and lets you see the contour of her throat, her beautiful rounded throat—ah, that's not giving her up now, is it?—What a confounded fool I am, to be sure! Anybody would say, if they could only have read my thoughts that moment, that I was really in love with this girl Selah!'

CHAPTER XIII

YE MOUNTAINS OF GILBOA!

The old Englischer Hof at Pontresina looked decidedly sleepy and misty at five o'clock on an August morning, when two sturdy British holiday-seekers, in knickerbockers and regular Alpine climbing rig, sat drinking their parting cup of coffee in the salle-a-manger, before starting to make the ascent of the Piz Margatsch, one of the tallest and by far the most difficult among the peaks of the Bernina range. There are few prettier villages in the Engadine than Pontresina, and few better hotels in all Switzerland than the old ivy-covered Englischer Hof. Yet on this particular morning, and at that particular hour, it certainly did look just a trifle cold and cheerless. 'He never makes very warm in the Engadine,' Carlo the waiter observed with a shudder, in his best English, to one of the two early risers: 'and he makes colder on an August morning here than he makes at Nice in full December.' For poor Carlo was one of those cosmopolitan waiters who follow the cosmopolitan tourist clientele round all the spas, health resorts, kurs and winter quarters of fashionable Europe. In January he and his brother, as Charles and Henri, handed round absinthes and cigarettes at the Cercle Nautique at Nice; in April, as Carlo and Enrico, they turned up again with water ices and wafer cakes in the Caffe Manzoni at Milan; and in August, the observant traveller might recognise them once more under the disguise of Karl and Heinrich, laying the table d'hote in the long and narrow old-fashioned dining-room of the Englischer Hof at Pontresina. Though their native tongue was the patois

Grant Allen

of the Canton Ticino, they spoke all the civilised languages of the world, 'and also German,' with perfect fluency, and without the slightest attempt at either grammar or idiomatic accuracy. And they both profoundly believed in their hearts that the rank, wealth, youth, beauty and fashion of all other nations were wisely ordained by the inscrutable designs of Providence for a single purpose, to enrich and reward the active, intelligent, and industrious natives of the Canton Ticino.

'Are the guides come yet?' asked Harry Oswald of the waiter in somewhat feeble and hesitating German. He made it a point to speak German to the waiters, because he regarded it as the only proper and national language of the universal Teutonic Swiss people.

'They await the gentlemans in the corridor,' answered Carlo, in his own peculiar and racy English; for he on his side resented the imputation that any traveller need ever converse with him in any but that traveller's own tongue, provided only it was one of the recognised and civilised languages of the world, or even German. They are a barbarous and disgusting race, those Tedeschi, look you well, Signor; they address you as though you were the dust in the piazza; yet even from them a polite and attentive person may confidently look for a modest, a very modest, but still a welcome trink-geld.

'Then we'd better hurry up, Oswald,' said Herbert Le Breton, 'for guides are the most tyrannical set of people on the entire face of this planet. I shall have another cup of coffee before I go, though, if the guides swear at me roundly in the best Roumansch for it, anyhow.'

'Your acquaintance with the Roumansch dialect being probably limited,' Harry Oswald answered, 'the difference between their swearing and their blessing would doubtless be reduced to a vanishing point. Though I've noticed that swearing is really a form of human speech everywhere readily understood of the people in spite of all differences of race or language. One touch of nature, you see; and swearing, after all, is extremely natural.'

'Are you ready?' asked Herbert, having tossed off his coffee. 'Yes? Then come along at once. I can feel the guides frowning at us through the partition.'

They turned out into the street, with its green-shuttered windows all still closed in the pale grey of early morning, and walked along with the three guides by the high road which leads through rocks and fir-trees up to the beginning of the steep path to the Piz Margatsch. Passing the clear emerald-green waterfall that rushes from under the lower melting end of the Morteratsch glacier, they took at once to the narrow track by the moraine along the edge of the ice, and then to the glacier itself, which is easy enough climbing, as glaciers go, for a good pedestrian. Herbert Le Breton, the older mountaineer of the two, got over the big blocks readily enough; but Harry, less accustomed to Swiss expeditions, lagged and loitered behind a little, and required more assistance from the guides every now and again than his sturdy companion.

'I'm getting rather blown at starting,' Harry called out at last to Herbert, some yards in front of him. 'Do you think the despotic guide would let us sit down and rest a bit if we asked him very prettily?'

'Offer him a cigar first,' Herbert shouted back, 'and then after a short and decent interval, prefer your request humbly in your politest French. The savage potentate always expects to be propitiated by gifts, as a preliminary to answering the petitions of his humble subjects.'

'I see,' Harry said, laughing. 'Supply before grievances, not grievances before supply.' And he halted a moment to light a cigar, and to offer one to each of the two guides who were helping him along on either side.

Thus mollified, the senior guide grudgingly allowed ten

minutes' halt and a drink of water at the bend by the corner of the glacier. They sat down upon the great translucent sea-green blocks and began talking with the taciturn chief guide.

'Is this glacier dangerous?' Harry asked.

'Dangerous, monsieur? Oh no, not as one counts glaciers. It is very safe. There are seldom accidents.'

'But there have been some?'

'Some, naturally. You don't climb mountains always without accidents. There was one the first time anyone ever made the ascent of the Piz Margatsch. That was fifty years ago. My uncle was killed in it.'

'Killed in it?' Harry echoed. 'How did it all happen, and where?'

'Yonder, monsieur, in a crevasse that was then situated near the bend at the corner, just where the great crevasse you see before you now stands. That was fifty years ago; since then the glacier has moved much. Its substance, in effect, has changed entirely.'

'Tell us all about it,' Herbert put in carelessly. He knew the guide wouldn't go on again till he had finished his whole story.

'It's a strange tale,' the guide answered, taking a puff or two at his cigar pensively and then removing it altogether for his set narrative—he had told the tale before a hundred times, and he had the very words of it now regularly by heart. 'It was the first time anyone ever tried to climb the Piz Margatsch. At that time, nobody in the valley knew the best path; it is my father who afterwards discovered it. Two English gentlemen came to Pontresina one morning; one might say you two gentlemen; but in those days there were not many tourists in the Engadine; the exploitation of the tourist had not yet begun to be developed. My father and my uncle were then the only two guides at Pontresina. The English gentlemen asked them to try with them the scaling of the Piz Margatsch. My uncle was afraid of it, but my father laughed down his fears. So they started. My uncle was dressed in a blue coat with brass buttons, and a pair of brown velvet breeches. Ah, heaven, I can see him yet, his white corpse in the blue coat and the brown velvet breeches!'

'But you can't be fifty yourself,' Harry said, looking at the tall long-limbed man attentively; 'no, nor forty, nor thirty either.'

'No, monsieur, I am twenty-seven,' the chief guide answered, taking another puff at his cigar very deliberately; 'and this was fifty years ago: yet I have seen his corpse just as the accident happened. You shall hear all about it. It is a tale from the dead; it is worth hearing.'

'This begins to grow mysterious,' said Herbert in English, hammering impatiently at the ice with the shod end of his alpenstock. 'Sounds for all the world just like the introduction to a Christmas number.'

'A young girl in the village loved my uncle,' the guide went on imperturbably; 'and she begged him not to go on this expedition. She was betrothed to him. But he wouldn't listen: and they all started together for the top of the Piz Margatsch. After many trials, my father and my uncle and the two tourists reached the summit. "So you see, Andreas," said my father, "your fears were all folly." "Half-way through the forest," said my uncle, "one is not yet safe from the wolf." Then they began to descend again. They got down past all the dangerous places, and on to this glacier, so well known, so familiar. And then my uncle began indeed to get careless. He laughed at his own fears; "Cathrein was all wrong," he said to my father, "we shall get down again safely, with Our Lady's assistance." So they reached at last the great crevasse. My father and one of the Englishmen got over without difficulty; but the other Englishman slipped; his footing failed him; and he was sinking, sinking, down, down, down, slipping quickly into the deep dark green abyss below. My uncle stretched out his hand over the edge: the Englishman caught it; and then my uncle missed his foothold, they both fell together and were lost to sight at once completely, in the invisible depths of the great glacier!'

'Well,' Herbert Le Breton said, as the man paused a moment. 'Is that all?'

'No,' the guide answered, with a tone of deep solemnity. 'That is not all. The glacier went on moving, moving, slowly, slowly, but always downward, for years and years. Yet no one ever heard anything more of the two lost bodies. At last one day, when I was seven years old, I went out playing with my brother, among the pine-woods, near the waterfall that rushes below there, from under the glacier. We saw something lying in the ice-cold water, just beneath the bottom of the ice-sheet. We climbed over the moraine; and there, oh heaven! we could see two dead bodies. They were drowned, just drowned, we thought: it might have been yesterday. One of them was short and thick-set, with the face of an Englishman: he was close-shaven, and, what seemed odd to us, he had on clothes which, though we were but children, we knew at once for the clothes of a long past fashion—in fact, a suit of the Louis dix-huit style. Tha other was a tall and handsome man, dressed in the unchangeable blue coat and brown velvet breeches of our own canton, of the Graubunden. We were very frightened about it, and so we ran away trembling and told an old woman who lived close by; her name was Cathrein, and her grandchildren used to play with us, though she herself was about the age of my father, for my father married very late. Old Cathrein came out with us to look; and the moment she saw the bodies, she cried out with a great cry, "It is he! It is Andreas! It is my betrothed, who was lost on the very day week when I was to be married. I should know him at once among ten thousand. It is many, many years now, but I have not forgotten his face—ah, my God, that face; I know it well!" And she took his hand in hers, that fair white young hand in her own old brown withered one, and kissed it gently. "And yet," she said, "he is five years older than me, this fair young man here; five years older than me!" We were frightened to hear her talk so, for we said to ourselves, "She must be mad;" so we ran home and brought our father. He looked at the dead bodies and at old Cathrein, and he said, "It is indeed true. He is my brother." Ah, monsieur, you would not have forgotten it if you had seen those two old people standing there beside the fresh corpses they had not seen for all those winters! They themselves had meanwhile grown old and grey and wrinkled; but the ice of the glacier had kept those others young, and fresh, and fair, and beautiful as on the day they were first engulfed in it. It was terrible to look at!'

'A most ghastly story, indeed,' Herbert Le Breton said, yawning; 'and now I think we'd better be getting under way again, hadn't we, Oswald?'

Harry Oswald rose from his seat on the block of ice unwillingly, and proceeded on his road up the mountain with a distinct and decided feeling of nervousness. Was it the guide's story that made his knees tremble slightly? was it his own inexperience in climbing? or was it the cold and the fatigue of the first ascent of the season to a man not yet in full pedestrian Alpine training? He did not feel at all sure about it in his own mind: but this much he knew with perfect certainty, that his footing was not nearly so secure under him as it had been during the earlier part of the climb over the lower end of the glacier.

By-and-by they reached the long sheer snowy slope near the Three Brothers. This slope is liable to slip, and requires careful walking, so the guides began roping them together. 'The stout monsieur in front, next after me,' said the chief guide, knotting the rope soundly round Herbert Le Breton: 'then Kaspar; then you, monsieur,' to Harry Oswald, 'and finally Paolo, to bring up the rear. The thin monsieur is nervous, I think; it's best to place him most in the middle.'

'If you really ARE nervous, Oswald,' Herbert said, not

unkindly, 'you'd better stop behind, I think, and let me go on with two of the guides. The really hard work, you know, has scarcely begun yet.'

'Oh dear, no,' Harry answered lightly (he didn't care to confess his timidity before Herbert Le Breton of all men in the world): 'I do feel just a little groggy about the knees, I admit; but it's not nervousness, it's only want of training. I haven't got accustomed to glacier-work yet, and the best way to overcome it is by constant practice. "Solvitur ambulando," you know, as Aldrich says about Achilles and the tortoise.'

'Very good,' Herbert answered drily; 'only mind, whatever you do, for Heaven's sake don't go and stumble and pull ME down on the top of you. It's the clear duty of a good citizen to respect the lives of the other men who are roped together with him on the side of a mountain.'

They set to work again, in single file, with cautious steps planted firmly on the treacherous snow, to scale the great white slope that stretched so temptingly before them. Harry felt his knees becoming at every step more and more ungovernable, while Herbert didn't improve matters by calling out to him from time to time, 'Now, then, look out for a hard bit here,' or 'Mind that loose piece of ice there,' or 'Be very careful how you put your foot down by the yielding edge yonder,' and so forth. At last, they had almost reached the top of the slope, and were just above the bare gulley on the side, when Harry's insecure footing on a stray scrap of ice gave way suddenly, and he begain to slip rapidly down the sheer slope of the mountain. In a second he had knocked against Paolo, and Paolo had begun to slip too, so that both were pulling with all their weight against Kaspar and the others in front. 'For Heaven's sake, man,' Herbert cried hastily, 'dig your alpen-stock deep into the snow.' At the same instant, the chief guide shouted in Roumansch to the same effect to Kaspar. But even as they spoke, Kaspar, pushing his feet hard against the snow, began to give way too; and the whole party seemed about to slip together down over the sheer rocky precipice of the great gulley on the right. It was a moment of supreme anxiety; but Herbert Le Breton, looking back with blood almost unstirred and calmly observant eye, saw at once the full scope of the threatening danger. 'There's only one chance,' he said to himself quietly. 'Oswald is lost already! Unless the rope breaks, we are all lost together!' At that very second, Harry Oswald, throwing his arms up wildly, had reached the edge of the terrible precipice; he went over with a piercing cry into the abyss, with the last guide beside him, and Kaspar following him close in mute terror. Then Herbert Le Breton felt the rope straining, straining, straining, upon the sharp frozen edge of the rock; for an inappreciable point of time it strained and crackled: one loud snap, and it was gone for ever. Herbert and the chief guide, almost upset by the sudden release from the heavy pull that was steadily dragging them over, threw themselves flat on their faces in the drifted snow, and checked their fall by a powerful muscular effort. The rope was broken and their lives were saved, but what had become of the three others?

They crept cautiously on hands and knees to the most practicable spot at the edge of the precipice, and the guide peered over into the great white blank below with eager eyes of horrid premonition. As he did so, he recoiled with awe, and made a rapid gesture with his hands, half prayer, half speechless terror. 'What do you see?' asked Herbert, not daring himself to look down upon the blank beneath him, lest he should be tempted to throw himself over in a giddy moment.

'Jesu, Maria,' cried the guide, crossing himself instinctively over and over again, 'they have all fallen to the very foot of the second precipice! They are lying, all three, huddled together on the ledge there just above the great glacier. They are dead, quite dead, dead before they reached the ground even. Great God, it is too terrible!'

Herbert Le Breton looked at the white-faced guide with just the faintest suspicion of a sneering curl upon his handsome features. The excitement of the danger was over now, and he

Grant Allen

had at once recovered his usual philosophic equanimity. 'Quite dead,' he said, in French, 'quite dead, are they? Then we can't be of any further use to them. But I suppose we must go down again at once to help recover the dead bodies!'

The guide gazed at him blankly with simple open-mouthed undisguised amazement. 'Naturally,' he said, in a very quiet voice of utter disgust and loathing. 'You wouldn't leave them lying there alone on the cold snow, would you?'

'This is really most annoying,' thought Herbert Le Breton to himself, in his rational philosophic fashion: 'here we are, almost at the summit, and now we shall have to turn back again from the very threshold of our goal, without having seen the view for which we've climbed up, and risked our lives too—all for a purely sentimental reason, because we won't leave those three dead men alone on the snow for an hour or two longer! it's a very short climb to the top now, and I could manage it by myself in twenty minutes. If only the chief guide had slid over with the others, I should have gone on alone, and had the view at least for my trouble. I could have pretended the accident happened on the way down again. As it is, I shall have to turn back ingloriously, re infecta. The guide will tell everybody at Pontresina that I went on, in spite of the accident; and then it would get into the English papers, and all the world would say that I was so dreadfully cruel and heartless. People are always so irrational in their ethical judgments. Oswald's quite dead, that's certain; nobody could fall over such a precipice as that without being killed a dozen times over before he even reached the bottom. A very painless and easy death too; I couldn't myself wish for a better one. We can't do them the slightest good by picking up their lifeless bodies, and yet a foolishly sentimental public opinion positively compels one to do it. Poor Oswald! Upon my soul I'm sorry for him, and for that pretty little sister of his too; but what's the use of bothering about it? The thing's done, and nothing that I can do or say will ever make it any better.'

So they turned once more in single file down by the great

glacier, and retraced their way to Pontresina without exchanging another word. To say the truth, the chief guide felt appalled and frightened by the presence of this impassive, unemotional British traveller, and did not even care to conceal his feelings. But then he wasn't an educated philosopher and man of culture like Herbert Le Breton.

Late that evening a party of twelve villagers brought back three stiff and mangled corpses on loose cattle hurdles into the village of Pontresina. Two of them were the bodies of two local Swiss guides, and the third, with its delicate face unscathed by the fall, and turned calmly upwards to the clear moonlight, was the body of Harry Oswald. Alas, alas, Gilboa! The beauty of Israel is slain upon thy high places.

CHAPTER XIV

'WHAT DO THESE HEBREWS HERE?'

From Calcombe Pomeroy Ernest had returned, not to Dunbude, but to meet the Exmoor party in London. There he had managed somehow—he hardly knew how himself—to live through a whole season without an explosion in his employer's family. That an explosion must come, sooner or later, he felt pretty sure in his own mind for several reasons: his whole existence there was a mistake and an anomaly, and he could no more mix in the end with the Exmoor family than oil can mix with vinegar, or vice versa. The round of dances and dinners to which he had to accompany his pupil was utterly distasteful to him. Lynmouth never learnt anything; so Ernest felt his own function in the household a perfectly useless one; and he was always on the eve of a declaration that he couldn't any longer put up with this, that, or the other 'gross immorality' in which Lynmouth was actively or passively encouraged by his father and mother. Still, there were two things which indefinitely postponed the smouldering outbreak. In the first place, Ernest wrote to, and heard from, Edie every day; and he believed he ought for Edie's sake to give the situation a fair trial, as long as he was able, or at least till he saw some other opening, which might make it possible within some reasonable period to marry her. In the second place, Lady Hilda had perceived with her intuitive quickness the probability that a cause of dispute might arise between her father and Ernest, and had made up her mind as far as in her lay to prevent its ever coming to a head. She didn't wish Ernest to leave his post in the household—so much originality was hardly again to be secured in a hurry—and therefore she laid herself out with all her ingenuity to smooth over all the possible openings for a difference of opinion whenever they occurred. If Ernest's scruples were getting the upper hand of his calmer judgment, Lady Hilda read the change in his face at once, and managed dexterously to draw off Lynmouth, or to talk over her mother quietly to acquiesce in Ernest's view of the question. If Lord Exmoor was beginning to think that this young man's confounded fads were really getting quite unbearable, Lady Hilda interposed some casual remark about how much better Lynmouth was kept out of the way now than he used to be in Mr. Walsh's time. Ernest himself never even suspected this unobtrusive diplomatist and peacemaker; but as a matter of fact it was mainly owing to Lady Hilda's constant interposition that he contrived to stop in Wilton Place through all that dreary and penitential London season.

At last, to Ernest's intense joy, the season began to show premonitory symptoms of collapsing from inanition. The twelfth of August was drawing nigh, and the coming-of-age of grouse, that most important of annual events in the orthodox British social calendar, would soon set free Lord Exmoor and his brother hereditary legislators from their arduous duty of acting as constitutional drag on the general advance of a great, tolerant, and easy-going nation. Soon the family would be off again to Dunbude, or away to its other moors in Scotland; and among the rocks and the heather Ernest felt he could endure Lord Exmoor and Lord Lynmouth a little more resignedly than among the reiterated polite platitudes and monotonous gaieties of the vacuous London drawing-rooms.

Lady Hilda, too, was longing in her own way for the season to be over. She had gone through another of them, thank goodness, she said to herself at times with a rare tinge of pensiveness, only to discover that the Hughs, and the Guys, and the Algies, and the Montys were just as fatuously inane as ever; and were just as anxious as before to make her share their fatuous inanity for a whole lifetime. Only fancy living with an

Grant Allen

unadulterated Monty from the time you were twenty to the time you were seventy-five—at which latter date he, being doubtless some five years older than one-self to begin with, would probably drop off quietly with suppressed gout, and leave you a mourning widow to deplore his untimely and lamented extinction for the rest of your existence! Why, long before that time you would have got to know his very thoughts by heart (if he had any, poor fellow!) and would be able to finish all his sentences and eke out all his stories for him, the moment he began them. Much better marry a respectable pork-butcher outright, and have at least the healthful exercise of chopping sausage-meat to fill up the stray gaps in the conversation. In that condition of life, they say, people are at any rate perfectly safe from the terrors of ennui. However, the season was over at last, thank Heaven; and in a week or so more they would be at dear old ugly Dunbude again for the whole winter. There Hilda would go sketching once more on the moorland, and if this time she didn't make that stupid fellow Ernest see what she was driving at, why, then her name certainly wasn't Hilda Tregellis.

A day or two before the legal period fixed for the beginning of the general grouse-slaughter, Ernest was sitting reading in the breakfast room at Wilton Place, when Lynmouth burst unexpectedly into the room in his usual boisterous fashion.

'Oh, I say, Mr. Le Breton,' he began, holding the door in his hand like one in a hurry, 'I want leave to miss work this morning. Gerald Talfourd has called for me in his dog-cart, and wants me to go out with him now immediately.'

'Not to-day, Lynmouth,' Ernest answered quietly. 'You were out twice last week, you know, and you hardly ever get your full hours for work at all since we came to London.'

'Oh, but look here, you know, Mr. Le Breton; I really MUST go to-day, because Talfourd has made an appointment for me. It's awful fun—he's going to have some pigeon-shooting.'

Ernest's countenance fell a little, and he answered in a graver voice than before, 'If that's what you want to go for, Lynmouth, I certainly can't let you go. You shall never have leave from me to go pigeon-shooting.'

'Why not?' Lynmouth asked, still holding the door-handle at the most significant angle.

'Because it's a cruel and brutal sport,' Ernest replied, looking him in the face steadily; 'and as long as you're under my charge I can't allow you to take part in it.'

'Oh, you can't,' said Lynmouth mischievously, with a gentle touch of satire in his tone. 'You can't, can't you! Very well, then, never mind about it.' And he shut the door after him with a bang, and ran off upstairs without further remonstrance.

'It's time for study, Lynmouth,' Ernest called out, opening the door and speaking to him as he retreated. 'Come down again at once, please, will you?'

But Lynmouth made no answer, and went straight off upstairs to the drawing-room. In a few minutes more he came back, and said in a tone of suppressed triumph, 'Well, Mr. Le Breton, I'm going with Talfourd. I've been up to papa, and he says I may "if I like to."'

Ernest bit his lip in a moment's hesitation. If it had been any ordinary question, he would have pocketed the contradiction of his authority—after all, if it didn't matter to them, it didn't matter to him—and let Lynmouth go wherever they allowed him. But the pigeon-shooting was a question of principle. As long as the boy was still nominally his pupil, he couldn't allow him to take any part in any such wicked and brutal amuse-ment, as he thought it. So he answered back quietly, 'No, Lynmouth, you are not to go. I don't think your father can have understood that I had forbidden you.'

'Oh!' Lynmouth said again, without a word of remonstrance, and went up a second time to the drawing-room.

In a few minutes a servant came down and spoke to Ernest. 'My lord would like to see you upstairs for a few minutes, if you please, sir.'

Ernest followed the man up with a vague foreboding that the deferred explosion was at last about to take place. Lord Exmoor was sitting on the sofa. 'Oh, I say, Le Breton,' he began in his good-humoured way, 'what's this that Lynmouth's been telling me about the pigeon-shooting? He says you won't let him go out with Gerald Talfourd.'

'Yes,' Ernest answered; 'he wanted to miss his morning's work, and I told him I couldn't allow him to do so.'

'But I said he might if he liked, Le Breton. Young Talfourd has called for him to go pigeon-shooting. And now Lynmouth tells me you refuse to let him go, after I've given him leave. Is that so?'

'Certainly,' said Ernest. 'I said he couldn't go, because before he asked you I had refused him permission, and I supposed you didn't know he was asking you to reverse my decision.'

'Oh, of course,' Lord Exmoor answered, for he was not an unreasonable man after his lights. 'You're quite right, Le Breton, quite right, certainly. Discipline's discipline, we all know, and must be kept up under any circumstances. You should have told me, Lynmouth, that Mr. Le Breton had forbidden you to go. However, as young Talfourd has made the engagement, I suppose you don't mind letting him have a holiday now, at my request, Le Breton, do you?'

Here was a dilemma indeed for Ernest. He hardly knew what to answer. He looked by chance at Lady Hilda, seated on the ottoman in the corner; and Lady Hilda, catching his eye, pursed up her lips visibly into the one word, 'Do.' But Ernest was inexorable. If he could possibly prevent it, he would not let those innocent pigeons be mangled and slaughtered for a lazy boy's cruel gratification. That was the one clear duty before him; and whether he offended Lord Exmoor or not, he had no choice save to pursue it.

'No, Lord Exmoor,' he said resolutely, after a long pause. 'I should have no objection to giving him a holiday, but I can't allow him to go pigeon-shooting.'

'Why not?' asked Lord Exmoor warmly.

Ernest did not answer.

'He says it's a cruel, brutal sport, papa,' Lynmouth put in parenthetically, in spite of an angry glance from Hilda; 'and he won't let me go while I'm his pupil.'

Lord Exmoor's face grew very red indeed, and he rose from the sofa angrily. 'So that's it, Mr. Le Breton!' he said, in a short sharp fashion. 'You think pigeon-shooting cruel and brutal, do you? Will you have the goodness to tell me, sir, do you know that I myself am in the habit of shooting pigeons at matches?'

'Yes,' Ernest answered, without flinching a muscle.

'Yes!' cried Lord Exmoor, growing redder and redder. 'You knew that, Mr. Le Breton, and yet you told my son you considered the practice brutal and cruel! Is that the way you teach him to honour his parents? Who are you, sir, that you dare set yourself up as a judge of me and my conduct? How dare you speak to him of his father in that manner? How dare you stir him up to disobedience and insubordination against his elders? How dare you, sir; how dare you?'

Ernest's face began to get red in return, and he answered with unwonted heat, 'How dare you address me so, yourself, Lord Exmoor? How dare you speak to me in that imperious manner? You're forgetting yourself, I think, and I had better

Grant Allen

leave you for the present, till you remember how to be more careful in your language. But Lynmouth is not to go pigeon-shooting. I object to his going, because the sport is a cruel and a brutal one, whoever may practise it. If I have any authority over him, I insist upon it that he shall not go. If he goes, I shall not stop here any longer. You can do as you like about it, of course, but you have my final word upon the matter. Lynmouth, go down to the study.'

'Stop, Lynmouth,' cried his father, boiling over visibly with indignation: 'Stop. Never mind what Mr. Le Breton says to you; do you hear me? Go out if you choose with Gerald Talfourd.'

Lynmouth didn't wait a moment for any further permission. He ran downstairs at once and banged the front door soundly after him with a resounding clatter. Lady Hilda looked imploringly at Ernest, and whispered half audibly, 'Now you've done it.' Ernest stood a second irresolute, while the Earl tramped angrily up and down the drawing-room, and then he said in a calmer voice, 'When would it be convenient, Lord Exmoor, that I should leave you?'

'Whenever you like,' Lord Exmoor answered violently. 'To-day if you can manage to get your things together. This is intolerable, absolutely intolerable! Gross and palpable impertinence; in my own house, too! "Cruel and brutal," indeed! "Cruel and brutal." Fiddlesticks! Why, it's not a bit different from partridge-shooting!' And he went out, closely followed by Ernest, leaving Lady Hilda alone and frightened in the drawing-room.

Ernest ran lightly upstairs to his own little study sitting-room. 'I've done it this time, certainly, as Lady Hilda said,' he thought to himself; 'but I don't see how I could possibly have avoided it. Even now, when all's done, I haven't succeeded in saving the lives of the poor innocent tortured pigeons. They'll be mangled and hunted for their poor frightened lives, anyhow. Well, now I must look out for that imaginary schoolmastership, and see what I can do for dear Edie. I shan't be sorry to get out of this after all, for the place was an impossible one for me from the very beginning. I shall sit down this moment and write to Edie, and after that I shall take out my portmanteau and get the man to help me put my luggage up to go away this very evening. Another day in the house after this would be obviously impossible.'

At that moment there came a knock at the door—a timid, tentative sort of knock, and somebody put her head inquiringly halfway through the doorway. Ernest looked up in sudden surprise. It was Lady Hilda.

'Mr. Le Breton,' she said, coming over towards the table where Ernest had just laid out his blotting-book and writing-paper: 'I couldn't prevent myself from coming up to tell you how much I admire your conduct in standing up so against papa for what you thought was right and proper. I can't say how greatly I admire it. I'm so glad you did as you did do. You have acted nobly.' And Hilda looked straight into his eyes with the most speaking and most melting of glances. 'Now,' she said to herself, 'according to all correct precedents, he ought to seize my hand fervently with a gentle pressure, and thank me with tears in his eyes for my kind sympathy.'

But Ernest, only looking puzzled and astonished, answered in the quietest of voices, 'Thank you very much, Lady Hilda: but I assure you there was really nothing at all noble, nothing at all to admire, in what I said or did in any way. In fact, I'm rather afraid, now I come to think of it, that I lost my temper with your father dreadfully.'

'Then you won't go away?' Hilda put in quickly. 'You think better of it now, do you? You'll apologise to papa, and go with us to Dunbude for the autumn? Do say you will, please, Mr. Le Breton.'

'Oh dear, no,' Ernest answered, smiling quietly at the bare idea of his apologising to Lord Exmoor. 'I certainly won't do that,

Grant Allen

whatever I do. To tell you the truth, Lady Hilda, I have not been very anxious to stop with Lynmouth all along: I've found it a most unprofitable tutorship—no sense of any duty performed, or any work done for society: and I'm not at all sorry that this accident should have broken up the engagement unexpectedly. At the same time, it's very kind of you to come up and speak to me about it, though I'm really quite ashamed you should have thought there was anything particularly praiseworthy or commendable in my standing out against such an obviously cruel sport as pigeon-shooting.'

'Ah, but I do think so, whatever you may say, Mr. Le Breton,' Hilda went on eagerly. 'I do think so, and I think it was very good of you to fight it out so against papa for what you believe is right and proper. For my own part, you know, I don't see any particular harm in pigeon-shooting. Of course it's very dreadful that the poor dear little things should be shot and wounded and winged and so forth; but then everything, almost, gets shot, you see—rabbits, and grouse, and partridges, and everything; so that really it's hardly worth while, it seems to me, making a fuss about it. Still, that's not the real question. You think it's wrong; which is very original and nice and proper of you; and as you think it's wrong, you won't countenance it in any way. I don't care, myself, whether it's wrong or not—I'm not called upon, thank goodness, to decide the question; but I do care very much that you should suffer for what you think the right course of action.' And Lady Hilda in her earnestness almost laid her hand upon his arm, and looked up to him in the most unmistakable and appealing fashion.

'You're very good, I'm sure, Lady Hilda,' Ernest replied, half hesitatingly, wondering much in his own mind what on earth she could be driving at.

There was a moment's pause, and then Hilda said pensively, 'And so we shall never walk together at Dunbude on the Clatter any more, Mr. Le Breton! We shall never climb again among the big boulders on those Devonshire hillsides! We shall never watch the red deer from the big pool on top of the sheep-walk! I'm sorry for it, Mr. Le Breton, very sorry for it. Oh, I do wish you weren't going to leave us!'

Ernest began to feel that this was really growing embarrassing. 'I dare say we shall often see one another,' he said evasively; for simple-minded as he was, a vague suspicion of what Lady Hilda wanted him to say had somehow forced itself timidly upon him. 'London's a very big place, no doubt; but still, people are always running together unexpectedly in it.'

Hilda sighed and looked at him again intently without speaking. She stood so, face to face with him across the table for fully two minutes; and then, seeming suddenly to awake from a reverie, she started and sighed once more, and turned at last reluctantly to leave the little study. 'I must go,' she said hastily; 'mamma would be very angry indeed with me if she knew I'd come here; but I couldn't let you leave the house without coming up to tell you how greatly I admire your spirit, and how very, very much I shall always miss you, Mr. Le Breton. Will you take this, and keep it as a memento?' As she spoke, she laid an envelope upon the table, and glided quietly out of the room.

Ernest took the envelope up with a smile, and opened it with some curiosity. It contained a photograph, with a brief inscription on the back, 'E. L. B., from Hilda Tregellis.'

As he did so, Hilda Tregellis, red and pale by turns, had rushed into her own room, locked the door wildly, and flung herself in a perfect tempest of tears on her own bed, where she lay and tossed about in a burning agony of shame and self-pity for twenty minutes. 'He doesn't love me,' she said to herself bitterly; 'he doesn't love me, and he doesn't care to love me, or want to marry me either! I'm sure he understood what I meant, this time; and there was no response in his eyes, no answer, no sympathy. He's like a block of wood—a cold, impassive, immovable, lifeless creature! And yet I could love him—oh, if only he would say a word to me in answer, how I could love him! I loved him when he stood up there and bearded papa in his own drawing-room, and asked him how dare he speak so, how dare he address him in such a manner; I KNEW then that I really loved him. If only he would let me! But he won't! To think that I could have half the Algies and Berties in London at my feet for the faintest encouragement, and I can't have this one poor penniless Ernest Le Breton, though I go down on my knees before him and absolutely ask him to marry me! That's the worst of it! I've humiliated myself before him by letting him see, oh, ever so much too plainly, that I wanted him to ask me; and I've been repulsed, rejected, positively refused and slighted by him! And yet I love him! I shall never love any other man as I love Ernest Le Breton.'

Poor Lady Hilda Tregellis! Even she too had, at times, her sentimental moments! And there she lay till her eyes were red and swollen with crying, and till it was quite hopeless to expect she could ever manage to make herself presentable for the Cecil Faunthorpes' garden-party that afternoon at Twickenham.

CHAPTER XV

EVIL TIDINGS

Ernest had packed his portmanteau, and ordered a hansom, meaning to take temporary refuge at Number 28 Epsilon Terrace; and he went down again for a few minutes to wait in the breakfast-room, where he saw the 'Times' lying casually on the little table by the front window. He took it up, half dreamily, by way of having something to do, and was skimming the telegrams in an unconcerned manner, when his attention was suddenly arrested by the name Le Breton, printed in conspicuous type near the bottom of the third column. He looked closer at the paragraph, and saw that it was headed 'Accident to British Tourists in Switzerland.' A strange tremor seized him immediately. Could anything have happened, then, to Herbert? He read the telegram through at once, and found this bald and concise summary before him of the fatal Pontresina accident:—

'As Mr. H. Oswald, F.R.S., of Oriel College, Oxford, and Mr. Le Breton, Fellow and Bursar of St. Aldate's College, along with three guides, were making the ascent of the Piz Margatsch, in the Bernina Alps, this morning, one of the party happened to slip near the great gulley known as the Gouffre. Mr. Oswald and two of the guides were precipitated over the edge of the cliff and killed immediately: the breaking of the rope at a critical moment alone saved the lives of Mr. Le Breton and the remaining guide. The bodies have been recovered this evening, and brought back to Pontresina.'

Grant Allen

Ernest laid down the paper with a thrill of horror. Poor Edie! How absolutely his own small difficulties with Lord Exmoor faded out of has memory at once in the face of that terrible, irretrievable calamity. Harry dead! The hope and mainstay of the family—the one great pride and glory of all the Oswalds, on whom their whole lives and affections centred, taken from them unexpectedly, without a chance of respite, without a moment's warning! Worst of all, they would probably learn it, as he did, for the first time by reading it accidentally in the curt language of the daily papers. Pray heaven the shock might not kill poor Edie!

There was only a minute in which to make up his mind, but in that minute Ernest had fully decided what he ought to do, and how to do it. He must go at once down to Calcombe Pomeroy, and try to lighten this great affliction for poor little Edie. Nay, lighten it he could not, but at least he could sympathise with her in it, and that, though little, was still some faint shade better than nothing at all. How fortunate that his difference with the Exmoors allowed him to go that very evening without a moment's delay. When the hansom arrived at the door, Ernest told the cabman to drive at once to Paddington Station. Almost before he had had time to realise the full meaning of the situation, he had taken a third-class ticket for Calcombe Road, and was rushing out of London by the Plymouth express, in one of the convenient and commodious little wooden horse-boxes which the Great Western Railway Company provide as a wholesome deterrent for economical people minded to save half their fare by going third instead of first or second.

Didcot, Swindon, Bath, Bristol, Exeter, Newton Abbot, all followed one after another, and by the time Ernest had reached Calcombe Road Station he had begun to frame for himself a definite plan of future action. He would stop at the Red Lion Inn that evening, send a telegram from Exeter beforehand to Edie, to say he was coming next day, and find out as much as possible about the way the family had borne the shock before he ventured actually to see them.

The Calcombe omnibus, drawn by two lean and weary horses, toiled its way slowly up the long steep incline for six miles to the Cross Foxes, and then rattled down the opposite slope, steaming and groaning, till it drew up at last with a sudden jerk and a general collapse in front of the old Red Lion Inn in the middle of the High Street. There Ernest put up for the present, having seen by the shutters at the grocer's shop on his way down that the Oswalds had already heard of Harry's accident. He had dinner by himself, with a sick heart, in the gloomy, close little coffee-room of the village inn, and after dinner he managed to draw in the landlord in person for a glass of sherry and half an hour's conversation.

'Very sad thing, sir, this 'ere causality in Switzerland,' said the red-faced landlord, coming round at once to the topic of the day at Calcombe, after a few unimportant preliminary generalities. 'Young Mr. Oswald, as has been killed, he lived here, sir; leastways his parents do. He was a very promising young gentleman up at Oxford, they do tell me—not much of a judge of horses, I should say, but still, I understand, quite the gentleman for all that. Very sad thing, the causality, sir, for all his family. 'Pears he was climbing up some of these 'ere Alps they have over there in them parts, covered with snow from head to foot in the manner of speaking, and there was another gentleman from Oxford with him, a Mr. Le Breton—'

'My brother,' Ernest put in, interrupting him; for he thought it best to let the landlord know at once who he was talking to.

'Oh, your brother, sir!' said the red-faced landlord, with a gleam of recognition, growing redder and hotter than ever; 'well, now you mention it, sir, I find I remember your face somehow. No offence, sir, but you're the young gentleman as come down in the spring to see young Mr. Oswald, aren't you?'

Ernest nodded assent.

'Ah, well, sir,' the landlord went on more freely—for of course all Calcombe had heard long since that Ernest was engaged to Edie Oswald—'you're one of the family like, in that case, if I may make bold to say so. Well, sir, this is a shocking trouble for poor old Mr. Oswald, and no mistake. The old gentleman was sort of centred on his son, you see, as the saying is: never thought of nobody else hardly, he didn't. Old Mr. Oswald, sir, was always a wonderful hand at figgers hisself, and powerful fond of measurements and such kinds of things. I've heard tell, indeed, as how he knew more mathematics, and trigononomy, and that, than the rector and the schoolmaster both put together. There's not one in fifty as knows as much mathematics as he do, I'll warrant. Well, you see, he brought up this son of his, little Harry as was—I can remember him now, running to and from the school, and figgerin' away on the slates, doin' the sums in algemer for the other boys when they went a-mitchin'—he brought him up like a gentleman, as you know very well, sir, and sent him to Oxford College: "to develop his mathematical talents, Mr. Legge," his father says to me here in this very parlour. What's the consequence? He develops that boy's talent sure enough, sir, till he comes to be a Fellow of Oxford College, they tell me, and even admitted into the Royal Society up in London. But this is how he did it, sir: and as you're a friend of the family like, and want to know all about it, no doubt, I don't mind tellin' you on the strict confidential, in the manner of speakin'.' Here the landlord drew his chair closer, and sipped the last drop in his glass of sherry with a mysterious air of very private and important disclosures. Ernest listened to his roundabout story with painful attention.

'Well, sir,' the landlord went on after a short and pensive pause, 'old Mr. Oswald's business ain't never been a prosperous one—though he was such a clover hand at figgers, he never made it remunerative; a bare livin' for the family, I don't mind sayin'; and he always spent more'n he ought to 'a done on Mr. Harry, and on the young lady too, sir, savin' your presence. So when Mr. Harry was goin' to Oxford to college, he come to me, and he says to me, "Mr. Legge," says he, "it's a very expensive thing sending my boy to the University," says he, "and I'm going to borrow money to send him with." "Don't you go a-doin' that, Mr. Oswald," says I; "your business don't justify you in doin' it, sir," says I. For you see, I knowed all the ins and outs of that there business, and I knowed he hadn't never made more'n enough just to keep things goin' decent like, as you may say, without any money saved or put by against a emergence. "Yes, I will, Mr. Legge," says he; "I can trust confidentially in my son's abilities," says he; "and I feel confidential he'll be in a position to repay me before long." So he borrowed the money on an insurance of Mr. Harry's life. Mr. Harry he always acted very honourable, sir; he was a perfect gentleman in every way, as YOU know, sir; and he began repayin' his father the loan as fast as he was able, and I daresay doin' a great deal for the family, and especially for the young lady, sir, out of his own pocket besides. But he still owed his father a couple of hundred pound an' more when this causality happened, while the business, I know, had been a-goin' to rack and ruin for the last three year. To-day I seen the agent of the insurance, and he says to me, "Legge," says he, most private like, "this is a bad job about young Oswald, I'm afeard, worse'n they know for." "Why, sir?" says I. "Well, Legge," says he, "they'll never get a penny of that there insurance, and the old gentleman'll have to pay up the defissit on his own account," says he. "How's that, Mr. Micklethwaite?" says I. "Because," says he, "there's a clause in the policy agin exceptional risks, in which is included naval and military services, furrin residences, topical voyages, and mountain-climbin'," says he; "and you mark my words," says he, "they'll never get a penny of it." In which case, sir, it's my opinion that old Mr. Oswald'll be clean broke, for he can't never make up the defissit out of his own business, can he now?'

Ernest listened with sad forebodings to the red-faced landlord's pitiful story, and feared in his heart that it was a bad look-out for the poor Oswalds. He didn't sleep much that evening, and next day he went round early to see Edie. The telegram he found would be a useless precaution, for the gossip of Calcombe Pomeroy had recognised him at once, and news had reached the Oswalds almost as soon as he arrived that young

Mr. Le Breton was stopping that evening at the Red Lion.

Edie opened the door for him herself, pale of face and with eyes reddened by tears, yet looking beautiful even so in her simple black morning dress, her mourning of course hadn't yet come home—and her deep white linen collar. 'It's very good of you to have come so soon, Mr. Le Breton,' she said, taking his hand quietly—he respected her sorrow too deeply to think of kissing her; 'he will be back with us to-morrow. Your brother is bringing him back to us, to lay him in our little churchyard, and we are all so very very grateful to him for it.'

Ernest was more than half surprised to hear it. It was an unusual act of kindly thoughtfulness on the part of Herbert.

Next day the body came home as Edie had said, and Ernest helped to lay it reverently to rest in Calcombe churchyard. Poor old Mr. Oswald, standing bowed and broken-hearted by the open grave side, looked as though he could never outlive that solemn burial of all his hopes and aspirations in a single narrow coffin. Yet it was wonderful to Ernest to see how much comfort he took, even in this terrible grief, from the leader which appeared in the 'Times' that morning on the subject of the Pontresina accident. It contained only a few of the stock newspaper platitudes of regret at the loss of a distinguished and rising young light of science—the ordinary glib commonplaces of obituary notices which a practised journalist knows so well how to adapt almost mechanically to the passing event of the moment; but they seemed to afford the shattered old country grocer an amount of consolation and solemn relief that no mere spoken condolences could ever possibly have carried with them. 'See what a wonderful lot they thought of our boy up in London, Mr. Le Breton,' he said, looking up from the paper tearfully, and wiping his big gold spectacles, dim with moisture. 'See what the "Times" says about him: "One of the ablest among our young academical mathematicians, a man who, if his life had been spared to us, might probably have attained the highest distinction in his own department of pure science." That's our Harry, Mr. Le Breton; that's what the

"Times" says about our dear, dead Harry! I wish he could have lived to read it himself, Edie—"a scholar of singularly profound attainments, whose abilities had recently secured him a place upon the historic roll of the Royal Society, and whom even the French Academy of Sciences had held worthy out of all the competitors of the civilised world, to be adjudged the highest mathematical honours of the present season." My poor boy! my poor, dear, lost boy! I wish you could have lived to hear it! We must keep the paper, Edie: we must keep all the papers; they'll show us at least what people who are real judges of these things thought about our dear, loved, lost Harry.'

Ernest dared hardly glance towards poor Edie, with the tears trickling slowly down her face; but he felt thankful that the broken-hearted old father could derive so much incomprehensible consolation from those cold and stereotyped conventional phrases. Truly a wonderful power there is in mere printer's ink properly daubed on plain absorbent white paper. And truly the human heart, full to bursting and just ready to break will allow itself to be cheated and cajoled in marvellous fashions by extraordinary cordials and inexplicable little social palliatives. The concentrated hopes of that old man's life were blasted and blighted for ever; and he found a temporary relief from that stunning shock in the artificial and insincere condolences of a stock leader-writer on a daily paper!

Walking back by himself in such sad meditations to the Red Lion, and sitting there by the open window, Ernest overheard a tremulous chattering voice mumbling out a few incoherent words at the Rector's doorway opposite. 'Oh, yes,' chirped out the voice in a tone of cheerful resignation, 'it's very sad indeed, very sad and shocking, and I'm naturally very sorry for it, of course. I always knew how it would be: I warned them of it; but they're a pig-headed, heedless, unmannerly family, and they wouldn't be guided by me. I said to him, "Now, Oswald, this is all very wrong and foolish of you. You go and put your son to Oxford, when he ought to be stopping at home, minding the shop and learning your business. You borrow money foolishly to send him there with. He'll go to Oxford;

he'll fall in with a lot of wealthy young gentlemen—people above his own natural station—he'll take up expensive, extravagant ways, and in the end he'll completely ruin himself. He won't pay you back a penny, you may depend upon it— these boys never do, when you make fine gentlemen of them; they think only of their cigars and their horses, and their dog-carts and so forth, and neglect their poor old fathers and mothers, that brought them up and scraped and saved to make fine gentlemen of them. You just take my advice, Oswald, and don't send him to college." But Oswald was always a presump-tuous, high-headed, independent sort of man, and instead of listening to me, what does he do but go and send this sharp boy of his up to Oxford. Well, now the boy's gone to Switzerland with one of the young Le Bretons—brother of the poor young man they've inveigled into what they call an engagement with Miss Edith, or Miss Jemima, or whatever the girl's name is—very well-connected people, the Le Bretons, and personal friends of the Archdeacon's—and there he's thrown himself over a precipice or something of the sort, no doubt to avoid his money-matters and debts and difficulties. At any rate, Micklethwaite tells me the poor old father'll have to pay up a couple of hundred pound to the insurance company: and how on earth he's ever to do it *I* don't know, for to my certain knowledge the rent of the shop is in arrears half-a-year already. But it's no business of mine, thank goodness!— and I only hope that exposure will serve to open that poor young Le Breton's eyes, and to warn him against having anything further to say to Miss Jemima. A designing young minx, if ever there was one! Poor young Le Breton's come down here for the funeral, I hear, which I must say was very friendly and proper and honourable of him; but now it's over, I hope he'll go back again, and see Miss Jemima in her true colours.'

Ernest turned back into the stuffy little coffee-room with his face on fire and his ears tingling with mingled shame and indignation. 'Whatever happens,' he thought to himself, 'I can't permit Edie to be subjected any longer to such insolence as this! Poor, dear, guileless, sorrowing little maiden! One would have thought her childish innocence and her terrible loss would have softened the heart even of such a cantankerous, virulent old harridan as that, till a few weeks were over, at least. She spoke of the Archdeacon: it must be old Miss Luttrell! Whoever it is, though, Edie shan't much longer be left where she can possibly come in contact with such a loathsome mass of incredible and unprovoked malice. That Edie should lose her dearly-loved brother is terrible enough; but that she should be exposed afterwards to be triumphed over in her most sacred grief by that bad old woman's querulous "I told you so" is simply intolerable!' And he paced up and down the room with a boiling heart, unable to keep down his righteous anger.

CHAPTER XVI

FLAT REBELLION

For the next fortnight Ernest remained at the Red Lion, though painfully conscious that he was sadly wasting his little reserve of funds from his late tutorship, in order to find out exactly what the Oswalds' position would be after the loss of poor Harry. Towards the end of that time he took Edie, pale and pretty in her simple new mourning, out once more into the Bourne Close for half an hour's quiet conversation. Very delicate and sweet and refined that tiny girlish face and figure looked in the plain unostentatious black and white of her great sorrow, and Ernest felt as he walked along by her side that she seemed to lean upon him naturally now; the loss of her main support and chief advisor in life seemed to draw her closer and closer every day to her one remaining prop and future husband.

'Edie,' he said to her, as they rested once more beside the old wooden bridge across the little river, 'I think it's time now we should begin to talk definitely over our common plans for the future. I know you'd naturally rather wait a little longer before discussing them; I wish for both our sakes we could have deferred it; but time presses, and I'm afraid from what I hear in the village that things won't go on henceforth exactly as they used to do with your dear father and mother.'

Edie coloured slightly as she answered, 'Then you've heard of all that already, Ernest'—she was learning to call him 'Ernest' now quite naturally. 'The Calcombe tattle has got round to you so soon! I'm glad of it, though, for it saves me the pain of having to tell you. Yes, it's quite true, and I'm afraid it will be a terrible, dreadful struggle for poor darling father and mother.' And the tears came up afresh, as she spoke, into her big black eyes—too familiar with them of late to make her even try to brush them away hastily from Ernest's sight with her little handkerchief.

'I'm sorry to know it's true,' Ernest said, taking her hand gently; 'very, very sorry. We must do what we can to lighten the trouble for them.'

'Yes,' Edie replied, looking at him through her tears; 'I mean to try. At any rate, I won't be a burden to them myself any longer. I've written already up to an agency in London to see whether they can manage to get me a place as a nursery-governess.'

'You a governess, Edie!' Ernest exclaimed hastily, with a gesture of deprecation. 'You a governess! Why, my own precious darling, you would never do for it!'

'Oh yes, indeed,' Edie answered quickly, 'I really think I could, Ernest. Of course I don't know very much—not judged by a standard like yours or our dear Harry's. Harry used to say all a woman could ever know was to find out how ignorant she was. Dear fellow! he was so very learned himself he couldn't under-stand the complacency of little perky, half-educated school-mistresses. But still, I know quite as much, I think, in my little way, as a great many girls who get good places in London as governesses. I can speak French fairly well, you know, and read German decently; and then dear Harry took such a lot of pains to make me get up books that he thought were good for me—history and so forth—and even to teach me a little, a very little, Latin. Of course I know I'm dreadfully ignorant; but not more so, I really believe, than a great many girls whom people consider quite well-educated enough to teach their daughters. After all, the daughters themselves are only women, too, you see, Ernest, and don't expect more than a smattering of book-knowledge, and a few showy fashionable accomplishments.'

'My dear Edie,' Ernest answered, smiling at her gently in spite of her tearful earnestness; 'you quite misunderstand me. It wasn't THAT I was thinking of at all. There are very few governesses and very few women anywhere who have half the knowledge and accomplishments and literary taste and artistic culture that you have; very few who have had the advantage of associating daily with such a man as poor Harry; and if you really wanted to get a place of the sort, the mere fact that you're Harry's sister, and that he interested himself in superintending your education, ought, by itself, to ensure your getting a very good one. But what I meant was rather this—I couldn't endure to think that you should be put to all the petty slights and small humiliations that a governess has always to endure in rich families. You don't know what it is, Edie; you can't imagine the endless devices for making her feel her dependence and her artificial inferiority that these great people have devised in their cleverness and their Christian condescension. You don't know what it is, Edie, and I pray heaven you may never know; but *I* do, for I've seen it—and, darling, I CAN'T let you expose yourself to it.'

To say the truth, at that moment there rose very vividly before Ernest's eyes the picture of poor shy Miss Merivale, the governess at Dunbude to little Lady Sybil, Lynmouth's younger sister. Miss Merivale was a rector's daughter—an orphan, and a very nice girl in her way; and Ernest had often thought to himself while he lived at the Exmoors', 'With just the slightest turn of Fortune's wheel that might be my own Edie.' Now, for himself he had never felt any sense of social inferiority at all at Dunbude; he was an Oxford man, and by the ordinary courtesy of English society he was always treated accordingly in every way as an equal. But there were galling distinctions made in Miss Merivale's case which he could not think of even at the time without a blush of ingenuous shame, and which he did not like now even to mention to pretty, shrinking, eager little Edie. One thing alone was enough to make his cheeks burn whenever he thought of it—a little thing, and yet how unendurable! Miss Merivale lunched with the family and with her pupil in the middle of the day, but she did not dine with them in the evening. She had tea by herself instead in Lady Sybil's little school-room. Many a time when Ernest had been out walking with her on the terrace just before dinner, and the dressing-gong sounded, he had felt almost too ashamed to go in at the summons and leave the poor little governess out there alone with her social disabilities. The gong seemed to raise such a hideous artificial barrier between himself and that delicately-bred, sensitive, cultivated English lady. That Edie should be subjected to such a life of affronts as that was simply unendurable. True, there are social distinctions of the sort which even Ernest Le Breton, communist as he was, could not practically get over; but then they were distinctions familiarised to the sufferers from childhood upward, and so perhaps a little less insupportable. But that Harry Oswald's sister—that Edie, his own precious delicate little Edie, a dainty English wild-flower of the tenderest, should be transplanted from her own appreciative home to such a chilly and ungenial soil as that—the very idea of it was horribly unspeakable.

'But, Ernest,' Edie answered, breaking in upon his bitter meditation, 'I assure you I wouldn't mind it a bit. I know—it's very dreadful, but then,'—and here she blushed one of her pretty apologetic little blushes—'you know I'm used to it. People in business always are. They expect to be treated just like servant—now THAT, I know you'll say, is itself a piece of hubris, the expression of a horrid class prejudice. And so it is, no doubt. But they do, for all that. As dear Harry used to say, even the polypes in aristocratic useless sponges at the sea-bottom won't have anything to say to the sponges of commerce. I'm sure nobody I could meet in a governess's place could possibly be worse in that respect than poor old Miss Catherine Luttrell.'

'That may be true, Edie darling,' Ernest answered, not caring to let her know that he had overheard a specimen of the Calcombe squirearchy, 'but in any case I don't want you to be troubled now, either with old Miss Luttrell or any other bitter old busybodies. I want to speak seriously to you about a very different project. Just look at this advertisement.'

He took a scrap of paper from his pocket and handed it to Edie. It ran thus:—

'WANTED at Pilbury Regis Grammar School, Dorset, a Third Classical Master. Must be a Graduate of Oxford or Cambridge; University Prizeman preferred. If unmarried, to take house duty. Commence September 20th. Salary, 200L a year. Apply, as above, to the Rev. J. Greatrex, D.D., Head Master.'

Edie read it through slowly. 'Well, Ernest?' she said, looking up from it into his face. 'Do you think of taking this mastership?'

'If I can get it,' Ernest answered. 'You see, I'm not a University Prizeman, and that may be a difficulty in the way; but otherwise I'm not unlikely to suit the requirements. Herbert knows something of the school—he's been down there to examine; and Mrs. Greatrex had a sort of distant bowing acquaintance with my mother; so I hope their influence might help me into it.'

'Well, Ernest?' Edie cried again, feeling pretty certain in her own heart what was coming next, and reddening accordingly.

'Well, Edie, in that case, would you care to marry at once, and try the experiment of beginning life with me upon two hundred a year? I know it's very little, darling, for our wants and necessities, brought up as you and I have been: but Herr Max says, you know, it's as much as any one family ought ever to spend upon its own gratifications; and at any rate I dare say you and I could manage to be very happy upon it, at least for the present. In any case it wnuld be better than being a governess. Will you risk it, Edie?'

'To me, Ernest,' Edie answered with her unaffected simplicity, 'it really seems quite a magnificent income. I don't suppose any of our friends or neighbours in Calcombe spend nearly as much as two hundred a year upon their own families.'

'Ah, yes, they do, darling. But that isn't the only thing. Two hundred a year is a very different matter in quiet, old-world, little Calcombe and in a fashionable modern watering-place like Pilbury Regis. We shall have to live in lodgings, Edie, and live very quietly indeed; but epen so I think it will be better than for you to go out and endure the humiliation of becoming a governess. Then I may understand that, if I can get this mastership, you'll consent to be married, Edie, before the end of September?'

'Oh, Ernest, that's dreadfully soon!'

'Yes, it is, darling; but you must have a very quiet wedding; and I can't bear to leave you here now any longer without Harry to cheer and protect you. Shall we look upon it as settled?'

Edie blushed and looked down as she answered almost inaudibly, 'As you think best, dear Ernest.'

So that very evening Ernest sent off an application to Pilbury Regis, together with such testimonials as he had by him, mentioning at the same time his intention to marry, and his recent engagement at Lord Exmoor's. 'I hope they won't make a point about the University Prize, Edie,' he said timidly; 'but I rather think they don't mean to insist upon it. I'm afraid it may be put in to some extent mainly as a bait to attract parents. Advertisements are often so very dishonest. At any rate, we can only try; and if I get it, I shall be able to call you my little wife in September.'

So soon after poor Harry's death he hardly liked to say much about how happy that consciousness would make him; but he sent off the letter with a beating heart, and waited anxiously for the head master's answer.

'Maria,' said Dr. Greatrex to his wife next morning, turning over the pile of letters at the breakfast table, 'who do you think has applied for the third mastership? Very lucky, really, isn't it?'

'Considering that there are some thirty millions of people in England, I believe, Dr. Greatrex,' said his wife with dignity, 'that some seventy of those have answered your advertisement, and that you haven't yet given me an opportunity even of guessing which it is of them all, I'm sure I can't say so far whether it's lucky or otherwise.'

'You're pleased to be satirical, my dear,' the doctor answered blandly; he was in too good a humour to pursue the opening further. 'But no matter. Well, I'll tell you, then; it's young Le Breton.'

'Not Lady Le Breton's son!' cried Mrs. Greatrex, forgetting her dignity in her surprise. 'Well, that certainly is very lucky. Now, if we could only get her to come down and stay with us for a week sometimes, after he's been here a little while, what a splendid advertisement it would be for the place, to be sure, Joseph!'

'Capital!' the head master said, eyeing the letter complacently as he sipped his coffee. 'A perfect jewel of a master, I should say, from every possible point of view. Just the sort of person to attract parents and pupils. "Allow me to introduce you to our third master, Mr. Le Breton; I hope Lady Le Breton was quite well when you heard from her last, Le Breton?" and all that sort of thing. Depend upon it, Maria, there's nothing in the world that makes a middle-class parent—and our parents are unfortunately all middle-class—prick up his ears like the faintest suspicion or echo of a title. "Very good school," he goes back and says to his wife immediately; "we'll send Tommy there; they have a master who's an honourable or something of the sort; sure to give the boys a thoroughly high gentlemanly tone." It's snobbery, I admit, sheer snobbery: but between ourselves, Maria, most people are snobs, and we have to live, professionally, by accommodating ourselves to their foolish prejudices.'

'At the same time, doctor,' said his wife severely, 'I don't think we ought to allow it too freely, at least with the door open.'

'You're quite right, my dear,' the head master answered submissively, rising at the same time to shut the door. 'But what makes this particular application all the better is that young Le Breton would come here straight from the Earl of Exmoor's where he has been acting as tutor to the son and heir, Viscount Lynmouth. That's really admirable, now, isn't it? Just consider the advantages of the situation. A doubtful parent comes to inspect the arrangements; sniffs at the dormitories, takes the gauge of the studies, snorts over the playground, condescends to approve of the fives courts. Then, after doing the usual Christian principles business and working in the high moral tone a little, we invite him to lunch, and young Le Breton to meet him. You remark casually in the most unconscious and natural fashion—I admit, my dear, that you do these little things much better than I do—"Oh, talking of cricket, Mr. Le Breton, your old pupil, Lord Lynmouth, made a splendid score the other day at the Eton and Harrow." Fixes the wavering parent like a shot. "Third master something or other in the peerage, and has been tutor to a son of Lord Exmoor's. Place to send your boys to if you want to make perfect gentlemen of them." I think we'd better close at once with this young man's offer, Maria. He's got a very decent degree, too; a first in Mods and Greats; really very decent.'

'But will he take a house-mastership do you think, doctor?' asked the careful lady.

'No, he won't; he's married or soon going to be. We must let him off the house duty.'

'Married!' said Mrs. Greatrex, turning it over cautiously.

'Who's he going to marry, I wonder? I hope somebody presentable.'

'Why, of course!' Dr. Greatrex answered, as who should feel shocked at the bare suggestion that a young man of Ernest Le Breton's antecedents could conceivably marry otherwise.

'His wife, or rather his wife that is to be, is a sister, he tells me, of that poor Mr. Oswald—the famous mathematician, you know, of Oriel—who got killed, you remember, by falling off the Matterhorn or somewhere, just the other day. You must have seen about it in the "Times."'

'I remember,' Mrs. Greatrex answered, in placid contentment; 'and I should say you can't do better than take him immediately. It'd be an excellent thing for the school, certainly. As the third mastership's worth only two hundred a year, of course he can't intend to marry upon THAT; so he must have means of his own, which is always a good thing to encourage in an under-master: or if his wife has money, that comes in the end to the same thing. They'll take a house of their own, no doubt; and she'll probably entertain—very quietly, I daresay; still, a small dinner now and then gives a very excellent tone to the school in its own way. Social considerations, as I always say, Joseph, are all-important in school management; and I think we may take it for granted that Mr. Le Breton would be socially a real acquisition.'

So it was shortly settled that Dr. Greatrex should write back accepting Ernest Le Breton as third master; and Mrs. Greatrex began immediately dropping stray allusions to 'Lady Le Breton, our new master's mother, you know,' among her various acquaintance, especially those with rising young families. The doctor and she thought a good deal of this catch they were making in the person of Ernest Le Breton. Poor souls, they little knew what sort of social qualities they were letting themselves in for. A firebrand or a bombshell would really have been a less remarkable guest to drop down straight into the prim and proper orthodox society of Pilbury Regis.

When Ernest received the letter in which Dr. Greatrex informed him that he might have the third mastership, he hardly knew how to contain his joy. He kissed Edie a dozen times over in his excitement, and sat up late making plans with her which would have been delightful but for poor Edie's lasting sorrow. In a short time it was all duly arranged, and Ernest began to think that he must go back to London for a day or two, to let Lady Le Breton hear of his change of plans, and got everything in order for their quiet wedding. He grudged the journey sadly, for he was beginning to understand now that he must take care of the pence for Edie's sake as well as for humanity's—his abstraction was individualising itself in concrete form—but he felt so much at least was demanded of him by filial duty, and, besides, he had one or two little matters to settle at Epsilon Terrace which could not so well be managed in his absence even by his trusty deputy, Ronald. So he ran up to town once more in a hurry, and dropped in as if nothing had happened, at his mother's house. It was no unusual matter for him to pass a fortnight at Wilton Place without finding time to call round at Epsilon Terrace to see Ronald, and his mother had not heard at all as yet of his recent change of engagement.

Lady Le Breton listened with severe displeasure to Ernest's account of his quarrel with Lord Exmoor. It was quite unnecessary and wrong, she said, to prevent Lynmouth from his innocent boyish amusements. Pigeon-shooting was practised by the very best people, and she was quite sure, therefore, there could be no harm of any sort in it. She believed the sport was countenanced, not only by bishops, but even by princes. Pigeons, she supposed, had been specially created by Providence for our use and enjoyment—'their final cause being apparently the manufacture of pigeon-pie,' Ronald suggested parenthetically: but we couldn't use them without killing them, unfortunately; and shooting was probably as painless a form of killing as any other. Peter or somebody, she distinctly remembered, had been specially commanded to arise, kill, and eat. To object to pigeon-shooting indeed, in Lady Le Breton's opinion, was clearly flying in the face of

Providence. Of Ronald's muttered reference to five sparrows being sold for two farthings, and yet not one of them being forgotten, she would not condescend to take any notice. However, thank goodness, the fault was none of hers; she could wash her hands entirely of all responsibility in the matter. She had done her best to secure Ernest a good place in a thoroughly nice family, and if he chose to throw it up at a moment's notice for one of his own absurd communistical fads, it was happily none of her business. She was glad, at any rate, that he'd got another berth, with a conscientious, earnest, Christian man like Dr. Greatrex. 'And indeed, Ernest,' she said, returning once more to the pigeon-shooting question, 'even your poor dear papa, who was full of such absurd religious fancies, didn't think that sport was unchristian, I'm certain; for I remember once, when we were quartered at Moozuffernugger in the North-West Provinces, he went out into a nullah near our compound one day, and with his own hand shot a man-eating tiger, which had carried off three little native children from the thanah; so that shows that he couldn't really object to sport; and I hope you don't mean to cast disrespect upon the memory of your own poor father!'. All of which profound moral and religious observations Ernest, as in duty bound, received with the most respectful and acquiescent silence.

And now he had to approach the more difficult task of breaking to his mother his approaching marriage with Edie Oswald. He began the subject as delicately as he could, dwelling strongly upon poor Harry Oswald's excellent position as an Oxford tutor, and upon Herbert's visit with him to Switzerland—he knew his mother too well to suppose that the real merits of the Oswald family would impress her in any way, as compared with their accidental social status; and then he went on to speak as gently as possible about his engagement with little Edie. At this point, to his exceeding discomfiture, Lady Le Breton adopted the unusual tactics of bursting suddenly into a flood of tears.

'Oh, Ernest,' she sobbed out inarticulately through her scented cambric handkerchief, 'for heaven's sake don't tell me that you've gone and engaged yourself to that designing girl! Oh, my poor, poor, misguided boy! Is there really no way to save you?'

'No way to save me!' exclaimed Ernest, astonished and disconcerted by this unexpected outburst.

'Yes, yes!' Lady Le Breton went on, almost passionately. 'Can't you manage somehow to get yourself out of it? I hope you haven't utterly compromised yourself! Couldn't dear Herbert go down to What's-his-name Pomeroy, and induce the father —a grocer, if I remember right—induce him, somehow or other, to compromise the matter?'

'Compromise!' cried Ernest, uncertain whether to laugh or be angry.

'Yes, compromise it!' Lady Le Breton answered, endeavouring to calm herself. 'Of course that Machiavellian girl has tried to drag you into it; and the family have aided and abetted her; and you've been weak and foolish—though not, I trust, wicked—and allowed them to get their net closed almost imperceptibly around you. But it isn't too late to withdraw even now, my poor, dear, deluded Ernest. It isn't too late to withdraw even now. Think of the disgrace and shame to the family! Think of your dear brothers and their blighted prospects! Don't allow this designing girl to draw you helplessly into such an ill-assorted marriage! Reflect upon your own future happiness! Consider what it will be to drag on years of your life with a woman, no longer perhaps externally attractive, whom you could never possibly respect or love for her own internal qualities! Don't go and wreck your own life, and your brothers' lives, for any mistaken and Quixotic notions of false honour! You mayn't like to throw her over, after you've once been inveigled into saying "Yes" (and the feeling, though foolish, does your heart credit); but reflect, my dear boy, such a promise, so obtained, can hardly be considered binding upon your conscience! I've no doubt dear Herbert, who's a capital man of business, would get them readily enough to agree to a compromise or a compensation.'

'My dear mother,'said Ernest white with indignation, but speaking very quietly, as soon as he could edge in a word, 'you quite misunderstand the whole question. Edie Oswald is a lady by nature, with all a lady's best feelings—I hate the word because of its false implications, but I can't use any other that will convey to you my meaning—and I love and admire and respect and worship her with all my heart and with all my soul. She hasn't inveigled me or set her cap at me, as you call it, in any way; she's the sweetest, timidest, most shrinking little thing that ever existed; on the contrary, it is I who have humbly asked her to accept me, because I know no other woman to whom I could give my whole heart so unreservedly. To tell you the truth, mother, with my ideas and opinions, I could hardly be happy with any girl of the class that you would call distinctively ladies: their class prejudices and their social predilections would jar and grate upon me at every turn. But Edie Oswald's a girl whom I could worship and love without any reserve—whom I can reverence for her beautiful character, her goodness, and her delicacy of feeling. She has honoured me by accepting me, and I'm going to marry her at the end of this month, and I want, if possible, to get your consent to the marriage before I do so. She's a wife of whom I shall be proud in every way; I wish I could think she would have equal cause to be proud of her husband.'

Lady Le Breton threw herself once more into a paroxysm of tears. 'Oh, Ernest,' she cried, 'do spare me! do spare me! This is too wicked, too unfeeling, too cruel of you altogether! I knew already you were very selfish and heartless and head-strong, but I didn't know you were quite so unmanageable and so unkind as this. I appeal to your better nature—for you HAVE a better nature—I'm sure you have a better nature: you're MY son, and you can't be utterly devoid of good impulses. I appeal confidently to your better nature to throw off this unhappy, designing, wicked girl before it is too late! She has made you forget your duty to your mother, but not, I hope, irrevocably. Oh, my poor, dear, wandering boy, won't you listen to the voice of reason? won't you return once more like the prodigal son, to your neglected mother and your forgotten duty?'

'My dear mother,' Ernest said, hardly knowing how to answer, 'you WILL persist in completely misunderstanding me. I love Edie Oswald with all my heart; I have promised to marry her, because she has done me the great and undeserved honour of accepting me as her future husband; and even if I wanted to break off the engagement (which it would break my own heart to do), I certainly couldn't break it off now without the most disgraceful and dishonourable wickedness. That is quite fixed and certain, and I can't go back upon it in any way.'

'Then you insist, you unnatural boy,' said Lady Le Breton, wiping her eyes, and assuming the air of an injured parent, 'you insist, against my express wish, in marrying this girl Osborne, or whatever you call her?'

'Yes, I do, mother,' Ernest answered quietly.

'In that case,' said Lady Le Breton, coldly, 'I must beg of you that you won't bring this lady, whether as your wife or otherwise, under my roof. I haven't been accustomed to associate with the daughters of tradesmen, and I don't wish to associate with them now in any way.'

'If so,' Ernest said, very softly, 'I can't remain under your roof myself any longer. I can go nowhere at all where my future wife will not be received on exactly the same terms that I am.'

'Then you had bettor go,' said Lady Le Breton, in her chilliest manner. 'Ronald, do me the favour to ring ihe bell for a cab for your brother Ernest.'

'I shall walk, thank you, mother,' said Ernest quietly. 'Good morning, dear Ronald.'

Ronald rose solemnly and opened the door for him. 'Therefore shall a man leave his father and mother,' he said in his clear, soft voice, 'and shall cleave unto his wife; and they twain shall be one flesh. Amen.'

Lady Le Breton darted a withering glance at her younger son as Ernest shut the door after him, and burst once more into a sudden flood of uncontrollable tears.

CHAPTER XVII

'COME YE OUT AND BE YE SEPARATE.'

Arthur Berkeley's London lodgings were wonderfully snug and comfortable for the second floor of a second-rate house in a small retired side street near the Embankment at Chelsea. He had made the most of the four modest little rooms, with his quick taste and his deft, cunning fingers:—four rooms, or rather boxes, one might almost call them; a bedroom each for himself and the Progenitor; a wee sitting-room for meals and music—the two Berkeleys would doubtless as soon have gone without the one as the other; and a tiny study where Arthur might work undisturbed at his own desk upon his new and original magnum opus, destined to form the great attraction of the coming season at the lately-opened Ambiguities Theatre. Things had prospered well with the former Oxford curate during the last twelve-month. His cantata at Leeds had proved a wonderful success, and had finally induced him to remove to London, and take to composing as a regular profession. He had his qualms about it, to be sure, as one who had put his hand to the plough and then turned back; he did not feel quite certain in his own mind how far he was justified in giving up the more spiritual for the more worldly calling; but natures like Arthur Berkeley's move rather upon passing feeling than upon deeper sentiment; and had he not ample ground, he asked himself, for this reconsideration of the monetary position? He had the Progenitor's happiness to insure before thinking of the possible injury to his non-existent parishioners. If he was doing Whippingham Parva or Norton-cum-Sutton out of an

Grant Allen

eloquent and valuable potential rector, if he was depriving the Church in the next half-century of a dignified and portly prospective archdeacon, he is at least making his father's last days brighter and more comfortable than his early ones had ever been. And then, was not music, too, in its own way, a service, a liturgy, a worship? Surely he could do higher good to men's souls—as they call them—to whatever little spark of nobler and better fire there might lurk within those dull clods of common clay he saw all around him—by writing such a work as his Leeds cantata, than by stringing together for ever those pretty centos of seventeenth-century conceits and nineteenth-century doubts or hesitations which he was accustomed to call his sermons! Whatever came of it, he must give up the miserable pittance of a curacy, and embrace the career open to the musical talents.

So he fitted up his little Chelsea rooms in his own economically sumptuous fashion with some bits of wall paper, a few jugs and vases, and an etching or two after Meissonier; planted the Progenitor down comfortably in a large easy-chair, with a melodious fiddle before him; and set to work himself to do what he could towards elevating the British stage and pocketing a reasonable profit on his own account from that familiar and ever-rejuvenescent process. He was quite in earnest, now, about producing a totally new effect of his own; and believing in his work, as a good workman ought to do, he wrought at it indefatigably and well in the retirement of a second-pair back, overlooking a yardful of fluttering clothes, and a fine skyline vista of bare, yellowish brick chimneys.

'What part are you working at to-day, Artie?' said the old shoemaker, looking over his son's shoulder at the blank music paper before him. 'Quartette of Biological Professors, eh?'

'Yes, father,' Berkeley answered with a smile. 'How do you think it runs now?' and he hummed over a few lines of his own words, set with a quaint lilt to his own inimitable and irresistible music:—

And though in unanimous chorus
We mourn that from ages before us
No single enaliosaurus
To-day should survive,

Yet joyfully may we bethink us,
With the earliest mammal to link us,
We still have the ornithorhyncus
Extant and alive!

'How do you think the score does for that, father, eh? Catching air rather, isn't it?'

'Not a better air in the whole piece, Artie; but, my boy, who do you think will ever understand the meaning of the words. The gods themselves won't know what you're driving at.'

'But I'm going to strike out a new line, Daddie dear. I'm not going to play to the gallery; I mean to play to the stalls and boxes.'

'Was there ever such a born aristocrat as this young parson is!' cried the old man, lifting up both his hands with a playful gesture of mock-deprecation. 'He's hopeless! He's terrible! He's incorrigible! Why, you unworthy son of a respectable Paddington shoemaker, if even the intelligent British artizans in the gallery don't understand you, how the dickens do you suppose the oiled and curled Assyrian bulls in the stalls and boxes will have a glimmering idea of what you're driving at? The supposition's an insult to the popular intelligence—in other words, to me, sir, your Progenitor.'

Berkeley laughed. 'I don't know about that, father,' he said, holding up the page of manuscript music at arm's length admiringly before him; 'but I do know one thing: this comic opera of mine is going to be a triumphant success.'

'So I've thought ever since you began it, Artie. You see, my boy, there's a great many points in its favour. In the first place you can write your own libretto, or whatever you call it; and you know I've always held that though that Wagner man was wrong in practice—a most inflated thunder-bomb, his Lohengrin—yet he was right in theory, right in theory, Artie; every composer ought to be his own poet. Well, then, again, you've got a certain peculiar vein of humour of your own, a kind of delicate semi-serious burlesque turn about you that's quite original, both in writing and in composing; you're a humourist in verse and a humourist in music, that's the long and the short of it. Now, you've hit upon a fresh lode of dramatic ore in this opera of yours, and if my judgment goes for anything, it'll bring the house down the first evening. I'm a bit of a critic, Artie; by hook or by crook, you know, paper or money, I've heard every good opera, comic or serious, that's been given in London these last thirty years, and I flatter myself I know something by this time about operatic criticism.'

'You're wrong about Wagner, father,' said Arthur, still glancing with paternal partiality at his sheet of manuscript: 'Lohengrin's a very fine work, a grand work, I assure you. I won't let you run it down. But, barring that, I think you're pretty nearly right in your main judgment. I'm not modest, and it strikes me somehow that I've invented a genre. That's about what it comes to.'

'If you'd confine yourself to your native tongue, Mr. Parson, your ignorant old father might have some chance of agreeing or disagreeing with you; but as he doesn't even know what the thingumbob you say you've invented may happen to be, he can't profitably continue the discussion of that subject. However, my only fear is that you may perhaps be writing above the heads of the audience. Not in the music, Artie; they can't fail to catch that; it rings in one's head like the song of a hedge warbler—tirree, tirree, lu-lu-lu, la-la, tirree, tu-whit, tu-whoo, tra-la-la—but in the words and the action. I'm half afraid that'll be over their heads, even in the gallery. What do you think you'll finally call it?'

'I'm hesitating, Daddy, between "Evolution" and "The Primate of Fiji." Which do you recommend—tell me?'

'The Primate, by all means,' said the old man gaily. 'And you still mean to open with the debate in the Fijian Parliament on the Deceased Grandmother's Second Cousin Bill?'

'No, I don't, Daddy. I've written a new first scene this week, in which the President of the Board of Trade remonstrates with the mermaids on their remissness in sending their little ones to the Fijian Board Schools, in order to receive primary instruction in the art of swimming. I've got a capital chorus of mermaids to balance the other chorus of Biological Professors on the Challenger Expedition. I consider it's a happy cross between Ariosto and Aristophanes. If you like, I'll give you the score, and read over the words to you.' 'Do,' said the old man, settling himself down in comfort in his son's easy-chair, and assuming the sternest air of an impartial critic. Arthur Berkeley read on dramatically, in his own clever airy fashion, suiting accent and gesture to the subject matter through the whole first three acts of that exquisitely humorous opera, the Primate of Fiji. Sometimes he hummed the tune over to himself as he went; sometimes he played a few notes upon his flute by way of striking the key-note; sometimes he rose from his seat in his animation, and half acted the part he was reading with almost unconscious and spontaneous mimicry. He read through the famous song of the President of the Local Government Board, that everybody has since heard played by every German band at the street corners; through the marvellously catching chorus of the superannuated tide-waiters; through the culminating dialogue between the London Missionary Society's Agent and the Hereditary Grand Sacrificer to the King of Fiji. Of course the recital lacked everything of the scenery and dresses that give it so much vogue upon the stage; but it had at least the charmingly suggestive music, the wonderful linking of sound to sense, the droll and inimitable intermixture of the plausible and the impossible which everybody has admired and laughed at in the acted piece.

The old shoemaker listened in breathless silence, keeping his eye fixed steadily all the time upon the clean copy of the score. Only once he made a wry face to himself, and that was in the chorus to the debate in the Fijian Parliament on the proposal to leave off the practice of obligatory cannibalism. The conservative party were of opinion that if you began by burying instead of eating your deceased wife, you might end by the atrocious practice of marrying your deceased wife's sister; and they opposed the revolutionary measure in that well known refrain:—

Of change like this we're naturally chary,
Nolumus leges Fijiae mutari.

That passage evidently gave the Progenitor deep pain.

'Stick to your own language, my boy,' he murmured; 'stick to your own language. The Latin may be very fine, but the gallery wil never understand it.' However, when Arthur finished at last, he drew a long breath, and laid down the roll of manuscript with an involuntary little cry of half-stifled applause.

'Artie,' he said rising from the chair slowly, 'Artie, that's not so bad for a parson, I can tell you. I hope the Archbishop won't be tempted to cite you for displaying an amount of originality unworthy of your cloth.'

'Father,' said Arthur, suddenly, after a short pause, with a tinge of pensiveness in his tone that was not usual with him, in speaking at least; 'Father, I often think I ought never to have become a parson at all.'

'Well, my boy,' said the old man, looking up at him sharply with his keen eyes, 'I knew that long ago. You've never really believed in the thing, and you oughtn't to have gone in for it from the very beginning. It was the music, and the dresses, and the decorations that enticed you, Artie, and not the doctrine.'

Arthur turned towards him with a pained expression. 'Father,' he said, half reproachfully, 'Father, dear father, dou't talk to me like that. Don't think I'm so shallow or so dishonest as to subscribe to opinions I don't believe in. It's a curious thing to say, a curious thing in this unbelieving age, and I'm half ashamed to say it, even to you; but do you know, father, I really do believe it: in my very heart of hearts, I fancy I believe every word of it.'

The old man listened to him compassionately and tenderly, as a woman listens to the fears and troubles of a little child. To him, that plain confession of faith was, in truth, a wonder and a stumbling-block. Good, simple-hearted, easy-going, logical-minded, sceptical shoemaker that he was, with his head all stuffed full of Malthus, and John Stuart Mill, and political economy, and the hard facts of life and science, how could he hope to understand the complex labyrinth of metaphysical thinking, and childlike faith, and aesthetic attraction, and historical authority, which made a sensitive man like Arthur Berkeley, in his wayward, half-serious, emotional fashion, turn back lovingly and regretfully to the fair old creed that his father had so long deserted? How strange that Artie, a full-grown male person, with all the learning of the schools behind him, should relapse at last into these childish and exploded mediaeval superstitions! How incredible that, after having been brought up from his babyhood upward on the strong meat of the agnostic philosophers, he should fall back in his manhood on the milk for babes administered to him by orthodox theology! The simple-minded old sceptic could hardly credit it, now that Arthur told him so with his own lips, though he had more than once suspected it when he heard him playing sacred music with that last touch of earnestness in his execution which only the sincerest conviction and most intimate realisation of its import can ever give. Ah well, ah well, good sceptical old shoemaker; there are perhaps more things in heaven and earth and in the deep soul of man than are dreamt of in your philosophy.

Still, though the avowal shocked and disappointed him a little, the old man could not find it in his heart to say one word of sorrow or disapproval, far less of ridicule or banter, to his dearly loved boy. He felt instinctively, what Herbert Le Breton could not feel, that this sentimental tendency of his son's, as he thought it, lay far too deep and seemed far too sacred for mere argument or common discussion. 'Perhaps,' he said to himself softly, 'Artie's emotional side has got the better of his intellectual. I brought him up without telling him any thing of these things, except negatively, and by way of warning against superstitious tendencies; and when he went to Oxford, and saw the doctrines tricked out in all the authority of a great hierarchy, with its cathedrals, and chapels, and choirs, and altars, and robes, and fal-lal finery, it got the better of him; got the better of him, very naturally. Artie's a cleverer fellow than his old father—had more education, and so on; and I'm fond of him, very fond of him; but his logical faculty isn't quite straight, somehow: he lets his feelings have too much weight and prominence against his calmer reason! I can easily understand how, with his tastes and leanings, the clericals should have managed to get a hold over him. The clericals are such insinuating cunning fellows. A very impressionable boy Artie was, always; the poetical temperament and the artistic temperament always is impressionable, I suppose; but shoe-making certainly does develop the logical faculties. Seems as though the logical faculties were situated in the fore-part of the brain, as they mark them out on the phrenological heads; and the leaning forward that gives us the shoemaker's forehead must tend to enlarge them—give them plenty of room to expand and develop!' Saying which thing to himself musingly, the father took his son's hand gently in his, and only smoothed it quietly as he looked deep into Arthur's eyes, without uttering a single word.

As for Arthur Berkeley, he sat silent, too, half averting his face from his father's gaze, and feeling a little blush of shame upon his cheek at having been surprised unexpectedly into such an unwonted avowal. How could he ever expect his father to understand the nature of his feelings! To him, good old man that he was, all these things were just matters of priestcraft and obscurantism—fables invented by the ecclesiastical mind as a means of getting fat livings and comfortable deaneries out of the public pocket. And, indeed, Arthur was well accustomed at Oxford to keeping his own opinions to himself on such subjects. What chance of sympathy or response was there for such a man as he in that coldly critical and calmly deliberative learned society? Not, of course, that all Oxford was wholly given over even then to extreme agnosticism. There were High Churchmen, and Low Churchmen, and Broad Churchmen enough, to be sure: men learned in the Fathers, and the Canons, and the Acts of the General Councils; men ready to argue on the intermediate state, or on the three witnesses, or on the heretical nature of the Old Catholic schism; men prepared with minute dogmatic opinions upon every conceivable or inconceivable point of abstract theology. There were people who could trace the Apostolic succession of the old Cornish bishops, and people who could pronounce authoritatively upon the exact distinction between justification and remission of sins. But for all these things Arthur Berkeley cared nothing. Where, then, among those learned exegetical theologians, was there room for one whose belief was a matter, not of reason and argument, but of feeling and of sympathy? He did not want to learn what the Council of Trent had said about such and such a dogma; he wanted to be conscious of an inner truth, to find the world permeated by an informing righteousness, to know himself at one with the inner essence of the entire universe. And though he could never feel sure whether it was all illusion or not, he had hungered and thirsted after believing it, till, as he told his father timidly that day, he actually did believe it somehow in his heart of hearts. Let us not seek to probe too deeply into those inner recesses, whose abysmal secrets are never perfectly clear even to the introspective eyes of the conscious self-dissector himself.

After a pause Arthur spoke again. He spoke this time in a very low voice, as one afraid to open his soul too much, even to his father. 'Dear, dear father,' he said, releasing his hand softly, 'you don't quite understand what I mean about it. It isn't because I don't believe, or try to believe, or hope I believe, that I think I ought never to have become a parson. In my way, as

Grant Allen

in a glass, darkly, I do strive my best to believe, though perhaps my belief is hardly more in its way than Ernest Le Breton's unbelieving. I do want to think that this great universe we see around us isn't all a mistake and an abortion. I want to find a mind and an order and a purpose in it; and, perhaps because I want it, I make myself believe that I have really found it. In that hope and belief, with the ultimate object of helping on whatever is best and truest in the world, I took orders. But I feel now that it was an error for me. I'm not the right man to make a parson. There are men who are born for that role; men who know how to conduct themselves in it decently and in seemly fashion; men who can quietly endure all its restraints, and can fairly rise to the height of all its duties. But I can't. I was intended for something lighter and less onerous than that. If I stop in the Church I shall do no good to myself or to it; if I come out of it, I shall make both parties freer, and shall be able to do more good in my own generation. And so, father, for the very same reasons that made me go into it, I mean to come out again. Not in any quarrel with it, nor as turning my back upon it, but just as the simple acknowledgment of a mistaken calling. It wouldn't be seemly, for example, for a parson to write comic operas. But I feel I can do more good by writing comic operas than by talking dogmatically about things I hardly understand to people who hardly understand me. So before I get this opera acted I mean to leave off my white tie, and be known in future, henceforth and for ever, as plain Arthur Berkeley.'

The old shoemaker listened in respectful silence. 'It isn't for me, Artie,' he said, as his son finished, 'to stand between a man and his conscience. As John Stuart Mill says in his essay on "Liberty," we must allow full play to every man's individuality. Wonderful man, John Stuart Mill; I understand his grand-father was a shoemaker. Well, I won't talk with you about the matter of conviction; but I never wanted you to be a parson, and I shall feel all the happier myself when you've ceased to be one.'

'And I,' said Arthur, 'shall feel all the freer; but if I had been able to remain where I was, I should have felt all the worthier, for all that.'

Grant Allen

CHAPTER XVIII

A QUIET WEDDING

Fate was adverse for the moment to Arthur Berkeley's well meant designs for shuffling off the trammels of his ecclesiastical habit. He was destined to appear in public at least once more, not only in the black coat and white tie of his everyday professional costume, but even in the flowing snowy surplice of a solemn and decorous spiritual function. The very next morning's post brought him a little note from Ernest Le Breton specially begging him, in his own name and Edie's, to come down to Calcombe Pomeroy, and officiate as parson at their approaching wedding. The note had cost Ernest a conscientious struggle, for he would have personally preferred to be married at a Registry Office, as being more in accordance with the duties of a good citizen, and savouring less of effete ecclesiastical superstition; but he felt he couldn't even propose such a step to Edie; she wouldn't have considered herself married at all, unless she were married quite regularly by a duly qualified clerk in holy orders of the Church of England as by law established. Already, indeed, Ernest was beginning to recognise with a sigh that if he was going to live in the world at all, he must do so by making at least a partial sacrifice of political consistency. You may step out of your own century, if you choose, yourself, but you can't get all the men and women with whom you come in contact to step out of it also in unison just to please you.

So Ernest had sat down reluctantly to his desk, and consented to ask Arthur Berkeley to assist at the important ceremony in his professional clerical capacity. If he was going to have a medicine man or a priest at all to marry him to the girl of his choice—a barbaric survival, at the best, he thought it—he would, at any rate, prefer having his friend Arthur—a good man and true—to having the fat, easy-going, purse-proud rector of the parish; the younger son of a wealthy family who had gone into the Church for the sake of the living, and who rolled sumptuously down the long hilly High Street every day in his comfortable carriage, leaning back with his fat hands folded complacently over his ample knees, and gazing abstractedly, with his little pigs'-eyes half buried in his cheek, at the beautiful prospect afforded him by the broad livery-covered backs of his coachman and his footman. Ernest could never have consented to lot that lazy, overfed, useless encumbrance on a long-suffering commonwealth, that idle gorger of dainty meats and choice wines from the tithes of the tolling, suffering people, bear any part in what was after all the most solemn and serious contract of his whole lifetime. And, to say the truth, Edie quite agreed with him on that point, too. Though her moral indignation against poor, useless, empty-headed old Mr. Walters didn't burn quite so fierce or so clear as Ernest's—she regarded the fat old parson, indeed, rather from the social point of view, as a ludicrously self-satisfied specimen of the lower stages of humanity, than from the political point of view, as a greedy swallower of large revenues for small work inefficiently performed—she would still have felt that his presence at her wedding jarred and grated on all the finer sensibilities of her nature, as out of accord with the solemn and tender associations of that supreme moment. To have been married by prosy old Mr. Walters, to have taken the final benediction on the greatest act of her life from those big white fat fingers, would have spoilt the reminiscence of the wedding day for her as long as she lived. But when Ernest suggested Arthur Berkeley's name to her, she acquiesced with all her heart in the happy selection. She liked Berkeley better than anybody else she had ever met, except Ernest; and she knew that his presence would rather add one more bright association to the day than detract from it in the coming years.

Her poor little wedding would want all the additions that friends could make to its cheerfulness, to get over the lasting gloom and blank of dear Harry's absence.

'You will come and help us, I know, Berkeley,' Ernest wrote to Arthur in his serious fashion. 'We feel there is nobody else we should so like to have present at our wedding as yourself. Come soon, too, for there are lots of things I want to talk over with you. It's a very solemn responsibility, getting married: you have to take upon yourself the duty of raising up future citizens for the state; and with our present knowledge of how nature works through the laws of heredity, you have to think whether you two who contemplate marriage are well fitted to act as parents to the generations that are to be. When I remember that all my own faults and failings may be handed on relentlessly to those that come after us—built up in the very fibre of their being—I am half appalled at my own temerity. Then, again, there is the inexorable question of money; is it prudent or is it wrong of us to marry on such an uncertainty? I'm afraid that Schurz and Malthas would tell us—very wrong. I have turned over these things by myself till I'm tired of arguing them out in my own head, and I want you to come down beforehand, so as to cheer me up a bit with your lighter and brighter philosophy. On the very eve of my marriage, I'm somehow getting dreadfully pessimistic.'

Arthur read the letter through impatiently and crumpled it up in his hands with a gesture of despondency. 'Poor little Miss Butterfly,' he said to himself, pityingly, 'was there ever such an abstraction of an ethical unit as this good, solemn, self-torturing Ernest! How will she ever live with him? How will he ever live with her? Poor little soul! Harry is gone like the sunshine out of her life; and now this well-meaning, gloomy, conscientious cloud comes caressingly to overspread her with the shadowing pall of its endless serious doubts and hesitations. Fancy a man who has won little Miss Butterfly's heart—dear little Miss Butterfly's gay, laughing, tender little heart—writing such a letter as that to the friend who's going to marry them! Upon my word, I've half a mind to go into the concientious scruples business on my own account! Have I any right to be a party to fettering poor airy fairy little Miss Butterfly, with a heavy iron chain for life and always, to this great lumbering elephantine moral Ernest? Am I justified in tying the cable round her dainty little neck with a silken thread, and then fastening it round his big leg with rivets of hardened steel on the patent Bessemer process? If a couple of persons, duly called by banns in their own respective parishes, or furnished with the right reverend's perquisite, a licence, come to me, a clerk in holy orders, and ask me to marry them, I've a vague idea that unless I comply I lay myself open to the penalties of praemunire, or something else equally awful and mysterious. But if the couple write and ask me to come down into Devonshire and marry them, that's quite another matter. I can lawfully answer, 'Non possumus.' There's a fine ecclesiastical ring, by the way, about answering 'Non possumus;' it sums up the entire position of the Church in a nutshell! Well, I doubt whether I ought to go; but as a matter of friendship, I'll throw overboard my poor conscience. It's used to the process by this time, no doubt, like eels to skinning; and as Hudibras says,

> However tender it may be,
> 'Tis passing blind where 'twill not see.

If she'd only have taken ME, now, who knows but I might in time have risen to be a Prebendary or even a Dean? 'They that have used the office of a deacon well, purchase to themselves a good degree,' Paul wrote to Timothy once; but it's not so now, it's not so now; preferment goes by favour, and the deacon must e'en shift as best he can on his own account.' So, in the end, Arthur packed up his surplice in his little handbag, and took his way peacefully down to Calcombe Pomeroy.

It was a very quiet, almost a sombre wedding, for the poor Oswalds were still enveloped in the lasting gloom of their great loss, and not much outward show or preparation, such as the female heart naturally delights in, could possibly be made under these painful circumstances. Still, all the world of

Calcombe came to see little Miss Oswald married to the grave gentleman from Oxford; and most of them gave her their hearty good wishes, for Edie was a general favourite with gentle and simple throughout the whole borough. Herbert was there, like a decorous gentleman, to represent the bridegroom's family, and so was Ronald, who had slipped away from London without telling Lady Le Breton, for fear of another distressful scone at the last moment. Arthur Berkeley read the service in his beautiful impressive manner, and looked his part well in his flowing white surplice. But as he uttered the solemn words, 'Whom God hath joined together, let no man put asunder,' the musical ring of his own voice sounded to his heart like the knell of his own one love—the funeral service over the only romance he could ever mix in throughout his whole lifetime. Poor fellow, he had taken the duty upon him with all friendly heartiness; but he felt an awful and lonely feeling steal over him when it was all finished, and when he knew that his little Miss Butterfly was now Ernest Le Breton's lawful wife for ever and ever.

In the vestry, after signing the books, Herbert and Ronald and some of the others insisted on their ancient right of kissing the bride in good old English fashion. But Arthur did not. It would not have been loyal. He felt in his heart that he had loved little Miss Butterfly too deeply himself for that; to claim a kiss would be abusing the formal dues of his momentary position. Henceforth he would not even think of her to himself in that little pet name of his brief Oxford dream: he would call her nothing in his own mind but Mrs. Le Breton.

Edie's simple little presents were all arranged in the tiny parlour behind the shop. Most of them were from her own personal friends: a few were from the gentry of the surrounding neighbourhood: but there were two handsomer than the rest: they came from outside the narrow little circle of Calcombe Pomeroy society. One was a plain gold bracelet from Arthur Berkeley; and on the gold of the inner face, though neither Edie nor Ernest noticed it, he had lightly cut with his knife on the soft metal the one word, 'Frustra.' The other was a dressing-case, with a little card inside, 'Miss Oswald, from Lady Hilda Tregellis.' Hilda had heard of Ernest's approaching wedding from Herbert (who took an early opportunity of casually lunching at Dunbude, in order to show that he mustn't be identified with his socialistic brother); and the news had strangely proved a slight salve to poor Hilda's wounded vanity—or, perhaps it would be fairer to say, to her slighted higher instincts. 'A country grocer's daughter!' she said to herself: 'the sister of a great mathematical scholar! How very original of him to think of marrying a grocer's daughter! Why, of course, he must have been engaged to her all along before he came here! And even if he hadn't been, one might have known at once that such a man as he is would never go and marry a girl whose name's in the peerage, when he could strike out a line for himself by marrying a grocer's daughter. I really like him better than ever for it. I must positively send her a little present. They'll be as poor as church mice, I've no doubt. I ought to send her something that'll be practically useful.' And by way of sending something practically useful, Lady Hilda chose at last a handsome silver-topped Russia leather dressing-case.

It was not such a wedding as Edie had pictured to herself in her first sweet maidenly fancies; but still, when they drove away alone in the landau from the side-door of the Red Lion to Calcombe Road Station, she felt a quiet pride and security in her heart from the fact that she was now the wedded wife of a man she loved so dearly as Ernest Le Breton. And even Ernest so far conquered his social scruples that he took first-class tickets, for the first time in his life, to Ilfracombe, where they were to spend their brief and hasty fragment of a poor little honeymoon. It's so extremely hard to be a consistent socialist where women are concerned, especially on the very day of your own wedding!

CHAPTER XIX

INTO THE FIRE

'Let me see, Le Breton,' Dr. Greatrex observed to the new master, 'you've taken rooms for yourself in West Street for the present—you'll take a house on the parade by-and-by, no doubt. Now, which church do you mean to go to?'

'Well, really,' Ernest answered, taken a little aback at the suddenness of the question, 'I haven't had time to think about it yet.'

The doctor frowned slightly. 'Not had time to think about it,' he repeated, rather severely. 'Not had time to think about such a serious question as your particular place of worship! You quite surprise me. Well, if you'll allow me to make a suggestion in the matter it would be that you and Mrs. Le Breton should take seats, for the present at least, at St. Martha's. The parish church is high, decidedly high, and I wouldn't recommend you to go there; most of our parents don't approve of it. You're an Oxford man, I know, and so I suppose you're rather high yourself; but in this particular matter I would strongly advise you to subordinate your own personal feelings to the parents' wishes. Then there's St. Jude's; St. Jude's is distinctly low—quite Evangelical in fact: indeed, I may say, scarcely what I should consider sound church principles at all in any way; and I think you ought most certainly to avoid it sedulously. Evangelicism is on the decline at present in Pilbury Regis. As to St. Barnabas—Barabbas they call it generally, a most irreverent joke, but, of course, inevitable—Barabbas is absolutely Ritualistic. Many of our parents object to it most strongly. But St. Martha's is a quiet, moderate, inoffensive church in every respect—sound and sensible, and free from all extremes. You can give no umbrage to anybody, even the most cantankerous, by going to St. Martha's. The High Church people fraternise with it on the one hand, and the moderate church people fraternise with it on the other, while as to the Evangelicals and the dissenters, they hardly contribute any boys to the school, or if they do, they don't object to unobtrusive church principles. Indeed, my experience has been, Le Breton, that even the most rabid dissenters prefer to have their sons educated by a sound, moderate, high-principled, and, if I may say so, neutral-tinted church clergyman.' And the doctor complacently pulled his white tie straight before the big gilt-framed drawing-room mirror.

'Then, again,' the doctor went on placidly in a bland tone of mild persuasion, 'there's the question of politics. Politics are a very ticklish matter, I can assure you, in Pilbury Regis. Have you any fixed political opinions of your own, Le Breton, or are you waiting to form them till you've had some little experience in your profession?'

'My opinions,' Ernest answered timidly, 'so far as they can be classed under any of the existing political formulas at all, are decidedly Liberal—I may even say Radical.'

The doctor bit his lip and frowned severely. 'Radical,' he said, slowly, with a certain delicate tinge of acerbity in his tone. 'That's bad. If you will allow me to interpose in the matter, I should strongly advise you, for your own sake, to change them at once and entirely. I don't object to moderate Liberalism—perhaps as many as one-third of our parents are moderate Liberals; but decidedly the most desirable form of political belief for a successful schoolmaster is a quiet and gentlemanly, but unswerving Conservatism. I don't say you ought to be an uncompromising old-fashioned Tory—far from it: that alienates not only the dissenters, but even the respectable

Grant Allen

middle-class Liberals. What is above all things expected in a schoolmaster is a central position in politics, so to speak—a careful avoidance of all extremes—a readiness to welcome all reasonable progress, while opposing in a conciliatory spirit all revolutionary or excessive changes—in short, an attitude of studied moderation. That, if you will allow me to advise you, Le Breton, is the sort of thing, you may depend upon it, that most usually meets the wishes of the largest possible number of pupils' parents.'

'I'm afraid,' Ernest answered, as respectfully as possible, 'my political convictions are too deeply seated to be subordinated to my professional interests.'

'Eh! What!' the doctor cried sharply. 'Subordinate your principles to your personal interests! Oh, pray don't mistake me so utterly as that! Not at all, not at all, my dear Le Breton. I don't mean that for the shadow of a second. What I mean is rather this,' and here the doctor cleared his throat and pulled round his white tie a second time, 'that a schoolmaster, considering attentively what is best for his pupils, mark you— we all exist for our pupils, you know, my dear fellow, don't we?—a schoolmaster should avoid such action as may give any unnecessary scandal, you see, or seem to clash with the ordinary opinion of the pupils' parents. Of course, if your views are fully formed, and are of a mildly Liberal complexion (put it so, I beg of you, and don't use that distressful word Radical), I wouldn't for the world have you act contrary to them. But I wouldn't have you obtrude them too ostentatiously—for your own sake, Le Breton, for your own sake, I assure you. Remember, you're a very young man yet: you have plenty of time before you to modify your opinions in: as you go on, you'll modify them—moderate them—bring them into harmony with the average opinions of ordinary parents. Don't commit yourself at present—that's all I would say to you— don't commit yourself at present. When you're as old as I am, my dear fellow, you'll see through all these youthful extravagances.'

'And as to the church, Mr. Le Breton,' said Mrs. Greatrex, with bland suggestiveness from the ottoman, 'of course, we regard the present very unsatisfactory arrangement as only temporary. The doctor hopes in time to get a chapel built, which is much nicer for the boys, and also more convenient for the masters and their families—they all have seats, of course, in the chancel. At Charlton College, where the doctor was an assistant for some years, before we came to Pilbury, there was one of the under-masters, a young man of very good family, who took such an interest in the place that he not only contributed a hundred pounds out of his own pocket towards building a chapel, but also got ever so many of his wealthy friends elsewhere to subscribe, first to that, and then to the organ and stained-glass window. We've got up a small building fund here ourselves already, of which the doctor's treasurer, and we hope before many years to have a really nice chapel, with good music and service well done—the kind of thing that'll be of use to the school, and have an excellent moral effect upon the boys in the way of religious training.'

'No doubt,' Ernest answered evasively, 'you'll soon manage to raise the money in such a place as Pilbury.'

'No doubt,' the doctor replied, looking at him with a searching glance, and evidently harbouring an uncomfortable suspicion, already, that this young man had not got the moral and religious welfare of the boys quite so deeply at heart as was desirable in a model junior assistant master. 'Well, well, we shall see you at school to-morrow morning, Le Breton: till then I hope you'll find yourselves quite comfortable in your new lodgings.'

Ernest went back from this visit of ceremony with a doubtful heart, and left Dr. and Mrs. Greatrex alone to discuss their new acquisition.

'Well, Maria,' said the doctor, in a dubious tone of voice, as soon as Ernest was fairly out of hearing, 'what do you think of him?'

'Think!' answered Mrs. Greatrex, energetically. 'Why, I don't think at all. I feel sure he'll never, never, never make a schoolmaster!'

'I'm afraid not,' the doctor responded, pensively. 'I'm afraid not, Maria. He's got ideas of his own, I regret to say; and, what's worse, they're not the right ones.'

'Oh, he'll never do,' Mrs. Greatrex continued, scornfully. 'Nothing at all professional about him in any way. No interest or enthusiasm in the matter of the chapel; not a spark of responsiveness even about the stained-glass window; hardly a trace of moral or religious earnestness, of care for the welfare and happiness of the dear boys. He wouldn't in the least impress intending parents—or, rather, I feel sure he'd impress them most unfavourably. The best thing we can do, now we've got him, is to play off his name on relations in society, but to keep the young man himself as far as possible in the background. I confess he's a disappointment—a very great and distressing disappointment.'

'He is, he is certainly,' the doctor acquiesced, with a sigh of regretfulness. 'I'm afraid we shall never be able to make much of him. But we must do our best—for his own sake, and the sake of the boys and parents, it's our duty, Maria, to do our best with him.'

'Oh, of course,' Mrs. Greatrex replied, languidly: 'but I'm bound to say, I'm sure it'll prove a very thankless piece of duty. Young men of his sort have never any proper sense of gratitude.'

Meanwhile, Edie, in the little lodgings in a side street near the school-house, had run out quickly to open the door for Ernest, and waited anxiously to hear his report upon their new employers.

'Well, Ernest dear,' she asked, with something of the old childish brightness in her eager manner, 'and what do you think of them?'

'Why, Edie,' Ernest answered, kissing her white forehead gently, 'I don't want to judge them too hastily, but I'm inclined to fancy, on first sight, that both the doctor and his wife are most egregious and unmitigated humbugs.'

'Humbugs, Ernest! why, how do you mean?'

'Well, Edie, they've got the moral and religious welfare of the boys at their very finger ends; and, do you know—I don't want to be uncharitable—but I somehow imagine they haven't got it at heart as well. However, we must do our best, and try to fall in with them.'

And for a whole year Ernest and Edie did try to fall in with them to the best of their ability. It was hard work, for though the doctor himself was really at bottom a kind-hearted man, with a mere thick veneer of professional humbug inseparable from his unhappy calling, Mrs. Greatrex was a veritable thorn in the flesh to poor little natural honest-hearted Edie. When she found that the Le Bretons didn't mean to take a house on the Parade or elsewhere, but were to live ingloriously in wee side street lodgings, her disappointment was severe and extreme; but when she incidentally discovered that Mrs. Le Breton was positively a grocer's daughter from a small country town, her moral indignation against the baseness of mankind rose almost to white heat. To think that young Le Breton should have insinuated himself into the position of third master under false pretences—should have held out as qualifications for the post his respectable connections, when he knew perfectly well all the time that he was going to marry somebody who was not in Society—it was really quite too awfully wicked and deceptive and unprincipled of him! A very bad, dishonest young man, she was very much afraid; a young man with no sense of truth or honour about him, though, of course, she wouldn't say so for the world before any of the parents, or do anything to injure the poor young fellow's future prospects if she could possibly help it. But Mrs.

Greatrex felt sure that Ernest had come to Pilbury of malice prepense, as part of a deep-laid scheme to injure and ruin the doctor by his horrid revolutionary notions. 'He does it on purpose,' she used to say; 'he talks in that way because he knows it positively shocks and annoys us. He pretends to be very innocent all the time; but at heart he's a malignant, jealous, uncharitable creature. I'm sure I wish he had never come to Pilbury Regis! And to go quarrelling with his own mother, too—the unnatural man! The only respectable relation he had, and the only one at all likely to produce any good or salutary effect upon intending parents!'

'My dear,' the doctor would answer apologetically, 'you're really quite too hard upon young Le Breton. As far as school-work goes, he's a capital master, I assure you—so conscientious, and hard-working, and systematic. He does his very best with the boys, even with that stupid lout, Blenkinsopp major; and he has managed to din something into them in mathematics somehow, so that I'm sure the fifth form will pass a better examination this term than any term since we first came here. Now that, you know, is really a great thing, even if he doesn't quite fall in with our preconceived social requirements.'

'I'm sure I don't know about the mathematics or the fifth form, Joseph,' Mrs. Geatrex used to reply, with great dignity. 'That sort of thing falls under your department, I'm aware, not under mine. But I'm sure that for all social purposes, Mr. Le Breton is really a great deal worse than useless. A more unchristian, disagreeable, self-opinionated, wrong-headed, objectionable young man I never came across in the whole course of my experience. However, you wouldn't listen to my advice upon the subject, so it's no use talking any longer about it. I always advised you not to take him without further enquiry into his antecedents; and you overbore me: you said he was so well-connected, and so forth, and would hear nothing against him; so I wish you joy now of your precious bargain. The only thing left for us is to find some good opportunity of getting rid of him.'

'I like the young man, as far as he goes,' Dr. Greatrex replied once, with unwonted spirit, 'and I won't get rid of him at all, my dear, unless he obliges me to. He's really well meaning, in spite of all his absurdities, and upon my word, Maria, I believe he's thoroughly honest in his opinions.'

Mrs. Greatrex only met this flat rebellion by an indirect remark to the effect that some people seemed absolutely destitute of the very faintest glimmering power of judging human character.

CHAPTER XX

LITERATURE, MUSIC, AND THE DRAMA

'The Primate of Fiji' was duly accepted and put into rehearsal by the astute and enterprising manager of the Ambiguities Theatre. 'It's a risk,' he said candidly, when he read the manuscript over, 'a decided risk, Mr. Berkeley; I acknowledge the riskiness, but I don't mind trying it for all that. You see, you've staked everything upon the doubtful supposition that the Public possesses a certain amount of elementary intelligence, and a certain appreciation of genuine original wit and humour. Your play's literature, good literature; and that's rather a speculative element to introduce into the regular theatre nowadays. Illegitimate, I should call it; decidedly illegitimate—but still, perhaps, worth trying. Do you know the story about old Simon Burbury, the horsedealer? Young Simon says to him one morning, "Father, don't you think we might manage to conduct this business of ours without always telling quite so many downright lies about it?" The old man looks back at him reproachfully, and says with a solemn shake of the head, "Ah, Simon, Simon, little did I ever think I should live to see a son of mine go in for speculation!" Well, my dear sir, that's pretty much how a modern manager feels about the literary element in the drama. The Public isn't accustomed to it, and there's no knowing how they may take it. Shakespeare, now, they stand readily enough, because he's an old-established and perfectly respectable family purveyor. Sheridan, too, of course, and one play of Goldsmith's, and a trifle or so of George Colman—all recognised and all tolerated because of their old prescriptive respectability. But for a new author to aim at being literary's rather presumptuous; now tell me yourself, isn't it? Seems as if he was setting himself up for a heaven-sent genius, and trying to sit upon the older dramatists of the present generation. Melodrama, sensation, burlesque—that's all right enough— perfectly legitimate; but a real literary comic opera, with good words and good music—it IS a little strong, for a beginner, Mr. Berkeley, you WILL acknowledge.'

'But don't you think,' Arthur answered, smiling good-humouredly at his cynical frankness, 'an educated and cultured Public is beginning to grow up that may, perhaps, really prefer a little literature, provided it's made light enough and attractive enough for their rapid digestion? Don't you think intelligent people are beginning to get just a trifle sick of burlesque, and spectacle, and sensation, and melodrama?'

'Why, my dear sir,' the manager answered promptly, 'that's the exact chance on which I'm calculating when I venture to accept your comic opera from an unknown beginner. It's clever, there's no denying that, and I hope the fact won't be allowed to tell against it: but the music's bright and lively; the songs are quaint and catching; the dialogue's brisk and not too witty; and there's plenty of business—plenty of business in it. I incline to think we can get together a house at the Ambiguities that'll enter into the humour of the thing, and see what your play's driving at. How did you learn all about stage requirements, though? I never saw a beginner's play with so little in it that was absolutely impossible.'

'I was a Shooting Star at Oxford,' Berkeley answered simply, 'so that I know something—like a despised amateur—about stage necessities; and I've written one or two little pieces before for private acting. Besides, Watkiss has helped me with all the technical arrangements of the little opera.'

'It'll do,' the manager answered, more confidently; 'I won't predict a success, because you know a manager should never prophesy unless he knows; but I think there's a Public in

London that'll take it in, just as they took in "Caste" and "Society," twenty years back, at the Prince of Wales's. Anyhow, I'm quite prepared to give it a fair trial.'

On the first night, Arthur Berkeley and the Progenitor went down in fear and trembling to the stage door of the Ambiguities. There was a full house, and the critics were all present, in some surprise at the temerity of this new man; for it was noised abroad already by those who had seen the rehearsals that 'The Primate of Fiji' was a fresh departure, after its own fashion, in the matter of English comic opera. The curtain rose upon the chorus of mermaids, and the first song was a decided hit. Still the Public, as becomes a first night, maintained a dignified and critical reserve. When the President of the Board of Trade, in full court costume, appeared upon the scene, in the midst of the very realistic long-haired sea-ladies, the audience was half shocked for a moment by the utter incongruity of the situation; but after a while they began to discover that the incongruity was part of the joke, and they laughed quietly a sedate and moderate laugh of suspended judgment. As the Progenitor had predicted, the gods were the first to enter into the spirit of the fun, and to give a hand to the Primate's first sermon. The scuntific professors on the Challenger Expedition took the fancy of the house a little more decidedly; and even the stalls thawed visibly when the professor of biology delivered his famous exposition of the evolution hypothesis to the assembled chiefs of Raratouga. But it was the one feeble second-hand old joke of the piece that really brought pit and boxes down together in a sudden fit of inextinguishable laughter. The professor of political economy enquired diligently, with note book in hand, of the Princess of Fiji, whether she thought the influence of the missionaries beneficial or otherwise; whether she considered these preachers of a new religion really good or not; to which the unsophisticated child of nature responded naively, 'Good, very good—roasted; but not quite so good boiled,' and the professor gravely entered the answer in his philosophic note-book. It was a very ancient jest indeed, but it tickled the ribs of the house mightily, as ancient jests usually do, and they burst forthwith into a hearty roar of genuine approval. Then Arthur began to breathe more freely. After that the house toned down again quietly, and gave no decided token of approbation till the end of the piece. When the curtain dropped there was a lull of hushed expectation for poor Arthur Berkeley; and at its close the house broke out into a storm of applause, and 'The Primate of Fiji' had firmly secured its position as the one great theatrical success of the present generation.

There was a loud cry of 'Author! Author!' and Arthur Berkeley, hardly knowing how he got there, or what he was standing on, found himself pushed from behind by friendly hands, on to the narrow space between the curtain and the footlights. He became aware that a very hot and red body, presumably himself, was bowing mechanically to a seething and clapping mass of hands and faces over the whole theatre. Backing out again, in the same semi-conscious fashion, with the universe generally reeling on more than one distinct axis all around him, he was seized and hand-shaken violently, first by the Progenitor, then by the manager, and then by half a dozen other miscellaneous and unknown persons. At last, after a lot more revolutions of the universe, he found himself comfortably pitched into a convenient hansom, with the Progenitor by his side; and hardly knew anything further till he discovered his own quiet supper table at the Chelsea lodgings, and saw his father mixing a strong glass of brandy and seltzer for him. to counteract the strength of the excitement.

Next morning Arthur Berkeley 'awoke, and found himself famous.' 'The Primate of Fiji' was the rage of the moment. Everybody went to hear it—everybody played its tunes at their own pianos—everybody quoted it, and adapted it, and used its clever catchwords as the pet fashionable slang expressions of the next three seasons. Arthur Berkeley was the lion of the hour; and the mantelpiece of the quiet little Chelsea study was ranged three rows deep with cards of invitation from people whose very names Arthur had never heard of six months before, and whom the Progenitor declared it was a sin and shame for any respectable young man of sound economical

Grant Allen

education even to countenance. There were countesses, and marchionesses, too, among the senders of those coronetted parallelograms of waste pasteboard, as the Progenitor called them—nay, there was even one invitation on the mantelpiece that bore the three strawberry leaves and other insignia of Her Grace the Duchess of Leicestershire.

'Can't you give us just ONE evening, Mr. Berkeley,' said Lady Hilda Tregellis, as she sat on the centre ottoman in Mrs. Campbell Moncrieff's drawing-room with Arthur Berkeley talking lightly to her about the nothings which constitute polite conversation in the nineteenth century. 'Just one evening, any day after the next fortnight? We should be so delighted if you could manage to favour us.'

'No, I'm afraid I can't, Lady Hilda,' Arthur answered. 'My evenings are so dreadfully full just now; and besides, you know, I'm not accustomed to so much society, and it unsettles me for my daily work. After all, you see, I'm a journeyman playwright now, and I have to labour at my unholy calling just like the theatrical carpenter.'

'How delightfully frank,' thought Lady Hilda. 'Really I like him quite immensely.—Not even the afternoon on Wednesday fortnight?' she went on aloud. 'You might come to our garden party on Wednesday fortnight.'

'Quite impossible,' Arthur Berkeley answered. 'That's my regular day at Pilbury Regis.'

'Pilbury Regis!' cried Lady Hilda, starting a little. 'You don't mean to say you have engagements, and in the thick of the season, too, at Pilbury Regis!'

'Yes, I have, every Wednesday fortnight,' Berkeley answered, with a smile. 'I go there regularly. You see, Lady Hilda, Wednesday's a half-holiday at Pilbury Grammar School; so every second week I run down for the day to visit an old friend of mine, who's also an acquaintance of yours, I believe,—Ernest Le Breton. He's married now, you know, and has got a mastership at the Pilbury Grammar School.'

'Then you know Mr. Le Breton!' cried Lady Hilda, charmed at this rapprochement of two delightfully original men. 'He is so nice. I like him immensely, and I'm so glad you're a friend of his. And Mrs. Le Breton, too; wasn't it nice of him? Tell me, Mr. Berkeley, was she really and truly a grocer's daughter?'

Berkeley's voice grew a little stiffer and colder as he answered, 'She was a sister of Oswald of Oriel, the great mathematician, who was killed last year by falling from the summit of a peak in the Bernina.'

'Oh, yes, yes, I know all about that, of course,' said Lady Hilda, quickly and carelessly. 'I know her brother was very clever and all that sort of thing; but then there are so many men who are very clever, aren't there? The really original thing about it all, you know, was that he actually married a grocer's daughter. That was really quite too delightfully original. I was charmed when I heard about it: I thought it was so exactly like dear Mr. Le Breton. He's so deliciously unconventional in every way. He was Lynmouth's tutor for a while, as you've heard, of course; and then he went away from us, at a moment's notice, so nicely, because he wouldn't stand papa's abominable behaviour, and quite right, too, when it was a matter of conscience—I dare say he's told you all about it, that horrid pigeon-shooting business. Well, and so you know Mrs. Le Breton—do tell me, what sort of person is she?'

'She's very nice, and very good, and very pretty, and very clever,' Arthur answered, a little constrainedly. 'I don't know that I can tell you anything more about her than that.'

'Then you really like her?' said Lady Hilda, warmly. 'You think her a fit wife for Mr. Le Breton, do you?'

'I think him a very lucky fellow indeed to have married such a charming and beautiful woman,' Arthur answered, quietly.

Lady Hilda noticed his manner, and read through it at once with a woman's quickness. 'Aha!' she said to herself: 'the wind blows that way, does it? What a very remarkable girl she must be, really, to have attracted two such men as Mr. Berkeley and Mr. Le Breton. I've lost one of them to her; I can't very well lose the other, too: for after Ernest Le Breton, I've never seen any man I should care to marry so much as Mr. Arthur Berkeley.'

'Lady Hilda,' said the hostess, coming up to her at that moment, 'you'll play us something, won't you? You know you promised to bring your music.'

Hilda rose at once with stately alacrity. Nothing could have pleased her better. She went to the piano, and, to the awe and astonishment of Mrs. Campbell Moncrieff, took out an arrangement of the Fijian war-dance from 'The Primate of Fiji.' It suited her brilliant slap-dash style of execution admirably; and she felt she had never played so well in her life before. The presence of the composer, which would have frightened and unnerved most girls of her age, only made Hilda Tregellis the bolder and the more ambitious. Here was somebody at least who knew something about it; none of your ordinary fashionable amateurs and mere soulless professional performers, but the very man who had made the music—the man in whose brain the notes had first gathered themselves together into speaking melody, and who could really judge the comparative merits of her rapid execution. She played with wonderful verve and spirit, so that Lady Exmoor, seated on the side sofa opposite, though shocked at first at Hilda's choice of a piece, glanced more than once at the wealthiest young commoner present (she had long since mentally resigned herself to the prospect of a commoner for that poor dear foolish Hilda), and closely watched his face to see what effect this unwonted outburst of musical talent might succeed in producing upon his latent susceptibilities. But Lady Hilda herself wasn't thinking of the wealthy commoner; she was playing straight at Arthur Berkeley: and when she saw that Arthur Berkeley's mouth had melted slowly into an approving smile, she played even more brilliantly and better than ever, after her bold, smart, vehement fashion. As she left the piano, Arthur said, 'Thank you; I have never heard the piece better rendered.' And Lady Hilda felt that that was a triumph which far outweighed any number of inane compliments from a whole regiment of simpering Algies, Monties, and Berties.

'You can't say any evening, then, Mr. Berkeley?' she said once more, as she held out her hand to him to say 'Good-night' a little later: 'not any evening at all, or part of an evening? You might really reconsider your engagements.'

Arthur hesitated visibly. 'Well, possibly I might manage it,' he said, wavering, 'though, I assure you, my evenings are very much more than full already.'

'Then don't make it an evening,' said Lady Hilda, pressingly. 'Make it lunch. After all, Mr. Berkeley, it's we ourselves who want to see you; not to show you off as a curiosity to all the rest of London. We have silly people enough in the evenings; but if you'll come to lunch with us alone one day, we shall have an opportunity of talking to you on our own account.'

Lady Hilda was tall and beautiful, and Lady Hilda spoke. as she always used to speak, with manifest sincerity. Now, it is not in human nature not to feel flattered when a beautiful woman pays one genuine homage; and Arthur Berkeley was quite as human, after all, as most other people. 'You're very kind,' he said, smiling. 'I must make it lunch, then, though I really ought to be working in the mornings instead of running about merely to amuse myself. What day will suit you best?'

'Oh, not to amuse yourself, Mr. Berkeley,' Hilda answered pointedly, 'but to gratify us. That, you know, is a work of benevolence. Say Monday next, then, at two o'clock. Will that do for you?'

'Perfectly,' Berkeley answered, taking her proffered hand extended to him with just that indefinable air of frankness which Lady Hilda knew so well how to throw into all her actions. 'Good evening. Wilton Place, isn't it!—Gracious heavens!' he thought to himself, as he glanced after her satin train sweeping slowly down the grand staircase, 'what on earth would the dear old Progenitor say if only he saw me in the midst of these meaningless aristocratic orgies. I am positively half-wheedled, it seems, into making love to an earl's daughter! If this sort of thing continues, I shall find myself, before I know it, connected by marriage with two-thirds of the British peerage. A beautiful woman, really, and quite queen-like in her manner when she doesn't choose rather to be unaffectedly gracious. How she sat upon that tall young man with the brown moustaches over by the mantelpiece! I didn't hear what she said to him, but I could see he was utterly crushed by the way he slank away with his tail between his legs, like a whipped spaniel. A splendid woman—and no doubt about it; looks as if she'd stepped straight out of the canvas of Titian, with the pearls in her hair and everything else exactly as he painted them. The handsomest girl I ever saw in my life—but not like Edie Le Breton. They say a man can only fall in love once in a lifetime. I wonder whether there's any truth in it! Well, well, you won't often see a finer woman in her own style than Lady Hilda Tregellis. Monday next, at two precisely; I needn't make a note of it—no fear of my forgetting.'

'I really do think,' Lady Hilda said to herself as she unrolled the pearls from her thick hair in her own room that winter evening, 'I almost like him better than I did Ernest Le Breton. The very first night I saw him at Lady Mary's I fell quite in love with his appearance, before I knew even who he was; and now that I've found out all about him, I never did hear anything so absolutely and delightfully original. His father a common shoemaker! That, to begin with, throws Ernest Le Breton quite into the shade! HIS father was a general in the Indian army—nothing could be more BANAL. Then Mr. Berkeley began life as a clergyman; but now he's taken off his white choker, and wears a suit of grey tweed like any ordinary English gentleman. So delightfully unconventional, isn't it? At last, to crown it all, he not only composes delicious music, but goes and writes a comic opera—such a comic opera! And the best of it is, success hasn't turned his head one atom. He doesn't run with vulgar eagerness after the great people, like your ordinary everyday successful nobody. He took no more notice of me, myself, at first, because I was Lady Hilda Tregellis, than if I'd been a common milkmaid; and he wouldn't come to our garden party because he wanted to go down to Pilbury Regis to visit the Le Bretons at their charity school or something! It was only after I played the war-dance arrangement so well—I never played so brilliantly in my life before—that he began to alter and soften a little. Certainly, these pearls do thoroughly become me. I think he looked after me when I was leaving the room just a tiny bit, as if he was really pleased with me for my own sake, and not merely because I happen to be called Lady Hilda Tregellis.'

Grant Allen

CHAPTER XXI

OFF WITH THE OLD LOVE.

'It's really very annoying, this letter from Selah,' Herbert Le Breton murmured to himself, as he carefully burnt the compromising document, envelope and all, with a fusee from his oriental silver pocket match-case. 'I had hoped the thing had all been forgotten by this time, after her long silence, and my last two judiciously chilly letters—a sort of slow refrigerating process for poor shivering naked little Cupid. But here, just at the very moment when I fancied the affair had quite blown over, comes this most objectionable letter, telling me that Selah has actually betaken herself to London to meet me; and what makes it more annoying still, I wanted to go up myself this week to dine at home with Ethel Faucit. Mother's plan about Ethel Faucit is exceedingly commendable; a girl with eight hundred a year, cultivated tastes, and no father or other encumbrances dragging after her. I always said I should like to marry a poor orphan. A very desirable young woman to annex in every way! And now, here's Selah Briggs—ugh! how could I ever have gone and entangled myself in my foolish days with a young woman burdened by such a cognomen!—here's Selah Briggs must needs run away from Hastings, and try to hunt me up on her own account in London. If I dared, I wouldn't go up to see her at all, and would let the thing die a natural death of inanition—sine Cerere et Baccho, and so forth—(I'm afraid, poor girl, she'll be more likely to find Bacchus than Ceres if she sticks in London); but the plain fact is, I don't dare—that's the long and the short of it. If I did,

Selah'd be tracking me to earth here in Oxford, and a nice mess that'd make of it! She doesn't know my name, to be sure; but as soon as she called at college and found nobody of the name of Walters was known there, she'd lie in wait for me about the gates, as sure as my name's Herbert Le Breton, and sooner or later she'd take it out of me, one way or the other. Selah has as many devils in her as the Gergesene who dwelt among the tombs, I'll be sworn to it; and if she's provoked, she'll let them all loose in a legion to crush me. I'd better see her and have it out quietly, once for all, than try to shirk it here in Oxford and let myself in at the end for the worse condemnation.'

Under this impression, Herbert Le Breton, leaning back in his well-padded oak armchair, ordered his scout to pack his portmanteau, and set off by the very first fast train for Paddington station. He would get over his interview with Selah Briggs in the afternoon, and return to Epsilon Terrace in good time for Lady Le Breton's dinner. Say what you like of it, Ethel Faucit and eight hundred a year, certe redditum, was a thing in no wise to be sneezed at by a judicious and discriminating person.

Herbert left his portmanteau in the cloakroom at Paddington, and drove off in a hansom to the queer address which Selah had given him. It was a fishy lodging of the commoner sort in a back street at Notting Hill, not far from the Portobello Road. At the top of the stairs, Selah stood waiting to meet him, and seemed much astonished when, instead of kissing her, as was his wont, he only shook her hand somewhat coolly. But she thought to herself that probably he didn't wish to be too demonstrative before the eyes of the lodging-house people, and so took no further notice of it.

'Well, Selah,' Herbert said, as soon as he entered the room, and seated himself quietly on one of the straight-backed wooden chairs, 'why on earth have you come to London?'

'Goodness gracious, Herbert,' Selah answered, letting loose the floodgates of her rapid speech after a week's silence, 'don't you go and ask me why I've done it. Ask me rather why I didn't go and do it long ago. Father, he's got more and more aggravating every day for the last twelve-month, till at last I couldn't atand him any longer. Prayer meetings, missionary meetings, convention meetings, all that sort of thing I could put up with somehow; but when it came to private exhortations and prayer over me with three or four of the godliest neighbours, I made up my mind not to put up with it one day longer. So last week I packed up two or three little things hurriedly, and left a note behind to say I felt I was too unregenerate to live in such spiritual company any longer; and came straight up here to London, and took these lodgings. Emily Lucas, she wrote to me from Hastings—she's the daughter of the hairdresser in our street, you know, and I told her to write to me to the Post-office. Emily Lucas wrote to me that there was weeping and gnashing of teeth, and swearing almost, when they found out I'd really left them. And well there might be, indeed, for I did more work for them (mostly just to get away for a while from the privileges) than they'll ever get a hired servant to do for them in this world, Herbert.' Herbert moved uneasily on his chair, as he noticed how glibly she called him now by his Christian name instead of saying 'Mr. Walters.' 'And Emily says,' Selah went on, without stopping to take breath for a second, 'that father put an advertisement at once into the "Christian Mirror"—pah, as if it was likely I should go buying or reading the "Christian Mirror," indeed—to say that if "S. B." would return at once to her affectionate and injured parents, the whole past would be forgotten and forgiven. Forgotten and forgiven! I should think it would, indeed! But he didn't ask me whether their eternal bothering and plaguing of me about my precious soul for twenty years past would also be forgotten and forgiven! He didn't ask me whether all their meetings, and conventions, and prayers, and all the rest of it, would be forgotten and forgiven! My precious soul! In Turkey they say the women have no souls! I often wished it had been my happy lot to be born in Turkey, and then, perhaps, they wouldn't have worried me so much about it. I'm sure I often said to them, "Oh don't bother on account of my poor unfortunate misguided little soul any longer. It's lost altogether, I don't doubt, and it doesn't in the least trouble me. If it was somebody else's, I could understand your being in such a fearful state of mind about it; but as it's only mine, you know, I'm sure it really doesn't matter." And then they'd only go off worse than ever,—mother doing hysterics, and so forth—and say I was a wicked, bad, abominable scoffer, and that it made them horribly frightened even to listen to me. As if I wasn't more likely to know the real value of my own soul than anybody else was!'

Herbert looked at her curiously and anxiously as she delivered this long harangue in a voluble stream, without a single pause or break; and then he said, in his quiet voice, 'How old are you, Selah?'

'Twenty-two,' Selah answered, carelessly. 'Why, Herbert?'

'Oh, nothing,' Herbert replied, turning away his eyes from her keen, searching gaze uncomfortably. He congratulated himself inwardly on the lucky fact that she was fully of age, for then at least he could only get into a row with her, and not with her parents. 'And now, Selah, do you know what I strongly advise you?'

'To get married at once,' Selah put in promptly.

Herbert drew himself up stiffly, and looked at her cautiously out of the corner of his eyes. 'No,' he said slowly, 'not to get married, but to go back again for the present to your people at Hastings. Consider, Selah, you've done a very foolish thing indeed by coming here alone in this way. You've compromised yourself, and you've compromised me. Indeed, if it weren't for the lasting affection I bear you'—he put this in awkwardly, but he felt it necessary to do so, for the flash of Selah's eyes fairly cowed him for the moment—'I wouldn't have come here at all this afternoon to see you. It might get us both into very serious trouble, and—and—and delay the prospect of our marriage. You see, everything depends upon my keeping my fellowship until I can get an appointment to marry on. Anything that risks loss of the fellowship is really a measurable danger for both of us.'

Selah looked at him very steadily with her big eyes, and Herbert felt that he was quailing a little under their piercing, withering inquisition. By Jove, what a splendid woman she was, though, when she was angry! 'Herbert,' she said, rising from her chair and standing her full height imperiously before him, 'Herbert, you're deceiving me. I almost believe you're shilly-shallying with me. I almost believe you don't ever really mean to marry me.'

Herbert moved uneasily upon his wooden seat. What was he to do? Should he make a clean breast of it forthwith, and answer boldly, 'Well, Selah, you have exactly diagnosed my mental attitude'? Or should he try to put her off a little with some meaningless explanatory platitudes? Or should he—by Jove, she was a very splendid woman!—should he take her in his arms that moment, kiss her doubts and fears away like a donkey, and boldly and sincerely promise to marry her? Pooh! not such a fool as all that comes to! not even with Selah before him now; for he was no boy any longer, and not to be caught by the mere vulgar charms of a flashy, self-asserting greengrocer's daughter.

'Selah,' he said at last, after a long pause, 'I strongly advise you once more to return to Hastings for the present. You'll find it better for you in the end. If your people are quite unendurable—as I don't doubt they are from what you tell me—you could look about meanwhile for a temporary appointment, say as'—he checked himself from uttering the word 'shop girl,' and substituted for it, 'draper's assistant.'

Selah looked at him angrily. 'What fools you men are about such things!' she said in a voice of utter scorn. 'When do you suppose I ever learnt the drapery? Or who do you suppose would ever give me a place in a shop of that sort without having learnt the drapery? I dare say you think it takes ten years to make one of you fine gentlemen at college, with your Greek and your Latin, but that the drapery, or the millinery, or the confectionery, comes by nature! However, that's not the question now. The question's simply this—Herbert Walters, do you or don't you mean to marry me?'

'I must temporise,' Herbert thought to himself, placidly. 'This girl's quite too unreservedly categorical! She eliminates modality with a vengeance!' 'Well, Selah,' he said in his calmest and most deliberate manner, 'we must take a great many points into consideration before deciding on that matter.' And then he went on to tell her what seemed to him the pros and cons of an immediate marriage. Couldn't she get a place meanwhile of some sort? Couldn't she let him have time to look about him? Couldn't she go back just for a few days to Hastings, until he could hear of something feasible for either of them? Selah interrupted him more than once with forcible interjectional observations such as 'bosh!' and 'rubbish!' and when he had finished she burst out once more into a long and voluble statement.

For more than an hour Herbert Le Breton and Selah Briggs fenced with one another, each after their own fashion, in the little fishy lodgings; and at every fresh thrust, Herbert parried so much the worse that at last Selah lost patience utterly, and rose in the end to the dignity of the situation. 'Herbert Walters,' she said, looking at him with unspeakable contempt, 'I see through your flimsy excuses now, and I feel certain you don't mean to marry me! You never did mean to marry me! You wanted to amuse yourself by making love to a poor girl in a country town, and now you'd like to throw her overboard and leave her alone to her own devices. I knew you meant that when you didn't write to me; but I wouldn't condemn you unheard; I gave you a chance to clear yourself. I see now you were trying to drop the acquaintance quietly, and make it seem as if I had backed out of it as well as you.'

Herbert felt the moment for breaking through all reserve had finally arrived. 'You admirably interpret my motives in the matter, Selah,' he said coldly. 'I don't think it would be just of me to interfere with your prospects in life any longer. I can't say how long it may be before I am able to afford marriage; and, meanwhile, I'm preventing you from forming a natural alliance with some respectable and estimable young man in your own station. I should be sorry to stand in your way any further; but if I could offer you any small pecuniary assistance at any time, either now or hereafter, you know I'd be very happy indeed to do so, Selah.'

The angry girl turned upon him fiercely. 'Selah!' she cried in a tone of crushing contempt. 'What do you mean by calling me Selah, sir? How dare you speak to me by my Christian name in the same breath you tell me you don't mean to marry me? How dare you have the insolence and impertinence to offer me money! Never say another word to me as long as you live, Herbert Walters; and leave me now, for I don't want to have anything more to say to you or your money for ever.'

Herbert took up his hat doubtfully. 'Selah!—Selah!—Miss Briggs, I mean,' he said, falteringly, for at that moment Selah's face was terrible to look at. 'I'm very sorry, I can assure you, that this interview—and our pleasant acquaintance—should unfortunately have had such a disagreeable termination. For my own part'—Herbert was always politic—'I should have wished to part with you in no unfriendly spirit. I should have wished to learn your plans for the future, and to aid you in forming a suitable settlement in life hereafter. May I venture to ask, before I go, whether you mean to remain in London or to return to Hastings? As one who has been your sincere friend, I should at least like to know what are your movements for the immediate present. How long do you mean to stop here, and when you leave these rooms where do you think you will next go to?'—'Confoundedly awkward,' he thought to himself, 'to have her prowling about and dogging one's footsteps here in London.'

Selah read through his miserable transparent little pretences at once with a woman's quick instinctive insight. 'Ugh!' she cried, pushing him away from her, figuratively, with a gesture of disgust, 'do you think, you poor suspicious creature, I want to go spying you or following you all over London? Are you afraid, in your sordid little respectable way, that I'll come up to Oxford to pry and peep into that snug comfortable fellowship of yours? Do you suppose I'm so much in love with you, Herbert Walters, that I can't let you go without wanting to fawn upon you and run after you ever afterwards! Pah! you miserable, pitiable, contemptible cur and coward, are you afraid even of a woman! Go away, and don't be frightened. I never want to see you or speak to you again as long as I live, you wretched, lying, shuffling hypocrite. I'd rather go back to my own people at Hastings a thousand times over than have anything more to do with you. They may be narrow-minded, and bigoted, and ignorant, and stupid, but at least they're honest—they're not liars and hypocrites. Go this minute, Herbert Walters, go away this minute, and don't stand there fiddling and quivering with your hat like a whipped schoolboy, but go at once, and take my eternal loathing and contempt for a parting present with you!'

Herbert held the door gingerly ajar for half a second, trying to think of a neat and appropriate epigram, but at that particular moment, for the life of him, he couldn't hit on one. So he closed the door after him quietly, and walking out alone into the street, immediately nailed a passing hansom. 'I didn't come out of that dilemma very creditably to myself, I must admit,' he thought with a burning face, as he rolled along quickly in the hansom; 'but anyhow, now I'm well out of it. The coast's all clear at last for Ethel Faucit. It's well to be off with the old love before you're on with the new, as that horrid vulgar practical proverb justly though somewhat coarsely puts it. Still, she's a perfectly magnificent creature, is Selah; and by Jove, when she got into that towering rage (and no wonder, for I won't be unjust to her in that respect), her tone and attitude would have done credit to any theatre. I should think Mrs. Siddons must have looked like that, say as Constance. Poor girl, I'm really sorry for her; from the very bottom of my heart, I'm really sorry for her. If it rested with me alone, hang me if I

Grant Allen

don't think I would positively have married her. But after all, the environment, you know, the environment is always too strong for us!'

Meanwhile, in the shabby lodgings near the Portobello Road, poor Selah, the excitement once over, was lying with her proud face buried in the pillows, and crying her very life out in great sobs of utter misery. The daydream of her whole existence was gone for ever: the bubble was burst; and nothing stood before her but a future of utter drudgery. 'The brute, the cur, the mean wretch,' she said aloud between her sobs; 'and yet I loved him. How beautifully he talked, and how he made me love him. If it had only been a common everyday Methodist sweetheart, now! but Herbert Walters! Oh, God, how I hate him, and how I did love him!'

When Herbert reached his mother's house in Epsilon Terrace, Lady Le Breton met him anxiously at the door. 'Herbert,' she said, almost weeping, 'my dear boy, what on earth should I do if it were not for you! You're the one comfort I have in all my children. Would you believe it—no, you won't believe it—as I was walking back here this afternoon with Mrs. Faucit (Ethel's aunt, of all people in the world), what do you think I saw, in our own main street, too, but a young man, decently dressed, in his shirt sleeves. No coat, I assure you, but only his shirt sleeves. Imagine my horror when he came up to us—Mrs. Faucit, too, you know—and said to me out loud, in the most unconcerned voice, "Well, mother!" I couldn't believe my eyes. Herbert, but I solemnly declare to you it was positively Ronald! You really could have knocked me down with a feather. Disgraceful, wasn't it, perfectly disgraceful!'

'How on earth did he come so?' asked Herbert, almost smiling in spite of himself.

'Why, do you know, Herbert,' Lady Le Breton answered somewhat obliquely, 'a few days since, I met him wheeling along a barrow full of coals for a dirty, grimy, ragged little girl from some alley or gutter somewhere. I believe they call the place the Mews—at the back of the terrace, you remember. He pretended the child wasn't big enough to wheel the coals, which was absurd, of course, or else her parents wouldn't have sent her; but I'm sure he really did it on purpose to annoy me. He never does these things when I'm not by to see; or if he does, I never see him. Now, that was bad enough in all conscience, wasn't it? but to-day what he did was still more outrageous. He met a poor man, as he calls him, in West-bourne Grove, who was one of his Christian brethren (is that the right expression?) and who declared he was next door to starving. So what must Ronald do, but run into a pawn-broker's—I shouldn't have thought he could ever have heard of such a place—and sell his coat, or something of the sort, and give the man (who was doubtless an impostor) all the money. Then he positively walked home in his shirt sleeves. I call it a most unchristian thing to do—and to walk straight into my very arms, too, as I was coming along with Mrs. Faucit.'

Herbert offered at once such condolences as were in his power. 'And are the Faucits coming to night?' he asked eagerly.

Lady Le Breton kissed him again gently on the forehead. 'Oh, Herbert,' she said warmly, 'I can't tell you what a comfort you always are to me. Oh yes, the Faucits are coming; and do you know, Herbert, my dear boy, I'm quite sure that old Mr. Faucit, the uncle, wouldn't at all object to the match, and that Ethel's really very much disposed indeed to like you immen-sely. You've only to follow up the advantage, my dear boy, and I don't for a moment think she'd ever refuse you. And I've been talking to Sir Sydney Weatherhead about your future, too, and he tells me (quite privately, of course) that, with your position and honours at Oxford, he fully believes he can easily push you into the first good vacant post at the Education Office; only you must be careful to say nothing about it beforehand, or the others will say it's a job, as they call it. Oh, Herbert, I really and truly can't tell you what a joy and a comfort you always are to me!'

CHAPTER XXII

THE PHILISTINES TRIUMPH

'My dear,' said Dr. Greatrex, looking up in alarm from the lunch table one morning, in the third term of Ernest Le Breton's stay at Pilbury, 'what an awful apparition! Do you know, I positively see Mr. Blenkinsopp, father of that odious boy Blenkinsopp major, distinctly visible to the naked eye, walking across the front lawn—on the grass too—to our doorway. The pupil's parent is really the very greatest bane of all the banes that beset a poor harassed overdriven school-master's unfortunate existence!'

'Blenkinsopp?' Mrs. Greatrex said reflectively. 'Blenkinsopp? Who is he? Oh, I remember, a tobacco-pipe manufacturer somewhere in the midland counties, isn't he? Mr. Blenkin-sopp, of Staffordshire, I always say to other parents—not Brosely—Brosely sounds decidedly commercial and unpresent-able. No nice people would naturally like their sons to mix with miscellaneous boys from a place called Brosely. Now, what on earth can he be coming here for, I wonder, Joseph?'

'Oh, *I* know,' the doctor answered with a deep-drawn sigh. 'I know, Maria, only too well. It's the way of all parents. He's come to inquire after Blenkinsopp major's health and progress. They all do it. They seem to think the sole object of a head-master's existence is to look after the comfort and morals of their own particular Tommy, or Bobby, or Dicky, or Harry. For heaven's sake, what form is Blenkinsopp major in? For heaven's sake, what's his Christian name, and age last birthday, and place in French and mathematics, and general state of health for past quarter? Where's the prompt-book, with house-master's and form-master's report, Maria? Oh, here it is, thank goodness! Let me see; let me see—he's ringing at the door this very instant. "Blenkinsopp... major... Charles Warrington... fifteen... fifth form... average, twelfth boy of twelve... idle, inattentive, naturally stupid; bad disposition... health invariably excellent... second eleven... bats well." That'll do. Run my eye down once again, and I shall remember all about him. How about the other? "Blenkinsopp... minor... Cyril Anastasius Guy Waterbury Macfarlane"—heavens, what a name!... "thirteen... fourth form... average, seventh boy of eighteen... industrious and well-meaning, but heavy and ineffective... health good... fourth eleven... fields badly." Ah, that's the most important one. Now I'm primed. Blenkinsopp major I remember something about, for he's one of the worst and most hopelessly stupid boys in the whole school—I've caned him frequently this term, and that keeps a boy green in one's memory; but Blenkinsopp minor, Cyril Anastasius Guy Thingumbob Whatyoumaycallit,—I don't remember HIM a bit. I suppose he's one of those inoffensive, mildly mediocre sort of boys who fail to impress their individuality upon one in any way. My experience is that you can always bear in mind the three cleverest boys at the top of each form, and the three stupidest or most mischievous boys at the bottom; but the nine or a dozen meritorious nobodies in the middle of the class are all so like one another in every way that you might as well try to discriminate between every individual sheep of a flock in a pasture. And yet, such is the natural contradictiousness and vexatious disposition of the British parent, that you'll always find him coming to inquire after just one of those very particular Tommies or Bobbies. Charles Warrington:—Cyril Anastasius Guy Whatyoumay—call it: that'll do: I shall remember now all about them.' And the doctor arranged his hair before the looking glass into the most professional stiffness, as a preparatory step to facing Mr. Blenkinsopp's parental inquiries in the head-master's study.

'What! Mr. Blenkinsopp! Yes, it is really. My dear sir, how DO you do? This is a most unexpected pleasure. We hadn't the least idea you were in Pilbury. When did you come here?'

'I came last night, Dr. Greatrex,' answered the dreaded parent respectfully: 'we've come down from Staffordshire for a week at the seaside, and we thought we might as well be within hail of Guy and Charlie.'

'Quite right, quite right, my dear sir,' said the doctor, mentally noting that Blenkinsopp minor was familiarly known as Guy, not Cyril; 'we're delighted to see you. And now you want to know all about our two young friends, don't you?'

'Well, yes, Dr. Greatrex; I SHOULD like to know how they are getting on.'

'Ah, of course, of course. Very right. It's such a pleasure to us when parents give us their active and hearty co-operation! You'd hardly believe, Mr. Blenkinsopp, how little interest some parents seem to feel in their boys' progress. To us, you know, who devote our whole time and energy assiduously to their ultimate welfare, it's sometimes quite discouraging to see how very little the parents themselves seem to care about it. But your boys are both doing capitally. The eldest—Blenkinsopp major, we call him; Charles Warrington, isn't it? (His home name's Charlie, if I recollect right. Ah, quite so.) Well, Charlie's the very picture of perfect health, as usual.' ('Health is his only strong point, it seems to me,' the doctor thought to himself instinctively. 'We must put that first and foremost.') 'In excellent health and very good spirits. He's in the second eleven now, and a capital batter: I've no doubt he'll go into the first eleven next term, if we lose Biddlecomb Tertius to the university. In work, as you know, he's not very great; doesn't do his abilities full justice, Mr. Blenkinsopp, through his dreadful inattention. He's generally near the bottom of the form, I'm sorry to say; generally near the bottom of the form.'

'Well, I dare say there's no harm in that, sir,' said Mr.

Blenkinsopp, senior, warmly. 'I was always at the bottom of the form at school myself, Doctor, but I've picked it up in after life; I've picked it up, sir, as you see, and I'm fully equal with most other people nowadays, as you'll find if you inquire of any town councilman or man of position down our way, at Brosely.'

'Ah, I dare say you were, Mr. Blenkinsopp,' the doctor answered blandly, with just the faintest tinge of unconscious satire, peering at his square unintelligent features as a fancier peers at the face of a bull-dog; 'I dare say you were now. After all, however clever a set of boys may be, one of them MUST be at the bottom of the form, in the nature of things, mustn't he? And your Charlie, I think, is only fifteen. Ah, yes; well, well; he'll do better, no doubt, if we keep him here a year or two longer. So then there's the second: Guy, you call him, if I remember right—Cyril Anastasius Guy—our Blenkinsopp minor. Guy's a good boy; an excellent boy: to tell you the plain truth, Mr. Blenkinsopp, I don't know much of him personally myself, which is a fact that tells greatly in his favour. Charlie I must admit I have to call up some times for reproof: Guy, never. Charlie's in the fifth form: Guy's seventh in the fourth. A capital place for a boy of his age! He's very industrious, you know—what we call a plodder. They call it a plodder, you see, at thirteen, Mr. Blenkinsopp, but a man of ability at forty.' Dr. Greatrex delivered that last effective shot point-blank at the eyes of the inquiring parent, and felt in a moment that its delicate generalised flattery had gone home straight to the parent's susceptible heart.

'But there's one thing, Doctor,' Mr. Blenkinsopp began, after a few minutes' further conversation on the merits and failings of Guy and Charlie, 'there's one other thing I feel I should like to speak to you about, and that's the teaching of your fifth form master, Mr. Le Breton. From what Charlie tells me, I don't quite like that young man's political ideas and opinions. It's said things to his form sometimes that are quite horrifying, I assure you; things about Property, and about our duty to the poor, and so on, that are positively enough to appal you. Now, for example, he told them—I don't quite like to repeat it, for it's sheer blasphemy I call it—but he told them in a Greek Testament lesson that the Apostles themselves were a sort of Republicans—Socialists, I think Charlie said, or else Chartists, or dynamiters. I'm not sure he didn't say St. Peter himself was a regular communist!'

Dr. Greatrex drew a long breath. 'I should think, Mr. Blenkinsopp,' he suggested blandly, 'Charlie must really have misunderstood Mr. Le Breton. You see, they've been reading the Acts of the Apostles in their Greek Testament this term. Now, of course, you remember that, during the first days of the infant Church, while its necessities were yet so great, as many as were possessors of lands or houses sold them, and brought the prices of the things that were sold, and laid them down at the apostles' feet; and distribution was made unto every man according as he had need. You see, here's the passage, Mr. Blenkinsopp, in the authorised version. I won't trouble you with the original. You've forgotten most of your Greek, I dare say: ah, I thought go. It doesn't stick to us like the Latin, does it? Now, perhaps, in expounding that passage, Mr. Le Breton may have referred in passing—as an illustration merely—to the unhappily prevalent modern doctrines of socialism and communism. He may have warned his boys, for example, against confounding a Christian communism like this, if I may so style it, with the rapacious, aggressive, immoral forms of communism now proposed to us, which are based upon the forcible disregard of all Property and all vested interests of every sort. I don't say he did, you know, for I haven't conferred with him upon the subject: but he may have done so; and he may even have used, as I have used, the phrase "Christian communism," to define the temporary attitude of the apostles and the early Church in this matter. That, perhaps, my dear sir, may be the origin of the misapprehension.'

Mr. Blenkinsopp looked hard at the three verses in the big Bible the doctor had handed him, with a somewhat suspicious glare. He was a self-made man, with land and houses of his own in plenty, and he didn't quite like this suggestive talk about selling them and laying the prices at the apostles' feet. It savoured to him both of communism and priestcraft. 'That's an awkward text, you know,' he said, looking up curiously from the Bible in his hand into the doctor's face, 'a very awkward text; and I should say it was rather a dangerous one to set too fully before young people. It seems to me to make too little altogether of Property. You know, Dr. Greatrex, at first sight it DOES look just a little like communism.'

'Precisely what Mr. Le Breton probably said,' the doctor answered, following up his advantage quickly. 'At first sight, no doubt, but at first sight only, I assure you, Mr. Blenkinsopp. If you look on to the fourth verse of the next chapter, you'll see that St. Peter, at least, was no communist,—which is perhaps what Mr. Le Breton really said. St. Peter there argues in favour of purely voluntary beneficence, you observe; as when you, Mr. Blenkinsopp, contribute a guinea to our chapel window:—you see, we're grateful to our kind benefactors: we don't forget them. And if you'll look at the Thirty-eighth Article of the Church of England, my dear sir, you'll find that the riches and goods of Christians are not common, as touching the right, title, and possession of the same as certain Anabaptists—(Gracious heavens, is he a Baptist, I wonder?—if so, I've put my foot in it)—certain Anabaptists do falsely boast—referring, of course, to sundry German fanatics of the time—followers of one Kniperdoling, a crazy enthusiast, not to the respectable English Baptist denomination; but that nevertheless every man ought, of such things as he possesseth, liberally to give alms to the poor. That, you see, is the doctrine of the Church of England, and that, I've no doubt, is the doctrine that Mr. Le Breton pointed out to your boys as the true Christian communism of St. Peter and the apostles.'

'Well, I hope so, Dr. Greatrex,' Mr. Blenkinsopp answered resignedly. 'I'm sure I hope so, for his own sake, as well as for his pupils'. Still, in these days, you know, when infidelity and Radicalism are so rife, one ought to be on one's guard against atheism and revolution, and attacks on Property in every form; oughtn't one, Doctor? These opinions are getting so rampant all around us, Property itself isn't safe. One really hardly knows what people are coming to nowadays. Why, last night I came down here and stopped at the Royal Marine, on the Parade, and having nothing else to do, while my wife was looking after the little ones, I turned into a hall down in Combe Street, where I saw a lot of placards up about a Grand National Social Democratic meeting. Well, I turned in, Dr. Greatrex, and there I heard a German refugee fellow from London—a white-haired man of the name of Schurts, or something of the sort'—Mr. Blenkinsopp pronounced it to rhyme with 'hurts'—'who was declaiming away in a fashion to make your hair stand on end, and frighten you half out of your wits with his dreadful communistic notions. I assure you, he positively took my breath away. I ran out of the hall at last, while he was still speaking, for fear the roof should fall in upon our heads and crush us to pieces. I declare to you, sir, I quite expected a visible judgment!'

'Did you really now?' said Dr. Greatrex, languidly. 'Well, I dare say, for I know there's a sad prevalence of revolutionary feeling among our workmen here, Mr, Blenkinsopp. Now, what was this man Schurz talking about?'

'Why, sheer communism, sir,' said Mr. Blenkinsopp, severely: 'sheer communism, I can tell you. Co-operation of workmen to rob their employers of profits; gross denunciation of capital and capitalists; and regular inciting of them against the Property of the landlords, by quoting Scripture, too, Doctor, by quoting the very words of Scripture. They say the devil can quote Scripture to his own destruction, don't they, Doctor? Well, he quoted something out of the Bible about woe unto them that join field to field, or words to that effect, to make themselves a solitude in the midst of the earth. Do you know, it strikes me that it's a very dangerous book, the Bible—in the hands of these socialistic demagogues, I mean. Look now, at that passage, and at what Mr. Le Breton said about Christian communism!'

'But, my dear Mr. Blenkinsopp,' the doctor cried, in a tone of gentle deprecation, 'I hope you don't confound a person like this man Schurz, a German refugee of the worst type, with our Mr. Le Breton, an Oxford graduate and an English gentleman of excellent family. I know Schurz by name through the papers: he's the author of a dreadful book called "Gold and the Proletariate," or something of that sort—a revolutionary work like Tom Paine's "Age of Reason," I believe—and he goes about the country now and then, lecturing and agitating, to make money, no doubt, out of the poor, misguided, credulous workmen. You quite pain me when you mention him in the same breath with a hard-working, conscientious, able teacher like our Mr. Le Breton.'

'Oh,' Mr. Blenkinsopp went on, a little mollified, 'then Mr. Le Breton's of a good family, is he? That's a great safeguard, at any rate, for you don't find people of good family running recklessly after these bloodthirsty doctrines, and disregarding the claims of Property.'

'My dear sir,' the doctor continued, 'we know his mother, Lady Le Breton, personally. His father, Sir Owen, was a distinguished officer-general in the Indian army in fact; and all his people are extremely well connected with some of our best county families. Nothing wrong about him in any way, I can answer for it. He came here direct from Lord Exmoor's, where he'd been acting as tutor to Viscount Lynmouth, the eldest son of the Tregellis family: and you may be sure THEY wouldn't have anybody about them in any capacity who wasn't thoroughly and perfectly responsible, and free from any prejudice against the just rights of property.'

At each successive step of this collective guarantee to Ernest Le Breton's perfect respectability, Mr. Blenkinsopp's square face beamed brighter and brighter, till at last when the name of Lord Exmour was finally reached, his mouth relaxed slowly into a broad smile, and he felt that he might implicitly trust the education of his boys to a person so intimately bound up with the best and highest interests of religion and Property in this kingdom. 'Of course,' he said placidly, 'that puts quite a different complexion upon the matter, Dr. Greatrex. I'm very glad to hear young Mr. Le Breton's such an excellent and trustworthy person. But the fact is, that Schurts man gave me quite a turn for the moment, with his sanguinary notions. I wish you could see the man, sir; a long white-haired, savage-bearded, fierce-eyed old revolutionist if ever there was one. It made me shudder to look at him, not raving and ranting like a madman—I shouldn't have minded so much if he'd a done that; but talking as cool and calm and collected, Doctor, about "eliminating the capitalist"—cutting off my head, in fact—as we two are talking here together at this moment. His very words were, sir, "we must eliminate the capitalist." Why, bless my soul,'—and here Mr. Blenkinsopp rushed to the window excitedly—'who on earth's this coming across your lawn, here, arm in arm with Mr. Le Breton, into the school-house? Man alive, Dr. Greatrex, whatever you choose to say, hanged if it isn't realty that German cut-throat fellow himself, and no mistake at all about it!'

Dr. Greatrex rose from his magisterial chair and glanced with dignified composure out of the window. Yes, there was positively no denying it! Ernest Le Breton, in cap and gown, with Edie by his side, was walking arm in arm up to the school-house with a long-bearded, large-headed German-looking man, whose placid powerful face the Doctor immediately recognised as the one he had seen in the illustrated papers above the name of Max Schurz, the defendant in the coming state trial for unlawfully uttering a seditious libel! He could hardly believe his eyes. Though he knew Ernest's opinions were dreadfully advanced, he could not have suspected him of thus consorting with positive murderous political criminals. In spite of his natural and kindly desire to screen his own junior master, he felt that this public exhibition of irreconcilable views was quite unpardonable and irretrievable. 'Mr. Blenkin-sopp,' he said gravely, turning to the awe-struck tobacco-pipe manufacturer with an expression of sympathetic dismay upon his practised face, 'I must retract all I have just been saying to you about our junior master. I was not aware of this. Mr. Le

Breton must no longer retain his post as an assistant at Pilbury Regis Grammar School.'

Mr. Blenkinsopp sank amazed into an easy-chair, and sat in dumb astonishment to see the end of this extraordinary and unprecedented adventure. The Doctor walked out severely to the school porch, and stood there in solemn state to await the approach of the unsuspecting offender.

'It's so delightful, dear Herr Max,' Ernest was saying at that exact moment, 'to have you down here with us even for a single night. You can't imagine what an oasis your coming has been to us both. I'm sure Edie has enjoyed it just as much as I have, and is just as anxious you should stop a little time here with us as I myself could possibly be.

'Oh, yes, Herr Schurz,' Edie put in persuasively with her sweet little pleading manner; 'do stay a little longer. I don't know when dear Ernest has enjoyed anything in the world so much as he has enjoyed seeing you. You've no idea how dull it is down here for him, and for me too, for that matter; everybody here is so borne, and narrow-minded and self-centred; nothing expansive or sympathetic about them, as there used to be about Ernest's set in dear, quiet, peaceable old Oxford. It's been such a pleasure to us to hear some conversation again that wasn't about the school, and the rector, and the Haigh Park people, and the flower show, and old Mrs. Jenkins's quarrel with the vicar of St. Barnabas. Except when Mr. Berkeley runs down sometimes for a Saturday to Monday trip to see us, and takes Ernest out for a good blow with him on the top of the breezy downs over yonder, we really never hear anything at all except the gossip and the small-talk of Pilbury Regis.'

'And what makes it worse, Herr Max,' said Ernest, looking up in the old man's calm strong face with the same reverent almost filial love and respect as ever, 'is the fact that I can't feel any real interest and enthusiasm in the work that's set before me. I try to do it as well as I can, and I believe Dr. Greatrex, who's a kind-hearted good sort of man in his way, is perfectly satisfied with it; but my heart isn't in it, you see, and can't be in it. What sort of good is one doing the world by dinning the same foolish round of Horace and Livy and Latin elegiacs into the heads of all these useless, eat-all, do-nothing young fellows, who'll only be fit to fight or preach or idle as soon as we've finished cramming them with our indigestible unserviceable nostrums!'

'Ah, Ernest, Ernest,' said Herr Max, nodding his heavy head gravely, 'you always WILL look too seriously altogether at your social duties. I can't get other people to do it enough; and I can't get you not to do it too much entirely. Remember, my dear boy, my pet old saying about a little leaven. You're doing more good by just unobtrusively holding your own opinions here at Pilbury, and getting in the thin end of the wedge by slowly influencing the minds of a few middle-class boys in your form, than you could possibly be doing by making shoes or weaving clothes for the fractional benefit of general humanity. Don't be so abstract, Ernest; concrete yourself a little; isn't it enough that you're earning a livelihood for your dear little wife here, whom I'm glad to know at last and to receive as a worthy daughter? I may call you, Edie, mayn't I, my daughter? So this is your school, is it? A pleasant building! And that stern-looking old gentleman yonder, I suppose, is your head master?'

'Dr. Greatrex,' said Edie innocently, stepping up to him in her bright elastic fashion, 'let me introduce you to our friend Herr Schurz, whose name I dare say you know—the German political economist. He's come down to Pilbury to deliver a lecture here, and we've been fortunate enough to put him up at our little lodging.'

The doctor bowed very stiffly. 'I have heard of Herr Schurz's reputation already,' he said with as much diplomatic politeness as he could command, fortunately bethinking himself at the right moment of the exact phrase that would cover the situation without committing him to any further courtesy towards the terrible stranger. 'Will you excuse my saying, Mrs. Le

Breton, that we're very busy this afternoon, and I want to have a few words with your husband in private immediately? Perhaps you'd better take Herr Schurz on to the downs' ('safer there than on the Parade, at any rate,' he thought to himself quickly), 'and Le Breton will join you in the combe a little later in the afternoon. I'll take the fifth form myself, and let him have a holiday with his friend here if he'd like one. Le Breton, will you step this way please?' And lifting his square cap with stern solemnity to Edie, the doctor disappeared under the porch into the corridor, closely followed by poor frightened and wondering Ernest.

Edie looked at Herr Max in dismay, for she saw clearly there was something serious the matter with the doctor. The old man shook his head sadly. 'It was very wrong of me,' he said bitterly: 'very wrong and very thoughtless. I ought to have remembered it and stopped away. I'm a caput lupinum, it seems, in Pilbury Regis, a sort of moral scarecrow or political leper, to be carefully avoided like some horrid contagion by a respectable, prosperous head-master. I might have known it, I might have known it, Edie; and now I'm afraid by my stupidity I've got dear Ernest unintentionally into a pack of troubles. Come on, my child, my poor dear child, come on to the downs, as he told us; I won't compromise you any longer by being seen with you in the streets, in the decent decorous whited sepulchres of Pilbury Regis.' And the grey old apostle, with two tears trickling unreproved down his wrinkled cheek, took Edie's arm tenderly in his, and led her like a father up to the green grassy slope that overlooks the little seaward combe by the nestling village of Nether Pilbury.

Meanwhile, Dr. Greatrex had taken Ernest into the breakfast-room—the study was already monopolised by Mr. Blenkin-sopp—and had seated himself nervously, with his hands folded before him, on a straight-backed chair There was a long and awkward pause, for the doctor didn't care to begin the interview; but at last he sighed deeply and said in a tone of genuine disappointment and difficulty, 'My dear Le Breton, this is really very unpleasant.'

Ernest looked at him, and said nothing.

'Do you know,' the doctor went on kindly after a minute, 'I really do like you and sympathise with you. But what am I to do after this? I can't keep you at the school any longer, can I now? I put it to your own common-sense. I'm afraid, Le Breton—it gives me sincere pain to say so—but I'm afraid we must part at the end of the quarter.'

Ernest only muttered that he was very sorry.

'But what are we to do about it, Le Breton?' the doctor continued more kindly than ever. 'What are we ever to do about it? For my own sake, and for the boys' sake, and for respectability's pake, it's quite impossible to let you remain here any longer. The first thing you must do is to send away this Schurz creature'—Ernest started a little—'and then we must try to let it blow over as best we can. Everybody'll be talking about it; you know the man's become quite notorious lately; and it'll be quite necessary to say distinctly, Le Breton, before the whole of Pilbury, that we've been obliged to dismiss you summarily. So much we positively MUST do for our own protection. But what on earth are we to do for you, my poor fellow? I'm afraid you've cut your own throat, and I don't see any way on earth out of it.'

'How so?' asked Ernest, half stunned by the suddenness of this unexpected dismissal.

'Why, just look the thing in the face yourself, Le Breton. I can't very well give you a recommendation to any other head master without mentioning to him why I had to ask you for your resignation. And I'm afraid if I told them, nobody else would ever take you.'

'Indeed?' said Ernest, very softly. 'Is it such a heinous offence to know so good a man as Herr Schurz—the best follower of the apostles I ever knew?'

'My dear fellow,' said the doctor, confidentially, with an unusual burst of outspoken frankness, 'so far as my own private feelings are concerned, I don't in the least object to your knowing Herr Schurz or any other socialist whatsoever. To tell you the truth, I dare say he really is an excellent and most well-meaning person at bottom. Between ourselves, I've always thought that there was nothing very heterodox in socialism; in fact, I often think, Le Breton, the Bible's the most thoroughly democratic book that ever was written. But we haven't got to deal in practice with first principles; we have to deal with Society—with men and women as we find them. Now, Society doesn't like your Herr Schurz, objects to him, anathematises him, wants to imprison him. If you walk about with him in public, Society won't send its sons to your school. Therefore, you should disguise your affection, and if you want to visit him, you should visit him, like Nicodemus, by night only.'

'I'm afraid,' said Ernest very fixedly, 'I shall never be able so far to accommodate myself to the wishes of Society.'

'I'm afraid not, myself, Le Breton,' the doctor went on with imperturbable good temper. 'I'm afraid not, and I'm sorry for it. The fact is, you've chosen the wrong profession. You haven't pliability enough for a schoolmaster; you're too isolated, too much out of the common run; your ideas are too peculiar. Now, you've got me to-day into a dreadful pickle, and I might very easily be angry with you about it, and part with you in bad blood; but I really like you, Le Breton, and I don't want to do that; so I only tell you plainly, you've mistaken your natural calling. What it can be I don't know; but we must put our two heads together, and see what we can do for you before the end of the quarter. Now, go up to the combe to your wife, and try to get that terrible bugbear of a German out of Pilbury as quickly and as quietly as possible. Good-bye for to-day, Le Breton; no coolness between us, for this, I hope, my dear fellow.'

Ernest grasped his hand warmly. 'You're very kind, Dr.

Greatrex,' he said with genuine feeling. 'I see you mean well by me, and I'm very, very sorry if I've unintentionally caused you any embarrassment.'

'Not at all, not at all, my dear fellow. Don't mention it. We'll tide it over somehow, and I'll see whether I can get you anything else to do that you're better fitted for.'

As the door closed on Ernest, the doctor just gently wiped a certain unusual dew off his gold spectacles with a corner of his spotless handkerchief. 'He's a good fellow,' he murmured to himself, 'an excellent fellow; but he doesn't manage to combine with the innocence of the dove the wisdom of the serpent. Poor boy, poor boy, I'm afraid he'll sink, but we must do what we can to keep his chin floating above the water. And now I must go back to the study to have out my explanation with that detestable thick-headed old pig of a Blenkinsopp! "Your views about young Le Breton," I must say to him, "are unfortunately only too well founded; and I have been compelled to dismiss him this very hour from Pilbury Grammar School." Ugh—how humiliating! the profession's really enough to give one a perfect sickening of life altogether!'

CHAPTER XXIII

THE STREETS OF ASKELON

Before the end of the quarter, two things occurred which made almost as serious a difference to Ernest's and Edie's lives as the dismissal from Pilbury Regis Grammar School. It was about a week or ten days after Herr Max's unfortunate visit that Ernest awoke one morning with a very curious and unpleasant taste in his mouth, accompanied by a violent fit of coughing. He knew what the taste was well enough; and he mentioned the matter casually to Edie a little later in the morning. Edie was naturally frightened at the symptoms, and made him go to see the school doctor. The doctor felt his pulse attentively, listened with his stethoscope at the chest, punched and pummelled the patient all over in the most orthodox fashion, and asked the usual inquisitorial personal questions about all the other members of his family. When he heard about Ronald's predisposition, he shook his head seriously, and feared there was really something in it. Increased vocal resonance at the top of the left lung, he must admit. Some tendency to tubercular deposit there, and perhaps even a slight deep-seated cavity. Ernest must take care of himself for the present, and keep himself as free as possible from all kind of worry or anxiety.

'Is it consumption, do you think, Dr. Sanders?' Edie asked breathlessly.

'Well, consumption, Mrs. Le Breton, is a very vague and indefinite expression,' said the doctor, tapping his white shirtcuff with his nail in his slowest and most deliberate manner. 'It may mean a great deal, or it may mean very little. I don't want in any way to alarm you, or to alarm your husband; but there's certainly a marked incipient tendency towards tubercular deposit. Yes, tubercular deposit... Well, if you ask me the question point-blank, I should say so... certainly... I should say it was phthisis, very little doubt of it... In short, what some people would call consumption.'

Ernest went home with Edie, comforting her all the way as well as he was able, and trying to make light of it, but feeling in his own heart that the look-out was decidedly beginning to gather blacker and darker than ever before them. Through the rest of that term he worked as well as he could; but Edie noticed every morning that the cough was getting worse and worse; and long before the time came for them to leave Pilbury he had begun to look distinctly delicate. Care for Edie and for the future was telling on him: his frame had never been very robust, and the anxieties of the last year had brought out the same latent hereditary tendency which had shown itself earlier and more markedly in the case of his brother Ronald.

Meanwhile, Dr. Greatrex was assiduous in looking about for something or other that Ernest could turn his hand to, and writing letters with indefatigable kindness to all his colleagues and correspondents: for though he was, as Ernest said, a most unmitigated humbug, that was really his only fault; and when his sympathies were once really aroused, as the Le Bretons had aroused them, there was no stone he would leave unturned if only his energy could be of any service to those whom he wished to benefit. But unfortunately in this case it couldn't. 'I'm at my wit's end what to do with you, Le Breton,' he said kindly one morning to Ernest: 'but how on earth I'm to manage anything, I can't imagine. For my own part, you know, though your conduct about that poor man Schurz (a well-meaning harmless fanatic, I dare say) was really a public scandal—from the point of view of parents I mean, my dear fellow, from the point of view of parents—I should almost be inclined to keep you on here in spite of it, and brave the public opinion of Pilbury Regis, if it depended entirely upon my own judgment. But in the management of a school, my dear boy, as you yourself must be aware, a head master isn't the sole and only authority; there are the governors, for example, Le Breton, and—and—and, ur, there's Mrs. Greatrex. Now, in all matters of social discipline and attitude, Mrs. Greatrex is justly of equal authority with me; and Mrs. Greatrex thinks it would never do to keep you at Pilbury. So, of course, that practically settles the question. I'm awfully sorry, Le Breton, dreadfully sorry, but I don't see my way out of it. The mischief's done already, to some extent, for all Pilbury knows now that Schurz came down here to stop with you at your lodgings: but if I were to keep you on they'd say I didn't disapprove of Schurz's opinions, and that would naturally be simple ruination for the school—simple ruination.'

Ernest thanked him sincerely for the trouble he had taken, but wondered desperately in his own heart what sort of future could ever be in store for them.

The second event was less unexpected, though quite equally embarrassing under existing circumstances. Hardly more than a month before the end of the quarter, a little black-eyed baby daughter came to add to the prospective burdens of the Le Breton family. She was a wee, fat, round-faced, dimpled Devonshire lass to look at, as far surpassing every previous baby in personal appearance as each of those previous babies, by universal admission, had surpassed all their earlier predecessors—a fact which, as Mr. Sanders remarked, ought to be of most gratifying import both to evolutionists and to philanthropists in general, as proving the continuous and progressive amelioration of the human race: and Edie was very proud of her indeed, as she lay placidly in her very plain little white robes on the pillow of her simple wickerwork cradle. But Ernest, though he learned to love the tiny intruder dearly afterwards, had no heart just then to bear the conventional congratulations of his friends and fellow-masters. Another mouth to feed, another life dependent upon him, and little enough, as it seemed, for him to feed it with. When Edie asked him what they should name the baby—he had just received an adverse answer to his application for a vacant secretaryship—he crumpled up the envelope bitterly in his hand, and cried out in his misery, 'Call her Pandora, Edie, call her Pandora; for we've got to the very bottom of the casket, and there is nothing at all left for us now but hope—and even of that very little!'

So they duly registered her name as Pandora; but her mother shortened it familiarly into Dot; and as little Dot she was practically known ever after.

Almost as soon as poor Edie was able to get about again, the time came when they would have to leave Pilbury Regis. The doctor's search had been quite ineffectual, and he had heard of absolutely nothing that was at all likely to suit Ernest Le Breton. He had tried Government offices, Members of Parliament, colonial friends, every body he knew in any way who miyht possibly know of vacant posts or appointments, but each answer was only a fresh disappointment for him and for Ernest. In the end, he was fain to advise his peccant under-master, since nothing else remained for it, that he had better go up to London for the present, take lodgings, and engage in the precarious occupation known as 'looking about for something to turn up.' On the morning when Edie and he were to leave the town, Dr. Greatrex saw Ernest privately in his own study.

'I wish very much I could have gone to the station to see you off, Le Breton,' he said, pressing his hand warmly; 'but it wouldn't do, you know, it wouldn't do, and Mrs. Greatrex wouldn't like it. People would say I sympathised secretly with your political opinions, which might offend Sir Matthew Ogle and others of our governors. But I'm sorry to get rid of you, really and sincerely sorry, my dear fellow; and apart from personal feeling, I'm sure you'd have made a good master in most ways, if it weren't for your most unfortunate socialistic notions. Get rid of them, Le Breton, I beg of you: do get rid of them. Well, the only thing I can advise you now is to try your hand, for the present only—till something turns up, you know—at literature and journalism. I shall be on the look-out for you still, and shall tell you at once of anything I may happen to hear of. But meanwhile, you must try to be earning something. And if at any time, my dear friend, you should be temporarily in want of money,'—the doctor said this in a shame-faced, hesitating sort of way, with not a little humming and hawing—'in want of money for immediate necessities merely, if you'll only be so kind as to write and tell me, I should consider it a pleasure and a privilege to lend you a ten pound note, you know—just for a short time, till you saw your way clear before you. Don't hesitate to ask me now, be sure; and I may as well say, write to me at the school, Le Breton, not at the school-house, so that even Mrs. Greatrex need never know anything about it. In fact, if you'll excuse me, I've put a small sum into this envelope—only twenty pounds—which may be of service to you, as a loan, as a loan merely; if you'll take it—only till something turns up, you know—you'll really be conferring a great favour upon me. There, there, my dear boy; now don't be offended: I've borrowed money myself at times, when I was a young man like you, and I hadn't a wife and family then as an excuse for it either. Put it in your pocket, there's a good fellow; you'll need it for Mrs. Le Breton and the baby, you see; now do please put it in your pocket.'

The tears rode fast and hot in Ernest's eyes, and he grasped the doctor's other hand with grateful fervour. 'Dear Dr. Greatrex,' he said as well as he was able, 'it's too kind of you, too kind of you altogether. But I really can't take the money. Even after the expenses of Edie's illness and of baby Dot's wardrobe, we have a little sum, a very little sum laid by, that'll help us to tide over the immediate present. It's too good of you, too good of you altogether. I shall remember your kindness for ever with the most sincere and heartfelt gratitude.'

As Ernest looked into the doctor's half-averted eyes, swimming and glistening just a little with sympathetic moisture, his heart smote him when he thought that he had ever described that good, kindly, generous man as an unmitigated humbug. 'It shows how little one can trust the mere outside shell of human beings,' he said to Edie, self-reproachfully, as they sat together in their hare third-class carriage an hour later. 'The humbug's just the conventional mask of his profession—necessary enough, I suppose, for people who are really going to live successfully in the world as we find it: the heart within him's a thousand times warmer and truer and more unspoiled than one could ever have imagined from the outer covering. He offered me his twenty pounds so delicately and considerately that but for my father's blood in me, Edie, for your sake, I believe I could almost have taken it.'

When they got to London, Ernest wished to leave Edie and Dot at Arthur Berkeley's rooms (he knew nowhere else to leave them), while he went out by himself to look about for cheap lodgings. Edie was still too weak, he said, to carry her baby about the streets of London in search of apartments. But Edie wouldn't hear of this arrangement; she didn't quite like going to Arthur's, and she felt sure she could bargain with the London landladies a great deal more effectually than a man like Ernest—which was an important matter in the present very reduced condition of the family finances. In the end it was agreed that they should both go out on the hunt together, but that Ernest should be permitted to relieve Edie by turns in taking care of the precious baby.

'They're dreadful people, I believe, London landladies,' said Edie, in her most housewifely manner; 'regular cheats and skinflints, I've always heard, who try to take you in on every conceivable point and item. We must be very careful not to let them get the better of us, Ernest, and to make full inquiries about all extras, and so forth, beforehand.'

They turned towards Holloway and the northern district, to look for cheap rooms, and they saw a great many, more or less dear, and more or less dirty and unsuitable, until their poor hearts really began to sink within them. At last, in despair, Edie turned up a small side street in Holloway, and stopped at a tiny house with a clean white curtain in its wee front bay window. 'This is awfully small, Ernest,' she said, despondently, 'but perhaps, after all, it might really suit us.'

The door was opened for them by a tall, raw-boned, hard-faced woman, the very embodiment and personification of Edie's ideal skinflint London landlady. Might they see the lodgings, Edie asked dubiously. Yes, they might, indeed, mum, answered the hard-faced woman. Edie glanced at Ernest significantly, as who should say that these would really never do.

The lodgings were very small, but they were as clean as a new pin. Edie began to relent, and thought, perhaps in spite of the landlady, they might somehow manage to put up with them. 'What was the rent?'

The hard-faced landlady looked at Edie steadily, and then answered 'Fifteen shillings, mum.'

'Oh, that's too much for us, I'm afraid,' said Edie ruefully. 'We don't want to go as high as that. We're very poor and quiet people.'

'Well, mum,' the landlady assented quickly, 'it is 'igh for the rooms, perhaps, mum, though I've 'ad more; but it IS 'igh, mum. I won't deny it. Still, for you, mum, and the baby, I wouldn't mind making it twelve and sixpence.'

'Couldn't you say half-a-sovereign?' Edie asked timidly, emboldened by success.

'Arf a suvveran, mum? Well, I 'ardly rightly know,' said the hard-faced landlady deliberately. 'I can't say without askin' of my 'usband whether he'll let me. Excuse me a minnit, mum; I'll just run down and ask 'im.'

Edie glanced at Ernest, and whispered doubtfully, 'They'll do, but I'm afraid she's a dreadful person.'

Meanwhile, the hard-faced landlady had run downstairs quickly, and called out in a pleasant voice of childish excitement to her husband. 'John, John,' she cried—'drat that man, where's he gone to. Oh, a smokin' of course, in the back kitching. Oh, John, there's the sweetest little lady you ever set eyes on, all in black, with a dear baby, a dear little speechless infant, and a invalid 'usband, I should say by the look of 'im, 'as come to ask the price of the ground floor lodgin's. And seein' she was so nice and kindlike, I told her fifteen shillings, instead of a suvveran; and she says, can't you let 'em for less? says she; and she was that pretty and engagin' that I says, well, for you I'll make it twelve and sixpence, mum, says I: and says she, you couldn't say 'arf a suvveran, could you? and says I, I'll ask my 'usband: and oh, John, I DO wish you'd let me take 'em at that, for a kinder, sweeter-lookin' dearer family I never did, an' that I tell you.'

John drew his pipe slowly out of his mouth—he was a big, heavy, coachman-built sort of person, in waistcoat and shirt-sleeves—and answered with a kindly smile, 'Why, Martha, if you want to take 'em for 'arf a suvveran, in course you'd ought to do it. Got a baby, pore thing, 'ave she now? Well, there, there, you just go this very minnit, and tell 'em as you'll take 'em.'

The hard-faced landlady went up the stairs again, only stopping a moment to observe parenthetically that a sweeter little lady she never did, and what was 'arf-a-crown a week to you and me, John? and then, holding the corner of her apron in her hand, she informed Edie that her 'usband was prepared to accept the ten shillings weekly.

'I'll try to make you and the gentleman comfortable, mum,' she said, eagerly; 'the gentleman don't look strong, now do he? We must try to feed 'im up and keep 'im cheerful. And we've got plenty of flowers to make the room bright, you see: I'm very fond of flowers myself, mum: seems to me as if they was sort of company to one, like, and when you water 'em and tend 'em always, I feel as if they was alive, and got to know one again, I do, and that makes one love 'em, now don't it, mum? To see 'em brighten up after· you've watered 'em, like that there maiden-'air fern there, why it's enough to make one love 'em the same as if they was Christians, mum.' There was a melting tenderness in her voice when she talked about the flowers that half won over Edie's heart, even in spite of her hard features.

'I'm glad you're so fond of flowers, Mrs.—. Oh, you haven't told us your name yet,' Edie said, beginning vaguely to suspect that perhaps the hard-faced landlady wasn't quite as bad as she looked to a casual observer.

'Alliss, mum,' the landlady answered, filling up Edie's interrogatory blank. 'My name is 'Alliss.'

'Alice what?' Edie asked again.

'Oh, no, mum, you don't rightly understand me,' the landlady replied, getting very red, and muddling up her aspirates more decidedly than ever, as people with her failing always do when they want to be specially deliberate and emphatic: 'not Halice, but 'Alliss; haitch, hay, hell, hell, hi, double hess—'Alliss: my full name's Martha 'Alliss, mum; my 'usband's John 'Alliss. When would you like to come in?'

'At once,' Edie answered. 'We've left our luggage at the cloak-room at Waterloo, and my husband will go back and fetch it, while I stop here with the baby.'

'Not that, he shan't, indeed, mum,' cried the hard-faced landlady, hastily; 'beggin' your pardon for sayin' so. Our John shall go—that's my 'usband, mum; and you shall give 'im the ticket. I wouldn't let your good gentleman there go, and 'im so tired, too, not for the world, I wouldn't. Just you give me the ticket, mum, and John shall go this very minnit and fetch it.'

'But perhaps your husband's busy,' said Ernest, reflecting upon the probable cost of cab hire; 'and he'll want a cab to fetch it in.'

'Bless your 'eart, sir,' said the landlady, busily arranging things all round the room meanwhile for the better accommodation of the baby, "e ain't noways busy 'e ain't. 'E's a lazy man, nowadays, John is: retired from business, 'e says, sir, and ain't got nothink to do but clean the knives, and lay the fires, and split the firewood, and such like. John were a coachman, sir, in a gentleman's family for most of 'is life, man and boy, these forty year, come Christmas; and we've saved a bit o' money between us, so as we don't need for nothink: and 'e don't want the cab, puttin' you to expense, sir, onnecessary, to bring the luggage round in. 'E'll just borrer the hand-barrer from the livery in the mews, sir, and wheel it round 'isself, in 'arf an hour, and make nothink of it. Just you give me the ticket, and set you right down there, and I'll make you and the lady a cup of tea at once, and John'll bring round the luggage by the time you've got your things off.'

Ernest looked at Edie, and Edie looked at Ernest. Could they have judged too hastily once more, after their determination to be lenient in first judgments for the future? So Ernest gave Mrs. Halliss the cloak-room ticket, and Mrs. Halliss ran down-stairs with it immediately. 'John,' the cried again, '—drat that man, where's 'e gone to? Oh, there you are, dearie! Just you put on your coat an' 'at as fast as ever you can, and borrer Tom Wood's barrer, and run down to Waterloo, and fetch up them two portmanteaus, will you? And you drop in on the way at the Waterfield. dairy—not Jenkins's: Jenkins's milk ain't good enough for them—and tell 'em to send round two penn'orth of fresh this very minnit, do y'ear, John, this very minnit, as it's extremely pertickler. And a good thing I didn't give you them two eggs for your dinner, as is fresh-laid by our own 'ens this mornin', and no others like 'em to be 'ad in London for love or money; and they shall 'ave 'em boiled light for their tea this very evenin'. And you look sharp, John,—drat the man, 'ow long 'e is—for I tell yon, these is reel gentlefolk, and them pore too, which makes it all the 'arder; and they've got to be treated the same in every respect as if they was paying a 'ole suvverin, bless their 'earts, the pore creechurs.'

'Pore,' said John, vainly endeavouring to tear on his coat with becoming rapidity under the influence of Mrs. Halliss's voluble exhortations. 'Pore are they, pore things? and so they may be. I've knowed the sons of country gentlemen, and that baronights too, Martha, as 'ad kep' their 'ounds, redooced to be that pore as they couldn't have afforded to a took our lodgings, even 'umble as they may be. Pore ain't nothink to do with it noways, as respecks gentility. I've lived forty years in gentlemen's families, up an' down, Martha, and I think I'd ought to know somethink about the 'abits and manners of the aristocracy. Pore ain't in the question at all, it ain't, as far as breedin' goes: and if they're pore, and got to be gentlefolks too all the same'—John spoke of this last serious disability in a tone of unfeigned pity—'why, Martha, wot I says is, we'd ought to do the very best we can for 'em any 'ow, now, oughtn't we?'

'Drat the man!' cried Mrs. Halliss again, impatiently; 'don't stand talkin' and sermonin' about it there no longer like a poll parrot, but just you run along and send in the milk, like a dear, will you? or that dear little lady'll have to be waitin' for her tea—and her with a month-old baby, too, the pretty thing, just to think of it!'

And indeed, long before John Halliss had got back again with the two wee portmanteaus—'I could 'a carried that lot on my 'ead,' he soliloquised when he saw them, 'without 'avin' troubled to wheel round a onnecessary encumbrance in the way of a barrer'—Mrs. Halliss had put the room tidy, and laid the baby carefully in a borrowed cradle in the corner, and brought up Edie and Ernest a big square tray covered by a snow-white napkin—'My own washin', mum'—and conveying a good cup of tea, a couple of crisp rolls, and two such delicious milky eggs as were never before known in the whole previous history of the county of Middlesex. And while they drank their tea, Mrs. Halliss insisted upon taking the baby down into the kitchen, so that they mightn't be bothered, pore things; for the pore lady must be tired with nursin' of it herself the livelong day, that she must: and when she got it into the kitchen, she was compelled to call over the back yard wall to Mrs. Bollond, the greengrocer's wife next door, with the ultimate view to getting a hare's brain for the dear baby to suck at through a handkerchief. And Mrs. Bollond, being specially so invited, came in by the area door, and inspected the dear baby; and both together arrived at the unanimous conclusion that little Dot was the very prettiest and sweetest child that ever sucked its fat little fingers, Lord bless her!

And in the neat wee parlour upstairs, Edie, pouring out tea from the glittering tin teapot into one of the scrupulously clean small whitey-gold teacups, was saying meanwhile to Ernest, 'Well, after all, Ernest dear, perhaps London landladies aren't all quite as black as they're usually painted.' A conclusion which neither Edie nor Ernest had ever after any occasion for altering in any way.

CHAPTER XXIV

THE CLOUDS BEGIN TO BREAK

And now, what were Ernest and Edie to do for a living! That was the practical difficulty that stared them at last plainly in the face—no mere abstract question of right and justice, of socialistic ideals or of political economy, but the stern, uncompromising, pressing domestic question of daily bread. They had come from Pilbury Regis with a very small reserve indeed in their poor lean little purses; and though Mrs. Halliss's lodgings might be cheap enough as London lodgings go, their means wouldn't allow them to stop there for many weeks together unless that hypothetical something of which they were in search should happen to turn up with most extraordinary and unprecedented rapidity. As soon as they were settled in at their tiny rooms, therefore, Ernest began a series of weary journeys into town, in search of work of some sort or another; and he hunted up all his old Oxford acquaintances in the Temple or elsewhere, to see if they could give him any suggestions towards a possible means of earning a livelihood. Most of them, he found to his surprise, though they had been great chums of his at college, seemed a little shy of him nowadays: one old Oxford friend, in particular, an impeccable man in close-cut frock coat and hat of shiny perfection, he overheard saying to another, he followed him accidentally up a long staircase in King's Bench Walk, 'Ah, yes, I met Le Breton in the Strand yesterday, when I was walking with a Q.C., too; he's married badly, got no employment, and looks awfully seedy. So very embarrassing, you know, now wasn't it?' And

Grant Allen

the other answered lightly, in the same unconcerned tone, 'Oh, of course, dreadfully embarrassing, really.' Ernest slank down the staircase again with a sinking heart, and tried to get no further hints from the respectabilities of King's Bench Walk, at least in this his utmost extremity.

Night after night, as the dusk was beginning to throw its pall over the great lonely desert of London—one vast frigid expanse of living souls that knew and cared nothing about him— Ernest turned back, foot-sore and heart-sick, to the cheery little lodgings in the short side-street at Holloway. There good Mrs. Halliss, whose hard face seemed to grow softer the longer you looked at it, had a warm clip of tea always ready against his coming: and Edie, with wee Dot sleeping placidly on her arm, stood at the door to welcome him back again in wife-like fashion. The flowers in the window bloomed bright and gay in the tiny parlour: and Edie, with her motherly cares for little Dot, seemed more like herself than ever she had done before since poor Harry's death had clouded the morning of her happy lifetime. But to Ernest, even that pretty picture of the young mother and her sleeping baby looked only like one more reminder of the terrible burden he had unavoidably yet too lightly taken upon him. Those two dear lives depended wholly upon him for their daily bread, and where that daily bread was ever to come from he had absolutely not the slightest notion.

There is no place in which it is more utterly dreary to be quite friendless than in teeming London. Still, they were not absolutely friendless even in that great lurid throng of jarring humanity, all eagerly intent on its own business, and none of it troubling its collective head about two such nonentities as Ernest and Edie. Ronald used to come round daily to see them and cheer them up with his quiet confidence in the Disposer of all things: and Arthur Berkeley, neglecting his West End invitations and his lady admirers, used to drop in often of an evening for a friendly chat and a rational suggestion or two.

'Why don't you try journalism, Le Breton?' he said to Ernest one night, as they sat discussing possibilities for the future in the little parlour together. 'Literature in some form or other's clearly the best thing for a man like you to turn his hand to. It demands less compliance with conventional rules than any other profession. No editor or publisher would ever dream of dismissing you, for example, because you invited your fire-brand friend Max Schurz to dinner. On the contrary, if it comes to that, he'd ask you what Herr Max thought about the future of trades unions and the socialist movement in Germany, and he'd advise you to turn it into a column and a half of copy, with a large type sensational heading, "A Comm-unistic Leader Interviewed. From our Special Correspondent."'

'But it's such a very useless, unsocialistic trade,' Ernest answered doubtfully. 'Do you think it would be quite right, Arthur, for a man to try and earn money by it? Of course it isn't much worse than school-mastering, I dare say; nobody can say he's performing a very useful function for the world by hammering a few lines of Ovid into the skull of poor stupid Blenkinsopp major, who after all will only use what he calls his education, if he uses it in any way at all, to enable him to make rather more money than any other tobacco-pipe manufacturer in the entire trade. Still, one does feel for all that, that mere writing of books and papers is a very unsatisfactory kind of work for an ethical being to perform for humanity. How much better, now, if one could only be a farm-labourer or a shoemaker!'

Arthur Berkeley looked across at him half angrily. 'My dear Ernest,' he said, in a severer voice than he often used, 'the time has gone by now for this economical puritanism of yours. It won't do any longer. You have to think of your child and of Mrs. Le Breton. Your first duty is to earn a livelihood for them and yourself; when you've done that satisfactorily, you may begin to think of the claims of humanity. Don't be vexed with me, my dear fellow, if I speak to you very plainly. You've lost your place at Pilbury because you wouldn't be practical. You might have known they wouldn't let you go hobnobbing publicly before the very eyes of boys and parents with a firebrand German Socialist. Mind, I don't say anything against Herr Schurz myself—what little I know about him is all in his favour—that he's a thorn in the side of those odious prigs, the political economists. I've often noticed that when a man wants to dogmatise to his heart's content without fear of contradiction, he invariably calls himself a political economist. Then if people differ from him, he smiles at them the benign smile of superior wisdom, and says superciliously, "Ah, I see you don't understand political economy!" Now, your Herr Schurz is a dissenter among economists, I believe—a sort of embryo Luther come to tilt with a German toy lance against their economical infallibilities; and I'm told he knows more about the subject than all the rest of them put together. Of course, if you like him and respect him—and I know you have one superstition left, my dear fellow—there's no reason on earth why you shouldn't do so; but you mustn't parade him too openly before the scandalised faces of respectable Pilbury. In future, you must be practical. Turn your hand to whatever you can get to do, and leave humanity at large to settle the debtor and creditor account with you hereafter.'

'I'll do my best, Berkeley,' Ernest answered submissively; 'and if you like, I'll strangle my conscience and try my hand at journalism.'

'Do, there's a good man,' Arthur Berkeley said, delighted at his late conversion. 'I know two or three editor fellows pretty well, and if you'll only turn off something, I'll ask them to have a look at it.'

Next morning, at breakfast, Ernest discussed the possibilities of this new venture very seriously with sympathising Edie. 'It's a great risk,' he said, turning it over dubiously in his mind; 'a great risk, and a great expense too, for nothing certain. Let me see, there'll be a quire of white foolscap to start with; that'll be a shilling—a lot of money as things go at present, Edie, isn't it?'

'Why not begin with half a quire, Ernest?' said his little wife, cautiously. 'That'd be only sixpence, you see.'

'Do they halve quires at the stationer's, I wonder?' Ernest went on still mentally reckoning. 'Well, suppose we put it at sixpence. Then we've got pens already by us, but not any ink— that's a penny—and there's postage, say about twopence; total ninepence. That's a lot of money, isn't it, now, for a pure uncertainty?'

'I'd try it, Ernest dear, if I were you,' Edie answered. 'We must do something, mustn't we, dear, to earn our living.'

'We must,' Ernest said, sighing. 'I wish it were anything but that; but I suppose what must be must be. Well, I'll go out a walk by myself in the quietest streets I can find, and try if I can think of anything on earth a man can write about. Arthur Berkeley says I ought to begin with a social article for a paper; he knows the "Morning Intelligence" people, and he'll try to get them to take something if I can manage to write it. I wonder what on earth would do as a social article for the "Morning Intelligence"! If only they'd let me write about socialism now! but Arthur says they won't take that; the times aren't yet ripe for it. I wish they were, Edie, I wish they were; and then perhaps you and I would find some way to earn ourselves a decent living.'

So Ernest went out, and ruminated quietly by himself, as well as he was able, in the least frequented streets of Holloway and Highgate. After about half an hour's excogitation, a brilliant idea at last flashed across him; he had found in a tobacconist's window something to write about! Your practised journalist doesn't need to think at all; he writes whatever comes uppermost without the unnecessarily troublesome preliminary of deliberate thinking. But Ernest Le Breton was only making his first experiment in the queer craft, and he looked upon himself as a veritable Watt or Columbus when he had actually discovered that hitherto unknown object, a thing to write about. He went straight back to good Mrs. Halliss's with his discovery whirling in his head, stopping only by the way at the stationer's, to invest in half a quire of white foolscap. 'The best's a shilling a quire, mister,' said the shopman; 'second best, tenpence.' Communist as he was, Ernest couldn't help noticing the unusual mode of address; but he took the cheaper quality quietly, and congratulated himself on his good luck in saving a penny upon the original estimate.

When he got home, he sat down at the plain wooden table by the window, and began with nervous haste to write away rapidly at his first literary venture. Edie sat by in her little low chair and watched him closely with breathless interest. Would it be a success or a failure? That was the question they were both every moment intently asking themselves. It was not a very important piece of literary workmanship, to be sure; only a social leader for a newspaper, to be carelessly skimmed to-day and used to light the fire to-morrow, if even that; and yet had it been the greatest masterpiece ever produced by the human intellect Ernest could not have worked at it with more conscientious care, or Edie watched him with profounder admiration. When Shakespeare sat down to write 'Hamlet,' it may be confidently asserted that neither Mistress Anne Shakespeare nor anybody else awaited the result of his literary labours with such unbounded and feverish anxiety. By the time Ernest had finished his second sheet of white foolscap—much erased and interlined with interminable additions and corrections—Edie ventured for a moment briefly to interrupt his creative efforts. 'Don't you think you've written as much as makes an ordinary leader now, Ernest?' she asked, apologetically. 'I'm afraid you're making it a good deal longer than it ought to be by rights.'

'I'm sure I don't know, Edie,' Ernest answered, gazing at the two laboured sheets with infinite dubitation and searching of spirit. 'I suppose one ought properly to count the words in an average leader, and make it the same length as they always are in the "Morning Intelligence." I think they generally run to just a column.'

'Of course you ought, dear,' Edie answered. 'Run out this

minute and buy one before you go a single line further.'

Ernest looked back at his two pages of foolscap somewhat ruefully. 'That's a dreadful bore,' he said, with a sigh: 'it'll just run away with the whole penny I thought I'd managed to save in getting the second quality of foolscap for fivepence. However, I suppose it can't be helped, and after all, if the thing succeeds, one can look upon the penny in the light of an investment. It's throwing a sprat to catch a whale, as the proverb says: though I'm afraid Herr Max would say that that was a very immoral capitalist proverb. How horribly low we must be sinking, Edie, when we come to use the anti-social language of those dreadful capitalists!'

'I don't think capitalists deal much in proverbs, dear,' said Edie, smiling in spite of herself; 'but you needn't go to the expense of buying a "Morning Intelligence," I dare say, for perhaps Mrs. Halliss may have an old one in the house; or if not, she might be able to borrow one from a neighbour. She has a perfect genius for borrowing, Mrs. Halliss; she borrows everything I want from somebody or other. I'll just run down to the kitchen this minute and ask her.'

In a few seconds Edie returned in triumph with an old soiled and torn copy of the 'Morning Intelligence,' duly procured by the ingenious Mrs. Halliss from the dairy opposite. It was a decidedly antiquated copy, and it had only too obviously been employed by its late possessor to wrap up a couple of kippered herrings; but it was still entire, so far as regarded the leaders at least, and it was perfectly legible in spite of its ancient and fish-like smell. To ensure accuracy, Ernest and Edie took a leader apiece, and carefully counted up the number of words that went to the column. They came on an average to fifteen hundred. Then Ernest counted his own manuscript with equal care—no easy task when one took into consideration the interlined or erased passages—and, to his infinite disgust, discovered that it only extended to seven hundred and fifty words. 'Why, Edie,' he said, in a very disappointed tone, 'how little it prints into! I should certainly have thought I'd written at least a whole column. And the worst of it is, I believe I've really said all I have to say about the subject.'

'What is it, Ernest dear?' asked Edie.

'Italian organ-boys,' Ernest answered. 'I saw on a placard in the news shop that one of them had been taken to a hospital in a starving condition.' He hardly liked to tell even Edie that he had stood for ten minutes at a tobacconist's window and read the case in a sheet of 'Lloyd's News' conspicuously hung up there for public perusal.

'Well, let me hear what you have written, Ernest dear, and then see if you couldn't expand it.'

Ernest read it over most seriously and solemnly—it was only a social leader, of the ordinary commonplace talky-talky sort; but to those two poor young people it was a very serious and solemn matter indeed—no less a matter than their own two lives and little Dot's into the bargain. It began with the particular case of the particular organ-boy who formed the peg on which the whole article was to be hung; it went on to discourse on the lives and manners of organ-boys in general; it digressed into the natural history of the common guinea-pig, with an excursus on the scenery of the Lower Apennines; and. it finished off with sundry abstract observations on the musical aspect of the barrel-organ and the aesthetic value of hurdy-gurdy performances. Edie listened to it all with deep attention.

'It's very good, Ernest dear,' she said, with wifely admiration, as soon as he had finished. 'Just like a real leader exactly; only, do you know, there aren't any anecdotes in it. I think a social leader of that sort ought always to have a lot of anecdotes. Couldn't you manage to bring in something about Fox and Sheridan, or about George IV. and Beau Brummel? They always do, you know, in most of the papers.'

Ernest gazed at her in silent admiration. 'How clever of you, Edie,' he said, 'to think of that! Why, of course there ought to be some anecdotes. They're the very breath of life to this sort of meaningless writing. Only, somehow, George IV. and Beau Brummel don't seem exactly relevant to Italian organ-grinders, now do they?'

'I thought,' said Edie, with hardly a touch of unintentional satire, 'that the best thing about anecdotes of that kind in a newspaper was their utter irrelevancy. But if Beau Brummel won't do, couldn't you manage to work in Guicciardini and the galleys? That's strictly Italian, you know, and therefore relevant; and I'm sure the newspaper leaders are extremely fond of that story about Guiccardini.'

'They are,' Ernest answered,'most undoubtedly; but perhaps for that very reason readers may be beginning to get just a little tired of it by this time.'

'I don't think the readers matter much,' said Edie, with a brilliant, flash of practical common-sense; 'at least, not nearly half as much, Ernest, as the editor.'

'Quite true,' Ernest replied, with another admiring look; 'but probably the editor more or less consults the taste and feelings of the readers. Well, I'll try to expand it a bit, and I'll manage to drag in an anecdote or two somehow—if not Guicciardini, at least something or other else Italian. You see Italy's a tolerably rich subject, because you can do any amount about Raffael, and Michael Angelo, and Leonardo, and so forth, not to mention Botticelli. The papers have made a dreadful run lately on Botticelli.'

So Ernest sat down once more at the table by the window, and began to interlard the manuscript with such allusions to Italy and the Italians as could suggest themselves on the spur of the moment to his anxious imagination. At the end of half an hour—about the time a practised hand would have occupied in writing the whole article—he counted words once more, and found there were still two hundred wanting. Two hundred more words to say about Italian organ-boys! Alas for the untrained human fancy! A master leader writer at the office of the 'Morning Intelligence' could have run on for ever on so fertile and suggestive a theme—a theme pregnant with unlimited openings for all the cheap commonplaces of abstract journalistic philanthropy; but poor Ernest, a 'prentice hand at the trade, had yet to learn the fluent trick of the accomplished news purveyor; he absolutely could not write without thinking about it. A third time he was obliged to recommit his manuscript, and a third time to count the words over. This time, oh joy, the reckoning came out as close as possible to the even fifteen hundred. Ernest gave a sigh of relief, and turned to read it all over again, as finally enlarged and amended, to the critical ears of admiring Edie.

There was anecdote enough now, in all conscience, in the article; and allusions enough to stock a whole week's numbers of the 'Morning Intelligence.' Edie listened to the whole tirade with an air of the most severe and impartial criticism. When Ernest had finished, she rose up and kissed him. 'I'm sure it'll do, Ernest,' she said confidently. 'It's exactly like a real leader. It's quite beautiful—a great deal more beautiful, in fact, than anything else I ever read in a newspaper: it's good enough to print in a volume.'

'I hope the editor'll think so,' Ernest answered, dubiously. 'If not, what a lot of valuable tenpenny foolscap wasted all for nothing! Now I must write it all out again clean, Edie, on fresh pieces.'

Newspaper men, it must be candidly admitted, do not usually write their articles twice over; indeed, to judge by the result, it may be charitably believed that they do not even, as a rule, read them through when written, to correct their frequent accidental slips of logic or English; but Ernest wrote out his organ-boy leader in his most legible and roundest hand, copperplate fashion, with as much care and precision as if it were his first copy for presentation to the stern writing-master of a Draconian board school. 'Editors are more likely to read your manuscript if it's legible, I should think, Edie,' he said, looking up at her with more of hope in his face than had often been seen in it of late. 'I wonder, now, whether they prefer it sent in a long envelope, folded in three; or in a square envelope, folded twice over; or in a paper cover, open like a pamphlet. There must be some recognised professional way of doing it, and I should think one's more likely to get it taken if one sends it in the regular professional fashion, than if one makes it look too amateurish. I shall go in for the long envelope; at any rate, if not journalistic, it's at least official.'

The editor of the 'Morning Intelligence' is an important personage in contemporary politics, and a man of more real weight in the world than half-a-dozen Members of Parliament for obscure country boroughs; but even that mighty man himself would probably have been a little surprised as well as amused (if he could have seen it) at the way in which Ernest and Edie Le Breton anxiously endeavoured to conciliate beforehand his merest possible personal fads and fancies. As a matter of fact, the question of the particular paper on which the article was written mattered to him absolutely less than nothing, inasmuch as he never looked at anything whatsoever until it had been set up in type for him to pass off-hand judgment upon its faults or its merits. His time was far too valuable to be lightly wasted on the task of deciphering crabbed manuscript.

In the afternoon, Berkeley called to see whether Ernest had followed his suggestion, and was agreeably surprised to find a whole article already finished. He glanced through the neatly written pages, and was still more pleased to discover that Ernest, with an unsuspected outburst of practicality and practicability, had really hit upon a possible subject. 'This may do, Ernest,' he said with a sigh of relief. 'I dare say it will. I know Lancaster wants leader writers, and I think this is quite good enough to serve his turn. I've spoken to him about you: come round with me now—he'll be at the office by four o'clock—and we'll see what we can do for you. It's absolutely useless sending anything to the editor of a daily paper without an introduction. You might write with the pen of the angel

Grant Allen

Gabriel, or turn out leaders which were a judicious mean between Gladstone, Burke, and Herbert Spencer, and it would profit you nothing, for the simple reason that he hasn't got the time to read them. He would toss Junius and Montesquieu into the waste paper basket, and accept copy on the shocking murder in the Borough Road from one of his regular contributors instead. He can't help himself: and what you must do, Ernest, is to become one of the regular ring, and combine to keep Junius and Montesquieu permanently outside.'

'The struggle for existence gives no quarter,' Ernest said sadly with half a sigh.

'And takes none,' Berkeley answered quickly. 'So for your wife's sake you must try your best to fight your way through it on your own account, for yourself and your family.'

The editor of the 'Morning Intelligence,' Mr. Hugh Lancaster, was a short, thick-set, hard-headed sort of man, with a kindly twinkle in his keen grey eyes, and a harassed smile playing continually around the corners of his firm and dose mouth. He looked as though he was naturally a good-humoured benevolent person, overdriven at the journalistic mill till half the life was worn out of him, leaving the benevolence as a wearied remnant, without energy enough to express itself in any other fashion than by the perpetual harassed smile. He saw Arthur Berkeley and Ernest Le Breton at once in his own sanctum, and took the manuscript from their hands with a languid air of perfect resignation. 'This is the friend you spoke of, is it, Berkeley?' he said in a wearied way. 'Well, well, we'll see what we can do for him.' At the same time he rang a tiny hand-bell. A boy, rather the worse for printer's ink, appeared at the summons. Mr. Lancaster handed him Ernest's careful manuscript unopened, with the laconic order, 'Press. Proof immediately.' The boy took it without a word. 'I'm very busy now,' Mr. Lancaster went on in the same wearied dispirited manner: 'come again in thirty-five minutes. Jones, show these gentlemen into a room somewhere.' And the editor fell back forthwith into his easy-chair and his original attitude of listless indifference. Berkeley and Ernest followed the boy into a bare back room, furnished only with a deal table and two chairs, and there anxiously awaited the result of the editor's critical examination.

'Don't be afraid of Lancaster, Ernest,' Arthur said kindly. 'His manner's awfully cold, I know, but he means well, and I really believe he'd go out of his way, rather than not, to do a kindness for anybody he thought actually in want of occupation. With most men, that's an excellent reason for not employing you: with Lancaster I do truly think it's a genuine recommendation.'

At the end of thirty-five minutes the grimy-faced office-boy returned with a friendly nod. 'Editor'll see you,' he said, with the Spartan brevity of the journalistic world—nobody connected with newspapers ever writes or speaks a single word unnecessarily, if he isn't going to be paid for it at so much per thousand—and Ernest followed him, trembling from head to foot, into Mr. Lancaster's private study.

The great editor took up the steaming hot proof that had just been brought him, and glanced down it carelessly with a rapid scrutiny. Then he turned to Ernest, and said in a dreamy fashion, 'This will do. We'll print this to-morrow. You may send us a middle very occasionally. Come here at four o'clock, when a subject suggests itself to you, and speak to me about it. My time's very fully occupied. Good morning, Mr. Le Breton. Berkeley, stop a minute, I want to talk with you.'

It was all done in a moment, and almost before Ernest knew what had happened he was out in the street again, with tears filling his eyes, and joy his heart, for here at last was bread, bread, bread, for Edie and the baby! He ran without stopping all the way back to Holloway, rushed headlong into the house and fell into Edie's arms, calling out wildly, 'He's taken it! He's taken it!' Edie kissed him half-a-dozen times over, and answered bravely, 'I knew he would, Ernest. It was such a splendid article.' And yet thousands of readers of the 'Morning

Intelligence' next day skimmed lightly over the leader on organ-boys in their ordinary casual fashion, without even thinking what hopes and fears and doubts and terrors had gone to the making of that very commonplace bit of newspaper rhetoric. For if the truth must be told, Edie's first admiring criticism was perfectly correct, and Ernest Le Breton's leader was just for all the world exactly the same as anybody else's.

Meanwhile, Arthur Berkeley had stayed behind as requested in Mr. Lancaster's study, and waited to hear what Mr. Lancaster had to say to him. The editor looked up at him wearily from his chair, passed his bread hand slowly across his bewildered forehead, and then said the one word, 'Poor?'

'Nothing on earth to do,' Berkeley answered.

'He might make a journalist, perhaps,' the editor gaid, sleepily. 'This social's up to the average. At any rate, I'll do my very best for him. But he can't live upon socials. We have too many social men already. What can he do? That's the question. It won't do to say he can write pretty nearly as well about anything that turns up as any other man in England can do. I can get a hundred young fellows in the Temple to do that, any day. The real question's this: is there anything he can write about a great deal better than all the other men in all England put together?'

'Yes, there is,' Berkeley answered with commendable promptitude, undismayed by Mr. Lancaster's excessive requirements. 'He knows more about communists, socialists, and political exiles generally, than anybody else in the whole of London.'

'Good,' the editor answered, brightening up, and speaking for a moment a little less languidly. 'That's good. There's this man Schurz, now, the German agitator. He's going to be tried soon for a seditious libel it seems, and he'll be sent to prison, naturally. Now, does your friend know anything at all of this fellow?'

'He knows him personally and intimately,' Berkeley replied, delighted to find that the card which had proved so bad a one at Pilbury Regis was turning up trumps in the more Bohemian neighbourhood of the Temple and Fleet Street. 'He can give you any information you want about Schurz or any of the rest of those people. He has associated with them all familiarly for the last six or seven years.'

'Then he takes an interest in politics,' said Mr. Lancaster, almost waking up now. 'That's good again. It's so very difficult to find young men nowadays, able to write, who take a genuine interest in politics. They all go off after literature and science and aesthetics, and other dry uninteresting subjects. Now, what does your average intelligent daily paper reader care, I should like to know, about literature and science and aesthetics and so forth? Well, he'll do, I've very little doubt: at any rate, I'll give him a trial. Perhaps he might be able to undertake this Great Widgerly disenfranchising case. Stop! he's poor, isn't he? I daresay he'd just as soon not wait for his money for this social. In the ordinary course, he wouldn't get paid till the end of the quarter; but I'll give you a cheque to take back to him now; perhaps he wants it. Poor fellow, poor fellow! he really looks very delicate. Depend upon it, Berkeley, I'll do anything on earth for him, if only he'll write tolerably.'

'You're awfully good,' Arthur said, taking the proffered cheque gratefully. 'I'm sure the money will be of great use to him: and it's very kind indeed of you to have thought of it.'

'Not at all, not at all,'the editor answered, collapsing dreamily. 'Good morning, good morning.'

At Mrs. Halliss's lodgings in Holloway, Edie was just saying to Ernest over their simple tea, 'I wonder what they'll give you for it, Ernest.' And Ernest had just answered, big with hope, 'Well, I should think it would be quite ten shillings, but I shouldn't be surprised, Edie, if it was as much as a pound;' when the door opened, and in walked Arthur Berkeley, with a cheque in his hand, which he laid by Edie's teacup. Edie took

Grant Allen

it up and gave a little cry of delight and astonishment. Ernest caught it from her hand in his eagerness, and gazed upon it with dazed and swimming vision. Did he read the words aright, and could it be really, 'Pay E. Le Breton, Esq., or order, three guineas'? Three guineas! Three guineas! Three real actual positive gold and silver guineas! It was almost too much for either of them to believe, and all for a single morning's light labour! What a perfect Eldorado of wealth and happiness seemed now to be opening out unexpectedly before them!

So much Arthur Berkeley, his own eyes glistening too with a sympathetic moisture, saw and heard before he went away in a happier mood and left them to their own domestic congratulations. But he did not see or know the reaction that came in the dead of night, after all that day's unwonted excitement, to poor, sickening, weary, over-burdened Ernest. Even Edie never knew it all, for Ernest was careful to hide it as much as possible from her knowledge. But he knew himself, though he would not even light the candle to see it, that he had got those three glorious guineas—the guineas they had so delighted in—with something more than a morning's labour. He had had to pay for them, not figuratively but literally, with some of his very life-blood.

CHAPTER XXV

HARD PRESSED

A week or two later, while 'The Primate of Fiji' was still running vigorously at the Ambiguities Theatre, Arthur Berkeley's second opera, 'The Duke of Bermondsey; or, the Bold Buccaneers of the Isle of Dogs,' was brought out with vast success and immense exultation at the Marlborough. There is always a strong tendency to criticise a little severely the second work of a successful beginner: people like to assume a knowing air, and to murmur self-complacently that they felt sure from the beginning he couldn't keep up permanently to his first level. But in spite of that natural tendency of the unregenerate human mind, and in spite, too, of a marked political bias on the author's part, 'The Duke of Bermondsey' took the town by storm almost as completely as 'The Primate of Fiji' had done before it. Everybody said that though the principles of the piece were really quite atrocious, when one came to think of them seriously, yet the music and the dialogue were crisp and brisk enough to float any amount of social or economical heresy that that clever young man, Mr. Arthur Berkeley, might choose to put into one of his amusing and original operas.

The social and economical heresies, of course, were partly due to Ernest Le Breton's insidious influence. At the same time that Berkeley was engaged in partially converting Ernest, Ernest was engaged in the counter process of partially converting Berkeley. To say the truth, the conversion was not a very difficult matter to effect; the neophyte had in him implicitly already the chief saving doctrines of the socialistic faith, or, if one must put it conversely, the germs of the disease were constitutionally implanted in his system, and only needed a little external encouragement to cring the poison out fully in the most virulent form of the complaint. The great point of 'The Duke of Bermondsey' consisted in the ridiculous contrast it exhibited between the wealth, dignity, and self-importance of the duke himself, and the squalid, miserable, shrinking poverty of the East-end purlieus from which he drew his enormous revenues. Ernest knew a little about the East-end from practical experience; he had gone there often with Ronald, on his rounds of mercy, and had seen with his own eyes those dens of misery which most people have only heard or read about. It was Ernest who had suggested this light satirical treatment of the great social problem, whose more serious side he himself had learnt to look at in Max Schurz's revolutionary salon; and it was to Ernest that Arthur Berkeley owed the first hint of that famous scene where the young Countess of Coalbrookdale converses familiarly on the natural beauties of healthful labour with the chorus of intelligent colliery hands, in the most realistic of grimy costumes, from her father's estates in Staffordshire. The stalls hardly knew whether to laugh or frown when the intelligent colliers respect-fully invited the countess, in her best Ascot flounces and furbelows, to enjoy the lauded delights of healthful mine labour in propria persona: but they quite recovered their good humour when the band of theatrical buccaneers, got up by the duke in Spanish costumes, with intent to deceive his lawless tenants in the East-end, came unexpectedly face to face with the genuine buccaneers of the Isle of Dogs, clothed in real costermonger caps and second-hand pilot-jackets of the marine-storedealers' fashionable pattern. It was all only the ridiculous incongruity of our actual society represented in the very faintest shades of caricature upon the stage; but it made the incongruities more incongruous still to see them crowded together so closely in a single concentrated tableau. Unthin-king people laughed uproariously at the fun and nonsense of the piece; thinking people laughed too, but not without an uncomfortable side twinge of conscientious remorse at the pity of it all. Some wise heads even observed with a shrug that when this sort of thing was applauded upon the stage, the fine old institutions of England were getting into dangerous contact with these pernicious continental socialistic theories. And no doubt those good people were really wise in their generation. 'When Figaro came,' Arthur Berkeley said himself to Ernest, 'the French revolution wasn't many paces behind on the track of the ages.'

'Better even than the Primate, Mr. Berkeley,' said Hilda Tregellis, as she met him in a London drawing-room a few days later. 'What a delightful scene, that of the Countess of Coalbrookdale! You're doing real good, I do believe, by making people think about these things more seriously, you know. As poor dear Mr. Le Breton would have said, you've got an ethical purpose—isn't that the word?—underlying even your comic operas. By the way, do you ever see the Le Bretons now? Poor souls, I hear they're doing very badly. The elder brother, Herbert Le Breton—horrid wretch!—he's here to-night; going to marry that pretty Miss Faucit, they say; daughter of old Mr. Faucit, the candle-maker—no, not candles, soap I think it is—but it doesn't matter twopence nowadays, does it? Well, as I was saying, you're doing a great deal of good with characters like this Countess of Coalbrookdale. We want more mixture of classes, don't we? more free intercourse between them; more familiarity of every sort. For my part, now, I should really very much like to know more of the inner life of the working classes.' 'If only he'd ask me to go to lunch,' she thought, 'with his dear old father, the super-annuated shoemaker! so very romantic, really!'

But Arthur only smiled a sphinx-like smile, and answered lightly, 'You would probably object to their treatment of you as much as the countess objected to the uupleasant griminess of the too-realistic coal galleries. Suppose you were to fall into the hands of a logical old radical workman, for example, who tore you to pieces, mentally speaking, with a shake or two of his big teeth, and calmly informed you that in his opinion you were nothing more than a very empty-headed, pretentious, ignorant young woman—perhaps even, after the plain-spoken vocabulary of hie kind, a regular downright minx and hussey?'

'Charming,' Lady Hilda answered, with perfect candour; 'so very different from the senseless adulation of all the Hughs, and Guys, and Berties! What I do love in talking to clever men, Mr. Berkeley, is their delicious frankness and transparency. If they think one a fool, they tell one so plainly, or at least they let one see it without any reserve. Now that, you know, is really such a very delightful trait in clever people's characters!'

'I don't know how you can have had the opportunity of judging, Lady Hilda,' Arthur answered, looking at her handsome open face with a momentary glance of passing admiration—Hilda Tregellis was improving visibly as she matured—'for no one can possibly ever have thought anything of the sort with you, I'm certain: and that I can say quite candidly, without the slightest tinge of flattery or adulation.'

'What! YOU don't think me a fool, Mr. Berkeley,' cried Lady Hilda, delighted even with that very negative bit of favourable appreciation. 'Now, that I call a real compliment, I assure you, because I know you clever people pitch your standard of intelligence so very, very high! You consider everybody fools, I'm sure, except the few people who are almost as clever as you yourselves are. However, to return to the countess: I do think there ought to be more mixture of classes in England, and somebody told me'—this was a violent effort to be literary on Hilda's part, by way of rising to the height of the occasion—'somebody told me that Mr. Matthew Arnold, who's so dreadfully satirical, and cultivated, and so forth, thinks exactly the same thing, you know. Why shouldn't the Countess of Coalbrookdale have really married the foreman of the colliers? I daresay she'd have been a great deal happier with a kind-hearted sensible man like him than with that lumbering, hunting, pheasant-shooting, horse-racing lout of a Lord Coalbrookdale, who would go to Norway on a fishing tour without her—now wouldn't she?'

'Very probably,' Berkeley answered: 'but in these matters we don't regard happiness only,—that, you see, would be mere base, vulgar, commonplace utilitarianism:—we regard much more that grand impersonal overruling entity, that unseen code of social morals, which we commonly call the CONVENANCES. Proper people don't take happiness into consideration at all, comparatively: they act religiously after the fashion that the CONVENANCES impose upon them.'

'Ah, but why, Mr. Berkeley,' Lady Hilda said, vehemently, 'why should the whole world always take it for granted that because a girl happens to be born the daughter of people whose name's in the peerage, she must necessarily be the slave of the proprieties, devoid of all higher or better instincts? Why should they take it for granted that she's destitute of any appreciation for any kind of greatness except the kind that's represented by a million and a quarter in the three per cents., or a great-great-grandfather who fought at the battle of Naseby? Why mayn't she have a spark of originality? Why mayn't she be as much attracted by literature, by science, by art, by... by... by beautiful music, as, say, the daughter of a lawyer, a doctor, or, or, or a country shopkeeper? What I want to know is just this, Mr. Berkeley: if people don't believe in distinctions of birth, why on earth should they suppose that Lady Mary, or Lady Betty, or Lady Winifred, must necessarily be more banale and vulgar-minded, and common-place than plain Miss Jones, or Miss Brown, or Miss Robinson? You admit that these other girls may possibly care for higher subjects: then why on earth shouldn't we, can you tell me?'

'Certainly,' Arthur Berkeley answered, looking down into Lady Hilda's beautiful eyes after a dreamy fashion, 'certainly there's no inherent reason why one person shouldn't have just as high tastes by nature as another. Everything depends, I suppose, upon inherited qualities, variously mixed, and afterwards modified by society and education.—It's very hot here, to-night, Lady Hilda, isn't it?'

'Very,' Lady Hilda echoed, taking his arm as she spoke. 'Shall we go into the conservatory?'

'I was just going to propose it myself,' Berkeley said, with a faint tremor thrilling in his voice. She was a very beautiful woman, certainly, and her unfeigned appreciation of his plays and his music was undeniably very flattering to him.

'Unless I bring him fairly to book this evening,' Hilda thought to herself as she swept with him gracefully into the conservatory, 'I shall have to fall back upon the red-haired hurlyburlying Scotch professor, after all—if I don't want to end by getting into the clutches of one of those horrid Monties or Algies!'

CHAPTER XXVI

IRRECLAIMABLE

The occasional social articles for the 'Morning Intelligence' supplied Ernest with work enough for the time being to occupy part of his leisure, and income enough to keep the ship floating somehow, if not securely, at least in decent fair-weather fashion. His frequent trips with Ronald into the East-end gave him something comparatively fresh to write about, and though he was compelled to conceal his own sentiments upon many points, in order to conform to that impersonal conscience, 'the policy of the paper,' he was still able to deal with subjects that really interested him, and in which he fancied he might actually be doing a little good. A few days after he had taken seriously to the new occupation, good Mrs. Halliss made her appearance in the tiny sitting-room one morning, and with many apologies and much humming and hawing ventured to make a slight personal representation to wondering little Edie.

'If you please, mum,' she said nervously, fumbling all the while with the corner of the table cloth she was folding on the breakfast-table, 'if I might make so bold, mum, without offence, I should like to say as me an' John 'as been talkin' it hover, an' we think now as your good gentleman 'as so much writin' to do, at 'is littery work, mum, as I may make bold to call it, perhaps you wouldn't mind, so as not to disturb 'im with the blessed baby—not as that dear child couldn't never disturb nobody, bless 'er dear 'eart, the darling, not even when she's cryin', she's that sweet and gentle,—but we thought, mum, as littery gentlemen likes to 'ave the coast clear, in the manner of speakin', and perhaps you wouldn't mind bein' so good as to use the little front room upstairs, mum, for a sort o' nursery, as I may call it, for the dear baby. It was our bedroom, that was, where John an' me used to sleep; but we've been an' putt our things into the front hattic, mum, as is very nice and comfortable in every way, so as to make room for the dear baby. An' if you won't take it as a liberty, mum, me an' John 'ud be more'n glad if you'd kindly make use of that there room for a sort of occasional nursery for the dear baby.'

Edie bit her lip hard in her momentary confusion. 'Oh, dear, Mrs. Halliss,' she said, almost crying at the kindly meant offer, 'I'm afraid we can't afford to have THREE rooms all for ourselves as things go at present. How much do you propose to charge us for the additional nursery?'

'Charge you for it, mum,' Mrs. Halliss echoed, almost indignantly; 'charge our lodgers for any little hextry accommodation like the small front room upstairs, mum—now, don't you go and say that to John, mum, I beg of you; for 'is temper's rather short at times, mum, thro' boin' asmatic and the rheumatiz, though you wouldn't think it to look at 'im, that you wouldn't; an' I'm reely afraid, mum, he might get angry if anybody was to holler 'im anythink for a little bit of hextry accommodation like that there. Lord bless your dear 'eart, mum, don't you say nothink more about that, I beg of you; for if John was to 'ear of it, he'd go off in a downright tearin' tantrum at the bare notion. An' about dinner, mum, you'll 'ave the cold mutton an' potatoes, and a bit of biled beetroot; and I'll just run round to the greengrocer's this moment to order it for early dinner.' And before Edie had time to thank her, the good woman was out of tha room again, and down in the kitchen at her daily preparations, with tears trickling slowly down both her hard red cheeks in her own motherly fashion.

So from that time forth, Ernest had the small sitting-room

entirely to himself, whenever he was engaged in his literary labours, while Edie and Dot turned the front bedroom on the first floor into a neat and commodious nursery. As other work did not turn up so rapidly as might have been expected, and as Ernest grew tired after a while of writing magazine articles on 'The Great Social Problem,' which were invariably 'declined with thanks' so promptly as to lead to a well-founded suspicion that they had never even been opened by the editor, he determined to employ his spare time in the production of an important economical volume, a treatise on the ultimate ethics of a labouring community, to be entitled 'The Final Rule of Social Right Living.' This valuable economical work he contin- ued to toil at for many months in the intervals of his other occupations; and when at last it was duly completed, he read it over at full length to dear little Edie, who considered it one of the most profoundly logical and convincing political treatises ever written. The various leading firms, however, to whom it was afterwards submitted with a view to publication, would appear, oddly enough, to have doubted its complete suitability to the tastes and demands of the reading public in the present century; for they invariably replied to Ernest's inquiries that they would be happy to undertake its production for the trilling sum of one hundred guineas, payable in advance; but that they did not see their way to accepting the risk and responsibility of floating so speculative a volume on their own account. In the end, the unhappy manuscript, after many refusals, was converted into cock-boats, hats, and paper dollies for little Dot; and its various intermediate reverses need enter no further into the main thread of this history. It kept Ernest busy in the spare hours of several months, and prevented him from thinking too much of his own immediate prospects, in his dreams for the golden future of humanity; and insomuch it did actually subserve some indirectly useful function; but on the other hand it wasted a considerable quantity of valuable tenpenny foolscap, and provided him after all with one more severe disappointment, to put on top of all the others to which he was just then being subjected. Clearly, the reading public took no paying interest in political economy; or if they did, then the article practically affected by the eternal laws of supply and demand was at least not the one meted out to them from the enthusiastic Schurzian pen of Ernest Le Breton.

One afternoon, not long after Ernest and Edie had taken rooms at Mrs. Halliss's, they were somewhat surprised at receiving the honour of a casual visit from a very unexpected and unusual quarter. Ronald was with them, talking earnestly over the prospects of the situation, when a knock came at the door, and to their great astonishment the knock was quickly followed by the entrance of Herbert. He had never been there before, and Ernest felt sure he had come now for some very definite and sufficient purpose. And so he had indeed: it was a strange one for him; but Herbert Le Breton was actually bound upon a mission of charity. We have all of us our feelings, no doubt, and Herbert Le Breton, too, in his own fashion, had his. Ernest was after all a good fellow enough at bottom, and his own brother: (a man can't for very rospect-ability's sake let his own brother go utterly to the dogs if he can possibly help it); and so Herbert had made up his mind, much against his natural inclination, to warn Ernest of the danger he incurred in having anything more to do or say with this insane, disreputable old Schurz fellow. For his own part, he hated giving advice; people never took it; and that was a deadly offence against his amour propre and a gross insult to his personal dignity; but still, in this case, for Ernest's sake, he determined after an inward struggle to swallow his own private scruples, and make an effort to check his brother on the edge of the abyss. Not that he would come to the point at once; Herbert was a careful diplomatic agent, and he didn't spoil his hand by displaying all his cards too openly at the outset; he would begin upon comparatively indifferent subjects, and lead round the conversation gradually to the perils and errors of pure Schurzianism. So he set out by admiring his niece's fat arms—a remarkable stretch of kindliness on Herbert's part, for of course other people's babies are well known to be really the most uninteresting objects in the whole animate universe—and then he passed on by natural transitions to Ernest's house-keeping arrangements, and to the prospects of journalism as a trade, and finally to the necessity for a journalist to consult the tastes of his reading public. 'And by the way, Ernest,' he said quietly at last, 'of course after this row at Pilbury, you'll drop the acquaintance of your very problematical German socialist.'

Edie started in surprise. 'What? Herr Schurz?' she said eagerly. 'Dear simple, kindly old Herr Schurz! Oh no, Herbert, that I'm sure he won't; Ernest will never drop HIS acquaintance, whatever happens.'

Herbert coughed drily. 'Then there are two of them for me to contend against,' he said to himself with an inward smile. 'I should really hardly have expected that, now. One would have said a priori that the sound common-sense and practical regard for the dominant feelings of society, which is so justly strong in most women, would have kept HER at any rate—with her own social disabilities, too—from aiding and abetting her husband in such a piece of egregious folly'—'I'm sorry to hear it, Mrs. Le Breton,' he went on aloud,—he never called her by her Christian name, and Edie was somehow rather pleased that he didn't: 'for you know Herr Schurz is far from being a desirable acquaintance. Quite apart from his own personal worth, of course—which is a question that I for my part am not called upon to decide—he's a snare and a stumbling-block in the eyes of society, and very likely indeed to injure Ernest's future prospects, as he has certainly injured his career in the past. You know he's going to be tried in a few weeks for a seditious libel and for inciting to murder the Emperor of Russia. Now, you will yourself admit, Mrs. Le Breton, that it's an awkward thing to be mixed up with people who are tried on a criminal charge for inciting to murder. Of course, we all allow that the Czar's a very despotic and autocratic sovereign, that his existence is an anomaly, and that the desire to blow him up is a very natural desire for every intelligent Russian to harbour privately in the solitude of his own bosom. If we were Russians ourselves, no doubt we'd try to blow him up too, if we could conveniently do so without detection. So much, every rational Englishman, who isn't blinded by prejudice or frightened by the mere sound of words, must at once frankly acknowledge. But unfortunately, you see, the mass of

Englishmen ARE blinded by prejudice, and ARE frightened by the mere sound of words. To them, blowing up a Czar is murder (though of course blowing up any number of our own black people isn't); and inciting to blow up the Czar, or doing what seems to most Englishmen equivalent to such incitement, as for example, saying in print that the Czar's government isn't quite ideally perfect and ought gradually and tentatively to be abolished—why, that, I say, is a criminal offence, and is naturally punishable by a term of imprisonment. Now, is it worth while to mix oneself up with people like that, Ernest, when you can just as easily do without having anything on earth to say to them?'

Edie's face burnt scarlet as she listened, but Ernest only answered more quietly—he never allowed anything that Herbert said to disturb his equanimity—'We don't think alike upon this subject, you know, Herbert; and I'm afraid the disagreement is fundamental. It doesn't matter so much to us what the world thinks as what is abstractly right; and Edie would prefer to cling to Herr Schurz, through good report and evil report, rather than to be applauded by your mass of Englishmen for having nothing to do with inciting to murder. We know that Herr Max never did anything of the kind; that he is the gentlest and best of men; and that in Russian affairs he has always been on the side of the more merciful methods, as against those who would have meted out to the Czar the harsher measure of pure justice.'

'Well,' Herbert answered bravely, with a virtuous determination not to be angry at this open insult to his own opinion, but to persevere in his friendly efforts for his brother's sake, 'we won't take Herr Max into consideration at all, but will look merely at the general question. The fact is, Ernest, you've chosen the wrong side. The environment is too strong for you; and if you set yourself up against it, it'll crush you between the upper and the nether mill-stone. It isn't your business to reform the world; it's your business to live in it; and if you go on as you're doing now, it strikes me that you'll fail at the outset in that very necessary first particular.'

'If I fail,' Ernest answered with a heavy heart, 'I can only die once; and after all every man can do no more than till to the best of his ability the niche in nature that he finds already cut out for him by circumstances.'

'My dear Ernest,' Herbert continued quietly, twisting himself a cigarette with placid deliberateness, as a preliminary to his departure; 'your great mistake in life is that you WILL persist in considering the universe as a cosmos. Now the fact is, it isn't a cosmos; it's a chaos, and a very poor one at that.'

'Ah, yes,' Ernest answered gravely; 'nobody recognises that fact more absolutely than I do; but surely it's the duty of man to try as far as in him lies to cosmise his own particular little corner of it.'

'In the abstract, certainly: as a race, most distinctly so; but as individuals, why, the thing's clearly impossible. There was one man who once tried to do it, and his name was Don Quixote.'

'There was another, I always thought,' Ernest replied more solemnly, 'and after his name we've all been taught as children to call ourselves Christians. At bottom, my ideal is only the Christian ideal.'

'But, my dear fellow, don't you see that the survival of the fittest must succeed in elbowing your ideal, for the present at least, out of existence? Look here, Ernest, you're going the wrong way to work altogether for your own happiness and comfort. It doesn't matter to me, of course; you can do as you like with yourself, and I oughtn't to interfere with you; but I do it because I'm your brother, and because I take a certain amount of interest in you accordingly. Now, I quite grant with you that the world's in a very unjust social condition at present. I'm not a fool, and I can't help seeing that wealth is very badly distributed, and that happiness is very unequally meted. But I don't feel called upon to make myself the martyr of the cause of readjustment for all that. If I were a working man, I should take up the side that you're taking up now; I

Grant Allen

should have everything to gain, and nothing to lose by it. But your mistake is just this, that when you might identify your own interests with the side of the "haves," as I do, you go out of your way to identify them with the side of the "have-nots," out of pure idealistic Utopian philanthropy. You belong by birth to the small and intrinsically weak minority of persons specially gifted by nature and by fortune; and why do you lay yourself out with all your might to hound on the mass of your inferiors till they trample down and destroy whatever gives any special importance, interest, or value to intellectual superiority, vigour of character, political knowledge, or even wealth? I can understand that the others should wish to do this; I can understand that they will inevitably do it in the long run; but why on earth do you, of all men, want to help them in pulling down a platform on which you yourself might, if you chose, stand well above their heads and shoulders?'

'Because I feel the platform's an unjust one,' Ernest answered, warmly.

'An excellent answer for them,' Herbert chimed in, in his coldest and calmest tone, 'but a very insufficient one for you. The injustice, if any, tells all in your own favour. As long as the mob doesn't rise up and tear the platform down (as it will one day), why on earth should you be more anxious about it than they are?'

'Because, Herbert, if there must be injustice, I would rather suffer it than do it.'

'Well, go your own way,' Herbert answered, with a calm smile of superior wisdom; 'go your own way and let it land you where it will. For my part, I back the environment. But it's no business of mine; I have done my best to warn you. Liberavi animam meam. You won't take my advice, and I must leave you to your own devices.' And with just a touch of the hand to Edie, and a careless nod to his two brothers, he sauntered out of the room without another word. 'As usual,' he thought to himself as he walked down the stairs, 'I go out of my way to give good advice to a fellow-creature, and I get only the black ingratitude of a snubbing in return. This is really almost enough to make even me turn utterly and completely selfish!'

'I wonder, Ernest,' said Ronald, looking up as Herbert shut the door gently behind him, 'how you and I ever came to have such a brother as Herbert!'

'I think it's easy enough to understand, Ronald, on plain hereditary principles.'

Ronald sighed. 'I see what you mean,' he said; 'it's poor mother's strain—the Whitaker strain—coming out in him.'

'I often fancy, Ronald, I can see the same two strains in varying intensity, running through all three of us alike. In Herbert the Whitaker strain is uppermost, and the Le Breton comparatively in abeyance; in me, they're both more or less blended; in you, the Le Breton strain comes out almost unadulterated. Yet even Herbert has more of a Le Breton in him than one might imagine, for he's with us intellectually; it's the emotional side only that's wanting to him. Even when members of a family are externally very much unlike one another in the mere surface features of their characters, I believe you can generally see the family likeness underlying it for all that.'

'Only you must know how to analyse the character to see it,' said Edie. 'I don't think it ever struck me before that there was anything in common between you and Herbert, Ernest, and yet now you point it out I believe there really is something after all. I'm sorry you told me, for I can't bear to think that you're like Herbert.'

'Oh, no,' Ronald put in hastily; 'it isn't Ernest who has something in him like Herbert; it's Herbert who has something in him like Ernest. There's a great deal of difference between the one thing and the other. Besides, he hasn't got enough of it, Edie, and Ernest has.'

CHAPTER XXVII

RONALD COMES OF AGE

'Strange,' Ronald Le Breton thought to himself, as he walked along the Embankment between Westminster and Waterloo, some weeks later—the day of Herr Max's trial,—'I had a sort of impulse to come down here alone this afternoon: I felt as if there was an unseen Hand somehow impelling me. Depend upon it, one doesn't have instincts of that sort utterly for nothing. The Finger that guides us guides us always aright for its own wise and unfathomable purposes. What a blessing and a comfort it is to feel that one's steps are continually directed from above, and that even an afternoon stroll through the great dreary town is appointed to us for some fit and sufficient reason! Look at that poor girl over there now, at the edge of the Embankment! I wonder what on earth she can have come here for. Why...how pale and excited she looks. What's she going so near the edge for? Gracious heavens! it can't be...yes...it is... no, no, but still it must be...that's what the Finger was guiding me here for this afternoon. There's no denying it. The poor creature's tempted to destroy herself. My instinct tells me so at once, and it never tells me wrong. Oh, Inscrutable Wisdom, help me, help me: give me light to act rightly! I must go up this very moment and speak to her!'

The girl was walking moodily along the edge of the bank, and looking in a dreamy fashion over the parapet into the sullen fast-flowing brown water below. An eye less keen than Ronald's might have seen in a moment, from her harassed weary face and her quick glance to right and left after the disappearing policeman, that she was turning over in her own mind something more desperate than any common everyday venture. Ronald stepped up to her hastily, and, firm in his conviction that the Finger was guiding him aright, spoke out at once with boldness on the mere strength of his rapid instinctive conjecture.

'Stop, stop,' he said, laying his hand gently on her shoulder: 'not for a moment, I beg of you, not for a moment. Not till you've at least told me what is your trouble.'

Selah turned round sharply and looked up in his face with a vague feeling of indefinable wonder. 'What do you mean?' she asked, in a husky voice. 'Don't do what? How do you know I was going to do anything?'

'You were going to throw yourself into the river,'Ronald answered confidently; 'or at least you were debating about it in your own soul. I know you were, because a sure Guide tells me so.'

Selah's lip curled a little at the sound of that familiar language. 'And suppose I was,' she replied, defiantly, in her reckless fashion; 'suppose I was: what's that to you or anybody, I should like to know? Are you your brother's keeper, as your own Bible puts it? Well, yes, then, perhaps I WAS going to drown myself: and if I choose, as soon as your back's turned, I shall go and do it still; so there; and that's all I have to say about it.'

Ronald turned his face towards her with an expression of the intensest interest, but before he could put in a single word, Selah interrupted him.

'I know what you're going to say,' she went on, looking up at him rebelliously. 'I know what you're going to say every bit as well as if you'd said it. You're one of these city missionary sort of people, you are; and you're going to tell me it's awfully wicked of me to try and destroy myself, and ain't I afraid of a terrible hereafter! Ugh! I hate and detest all that mummery.'

Ronald looked down upon her in return with a sort of silent wondering pity. 'Awfully wicked,' he said slowly, 'awfully wicked! How meaningless! How incomprehensible! Awfully wicked to be friendless, or poor, or wretched, or unhappy! Awfully wicked to be driven by despair, or by heartlessness, to such a pitch of misery or frenzy that you want to fling yourself wildly into the river, only to be out of it all, anywhere, in a minute! Why you poor, unhappy girl, how on earth can you possibly help it?'

There was something in the tone of his earnest voice that melted for a moment even Selah Briggs's pride and vehemence. It was very impertinent of him to try and interfere with her purely personal business, no doubt, but he seemed to do so in a genuinely kindly rather than in a fussy interfering spirit. At any rate he didn't begin by talking to her that horrid cant about the attempt to commit suicide being so extremely wicked! If he had done that, Selah would have felt it was not only an unwarrantable intrusion upon her liberty of action, but a grotesque insult to her natural intelligence as well.

'I've a right to drown myself if I choose,' she faltered out, leaning faintly as she spoke against the parapet, 'and nobody else has any possible right to hinder or prevent me. If you people make laws against my rights in that matter, I shall set your laws aside whenever and wherever it happens to suit my personal convenience.'

'Exactly so,' Ronald answered, in the same tone of gentle and acquiescent persuasion. 'I quite agree with you. It's as clear as daylight that every individual human being has a perfect right to put an end to his own life whenever it becomes irksome or unpleasant to him; and nobody else has any right whatever to interfere with him. The prohibitions that law puts upon our freedom in that respect are only of a piece with the other absurd restrictions of our existing unchristian legislation—as opposed to the spirit of the Word as the old rule that made us bury a suicide at four cross roads with a hideously barbarous and brutal ceremonial. They're all mere temporary survivals from a primitive paganism: the truth shall make us free. But though we mayn't rightly interfere, we may surely inquire in a brotherly spirit of interest, whether it isn't possible for us to make life less irksome for those who, unhappily, want to get rid of it. After all, the causes of our discontent are often quite removable. Tell me, at least, what yours are, and let me see whether I'm able to do anything towards removing them.'

Selah hung back a little sullenly. This was a wonderful mixture of tongues that the strange young man was talking in! When he spoke about the right and wrong of suicide, ethically considered, it might have been Herbert Walters himself who was addressing her: when he glided off sideways to the truth and the Word, it might have been her Primitive Methodist friends at Hastings, in full meeting assembled. And, by the way, he reminded her strangely, somehow, of Herbert Walters! What manner of man could he be, she wondered, and what strange sort of new Gospel was this that he was preaching to her?

'How do I know who you are?' she asked him, carelessly. 'How do I know what you want to know my story for? Perhaps you're only trying to get something out of me.'

'Trust me,' Ronald said simply. 'By faith we live, you know. Only trust me.'

Selah answered nothing.

'Come over here to the bench by the garden,' Ronald went on earnestly. 'We can talk there more at our leisure. I don't like to see you leaning so close to the parapet. It's a temptation; I know it's a temptation.'

Seiah looked at him again inquiringly. She had never before met anybody so curious, she fancied. 'Aren't you afraid of being seen sitting with me like this,' she said, 'on the Embankment benches? Some of your fine friends might come by and wonder who on earth you had got here with you.' And, indeed, Selah's dress had grown vory shabby and poor-looking

Grant Allen

during a long and often fruitless search for casual work or employment in London.

But Ronald only surveyed her gently from head to foot with a quiet smile, and answered softly, 'Oh, no; there's no reason on earth why we shouldn't sit down and talk together; and even if there were, my friends all know me far too well by this time to be surprised at anything I may do, when the Hand guides me. If you will only sit down and tell me your story, I should like to see whether I could possibly do anything to help you.'

Selah let him lead her in his gentle half-womanly fashion to the bench, and sat down beside him mechanically. Still, she made no attempt to begin her pitiful story. Ronald suspected for a second some special cause for her embarrassment, and ventured to suggest a possible way out of it. 'Perhaps,' he said timidly, 'you would rather speak to some older and more fatherly man about it, or to some kind lady. If so, I have many good friends in London who would listen to you with as much interest and attention as I should.'

The old spirit flared up in Selah for a second, as she answered quickly, 'No, no, sir, it's nothing of that sort. I can tell YOU as well as I can tell anybody. If I've been unfortunate, it's been through no fault of my own, thank goodness, but only through the hard-heartedness and unkindness of other people. I'd rather speak to you than to anyone else, because I feel some-how—why, I don't know—as if you had something or other really good in you.'

'I beg your pardon,' Ronald said hastily, 'for even suggesting it but you see, I often have to meet a great many people who've been unhappy through a great many different causes, and that leads one occasionally for a time into mistaken inferences. Let me hear all your history, please, and I firmly believe, through the aid that never forsakes us, I shall be able to do something or other to help you in your difficulties.'

Thus adjured, Selah began and told her whole unhappy history through, without pause or break, into Ronald's quietly sympathetic ear. She told him quite frankly and fully how she had picked up the acquaintance of a young Mr. Walters from Oxford at Hastings: how this Mr. Walters had led her to believe he would marry her: how she had left her home hurriedly, under the belief that he would be induced to keep his promise: how he had thrown her over to her own devices: and how she had ever since been trying to pick up a precarious livelihood for herself in stray ways as a sempstress, work for which she wag naturally very ill-fitted, and for which she had no introductions. She slurred over nothing on either side of the story; and especially she did not forget to describe the full measure of her troubles and trials from her Methodist friends at Hastings. Ronald shook his head sympathetically at this stage of the story. 'Ah, I know, I know,' he muttered, half under his breath; 'nasty pious people! Very well meaning, very devout, very earnest, one may be sure of it—but oh! what terrible soul-killing people to live among! I can understand all about it, for I've met them often—Sabbath-keeping folks; preaching and praying folks; worrying, bothering, fussy-religious folks: formalists, Pharisees, mint-anise and-cummin Christians: awfully anxious about your soul, and so forth, and doing their very best to make you as miserable all the time as a slave at the torture! I don't wonder you ran away from them.'

'And I wasn't really going to drown myself, you know, when you spoke to me.' Selah said, quite apologetically. 'I was only just looking over into the beautiful brown water, and thinking how delicious it would be to fling oneself in there, and be carried off down to the sea, and rolled about for ever into pebbles on the shingle, and there would be an end of one altogether—oh, how lovely!'

'Very natural,' Ronald answered calmly. 'Very natural. Of course it would. I've often thought the same thing myself. Still, one oughtn't, if possible, to give way to these impulses: one ought to do all that's in one's power to prevent such a miserable termination to one's divinely allotted existence. After all, it is His will, you see, that we should be happy.'

When Selah had quite finished all her story, Ronald began drawing circles in the road with the end of his stick, and perpending within himself what had better be done about it, now that all was told him. 'No work,' he said, half to himself; 'no money; no food. Why, why, I suppose you must be hungry.'

Selah nodded assent.

'Will you allow me to offer you a little lunch?' he asked, hesitatingly, with something of Herbert's stately politeness. Even in this last extremity, Ronald felt instinctively what was due to Selah Briggs's natural sentiments of pride and delicacy. He must speak to her deferentially as if she were a lady, not give her alms as if she were a beggar.

Then for the first time that day Selah burst suddenly into tears. 'Oh, sir,' she said, sobbing, 'you are very kind to me.'

Ronald waited a moment or two till her eyes were dry, and then took her across the gardens and into Gatti's. Any other man might have chosen some other place of entertainment under the circumstances, but Ronald, in his perfect simplicity of heart, looked only for the first shop where he could get Selah the food she needed. He ordered something hot hastily, and, when it came, though he had had his own lunch already, he played a little with a knife and fork himself for show's sake, in order not to seem as if he were merely looking on while Selah was eating. These little touches of feeling were not lost upon Selah: she noticed them at once, and recognised in what Ernest would have called her aboriginal unregenerate vocabulary that she was dealing with a true gentleman.

'Walters,' Ronald said, pausing a second with a bit of chop poised lightly on the end of his fork; 'let me see—Walters. I don't know any man of that name, myself, but I've had two brothers at Oxford, and perhaps one of them could tell me who he is. Walters—Walters. You said your own name was Miss Briggs, I think, didn't you? My name's Ronald

Le Breton.'

'How curious,' Selah said, colouring up. 'I'm sure I remember Mr. Walters talking more than once to me about his brother Ronald.'

'Indeed,' Ronald answered, without even a passing tinge of suspicion. That any man should give a false name to other people with intent to deceive was a thing that would never have entered into his simple head—far less that his own brother Herbert should be guilty of such a piece of disgraceful meanness.

'I think,' Ronald went on, as soon as Selah had finished her lunch, 'you'd better come with me back to my mother's house for the present. I suppose, now you've talked it over a little, you won't think of throwing yourself into the river any more for to-day. You'll postpone your intention for the present, won't you? Adjourn it sine die till we can see what can be done for you.'

Selah smiled faintly. Even with the slight fresh spring of hope that this chance rencontre had roused anew within her, it seemed rather absurd and childish of her to have meditated suicide only an hour ago. Besides, she had eaten and drunk since then, and the profoundest philosophers have always frankly admitted that the pessimistic side of human nature is greatly mitigated after a good dinner.

Ronald called a hansom, and drove up rapidly to Epsilon Terrace. When he got there, he took Selah into the little back breakfast room, regardless of the proprieties, and began once more to consider the prospects of the future.

'Is Lady Le Breton in?' he asked the servant: and Selah noticed with surprise and wonder that this strange young man's mother was actually 'a lady of title,' as she called it to herself in her curious ordinary language.

Grant Allen

'No, sir,' the girl answered; 'she have been gone out about an hour.'

'Then I must leave you here while I go out and get you lodgings for the present,' Ronald said, quietly; 'you won't object to my doing that, of course: you can easily pay me back from your salary as soon as we succeed in finding you some suitable occupation. Let me see, where can I put you for the next fortnight? Naturally you wouldn't like to live with religious people, would you?'

'I hate them,' Selah answered vigorously.

'Of course, of course,' Ronald went on, as if to himself. 'Perfectly natural. She hates them! So should I if I'd been bothered and worried out of my life by them in the way she has. I hate them myself—that kind: or, rather, it's wrong to say that of them, poor creatures, for they mean well, they really mean well at bottom, in their blundering, formal, pettifogging way. They think they can take the kingdom of Heaven, not by storm, but by petty compliances, like servile servants who have to deal with a capricious, exacting master. Poor souls, they know no better. They measure the universe by the reflection in their muddy mill-pond. Nasty pious people is what I always call them; nasty pious people: little narrow souls, trying hard to be Christians after their lights, and only attaining, after all, to a sort of second-hand diluted Judaism, a religion of cup-washing, and phylacteries, and new moons, and sabbaths, and daily sacrifices. However, that's neither here nor there. I won't hand you over, Miss Briggs, to any of those poor benighted people. No, nor to any religious people at all. It wouldn't suit you: you want to be well out of it. I know the very place for you. There are the Baumanns: they'd be glad to let a room: Baumann's a German refugee, and a friend of Ernest's: a good man, but a secularist. THEY wouldn't bother you with any religion: poor things, they haven't got any. Mrs. Baumann's an excellent woman—educated, too; no objection at all in any way to the Baumanns. They're people I like and respect immensely—every good quality they have; and I'm often grieved to think such excellent people should be deprived of the comfort and pleasure of believing. But, then, so's my dear brother Ernest; and you know, they're none the worse for it, apparently, any of them: indeed, I don't know that there's anybody with whom I can talk more sympathetically on spiritual matters than dear Ernest. Depend upon it, most of the most spiritually-minded people nowadays are outside all the churches altogether.'

Selah listened in blank amazement to this singular avowal of heterodox opinion from an obviously religious person. What Ronald Le Breton could be she couldn't imagine; and she thought with an inward smile of the very different way in which her friends at Hastings would have discussed the spiritual character of a wicked secularist.

Just at that moment a latch-key turned lightly in the street door, and two sets of footsteps came down the passage to Lady Le Breton's little back breakfast-room. One set turned up the staircase, the other halted for a second at the breakfast-room doorway. Then the door opened gently, and Herbert Le Breton and Selah Briggs stood face to face again in blank astonishment.

There was a moment's pause, as Selah rose with burning cheeks from the chair where she was sitting; and neither spoke a word as they looked with eyes of mutual suspicion and dislike into each other's faces. At last Herbert Le Breton turned with some acerbity to his brother Ronald, and asked in a voice of affected contempt, 'Who is this woman?'

'This LADY'S name is Miss Briggs,' Ronald answered, pointedly, but, of course, quite innocently.

'I needn't ask you who this man is,' Selah said, with bitter emphasis. 'It's Herbert Walters.'

A horrible light burst in upon Ronald instantaneously as she uttered the name; but he could not believe it; he would not believe it: it was too terrible, too incredible. 'No, no,' he said falteringly, turning to Selah; 'you must be mistaken. This is not Mr. Walters. This is my brother, Herbert Le Breton.'

Selah gazed into Herbert's slinking eyes with a concentrated expression of scorn and disgust. 'Then he gave me a false name,' she said, slowly, fronting him like a tigress. 'He gave me a false name, it seems, from the very beginning. All through, the false wretch, all through, he actually meant to deceive me. He laid his vile scheme for it beforehand. I never wish to see you again, you miserable cur, Herbert Le Breton, if that's your real name at last. I never wish to see you again: but I'm glad I've done it now by accident, if it were only to inflict upon you the humiliation of knowing that I have measured the utmost depth of your infamy! You mean, common, false scoundrel, I have measured to the bottom the depth of your infamy!'

'Oh, don't,' Ronald said imploringly, laying his hand upon her arm. 'He deserves it, no doubt; but don't glory over his humiliation.' He had no need to ask whether she spoke the truth; his brother's livid and scarlet face was evidence enough against him.

Herbert, however, answered nothing. He merely turned angrily to Ronald. 'I won't bandy words,' he said constrainedly in his coldest tone, 'with this infamous woman whom you have brought here on purpose to insult me; but I must request you to ask her to leave the house immediately. Your mother's home is no place to which to bring people of such a character.'

As he spoke, the door opened again, and Lady Le Breton, attracted by the sound of angry voices, entered unexpectedly. 'What does all this riot mean, Herbert?' she asked, imperiously. 'Who on earth is this young woman that Ronald has brought into my own house, actually without my permission?'

Herbert whispered a few words quietly into her ear, and then left the room hurriedly with a stiff and formal bow to his brother Ronald. Lady Le Breton turned round to the culprit severely.

'Disgraceful, Ronald!' she cried in her sternest and most angry voice; 'perfectly disgraceful! You aid and abet this wretched creature—whose object is only to extort money by false pretences out of your brother Herbert—you aid and abet her in her abominable stratagems, and you even venture to introduce her clandestinely into my own breakfast-room. I wonder you're not ashamed of yourself. What on earth can you mean by such extraordinary, such unChristian conduct? Go to your own room this moment, sir, and ask this young woman to leave the house immediately.'

'I shall go without being asked,' Selah said, proudly, her big eyes flashing defiance haughtily into Lady Le Breton's. 'I don't know who you all may be, or what this gentleman who brought me here may have to do with you: but if you are in any way connected with that wretch Herbert Le Breton, who called himself Herbert Walters for the sake of deceiving me, I don't want to have anything further to say to any of the whole pack of you. Please stand out of my way,' she went on to Ronald, 'and I shall have done with you all together this very instant. I wish to God I had never seen a single one of you.'

'No, no, not just yet, please,' Ronald put in hastily. 'You mustn't go just yet, I implore you, I beg of you, till I have explained to my mother, before you, how this all happened; and then, when you go, I shall go with you. Though I have the misfortune to be the brother of the man who gave you a false name in order to deceive you, I trust you will still allow me to help you as far as I am able, and to take you to my German friends of whom I spoke to you.'

'Ronald,' Lady Le Breton cried, in her most commanding tone, 'you must have taken leave of your senses. How dare you keep this person a moment longer in my house against my wish, when even she herself is anxious to quit it? Let her go at once, let her go at once, sir.'

'No, mother,' Ronald answered firmly. 'We are commanded in the Word to obey our parents in all things, "in the Lord." I think you've forgotten that proviso, mother, "in the Lord." Now, mother, I will tell you all about it.' And then, in a rapid sketch, Ronald, with his back planted solidly against the door, told his mother briefly all he knew about Selah Briggs, how he had found her, how he had brought her home not knowing who she was, and how she had recognised Herbert as her unfaithful lover. Lady Le Breton, when she saw that escape was practically impossible, flung herself back in an easy-chair, where she swayed herself backward and forward gently all the while, without once lifting her eyes towards Ronald, and sighed impatiently from time to time audibly, as if the story merely bored her. As for poor Selah, she stood upright in front of Ronald without a word, looking neither to the right nor to the left, and waiting eagerly for the story to be finished.

When Ronald had said his say, Lady Le Breton looked up at last and said simply, with a pretended yawn, 'Now, Ronald, will you go to your own room?'

'I will not,' Ronald answered, in a soft whisper. 'I will go with this lady to the rooms of which I have spoken to her.'

'Then,' Lady Le Breton said coldly, 'you shall not return here. It seems I'm to lose all my children, one after another, by their extraordinary rebelliousness!'

'By your own act—yes,' Ronald answered, very calmly. 'You forgot that last Thursday was my birthday, I daresay, mother; but I didn't forget it; it was; and I came of age then. I'm my own master now. I've stopped here as long as I could, mother, because of the commandment: but I can't stop here any longer. I shall go to Ernest's for to-night as soon as I've got rooms for this lady.'

'Good evening,' Lady Le Breton said, bowing frigidly, without another word.

'Good evening, mother,' Ronald replied, in his natural voice. 'Miss Briggs, will you come with me? I'm very sorry that this unhappy scene should have been inflicted upon you against my will; but I hope and pray that you won't have lost all confidence in my wish to help you, in spite of these unfortunate accidents.'

Selah followed him blindly, in a dazzled fashion, out on to the flagstones of Epsilon Terrace.

'Dear me, dear me,' moaned Lady Le Breton, sinking back vacantly once more, with an air of resignation after her efforts, into the easy-chair: 'was there ever a mother so plagued and burdened with unnatural and undutiful sons as I am? If it weren't for dear Herbert, I'm sure I don't know what I should ever do between them. Ronald, too, who always pretended to be so very, very religious! To think that he should go and uphold the word of a miserable, abandoned, improper adventuress against his own brother Herbert! Atrocious, perfectly atrocious! Where on earth he can have picked up such a woman I'm positively at a loss to imagine. But it's exactly like his poor dear father: I remember once when we were stationed at Moozuffernugger, in the North-West Provinces, with the 14th Bengal, poor Owen absolutely insisted on taking up the case of some Eurasian waman, who pretended she'd been badly treated by young Walker of our regiment! I call it quite improper—almost unseemly—to meddle in the affairs of such people. I daresay Herbert has had something or other to say to this horrid girl; young men will be young men, and in the army we know how to make allowances for that sort of thing: but that Ronald should positively think of bringing such a person into my breakfast-room is not to be heard of. Ronald's a pure Le Breton—that's undeniable, thank goodness; not a single one of the good Whitaker points to be found in all his nature. However, poor dear Sir Owen, in spite of all his nonsense, was at least an officer and a gentleman; whereas the nonsense these boys have picked up at Oxford and among their German refugee people is both irreligious, and, I may even say, indecent, or, to put it in the mildest way, indecorous.

Grant Allen

I wish with all my heart I'd never sent them to Oxford. I've always thought that if only Ernest had gone in for a direct commission, he'd soon have got all that absurd revolutionary rubbish knocked out of him in a mess-room! But it's a great comfort to me to think I have one real blessing in dear Herbert, who's just such a son as any mother might well be thoroughly proud of in every way!'

While Lady Le Breton was thus communing with herself in the breakfast-room, and while Herbert was trying to patch up a hollow truce with his own much-bruised self-respect in his own bedroom, Ronald was taking poor dazed and wearied Selah round to the refuge of the Baumanns' hospitable roof. As soon as that matter was temporarily arranged to the mutual satisfaction of all the parties concerned, Ronald walked over alone to Ernest's little lodgings at Holloway. He would sleep there that night, and send round a letter to Amelia, the house-maid, in the morning, asking her to pack up his things and forward them at once to Mrs. Halliss's. For himself, he did not propose, unless circumstances compelled it, again to enter his mother's rooms, except by her own express invitation. After all, he thought, even his little income, if clubbed with Edie and Ernest's, would probably help them all to live now in tolerable comfort.

So he told Edie all his story, and Edie listened to it with an approving smile. 'I think, dear Ronald,' she said, taking his hand in hers, 'you did quite right—quite as Ernest himself would have done under the circumstances.'

'Where's Ernest?' asked Ronald, half smiling at that naive wifely standard of right conduct.

'Gone with Mr. Berkeley to the trial,' Edie answered.

'The trial! What trial?'

'Oh, don't you know? Herr Max's. They're trying him to-day for littering a seditious libel and inciting to murder the chief of the Third Section at St. Petersburg.'

'But he said nothing at all,' Ronald cried in astonishment. 'I read the article myself. He said nothing that any Englishman mightn't have said under the same circumstances. Why, I could have written the libel, as they call it, myself, even, and I'm not much of a politician either! They can't ever be trying him in a country like England for anything so ridiculously little as that!'

'But they are,' Edie answered quietly; 'and dear Ernest's dreadfully afraid the verdict will go against him.'

'Nonsense,' Ronald answered with natural confidence. 'No English jury would ever convict a man for speaking up like that against an odious and abominable tyranny.'

Very late in the afternoon, Ernest and Berkeley returned to the lodgings. Ernest's face was white with excitement, and his lips were trembling violently with suppressed emotion. His eyes were red and swollen. Edie hardly needed to ask in a breathless whisper of Arthur Berkeley, 'What verdict?'

'Guilty,' Arthur Berkeley answered with a look of unfeigned horror and indignation. He had learnt by this time quite to take the communistic view of such questions.

'Guilty,' Ronald cried, jumping up from his chair in astonishment. 'Impossible! And what sentence?'

'Twelve months' hard labour,' Berkeley answered, slowly and remorsefully.

'An atrocious sentence!' Ronald exclaimed, turning red with excitement. 'An abominable sentence! A most malignant and vindictive sentence! Who was the judge, Arthur?'

'Bassenthwaite,' Berkeley replied half under his breath.

'And may the Lord have mercy upon his soul!' said Ronald solemnly,

But Ernest never said a single word. He only sat down and ate his supper in silence, like one stunned and dazzled. He didn't even notice Ronald's coming. And Edie knew by his quick breath and his face alternately flushed and pallid that there would be another crisis in his gathering complaint before the next morning.

CHAPTER XXVIII

TELL IT NOT IN OATH

As they sat silent in that little sitting-room after supper, a double knock at the door suddenly announced the arrival of a telegram for Ernest. He opened it with trembling lingers. It was from Lancaster:—'Come down to the office at once. Schurz has been sentenced to a year's imprisonment, and we want a leader about him for to-morrow.' The telegram roused Ernest at once from his stupefied lethargy. Here was a chance at last of doing something for Max Schurz and for the cause of freedom! Here was a chance of waking up all England to a sense of the horrible crime it had just committed through the voice of its duly accredited judicial mouthpiece! The country was trembling on the brink of an abyss, and he, Ernest Le Breton, might just be in time to save it. The Home Secretary must be compelled by the unanimous clamour of thirty millions of free working people to redress the gross injustice of the law in sending Max Sohurz, the greatest, noblest, and purest-minded of mankind, to a common felon's prison! Nothing else on earth could have moved Ernest, jaded and dispirited as he was at that moment, to the painful exertion of writing a newspaper leader after the day's fatigues and excitements, except the thought that by doing so he might not only blot out this national disgrace, as he considered it, but might also help to release the martyr of the people's rights from his incredible, unspeakable punishment. Flushed and feverish though he was, he rose straight up from the table, handed the telegram to Edie without a word, and started off alone to hail a

Grant Allen

hansom cab and drive down immediately to the office. Arthur Berkeley, fearful of what might happen to him in his present excited state, stole out after him quietly, and followed him unperceived in another hansom at a little distance.

When Ernest got to the 'Morning Intelligence' buildings, he was shown up at once into the editorial room. He expected to find Mr. Lancaster at the same white heat of indignation as himself; but to his immense surprise he actually found him in the usual sleepy languid condition of apathetic impartiality. 'I wired for you, Le Breton,' the impassive editor said calmly, 'because I understand you know all about this man Schurz, who has just got his twelve months' imprisonment this evening. I suppose, of course, you've heard already all about it.'

'I've been at the trial all day,' Ernest answered, 'and myself heard the verdict and sentence.'

'Good,' Mr. Lancaster said, with a dreamy touch of approval in his tone. 'That's good journalism, certainly, and very smart of you. Helps you to give local colour and realistic touches to the matter. But you ought to have called in here to see me immediately. We shall have a regular reporter's report of the trial, of course; but reporters' reports are fearfully and wonderfully lifeless. If you like, besides the leader, you might work up a striking headed article on the Scene in Court. This is an important case, and we want something more about it than mere writing, you know; a little about the man himself and his personal history, which Berkeley tells me you're well acquainted with. He's written something called "Gold and the Proletariate," or whatever it is; just tell our readers all about it. As to the leader, say what you like in it—of course I shall look over the proof, and tone it down a bit to suit the taste of our public—we appeal mainly to the mercantile middle class, I need hardly say; but you know the general policy of the paper, and you can just write what you think best, subject to subsequent editorial revision. Get to work at once, please, as the articles are wanted immediately, and send down slips as fast as they're written to the printers.'

Ernest could hardly contain his surprise at Mr. Lancaster's calmness under such unheard-of circumstances, when the whole laborious fabric of British liberties was tottering visibly to its base—but he wisely concluded to himself that the editor had to see articles written about every possible subject every evening—from a European convulsion to a fire at a theatre,— and that use must have made it in him a property of easiness. When a man's obliged to work himself up perpetually into a state of artificial excitement about every railway accident, explosion, shipwreck, earthquake, or volcanic eruption, in Europe, Asia, Africa, America, and the islands of the Pacific Ocean, why then, Ernest charitably said to himself, his sympathies must naturally end by getting a trifle callous, especially when he's such a very apathetic person to start with as this laconic editorial Lancaster. So he turned into the little bare box devoted to his temporary use, and began writing with perfectly unexampled and extraordinary rapidity at his leader and his article about the injured and martyred apostle of the slighted communistic religion.

It was only a few months since Ernest had, with vast toil and forethought, spun slowly out his maiden newspaper article on the Italian organ-boy, and now he found himself, to his own immense surprise, covering sheet after sheet of paper in feverish haste with a long account of Max Schurz's splendid life and labours, and with a really fervid and eloquent appeal to the English people not to suffer such a man as he to go helplessly and hopelessly to an English prison, at the bare bidding of a foreign despot. He never stopped for one moment to take thought, or to correct what he had written; in the excitement of the moment his pen travelled along over the paper as if inspired, and he found the words and thoughts thronging his brain almost faster than his lagging hand could suffice to give them visible embodiment. As each page was thrown off hurriedly, he sent it down, still pale and wet, to the printers in the office; and before two o'clock in the morning, he had full proofs of all he had written sent up to him for final correction. It was a stirring and vigorous leader, he felt quite certain himself as he read it over; and he thought with a

Grant Allen

swelling breast that it would appear next day, with all the impersonal authority of the 'Morning Intelligence' stamped upon its face, at ten thousand English breakfast tables, where it might rouse the people in their millions to protest sternly before it was too late against this horrid violation of our cherished and boasted national hospitality.

Meanwhile, Arthur Berkeley had stopped at the office, and run in hastily for five minutes' talk with the terrible editor. 'Don't say anything to shock Le Breton, I beg of you, Lancaster,' he said, 'about this poor man Schurz who has just been sent for a year to prison. It's a very hard case, and I'm awfully sorry for the man myself, though that's neither here nor there. I can see from your face that you, for your part, don't sympathise with him; but at any rate, don't say anything about it to hurt Le Breton's feelings. He's in a dreadfully feverish and excited condition this evening; Max Schurz has always been to him almost like a father, and he naturally takes his sentence very bitterly to heart. To tell you the truth, I regret it a great deal myself, I know a little of Schurz, through Le Breton, and I know what a well-meaning, ardent, enthusiastic person he really is, and how much good actually underlies all his chaotic socialistic notions. But at any rate, I do beg of you, don't say anything to further excite and hurt poor Le Breton.'

'Certainly not,' the editor answered, smoothing his large hands softly one over the other. 'Certainly not; though I confess, as a practical man, I don't sympathise in the least with this preposterous German refugee fellow. So far as I can learn, he's been at the bottom of half the revolutionary and insurrectionary movements of the last twenty years—a regular out-and-out professional socialistic incendiary.'

'You wouldn't say so,' Berkeley replied quietly, 'if you'd seen more of him, Lancaster.' But being a man of the world, and having come mainly on Ernest's account, he didn't care to press the abstract question of Herr Max's political sincerity any further.

'Well,' the editor went on, a little testily, 'be that as it may, I won't discuss the subject with your friend Le Breton, who's really a nice, enthusiastic young fellow, I think, as far as I've seen him. I'll simply let him write to-night whatever he pleases, and make the necessary alterations in proof afterwards, without talking it over with him personally at all. That'll avoid any needless discussion and ruffling of his supersensitive communistic feelings. Poor fellow, he looks very ill indeed to-night. I'm really extremely sorry for him.'

'When will he be finished?' asked Arthur.

'At two,' the editor answered.

'I'll send a cab for him,' Arthur said; 'there'll be none about at that hour, probably. Will you kindly tell him it's waiting for him?'

At two o'clock or a little after, Ernest drove home with his heart on fire, full of eagerness and swelling hope for to-morrow morning. He found Edie waiting for him, late as it was, with a little bottle of wine—an unknown luxury at Mrs. Halliss's lodgings—and such light supper as she thought he could manage to swallow in his excitement. Ernest drank a glass of the wine, but left the supper untasted. Then he went to bed, and tossed about uneasily till morning. He couldn't sleep through his anxiety to see his great leader appear in all the added dignity of printer's ink and rouse the slumbering world of England up to a due sense of Max Schurz's wrongs and the law's incomprehensible iniquity.

Before seven, he rose very quietly, dressed himself without saying a word, and stole out to buy an early copy of the 'Morning Intelligence.' He got one at the small tobacconist's shop round the corner, where he had taken his first hint for the Italian organ-boy leader. It was with difficulty that he could contain himself till he was back in Mrs. Halliss's little front parlour; and there he tore open the paper eagerly, and turned to the well-remembered words at the beginning of his desperate appealing article. He could recollect the very run of every clause and word he had written: 'No Englishman can read without a thrill of righteous indignation,' it began,'the sentence passed last night upon Max Schurz, the author of that remarkable economical work, "Gold and the Proletariate." Herr Schurz is one of those numerous refugees from German despotism who have taken advantage of the hospitable welcome usually afforded by England to the oppressed of all creeds or nations'—and so forth, and so forth. Where was it now? Yes, that was it, in the place of honour, of course—the first leader under the clock in the 'Morning Intelligence.' His eye caught at once the opening key-words, 'No Englishman.' Sinking down into the easy-chair by the flowers in the window he prepared to run it through at his leisure with breathless anxiety.

'No Englishman can read without a feeling of the highest approval the sentence passed last night upon Max Schurz, the author of that misguided economical work, "Gold and the Proletariate." Herr Schurz is one of those numerous refugees from German authority, who have taken advantage of the hospitable welcome usually afforded by England to the oppressed of all creeds or nations, in order to hatch plots in security against the peace of sovereigns or governments with which we desire always to maintain the most amicable and cordial relations.' Ernest's eyes seemed to fail him. The type on the paper swam wildly before his bewildered vision. What on earth could this mean? It was his own leader, indeed, with the very rhythm and cadence of the sentences accurately preserved, but with all the adjectives and epithets so ingeniously altered that it was turned into a crushing condemnation of Max Schurz, his principles, his conduct, and his ethical theories. From beginning to end, the article appealed to the common-sense of intelligent Englishmen to admire the dignity of the law in thus vindicating itself against the atrocious schemes of a dangerous and ungrateful political exile who had abused the hospitality of a great fres country to concoct vile plots against the persons of friendly sovereigns and innocent ministers on the European continent.

Ernest laid down the paper dreamily, and leant back for a moment in his chair, to let his brain recover a little from the reeling dizziness of that crushing disappointment. Then he turned in a giddy mechanical fashion to the headed article on the fourth page. There the self-same style of treatment met once more his astonished gaze. All the minute facts as to Max Schurz's history and personality were carefully preserved; the description of his simple artisan life, his modest household, his Sunday evening receptions, his great following of earnest and enthusiastic refugees—every word of all this, which hardly anyone else could have equally well supplied, was retained intact in the published copy; yet the whole spirit of the thing had utterly evaporated, or rather had been perverted into the exact opposite unsympathetic channel. Where Ernest had written 'enthusiasm,' Lancaster had simply altered the word to 'fanaticism;' where Ernest had spoken of Herr Max's 'single-hearted devotion,' Lancaster had merely changed the phrase into 'undisguised revolutionary ardour.' The whole paper was one long sermon against Max Schurz's Utopian schemes, imputing to him not only folly but even positive criminality as well. We all know how we all in England look upon the foreign political refugee—a man to be hit again with impunity, because he has no friends; but to Ernest, who had lived so long in his own little socialistic set, the discovery that people could openly say such things against his chosen apostle at the very moment of his martyrdom, was a hideous and blinding disill-usionment. He put the paper down upon the table once more, and buried his face helplessly between his burning hands.

The worst of it all was this: if Herr Max ever saw those articles he would naturally conclude that Ernest had been guilty of the basest treachery, and that too on the very day when he most needed the aid and sympathy of all his followers. With a thrill of horror he thought in his own soul that the great leader might suspect him for an hour of being the venal Judas of the little sect.

How Ernest ever got through that weary day he did not know himself; nothing kept him up through it except his burning

Grant Allen

indignation against Lancaster's abominable conduct. About eleven o'clock, Arthur Berkeley called in to see him. 'I'm afraid you've been a little disappointed,' he said, 'about the turn Lancaster has given to your two articles. He told me he meant to alter the tone so as to suit the policy of the paper, and I see he's done so very thoroughly. You can't look for much sympathy from commonplace, cold, calculating Englishmen for enthusiastic natures like Herr Max's.'

Ernest turned to him in blank amazement. He had expected Berkeley to be as angry as himself at Lancaster's shameful mutilation of his appealing leader; and he found now that even Berkeley accepted it as an ordinary incident in the course of journalistic business. His heart sank within him as he thought how little hope there could be of Herr Max's liberation, when even his own familiar friend Berkeley looked upon the matter in such a casual careless fashion.

'I shall never write another word for the "Morning Intelligence,"' he cried vehemently, after a moment's pause. 'If we starve for it, I shall never write another word in that wicked, abominable, dishonourable paper. I can die easily enough, heaven knows, without a murmur: but I can't be disloyal to dear Herr Max, and to all my innate ingrained principles.'

'Don't say that, Ernest,' Berkeley answered gently. 'Think of Mrs. Le Breton and the baby. The luxury of starvation for the sake of a cause is one you might venture to allow yourself if you were alone in the world as I am, but not one which you ought to force unwillingly upon your wife and children. You've been getting a trifle more practical of late under the spur of necessity; don't go and turn impossible again at the supreme moment. Whatever happens, it's your plain duty to go on writing for the "Morning Intelligence." You say with your own hand only what you think and believe yourself: the editor alone is responsible for the final policy of the paper.'

Ernest only muttered slowly to himself,—'Never, never, never!'

Still, though the first attempt had failed, Ernest did not wholly give up his hopes of doing something towards the release of Herr Max from that unutterable imprisonment. He drew up a form of petition to the Home Secretary, in which he pointed out the reasons for setting aside the course of the law in the case of this particular political prisoner. With feverish anxiety he ran about London for the next two days, trying to get influential signatures to his petition, and to rouse the people in their millions to demand the release of the popular martyr. Alas for the stolid indifference of the British public! The people in their millions sat down to eat and drink, and rose up to play, exactly as if nothing unusual in any way had happened. Most of them had never heard at all of Herr Max, or of 'Gold and the Proletariate,' and those who had heard understood for the most part that he was a bad lot who was imprisoned for trying nefariously to blow up the Emperor of Rooshia. Crowds of people nightly besieged the doors of the Ambiguities and the Marlborough, to hear the fate of 'The Primate of Fiji' and 'The Duke of Bermondsey;' but very few among the millions took the trouble to sign their names to Ernest Le Breton's despairing petition. Even the advanced radicals of the market-place, the men who figured largely at Trafalgar Square meetings and Agricultural Labourers' Unions, feared to damage their reputation for moderation and sobriety by getting themselves mixed up with a continental agitator like this man Schurz that people were talking about. The Irish members expressed a pious horror of the very word dynamite: the working-man leaders hemmed and hawed, and regretted their inability, in their very delicate position, to do anything which might seem like countenancing Russian nihilism. In the end, Ernest sent, in his petition with only half a dozen unknown signatures; and the Home Secretary's private prompter threw it into the waste-paper basket entire, without even taking the trouble to mention its existence to his harassed and overburdened chief. Just a Marylebone communist refugee in prison! How could a statesman with half the bores and faddists of England on his troubled hands, find time to look at uninfluential petitions about an insignificant worthless nobody like that?

So gentle, noble-natured, learned Herr Max went to prison and served his year there uncomplainingly, like any other social malefactor; and Society talked about his case with languid interest for nearly a fortnight, and then straightway found a new sensation, and forgot all about him. But there are three hundred and sixty-five days of twenty-four hours each in every year; and for every one of those days Herr Max and Herr Max's friends never forgot for an hour together that he was in prison.

And at the end of the week Ernest got a letter from Lancaster, enclosing a cheque for eight guineas. That is a vast sum of money, eight guineas: just think of all the bread, and meat, and tea, and clothing one can buy with it for a small family! 'My dear Le Breton,' the editor wrote—in his own hand, too; a rare honour; for he was a kindly man, and he had learned, much to his surprise, from Arthur Berkeley, that Ernest was angry at his treatment of the Schurzian leader: 'My dear Le Breton, I enclose cheque for eight guineas, for your two articles. I hope you didn't mind the way I was obliged to cut them up in some unessential details, so as to suit the policy of the paper. I kept whatever was really most distinctive as embodying special information in them. You know we are above all things strictly moderate. Please send us another social shortly.'

It was a kind letter, undoubtedly a kind and kindly-meant letter: but Ernest flung it from him as though he had been stung by a serpent or a scorpion. Then he handed the cheque to Edie in solemn silence, to see what she would do with it. He merely wanted to try her constancy. For himself, he would have felt like a Judas indeed if he had taken and used their thirty pieces of silver.

Edie looked at the cheque intently and sighed a deep sigh of regret. How could she do otherwise? They were so very poor, and it was such an immense sum of money! Then she rose quietly without saying a word, and lighted a match from the box on the mantelpiece. She held the cheque firmly between her finger and thumb till it was nearly burnt, end let it drop slowly at last into the empty fireplace. Ernest rose up and kissed her tenderly. The leaden weight of the thirty pieces of silver was fairly off their united conscience. They had made what reparation they could for the evil of that unhappy, undesigned leader. After all Ernest had wasted the last remnant of his energy on one eventful evening, all for nothing.

As Edie sat looking wistfully at the smouldering fragments of the burnt cheque, Ernest roused her again by saying quietly, 'To-day's Saturday. Have we got anything for to-morrow's dinner, Edie?'

'Nothing,' Edie answered, simply. 'How much money have you left, Ernest?'

'Sixpence,' Ernest said, without needing to consult his empty purse for confirmation—he had counted the pence, as they went, too carefully for that already. 'Edie, I'm afraid we must go at last to the poor man's banker till I can get some more money.'

'Oh, Ernest—not—not—not the pawnbroker!'

'Yes, Edie, the pawnbroker.'

The tears came quickly into Edie's eyes, but she answered nothing. They must have food, and there was no other way open before them. They rose together and went quietly into the bedroom. There they gathered together the few little trinkets and other things that might be of use to them, and Ernest took down his hat from the stand to go out with them to the pawnbroker's.

As he turned out he was met energetically on the landing by a stout barricade from good Mrs. Halliss. 'No, sir, not you, sir,' the landlady said firmly, trying to take the parcel from him as he went towards the door. 'I beg your pardon, sir, for 'avin' over'eard what wasn't meant for me to 'ear, no doubt, but I couldn't 'elp it, sir, and John an' me can't allow nothink of this sort, we can't. We're used to this sort o' things, sir, John and me is; but you and the dear lady isn't used to 'em, sir, and didn't nought to be neither, and John an' me can't allow it, not anyhow.'

Ernest turned scarlet with shame, but could say nothing. Edie only whispered softly, 'Dear, dear Mrs. Halliss, we're so sorry, but we can't help it.'

''Elp it, ma'am,' said Mrs. Halliss, herself almost crying, 'nor there ain't no reason why you should try to 'elp it neither. As I says to John, "John," says I, "there ain't no 'arm in it, noways," says I, "but I can't stand by," says I, "and see them two poor dear young creechurs," meanin' no offence, ma'am, "a-pawning of their own jewelry and things to go and pay for their Sunday's dinner." And John, 'e says, says 'e, "Quite right, Martha," says 'e; "don't let 'em, my dear," says 'e. "The Lord has prospered us a bit in our 'umble way, Martha," says 'e, "and we ain't got no cause to want, we ain't; and if the dear lady and the good gentleman wouldn't take it as a liberty," says 'e, "it 'ud be better they should just borrer a pound or two for a week from us," says 'e, beggin' your pardon, ma'am, for 'intin' of it, "than that there Mr. Le Breting, as ain't accustomed to such places nohow, should go a-makin' acquaintance, for the fust time of his life, as you may say, with the inside of a pawnbroker's shop," says 'e. "John," says I, "it's my belief the lady and gentleman 'ud be insulted," says I, "though they ARE the sweetest unassoomin'est young gentlefolk I ever did see," says I, "if we were to go as tin' them to accept the loan of money from the likes of you and me, John, as is no better, by the side of them, nor old servants, in the manner o' speakin'.'" "Insulted," says 'e; "not a bit of it, they needn't, Martha," says 'e, "for I knows the ways of the aristocracy," says 'e, "and I knows as there's many a gentleman as owns 'is own 'osses and 'is own 'ounds as isn't afraid to borrer a pound or so from 'is own coachman, or even from 'is own groom—not but what to borrer from a groom is lowerin'," says 'e, "in a tempory emergency. Mind you, Martha," says 'e, "a tempory emergency is a thing as may 'appen to landed gentlefolks any day," says 'e.

"It's like a 'ole in your coat made by a tear," says 'e; "a haccident as may 'appen to-morrer to the Prince of Wales 'isself upon the 'untin' field," 'e says. "Well, then, John," says I, "I'll just go an' speak to 'em about it, this very minnit," says I, and if I might make so bold, ma'am, without seemin' too presumptious, I should be very glad if you'd kindly allow me, ma'am, to lend Mr. Le Breting a few suvverins till 'e gets 'is next remittances, ma'am.'

Edie looked at Ernest, and Ernest looked at Edie and the landlady; and then they all three burst out crying together without further apology. Perhaps it was the old Adam left in Ernest a little; but though he could stand kindness from Dr. Greatrex or from Mr. Lancaster stoically enough, he couldn't watch the humble devotion of those two honest-hearted simple old servants without a mingled thrill of shame and tenderness. 'Mrs. Halliss,' he said, catching up the landlady's hard red hand gratefully in his own, 'you are too good and too kind, and too considerate for us altogether. I feel we have done nothing to deserve such great kindness from you. But I really don't think it would be right of us to borrow from you when we don't even know how long it may be before we're able to return your money or whether we shall ever be able to return it at all. We're so much obliged to you, so very very much obliged to you, dear Mrs. Halliss, but I think we ought as a matter of duty to pawn these few little things rather than run into debt which we've no fair prospect at present of ever redeeming.'

'HAS you please, sir,' Mrs. Halliss said gently, wiping her eyes with her snow-white apron, for she saw at once that Ernest really meant what he said. 'Not that John an' me would think of it for a minnit, sir, so long as you wouldn't mind our takin' the liberty; but any'ow, sir, we can't allow you to go out yourself and go to the pawnbroker's. It ain't no fit place for the likes of you, sir, a pawnbroker's ain't, in all that low company; and I don't suppose you'd rightly know 'ow much to hask on the articles, neither. John, 'e ain't afeard of goin'; an' 'e says, 'e insists upon it as 'e's to go, for 'e don't think, sir, for the honour of the 'ouse, 'e says, sir, as a lodger of ours ought to be seen a-goin' to the pawnbroker's. Just you give them things right over to John, sir, and 'e'll get you a better price on 'em by a long way nor they'd ever think of giving a gentleman like you, sir.'

Ernest fought off the question in a half-hearted fashion for a little while, but Mrs. Halliss insisted upon it, and after a short time Ernest gave way, for to say the truth he had very vague ideas himself as to how he ought to proceed in a pawnbroking expedition. Mrs. Halliss ran down the kitchen stairs quickly, for fear he should change his mind as soon as her back was turned, and called out gaily to her husband in the first delight of her unexpected triumph.

'John,' she cried, '—drat that man, where is 'e? John, dear, you just putt your 'at on, and purtend to run round the corner a bit to Aston's the pawnbroker's. The Lord have mercy upon me for the stories I've been a-tellin' of 'em, but I couldn't bear to see them two pore things a-pawnin' their little bits of jewelry and sich, and Mr. Le Breting, too, 'im as ain't fit to go knockin' together with underbred folks like pawnbrokers. So I told 'im as you'd take 'em round and pawn 'em for 'im yourself; not as I don't suppose you've never pawned nothink in your 'ole life, John, leastways not since ever you an' me kep' company, for afore that I suppose you was purty much like other young men is, John, for all you shakes your 'ead at it now so innocent like. But you just run round, there's a dear, and make as if you was goin' to the pawnbroker's, and then you come straight 'ome again unbeknown to 'em. I ain't a goin' to let them two pore dears go pawnin' their things for a dinner nohow. You take them two suvverins out of your box, John, and putt away these 'ere little things for the present time till the pore souls is able to pay us, and if they never don't, small matter neither. Now you go fast, John, there's a dear, and come back, and mind you give them two suvverins to Mr. Le Breting as natural like as ever you're able.'

'Pawn 'em,' John said in a pitying voice, 'no indeed, it ain't come to that yet, I should 'ope, that they need go a-pawnin' their effects while we've got a suvverin or two laid by in our box, Martha. Not as anybody need be ashamed of pawnin' on occasions, for that matter,—I don't say as a reg'lar thing, but now an' then on occasions, as you may call it; for even in the best dookal families, I've 'eard tell they DO sometimes 'ave to pawn the dimonds, so that pawnin' ain't in the runnin' noways, bless you, as respects gentility. Not as I'd like to go into a pawnshop myself, Martha, as I've always been brought up respectable; but when you send for Mr. Hattenborough to your own ressydence and say quite commandin' like, "'Er Grace 'ud be obleeged if you'd wait upon 'er in Belgrave Square to hinspeck 'er dimonds as I want to raise the wind on 'em," why, that's quite another matter nat'rally.'

When honest John came back in a few minutes and handed the two sovereigns over to Ernest, he did it with such an unblushing face as might have won him applause on any stage for its perfect naturalness. 'Lor' bless your 'eart, sir,' he said in answer to Ernest's shamefaced thanks, touching the place where his hat ought to be mechanically, 'it ain't nothing, sir, that ain't. If it weren't for the dookal families of England, sir, it's my belief the pawnbrokin' business wouldn't be worth mentioning in the manner o' speakin'.'

That evening, Ernest paced up and down the little parlour rather moodily for half an hour with three words ringing perpetually in his dizzy ears-the 'Never, never, never,' he had used so short a tune since about the 'Morning Intelligence.' He must get money somehow for Dot and Edie! he must get money somehow to pay good Mrs. Halliss for their board and lodging! There was only one way possible. Fight against it as he would, in the end he must come back to that inevitable conclusion. At last he sat down with a gloomy face at the centre table, and pulled out a sheet of blank foolscap.

'What are you going to do, Ernest?' Edie asked him.

Ernest groaned. 'I'm writing a social for the "Morning

Grant Allen

Intelligence," Edie,' he answered bitterly.

'Oh, Ernest!' Edie said with a face of horror and surprise. 'Not after the shameful way they've treated poor Max Schurz!'

Ernest groaned again. 'There's nothing else to be done, Edie,' he said, looking up at her despondently. 'I must earn money somehow to keep the house going.'

It is the business of the truthful historian to narrate facts, not to palliate or extenuate the conduct of the various actors. Whether Ernest did right or wrong, at least he did it; he wrote a playful social for Monday's 'Morning Intelligence,' and carried it into the office on Sunday afternoon himself, beause there was no postal delivery in the London district.

That night, he lay awake once more for hours together, tossing and turning, and reflecting bitterly on his own baseness and his final moral downfall. Herbert was right, after all. The environment was beginning to conquer. He could hold out no longer. Herr Max was in prison; the world was profoundly indifferent; he himself had fallen away like Peter; and there was nothing left for him now but to look about and find himself a dishonourable grave.

And Dot? And Edie? What was to become of them after? Ah me, for the pity of it when a man cannot even crawl quietly into a corner and die in peace like a dog, without being tortured by fears and terrors beforehand as to what will come to those he loves far better than life when he himself is quietly dead and buried out of the turmoil!

CHAPTER XXIX

A MAN AND A MAID

IF Ernest and Edie had permitted it, Ronald Le Breton would have gone at once, after his coming of age, to club income and expenditure with his brother's household. But, as Edie justly remarked, when he proposed it, such a course would pretty nearly have amounted to clubbing HIS income with THEIR expenditure; and even in their last extreme of poverty that was an injustice which neither she nor her husband could possibly permit. Ronald needed all his little fortune for his own simple wants, and though they themselves starved, they couldn't bear to deprive him of the small luxuries which had grown into absolute necessaries for one so feeble and weak. Indeed, ill as Ernest himself now was, he had never outgrown the fixed habit of regarding Ronald as the invalid of the family; and to have taken anything, though in the direst straits, from him, would have seemed like robbing the helpless poor of their bare necessities. So Ronald was fain at last to take lodgings for himself with a neighbour of good Mrs. Halliss's, and only to share in Ernest's troubles to the small extent of an occasional loan, which Edie would have repaid to time if she had to go without their own poor little dinner for the sake of the repayment.

Meanwhile, Ronald had another interest on hand which to his enthusiastic nature seemed directly imposed upon him by the finger of Providence—to provide a home and occupation for poor Selah, whom Herbert had cast aside as a legacy to him. As soon as he had got settled down to his own new mode of life in the Holloway lodgings, he began to look about for a fit place for the homeless girl—a place, he thought to himself, which must combine several special advantages; plenty of work—she wanted that to take her mind off brooding; good, honest, upright people; and above all, no religion. Ronald recognised that last undoubted requirement as of absolutely paramount importance. 'She'll stand any amount of talk or anything else from me,' he said to himself often, 'because she knows I'm really in earnest; but she wouldn't stand it for a moment from those well-meaning, undiscriminating, religious busy-bodies, who are so awfully anxious about other people's souls, though they never seem for a single minute to consider in any way other people's feelings.' After a little careful hunting among his various acquaintances, however, he found at last a place that would exactly suit Selah at a stationer's in Netting Hill; and there he put her—with full confidence that Selah would do the work entrusted to her well and ably, if not from conscientiousness, at least from personal pride, 'which, after all,' Roland soliloquised dreamily, 'is as good a substitute for the genuine article as one can reasonably expect to find in poor fallen human nature.'

'I wish, Mr. Le Breton,' Selah said, quite timidly for her (maidenly reserve, it must be admitted, was not one of Selah Briggs's strong points), 'that I wasn't going to be quite so far from you as Notting Hill. If I could see you sometimes, you know, I should feel that it might keep me more straight—keep me away from the river in future, I mean. I can't stand most people's preaching, but somehow, your preaching seems to do me more good than harm, really, which is just the exact opposite way, it seems to me, from everybody else's.'

Ronald smiled sedately. 'I'm glad you want to see me sometimes,' he said, with a touch of something very like gallantry in his tone that was wholly unusual with him. 'I shall walk over every now and then, and look you up at your lodgings over yonder; and besides, you can come on Sundays to dear Edie's, and I shall be able to meet you there once a fortnight or thereabouts. But I'm not going to let you call me Mr. Le

Breton any longer; it isn't friendly: and, what's more, it isn't Christian. Why should there be these artificial barriers between soul and soul, eh, Selah? I shall call you Selah in future: it seems more genuine and heartfelt, and unencumbered with needless conventions, than your misters and misses. After all, why should we keep up such idle formalities between brethren and fellow-workers?'

Selah started a little—she knew better than Ronald himself did what such first advances really led to. 'Oh, Mr. Le Breton,' she said quickly, 'I really can't call you Ronald. I can never call any other man by his Christian name as long as I live, after—your brother.'

'You mistake me, Selah,' Ronald put in hastily, with his quaint gravity. 'I mean it merely as a sign of confidence and a mark of Christian friendship. Sisters call their brothers by their Christian names, don't they? So there can be no harm in that, surely. It seems to me that if you call me Mr. Le Breton, you're putting me on the footing of a man merely; if you call me Ronald, you're putting me on the footing of a brother, which is really a much more harmless and unequivocal position for me to stand in. Do, please, Selah, call me Ronald.'

'I'm afraid I can't,' Selah answered. 'I daren't. I mustn't.' But she faltered a little for a moment, notwithstanding.

'You must, Selah,' Ronald said, with all the force of his enthusiastic nature, fixing his piercing eyes full upon her. 'You must, I tell you. Call me Ronald.'

'Very well—Ronald,' Selah said at last, after a long pause. 'Good-bye, now. I must be going. Good-bye, and thank you. Thank you. Thank you.' There was a tear quivering even in Selah Briggs's eye, as she held his hand lingeringly a moment in hers before releasing it. He was a very good fellow, really, and he had been so very kind, too, in interesting himself about her future.

'What a marvellous thread of sameness,' Ronald thought to himself, as he walked back rapidly to his solitary lodgings, 'runs through the warp and woof of a single family, after all! What an underlying unity of texture there must be throughout, in all its members, however outwardly dissimilar they may seem to be from one another! One would say at first sight there was very little, if anything, in common between me and Herbert. And yet this girl interests me wonderfully. Of course I'm not in love with her—the notion of MY falling in love with anybody is clearly too ridiculous. But I'm attracted by her, drawn towards her, fascinated as it were; I feel a sort of curious spell upon me whenever I look into her deep big eyes, flashing out upon one with their strange luminousness. It isn't merely that the Hand has thrown her in my way: that counts for something, no doubt, but not for everything. Besides, the Hand doesn't act blindly—nay, rather, acts with supreme wisdom, surpassing the powers or the comprehension of man. When it threw Selah Briggs in my way, depend upon it, it was because the Infinite saw in me something that was specially adapted to her, and in her something that was specially adapted to me. The instrument is duly shaped by inscrutable Wisdom for its own proper work. Now, whatever interests ME in her, must have also interested Herbert in her equally and for the same reason. We're drawn towards her, clearly; she exercises over both of us some curious electric power that she doesn't exercise, presumably, over other people. For Herbert must have been really in love with her—not that I'm in love with her, of course; but still, the phenomena are analogous, even if on a slightly different plane—Herbert must have been really in love with her, I'm sure, or such a prudent man as he is would never have let himself get into what he would consider such a dangerous and difficult entanglement. Yes, clearly, there's something in Selah Briggs that seems to possess a singular polarity, as Ernest would call it, for the Le Breton character and individuality!

'And then, it cuts both ways, too, for Selah was once desperately in love with Herbert: of that I'm certain. She must have been, to judge from the mere strength of the final revulsion. She's a girl of intensely deep passions—I like people to have some depth to their character, even if it's only in the way of passion—and she'd never have loved him at all without loving him fervently and almost wildly: hers is a fervent, wild, indomitable nature. Yes, she was certainly in love with Herbert; and now, though of course I don't mean to say she's in love with me (I hope it isn't wrong to think in this way about an unmarried girl), still I can't help seeing that I have a certain influence over her in return—that she pays much attention to what I say and think, considers me a person worth considering, which she doesn't do, I'm sure, with most other people. Ah, well, there's a vast deal of truth, no doubt, in these new hereditary doctrines of Darwin's and Galton's that Herbert and Ernest talk about so much; a family's a family, that's certain, not a mere stray collection of casual acquaintances. How the likeness runs through the very inmost structure of our hearts and natures! I see in Selah very much what Herbert saw in Selah: Selah sees in me very much what she saw in Herbert. Extraordinary insight into human nature men like Darwin and Galton have, to be sure? And David, too, what a marvellous thinker he was, really! What unfathomed depths of meaning lie unexpected in that simple sentence of his, "I am fearfully and wonderfully made." Fearfully and wonderfully, indeed, when one remembers that from one father and mother Herbert and I have both been compounded, so unlike in some things that we scarcely seem to be comparable with one another (look at Herbert's splendid intellect beside mine!), so like in others that Selah Briggs—goodness gracious, what am I thinking of? I was just going to say that Selah Briggs falls in love first with one of us and then with the other. I do hope and trust it isn't wrong of me to fill my poor distracted head so much with these odd thoughts about that unfortunate girl, Selah!'

CHAPTER XXX

THE ENVIRONMENT FINALLY TRIUMPHS

Winter had come, and on a bitter cold winter's night, Ernest Le Breton once more received an unexpected telegram asking him to hurry down without a moment's delay on important business to the 'Morning Intelligence' office. The telegram didn't state at all what the business was; it merely said it was urgent and immediate without in any way specifying its nature. Ernest sallied forth in some perturbation, for his memories of the last occasion when the 'Morning Intelligence' required his aid on important business were far from pleasant ones; but for Edie's sake he felt he must go, and so he went without a murmur.

'Sit down, Le Breton,' Mr. Lancaster said slowly when Ernest entered. 'The matter I want to see you about's a very peculiar one. I understand from some of my friends that you're a son of Sir Owen Le Breton, the Indian general.'

'Yes, I am,' Ernest answered, wondering within himself to what end this curious preamble could possibly be leading up. If there's any one profession, he thought, which is absolutely free from the slightest genealogical interest in the persons of its professors, surely that particular calling ought to be the profession of journalism.

'Well, so I hear, Le Breton. Now, I believe I'm right in saying, am I not, that it was your father who first subdued and organised a certain refractory hill-tribe on the Tibetan frontier, known as the Bodahls, wasn't it?'

'Quite right,' Ernest replied, with a glimmering idea slowly rising in his mind as to what Mr. Lancaster was now driving at.

'Ah, that's good, very good indeed, certainly. Well, tell me, Le Breton, do you yourself happen to know anything on earth about these precious insignificant people?'

'I know all about them,' Ernest answered quickly. 'I've read all my father's papers and despatches, and seen his maps and plans and reports in our house at home from my boyhood upward. I know as much about the Bodahls, in fact, as I know about Bayswater, or Holborn, or Fleet Street.'

'Capital, capital,' the editor said, fondling his big hands softly; 'that'll exactly suit us. And could you get at these plans and papers now, this very evening, just to refresh the gaps in your memory?'

'I could have them all down here,' Ernest answered, 'at an hour's notice.'

'Good,' the editor said again. 'I'll send a boy for them with a cab. Meanwhile, you'd better be perpending this telegram from our Simla correspondent, just received. It's going to be the question of the moment, and we should very much like you to give us a leader of a full column about the matter.'

Ernest took the telegram and read it over carefully. It ran in the usual very abbreviated newspaper fashion: 'Russian agents revolted Bodahls Tibetan frontier. Advices Peshawur state Russian army marching on Merv. Bodahls attacked Commissioner, declared independence British raj.'

'Will you write us a leader?' the editor asked, simply.

Ernest drew a long breath. Three guineas! Edie, Dot, an empty exchequer! If he could only have five minutes to make his mind up! But he couldn't. After all, what did it matter what he said about these poor unknown Bodahls? If HE didn't write the leader, somebody else who knew far less about the subject than he did would be sure to do it. He wasn't responsible for that impalpable entity 'the policy of the paper.' Beside the great social power of the 'Morning Intelligence,' of the united English people, what was he, Ernest Le Breton, but a miserable solitary misplaced unit? One way or the other, he could do very little indeed, for good or for evil. After half a minute's internal struggle, he answered back the editor faintly, 'Yes, I will.' 'For Edie,' he muttered half audibly to himself; 'I must do it for dear Edie.'

'And you'll allow me to make whatever alterations I think necessary in the article to suit the policy of the paper?' the editor asked once more, looking through him with his sleepy keen grey eyes. 'You see, Le Breton, I don't want to annoy you, and I know your own principles are rather peculiar; but of course all we want you for is just to give us the correct state-ment of facts about these outlandish people. All that concerns our own attitude towards them as a nation falls naturally under the head of editorial matter. You must see yourself that it's quite impossible for us to let any one single contributor dictate from his own standpoint the policy of the paper.'

Ernest bent his head slowly. 'You're very kind to argue out the matter with me so, Mr. Lancaster,' he said, trembling with excitement. 'Yes, I suppose I must bury my scruples. I'll write a leader about these Bodahls, and let you deal with it afterwards as you think proper.'

They showed him into the bare little back room, and sent a boy up with a hastily written note to Ronald for the maps and papers. There Ernest sat for an hour or two, writing away for very life, and putting on paper everything that he knew about the poor Bodahls. By two o'clock, the proofs had all come up to him, and he took his hat in a shamefaced manner to sally out into the cold street, where he hoped to hide his rising remorse and agony under cover of the solitary night. He knew too well what 'the policy of the paper' would be, to venture upon asking any questions about it. As he left the office, a boy brought him down a sealed envelope from Mr. Lancaster. With his usual kindly thoughtfulness the editor had sent him at once the customary cheque for three guineas. Ernest folded it up with quivering fingers, and felt the blood burn in his cheeks as he put it away in his waistcoat pocket. That accursed money! For it he had that night sold his dearest principles! And yet, not for it, not for it, not for it—oh, no, not for it, but for Dot and Edie!

The boy had a duplicate proof in his other hand, and Ernest saw at once that it was his own leader, as altered and corrected by Mr. Lancaster. He asked the boy whether he might see it; and the boy, knowing it was Ernest's own writing, handed it to him at once without further question. Ernest did not dare to look at it then and there for fear he should break down utterly before the boy; he put it for the moment into his inner pocket, and buttoned his thin overcoat tightly around him. It was colder still in the frosty air of early morning, and the contrast to the heated atmosphere of the printing house struck him with ominous chill as he issued slowly forth into the silent precincts of unpeopled Fleet Street.

It was a terrible memorable night, that awful Tuesday; the coldest night known for many years in any English winter. Snow lay deep upon the ground, and a few flakes were falling still from the cloudy sky, for it was in the second week of January. The wind was drifting it in gusty eddies down the long streets, and driving the drifts before it like whirling dust in an August storm. Not a cab was to be seen anywhere, not even a stray hansom crawling home from clubs or theatres; and Ernest set out with a rueful countenance to walk as best he might alone through the snow all the way to Holloway. It is a long and dreary trudge at any time; it seemed very long and dreary indeed to Ernest Le Breton, with his delicate frame and weak chest, battling against the fierce wind on a dark and snowy winter's night, and with the fever of a great anxiety and a great remorse silently torturing his distracted bosom. At each step he took through the snow, he almost fancied himself a hunted Bodahl. Would British soldiers drive those poor savage women and children to die so of cold and hunger on their snowy hilltops? Would English fathers and mothers, at home at their ease, applaud the act with careless thoughtlessness as a piece of our famous spirited foreign policy? And would his own article, written with his own poor thin cold fingers in that day's 'Morning Intelligence,' help to spur them on upon that wicked and unnecessary war? What right had we to conquer the Bodahls? What right had we to hold them in subjection or to punish them for revolting? And above all, what right had he, Ernest Le Breton, upon whose head the hereditary guilt of the first conquest ought properly to have weighed with such personal heaviness—what right had he, of all men, directly or indirectly, to aid or abet the English people in their immoral and inhuman resolve? Oh, God, his sin was worse than theirs; for they sinned, thinking they did justly; but as for him, he sinned against the light; he knew the better, and, bribed by gold, he did the worse. At that moment, the little slip of printed paper in his waistcoat pocket seemed to burn through all the frosts of that awful evening like a chain of molten steel into his very marrow!

Trudging on slowly through the white stainless snow, step by step,—snow that cast a sheet of pure white even over the narrow lanes behind the Farringdon Road,—cold at foot and hot at heart, he reached at last the wide corner by the Angel at Islington. The lights in the windows were all out long ago, of course, but the lamps outside were still flaring brightly, and a solitary policeman was standing under one of them, trying to warm his frozen hands by breathing rapidly on the curved and distorted fingers. Ernest was very tired of his tramp by that time, and emboldened by companionship he stopped awhile to rest himself in the snow and wind under the opposite lamp-light. Putting his back against the post, he drew the altered proof of his article slowly out of his inner pocket. It had a strange fascination for him, and yet he dreaded to look at it. With an effort, he unfolded it in his stiff fingers, and held the paper up to the light, regardless of the fact that the policeman was watching his proceedings with the interest naturally due from a man of his profession to a suspicious-looking character who was probably a convicted pickpocket. The first sentence once more told him the worst. There was no doubt at all about it. The three guineas in his pocket were the price of blood!

'The insult to British prestige in the East,' ran that terrible opening paragraph, 'implied in the brief telegram which we publish this morning from our own Correspondent at Simla, calls for a speedy and a severe retribution. It must be washed out in blood.' Blood, blood, blood! The letters swam before his eyes. It was this, then, that he, the disciple of peace-loving Max Schurz, the hater of war and conquest, the foe of unjust British domination over inferior races—it was this that he had helped to make plausible with his special knowledge and his ready pen! Oh, heaven, what reparation could he make for this horrid crime he had knowingly and wilfully committed? What could he do to avoid the guilt of those poor savages' blood upon his devoted head? In one moment he thought out a hundred scenes of massacre and pillage—scenes such as he knew only too well always precede and accompany the blessings of British rule in distant dependencies. The temptation had been strong—the money had been sorely wanted—there was very little food in the house; but how could he ever have yielded to such a depth of premeditated wickedness! He folded the piece of paper into his pocket once more, and buried his face in his hands for a whole minute. The policeman now began to suspect that he was not so much a pickpocket as an escaped lunatic.

And so he was, no doubt. Of course we who are practical men of the world know very well that all this foolish feeling on Ernest Le Breton's part was very womanish and weak and overwrought; that he ought to have done the work that was set before him, asking no questions for conscience' sake; and that he might honestly have pocketed the three guineas, letting his supposed duty to a few naked brown people somewhere up in the Indian hill-country take care of itself, as all the rest of us always do. But some allowance must naturally be made for his peculiar temperament and for his particular state of health. Consumptive people are apt to take a somewhat hectic view of life in every way; they lack the common-sense ballast that makes most of us able to value the lives of a few hundred poor distant savages at their proper infinitesimal figure. At any rate, Ernest Le Breton, as a matter of fact, rightly or wrongly, did take this curious standpoint about things in general; and did then and there turn back through the deep snow, all his soul burning within him, fired with dire remorse, and filled only with one idea—how to prevent this wicked article to which he had contributed so many facts and opinions from getting printed in to-morrow's paper. True, it was not he who had put in the usual newspaper platitudes about the might of England, and the insult to the British flag, and the immediate necessity for a stern retaliation; but all that vapouring wicked talk (as he thought it) would go forth to the world fortified by the value of his special facts and his obviously intimate acquaintance with the whole past history of the Bodahl people. So he turned back and battled once more with the wind and snow as far as Fleet Street; and then he rushed excitedly into the 'Morning Intelligence' office, and asked with the wildness of despair to see the editor.

Mr. Lancaster had gone home an hour since, the porter said; but Mr. Wilks, the sub-editor, was still there, superintending the printing of the paper, and if Ernest liked, Mr. Wilks would see him immediately.

Ernest nodded assent at once, and was forthwith ushered up into Mr. Wilks's private sanctum. The sub-editor was a dry, grizzly-bearded man, with a prevailing wolfish greyness of demeanour about his whole person; and he shook Ernest's proffered hand solemnly, in the dreary fashion that is always begotten of the systematic transposition of night and day.

'For heaven's sake, Mr. Wilks,' Ernest cried imploringly, 'I want to know whether you can possibly suppress or at least alter my leader on the Bodahl insurrection!'

Mr. Wilks looked at him curiously, as one might look at a person who had suddenly developed violent symptoms of dangerous insanity. 'Suppress the Bodahl leader,' he said slowly like one dreaming. 'Suppress the Bodahl leader! Impossible! Why, it's the largest type heading in the whole of to-day's paper, is this Bodahl business. "Shocking Outrage upon a British Commissioner on the Indian Frontier. Revolt of the Entire Bodahl Tribe. Russian Intrigue in Central Asia. Dangerous Position of the Viceroy at Simla." Oh, dear me, no; not to have a leader upon THAT, my dear sir, would be simply suicidal!'

'But can't you cut out my part of it, at least,' Ernest said anxiously. 'Oh, Mr. Wilks, you don't know what I've suffered to-night on account of this dreadful unmerited leader. It's wicked, it's unjust, it's abominable, and I can't bear to think that I have had anything to do with sending it out into the world to inflame the passions of unthinking people! Do please try to let my part of it be left out, and only Mr. Lancaster's, at least, be printed.'

Mr. Wilks looked at him again with the intensest suspicion.

'A sub-editor,' he answered evasively, 'has nothing at all to do with the politics of a paper. The editor alone manages that department on his own responsibility. But what on earth would you have me do? I can't stop the machines for half an hour, can I, just to let you have the chance of doctoring your leader? If you thought it wrong to write it, you ought never to have written it; now it's written it must certainly stand.'

Ernest sank into a chair, and said nothing; but he turned so deadly pale that Mr. Wilks was fain to have recourse to a little brown flask he kept stowed away in a corner of his desk, and to administer a prompt dose of brandy and water.

'There, there,' he said, in the kindest manner of which he was capable, 'what are you going to do now? You can't be going out again in this state and in this weather, can you?'

'Yes, I am,' Ernest answered feebly. 'I'm going to walk home at once to Holloway.'

'To Holloway!' the sub-editor said in a tone of comparative horror. 'Oh! no, I can't allow that. Wait here an hour or two till the workmen's trains begin running. Or, stay; Lancaster left his brougham here for me to-night, as I have to be off early to-morrow on business; I'll send you home in that, and let Hawkins get me a cab from the mews by order.'

Ernest made no resistance; and so the sub-editor sent him home at once in Lancaster's brougham.

When he got home in the early grey of morning, he found Edie still sitting up for him in her chair, and wondering what could be detaining him so long at the newspaper office. He threw himself wildly at her feet, and, in such broken sentences as he was able to command, he told her all the pitiful story. Edie soothed him and kissed him as he went along, but never said a word for good or evil till he had finished.

'It was a terrible temptation, darling,' she said softly: 'a terrible temptation, indeed, and I don't wonder you gave way to it; but we mustn't touch the three guineas. As you say rightly, it's blood-money.'

Ernest drew the cheque slowly from his pocket, and held it hesitatingly a moment in his hand. Edie looked at him curiously.

'What are you going to do with it, darling?' she asked in a low voice, as he gazed vacantly at the last dying embers in the little smouldering fireplace.

'Nothing, Edie dearest,' Ernest answered huskily, folding it up and putting it away in the drawer by the window. They neither of them dared to look the other in the face, but they bad not the heart to burn it boldly. It was blood-money, to be sure; but three guineas are really so very useful!

Four days later, little Dot was taken with a sudden illness. Ernest and Edie sat watching by her little cradle throughout the night, and saw with heavy hearts that she was rapidly growing feebler. Poor wee soul, they had nothing to keep her for: it would be better, perhaps, if she were gone; and yet, the human heart cannot be stifled by such calm deliverances of practical reason; it WILL let its hot emotions overcome the cold calculations of better and worse supplied it by the unbiassed intellect.

All night long they sat there tearfully, fearing she would not live till morning; and in the early dawn they sent round hastily for a neighbouring doctor. They had no money to pay him with, to be sure; but that didn't much matter; they could leave it over for the present, and perhaps some day before long Ernest might write another social, and earn an honest three guineas. Anyhow, it was a question of life and death, and they could not help sending for the doctor, whatever difficulty they might afterwards find in paying him.

The doctor came, and looked with the usual professional seriousness at the baby patient. Did they feed her entirely on London milk? he asked doubtfully. Yes, entirely. Ah! then that was the sole root of the entire mischief. She was very dangerously ill, no doubt, and he didn't know whether he could pull her through anyhow; but if anything would do it, it was a change to goat's milk. There was a man who sold goat's milk round the corner. He would show Ernest where to find him.

Ernest looked doubtfully at Edie, and Edie looked back again at Ernest. One thought rose at once in both their minds. They had no money to pay for it with, except—except that dreadful cheque. For four days it had lain, burning a hole in Ernest's heart from its drawer by the window, and he had not dared to change it. Now he rose without saying a word, and opened the drawer in a solemn, hesitating fashion. He looked once more at Edie inquiringly; Edie nodded a faint approval. Ernest, pale as death, put on his hat, and went out totteringly with the doctor. He stopped on the way to change the cheque at the

Grant Allen

baker's where they usually dealt, and then went on to the goat's milk shop. How that sovereign he flung upon the counter seemed to ring the knell of his seif-respect! The man who changed it noticed the strangeness of Ernest's look, and knew at once he had not come by the money honestly. He rang it twice to make sure it was good, and then gave the change to Ernest. But Dot, at least, was saved; that was a great thing. The milk arrived duly every morning for some weeks, and, after a severe struggle, Dot grew gradually better. While the danger lasted, neither of them dared think much of the cheque; but when Dot had got quite well again, Ernest was concious of a certain unwonted awkwardness of manner in talking to Edie. He knew perfectly well what it meant; they were both accomplices in crime together.

When Ernest wrote his 'social' after Max Schurz's affair, he felt he had already touched the lowest depths of degradation. He knew now that he had touched a still lower one. Oh! horrible abyss of self-abasement!—he had taken the blood-money. And yet, it was to save Dot's life! Herbert was right, after all: quite right. Yes, yes, all hope was gone: the environment had finally triumphed.

In the awful self-reproach of that deadly remorse for the acceptance of the blood-money, Ernest Le Breton felt at last in his heart that surely the bitterness of death was past. It would be better for them all to die together than to live on through such a life of shame and misery. Ah, Peter, Peter, you are not the only one that has denied his Lord and Master!

And yet, Ernest Le Breton had only written part of a newspaper leader about a small revolt of the Bodahls. And he suffered more agony for it than many a sensitive man, even, has suffered for the commission of some obvious crime.

'I say, Berkeley,' Lancaster droned out in the lobby of their club one afternoon shortly afterwards, 'what on earth am I ever to do about that socialistic friend of yours, Le Breton? I can't ever give him any political work again, you know. Just fancy!

first, you remember, I set him upon the Schurz imprisonment business, and he nearly went mad then because I didn't back up Schurz for wanting to murder the Emperor of Russia. After that, just now the other day, I tried him on the Bodahl business, and hang me if he didn't have qualms of conscience about it afterwards, and trudge back through all the snow that awful Tuesday, to see if he couldn't induce Wilks to stop the press, and let him cut it all out at the last moment! He's as mad as a March hare, you know, and if it weren't that I'm really sorry for him I wouldn't go on taking socials from him any longer. But I will; I'll give him work as long as he'll do it for me on any terms; though, of course, it's obviously impossible under the circumstances to let him have another go at politics, isn't it?'

'You're really awfully kind, Lancaster,' Berkeley answered warmly. 'No other fellow would do as much for Le Breton as you do. I admit he's absolutely impracticable, but I would give more than I can tell you if only I thought he could be made to pull through somehow.'

'Impracticable!' the editor said shortly, 'I believe you, indeed. Why, do you remember that ridiculous Schurz business? Well, I sent Le Breton a cheque for eight guineas for that lot, and can you credit it, it's remained uncashed from that day to this. I really think he must have destroyed it.'

'No doubt,' Arthur answered, with a smile. 'And the Bodahls? What about them?'

'Oh! he kept that cheque for a few days uncashed—though I'm sure he wanted money at the time; but in the end, I'm happy to say, he cashed it.'

Arthur's countenance fell ominously.

'He did!' he said gloomily. 'He cashed it! That's bad news indeed, then. I must go and see them to-morrow morning early. I'm afraid they must be at the last pitch of poverty before they'd consent to do that. And yet, Solomon says, men do not despise a thief if he steal to satisfy his soul when he is hungry. And Le Breton, after all, has a wife and child to think of.'

Lancaster stared at him blankly, and turned aside to glance at the telegrams, saying to himself meanwhile, that all these young fellows of the new school alike were really quite too incomprehensible for a sensible, practical man like himself to deal with comfortably.

CHAPTER XXXI

DE PROFUNDIS

After all Ernest didn't get many more socials to write for the 'Morning Intelligence,' as it happened; for the war that came on shortly after crowded such trifles as socials fairly out of all the papers, and he had harder work than ever to pick up a precarious living somehow by the most casual possible contributions. Of course he tried many other channels; but he had few introductions, and then his views were really so absurdly ultra that no reasonable editor could ever be expected to put up with them. He got tired at last of seeing his well-meant papers return to him, morning after morning, with the unvarying legend, 'Declined with thanks;' and he might have gone to the wall utterly but for the kindly interest which Arthur Berkeley still took in his and Edie's future. On the very day after his conversation with Lancaster at the club Arthur dropped round casually at Holloway, and brought with him a proposal which he said had just been made him by a colonial newsagent. It was a transparent little ruse enough; but Ernest and Edie were not learned in the ways of the world and did not suspect it so readily as older and wiser heads might probably have done. Would Ernest supply a fortnightly letter, to go by the Australian mail, to the Paramatta 'Chronicle and News,' containing London political and social gossip of a commonplace kind—just the petty chit-chat he could pick up easily out of 'Truth' and the 'World'—for the small sum of thirty shillings a letter?

Grant Allen

Yes, Ernest thought he could manage that.

Very well, then. The letter must be sent on alternate Wednesdays to the colonial newsagent's address, and it would be duly forwarded by mail to the office of the Paramatta 'Chronicle.' A little suspicious, that item, Berkeley thought, but Ernest swallowed it like a child and made no comment. It must be addressed to 'Paramatta, care of Lane & Co.,' and the payments would be made fortnightly through the same agency. Arthur watched his friend's face narrowly at this point again; but Ernest in his simple-minded, unsuspecting wasy, never noticed the obvious meaning of this little deception. He thanked Arthur over and over again for his kindness, but he never guessed how far it extended. The letters kept him employed for two days a week, or thereabouts, and though they never got to Paramatta, nor any farther than Arthur Berkeley's own study in the little house he had taken for himself at Chelsea, they were regularly paid for through the colonial newsagents, by means of a cheque which really owed its ultimate origin to Arthur Berkeley himsslf. Fifteen shillings a week is not a large fortune, certainly; but still it is considerably better than nothing, when you come to try both methods of living by practical experience.

Even so, however, Ernest and Edie had a hard struggle, with their habits of life and Ernest's delicate health, to make both ends meet upon that modest income. They found the necessity for recourse to the imaginary pawnbroker growing upon them with alarming rapidity; and though the few small articles that they sent out for that purpose never really went beyond kind Mrs. Halliss's kitchen dresser, yet so far as Ernest and Edie were concerned, the effect was much the same as if they had been really pledged to the licensed broker. The good woman hid them away carefully in the back drawers of the dresser, sending up as much money for the poor little trinkets as she thought it at all credible that any man in his senses could possibly advance—if she had given altogether too much, she thought it probable that even the unsuspicious Le Bretons would detect the kindly deception—at the time remarking to

John that 'if ever them pore dear young creechurs was able to redeem 'em again, why, well an' good; an' if not, why, they could just find some excuse to give 'em back to the dear lady after pore Mr. Le Breting was dead an' gone, as he must be, no doubt, afore many months was over.' What wretched stuff that is that some narrow-minded cynics love to talk, after their cheap moralising fashion, about the coldness and cruelty of the world! The world is not cold and cruel; it is brimming over everywhere with kindliness and warmth of heart; and you have only got to put yourself into the proper circumstances in order to call forth at once on every hand, and in all classes, its tenderest and truest sympathies. None but selfish, unsympathetic people themselves ever find it otherwise in the day of trouble. It is not the world that is cold and heartless—it is not the individual members of the world that are cruel and unkind—it is the relentless march of circumstances—the faulty organisation which none of us can control, and for which none of us is personally responsible, that grinds us to powder under its Juggernaut wheels. Private kindliness is for ever trying, feebly and unsuccessfully, but with its best efforts, to undo the evil that general mismanagement is for ever perpetrating in its fateful course.

One day, a few weeks later, Arthur Berkeley called in again, and on the stairs he met a child playing—a neighbour's child whom good Mrs. Halliss allowed to come in and amuse herself while the mother went out charing. The girl had a bright gold object in her hand; and Arthur, wondering how she came by it, took it from her and looked at it curiously. He recognised it in a moment for what it was—a gold bracelet, a well remembered gold bracelet—the very one that he himself had given as a wedding present to poor Edie. He turned it over and looked closely at the inside: cut into the soft gold he saw the one word 'Frustra,' that he himself had carved into it with his penknife the night before the memorable wedding.

'Where did you get this?' he asked the child.

'Mrs. 'Alliss give it me,' the little one answered, beginning to cry.

Arthur ran lightly down the steps again, and knocked at the door of Mrs. Halliss's kitchen, with the tell-tale bracelet in his hand. Mrs. Halliss opened the dcor to him respectfully, and after a faint attempt at innocent prevarication, felt bound to let out all the pitiful little secret without further preamble. So Arthur, good, kind-hearted, delicate-souled Arthur, took his seat sadly upon one of the hard wooden kitchen chairs, and waited patiently while Mrs. Halliss and honest John, in their roundabout inarticulate fashion, slowly unfolded the story how them two pore young creechurs upstairs had been druv that low through want of funs that Mrs. Le Breting, God bless 'er 'eart, 'ad 'ad to pawn her poor little bits of jewelry and such like: and how they 'adn't 'ad the face to go an' pawn it for her, and so 'ad locked it up in their drawers, and waited hopefully for better times. Arthur listened to all this with an aching heart, and went home alone to ponder on the best way of still further assisting them.

The only thing that occurred to him was a plan for giving Edie, too, a little relief, in the way of what she might suppose to be money-getting occupation. She used to paint a little in water-colours, he remembered, in the old days; so he put an advertisement in a morning paper, which he got Mrs. Halliss to show Edie, asking for drawings of orchids, the flowers to be supplied and accurately copied by an amateur at a reasonable price. Edie fell into the harmless friendly trap readily enough, and was duly supplied with orchids by a florist in Regent Street, who professed to receive his instructions from the advertiser. The pictures were all produced in due time, and were sent to a fixed address, where a gentleman in a hansom used to call for them at regular intervals. Arthur Berkeley kept those poor little water-colours long afterwards locked up in a certain drawer all by themselves: they were sacred mementoes to him of that old hopeless love for the little Miss Butterfly of his Oxford days.

With the very first three guineas that Edie earned, carefully saved and hoarded out of her payments for the water-colours, she insisted in the pride of her heart that Ernest should go and visit a great London consulting physician. Sir Antony Wraxall was the best specialist in town on the subject of consumption, she had heard, and she was quite sure so clever a man must do Ernest a great deal of good, if he didn't even permanently cure him.

'It's no use, Edie darling,' Ernest said to her imploringly. 'You'll only be wasting your hard-earned money. What I want is not advice or medicine; I want what no doctor on earth can possibly give me—relief from this terrible crushing responsibility.'

But Edie would bear no refusal. It was HER money, she said, the first she had ever earned in her whole life, and she should certainly do as she herself liked with it. Sir Antony Wraxall, she was quite confident, would soon be able to make him better.

So Ernest, overborne by her intreaties, yielded at last, and made an appointment with Sir Antony Wraxall. He took his quarter-hour in due form, and told the great physician all his symptoms as though he believed in the foolish farce. Sir Antony held his head solemnly on one side, weighed him with puritanical scrupulosity to a quarter of an ounce on his delicate balance, listened attentively at the chest with his silver-mounted stethoscope, and perpended the net result of his investigation with professional gravity; then he gave Edie his full advice and opinion to the maximum extent of five minutes.

'Your husband's case is not a hopeful one, Mrs. Le Breton,' he said solemnly, 'but still, a great deal may be done for him.' Edie's face brightened visibly. 'With care, his life may be prolonged for many years,—I may even say, indeed, quite indefinitely.' Edie smiled with joy and gratitude. 'But you must strictly observe my rules and directions—the same that I've just given in a similar case to the Crown Prince of Servia who was here before you. In the first place, your husband must give up work altogether. He must be content to live perfectly and absolutely idle. Then, secondly, he must live quite away from England. I should recommend the Engadine in summer, and Algeria or the Nile trip every winter; but, if that's beyond your means—and I understand from Mr. Le Breton that you're in somewhat straitened circumstances—I don't object to Catania, or Malaga, or even Mentone and the Riviera. You can rent furnished villas for very little on the Riviera. But he must in no case come farther north, even in summer, than the Lake of Geneva. That, I assure you, is quite indispensable, if he wishes to live another twelvemonth. Take him south at once, in a coupe-lit of course, and break the journey once or twice at Lyons and Marseilles. Next, as to diet, he must live generously—very generously. Don't let him drink claret; claret's poor sour stuff; a pint of good champagne daily, or a good, full-bodied, genial vintage Burgundy would be far better and more digestible for him. Oysters, game, sweetbreads, red mullet, any little delicacy of that sort as much as possible. Don't let him walk; let him have carriage exercise daily; you can hire carriages for a mere trifle monthly at Cannes and Mentone. Above all things, give him perfect freedom from anxiety. Allow him to concentrate his whole attention on the act of getting well, and you'll find he'll improve astonishingly in no time. But if you keep him here in England and feed him badly and neglect my directions, I can't answer for his getting through another winter....Don't disturb yourself, I beg of you; don't, pray, give way to tears; there is really no occasion for it, my dear madam, no occasion for it at all, if you'll only do as I tell you....Quite right, thank you. Good morning.—Next case, McFarlane.— Good morning. Good morning.'

So that was the end of weeping little Edie's poor hardly-spared three guineas.

The very next day Arthur Berkeley happened to mount the stairs quietly, at an earlier hour than usual, and knocked at the door of Ernest's lodging. There was no answer, so he turned the handle, and entered by himself. The remains of breakfast lay upon the table. Arthur did not want to spy, but he couldn't help remarking that these remains were extremely meagre and scanty. Half a loaf of bread stood upon a solitary plate in the centre; a teapot and two cups occupied one side; and—that was all. In spite of himself, he couldn't restrain his curiosity, and he looked more closely at the knives and plates. Not a mark of anything but crumbs upon them, not even butter! He looked into the cups. Nothing but milkless tea at the bottom! Yes, the truth was only too evident; they had had no meat for breakfast, no butter, no milk, no sugar; it was quite clear that the meal had consisted entirely of dry bread with plain tea—call it hot water—and that for a dying man and a delicate over-worked lady! Arthur looked at that pitiable breakfast-table with a twinge of remorse, and the tears rose sharply and involuntarily into his eyes. He had not done enough for them, then; he had not done enough for them.

Poor little Miss Butterfly! and had it really come to this! You, so bright, so light, so airy, in want, in positive want, in hunger even, with your good, impossible, impracticable Ernest! Had it come to this! Bread and water; dry bread and water! Down tears, down; a man must be a man; but, oh, what a bitter sight for Arthur Berkeley! And yet, what could he do to mend it? Money they would not take; he dare not even offer it; and he was at his wit's end for any other contrivance for serving them without their knowledge. He must do what he could; but how he was to do it, he couldn't imagine.

As he stood there, ruminating bitterly over that poor bare table, he thought he heard sounds above, as of Edie coming downstairs with Dot on her shoulder. He knew she would not like to know that he had surprised the secret of their dire poverty; and he turned silently and cautiously to descend the stair. There was only just time enough to get away, for Edie was even then opening the door of the nursery. Noiselessly, with cat-like tread, he crept down the steps once more, and heard Edie descending, and singing as she came down to Dot. It was a plaintive little song, in a sad key—a plaintive little song of his own—but not wholly distressful, Arthur thought; she could still sing, then, to her baby! With the hot tears rising a second time to his eyes, he groped his way to the foot of the staircase. There he brushed them hurriedly aside with his hand, and turned out into the open street. The children were playing and tumbling in the sun, and a languid young man in a faultless frock coat and smooth silk hat was buying a showy button-hole flower from the little suburban florist's opposite.

With a heavy heart Arthur Berkeley turned homeward to his own cosy little cottage; that modest palace of art which he had once hoped little Miss Butterfly might have shared with him. He went up the steps, and turned quickly into his own small study. The Progenitor was there, sitting reading in an easy-chair. 'At least,' Arthur thought to himself, 'I have made HIS old age happy. If I could only do as much for little Miss Butterfly! for little Miss Butterfly! for little Miss Butterfly! If I could only do as much for her, oh, how happy and contented I should be!'

He flung himself down on his own sofa, and brushed big eyes nervously with his handkerchief before he dared lookup again towards the Progenitor. 'Father,' he said, clutching his watch-chain hard and playing with it nervously to keep down his emotion, 'I'm afraid those poor Le Bretons are in an awfully bad way. I'm afraid, do you know, that they actually haven't enough to eat! I went into their rooms just now, and, would you believe it, I found nothing on the table for breakfast but dry bread and tea!'

The Progenitor looked up quietly from the volume of Morley's 'Voltaire' which he was at that moment placidly engaged in devouring. 'Nothing but dry bread and tea,' he said, in what seemed to Arthur a horribly unconcerned tone. 'Really, hadn't they? Well, I dare say they ARE very badly off, poor people. But after all, you know, Artie, they can't be really poor, for Le Breton told me himself he was generally earning fifteen shillings or a pound a week, and that, you see, is really for three people a very good income, now isn't it?'

Arthur, delicate-minded, gentle, chivalrous Arthur, gazed in surprise and sudden distress at that dear, good, unselfish old father of his. How extraordinary that the kindly old man couldn't grasp the full horror of the situation! How strange that he, who would himself have been so tender, so considerate, so womanly in his care and sympathy towards anything that seemed to him like real poverty or real suffering, should have been so blinded by his long hard workingman life towards the peculiar difficulties and trials of classes other than his own as not to recognise the true meaning of that dreadful disclosure! Arthur was not angry with him—he felt too fully at that moment what depths of genuine silent hardship uncomplainingly endured were implied in the stoically calm frame of mind which could treat Edie Le Breton's penury of luxuries as a comparatively slight matter: after all, his father was right at bottom; such mere sentimental middle-class poverty is as nothing to the privations of the really poor; yet he could not help feeling a little disappointed for all that. He wanted sympathy in his pity, and he could clearly expect none here. 'Why, father,' he cried bitterly, 'you don't throw yourself into the position as you ought to do. A pound a week, paid regularly, would be a splendid income of course for people brought up like you or me. But just consider how those two young people have been brought up! Consider their wants and their habits! Consider the luxury they have been accustomed to! And then think of their being obliged to want now almost for food in their last extremity!'

His father answered in the same quiet tone—not hardly, but calmly, as though he were discussing a problem in political economy instead of the problem of Edie Le Breton's happiness—'Well, you see, it's all a matter of the standard of comfort. These two friends of yours have been brought up above their future; and now that they're got to come down to their natural level, why, of course, they feel it, depend upon it, they feel it. Their parents, of course, shouldn't have accustomed them to a style of life above their station. Good dry bread, not too stale, does nobody any harm: still, I dare say they don't like coming down to it. But bless your heart, Artie, if you'd seen the real want and poverty that I've seen, my boy—the actual hunger and cold and nakedness that I've known honest working people brought down to by no work, and nothing but the House open before them, or not that even, you wouldn't think so much of the sentimental grievances of people who are earning fifteen shillings a week in ease and comfort.'

'But, Father,' Arthur went on, scarcely able to keep down the rising tone of indignation at such seeming heartlessness, 'Ernest doesn't earn even that always. Sometimes he earns nothing, or next to nothing; and it's the uncertainty and insecurity that tells upon them even more than the poverty itself. Oh, Father, Father, you who have always been so good and kind, I never heard you speak so cruelly about anyone before as you're speaking now about that poor, friendless, helpless, penniless, heart-broken little woman!'

The old shoemaker caught at the word suddenly, and looking him through and through with an unexpected gleam of discovery, laid down the life of Voltaire on the table with a bang, and sat straight upright in his chair, nodding his head, and muttering slowly to himself, 'Little woman—he said "little woman!" Poor Artie, Poor Artie!' in a tone of inexpressible pity. At last he turned to Arthur and cried with a voice of womanly tenderness, 'My boy, my boy, I didn't know before it was the lassie you were thinking of; I thought it was only poor young Le Breton. I see it all now; I've surprised your secret; you've let it out to me without knowing it. Oh, Artie, if that's She, I'm sorry for her, and I'm sorry for you, my boy, from the bottom of my heart. If that's She, Artie, we'll put our heads together, and see what plan we can manage to save her from what she has never been accustomed to. Don't think too hardly of your old Progenitor, Artie; he hasn't mixed with these people all his life, and learned to sympathise with them as you've done, my son; he doesn't understand them or know their troubles as you do: but if that's her that you told me about one day, we shall find the means to make her happy and comfortable yet, if we have to starve for it. Dear Arthur, do not think I could be harsh or unfeeling for a moment to the woman that you ever once in passing fixed your heart upon.

Let's talk it over and think it over, and sooner or later we'll surely find the way to accomplish it.'

CHAPTER XXXII

PRECONTRACT OF MARRIAGE

Whether Ronald Le Breton's abstruse speculations on the theory of heredity were well founded or not, it certainly did happen, at any rate, that the more he saw of Selah Briggs the better he liked her; and the more Selah saw of him the better she liked him in return. Curiously enough, too, Selah did actually recognise in him what he fancied he recognised in himself, that part of his brother's nature (not all wholly assumed) which was just what Selah had first been drawn to admire in Herbert himself. It wasn't merely the originality of his general point of view: it was something more deep-seated and undefinable than that—in a word, his idiosyncrasy. Selah Briggs, with her peculiar fiery soul and rebellious nature, found in both the Le Bretons something that seemed at once to satisfy her wants, to fulfil her desires, to saturate her affinities: and with Ronald, as with Herbert before, she was conscious of a certain awe and respect which was all the more pleasant to her because her untamed spirit had never felt anything like it with any other human being. She didn't understand them, and she didn't want to understand them: that constituted just the very charm of their whole personality to her peculiar fancy. All the other people she had ever met were as transparent as glass, for good or for evil; she could see through all their faults and virtues as easily as one sees through a window: the Le Bretons were to her inscrutable, novel, incomprehensible, inexplicable, and she prized them for their very inscrutability. And so it came to pass, that almost by a process of natural and imperceptible transference, she passed on at last to Ronald's account very much the same intensity of feeling that she had formerly felt towards his brother Herbert.

But at the same time, Selah never for a moment let him see it. She was too proud to confess now that she could ever love another man: the Mr. Walters she had once believed in had never, never, never existed: and she would raise no other idol in future to take the place of that vanished ideal. She was grateful to Ronald, and even fond of him: but that was all-outwardly at least. She never let him see, by word or act, that in her heart of hearts she was beginning to love him. And yet Ronald instinctively knew it. He himself could not have told you why; but he knew it. Even a woman cannot hide a secret from a man with that peculiarly penetrating intuitive temperament which belongs to sensitive, delicate types like Ronald Le Breton's.

One Sunday evening, when Selah had been spending a few hours at Edie's lodgings (Ronald always made it an excuse for finding them a supper, on the ground that Selah was really his guest, though he could not conveniently ask her to his own rooms), he walked home towards Notting Hill with Selah; and as they crossed the Regent's Park, he took the opportunity to say something to her that he had had upon his mind for a few weeks past, in some vague, indefinite, half-unconscious fashion.

'Selah,' he began, a little timidly, 'don't you think it's very probable we shan't have Ernest here much longer with us?'

'I'm afraid it is, Ronald,' Selah answered. She had got quite accustomed now to calling him Ronald. With such a poor, weak, sickly fellow as that, why really, after all, it did not much matter.

'Well, Selah,' Ronald went on, gravely, his eyes filling with tears as he spoke, 'in that case, you know, I can't think what's to become of poor Edie. It's a dreadful contingency to talk about, Selah, and I can't bear talking about it; but we MUST face these things, however terrible, mustn't we? and in this case one's absolutely bound to face it for poor Edie's sake as well as for Ernest's. Selah, she must have a home to go to, when dear Ernest's taken from us.'

'I'm very sorry for her, Ronald,' Selah answered, with unusual softness of manner, 'but I really don't see how a home can possibly be provided for her.'

'I do,' Ronald answered, more calmly; 'and for their sakes, Selah, I want you to help me in trying to provide it.'

'How?' Selah asked, looking up in his face curiously, as they passed into a ray of lamplight.

'Listen, Selah, and I'll tell you. Why, by marrying me.'

'Never?' Selah answered, firmly, and with a decided tinge of the old Adam in her trembling voice. 'Never, Ronald! Never, never, never!'

'Wait a minute, Selah,' Ronald pleaded, 'till you've heard the end of what I have to say to you. Consider that when dear Ernest's gone (oh! Selah, you must excuse me; it makes me cry so to think of it), there'll be nowhere on earth for poor little Edie and Dot to go to.'

'Did ever a man propose to a girl so extraordinarily in all this world,' Selah thought to herself, angrily. 'He actually expects me to marry him in order to provide a home for his precious sister-in-law. That's really carrying unselfishness a step too far, I call it.'

'Edie couldn't come and live with me, of course,' Ronald went on, quickly, 'if I were a bachelor; but if I were married, why then, naturally, she and Dot could come and live with us; and she could earn a little money somehow, no doubt; and, at any rate, it'd be better for her than starvation.'

Selah stopped a minute, and tapped the hard ground two or three times angrily with the point of her umbrella. 'And me, Ronald?' she said in a curious defiant voice. 'And ME? I suppose you've forgotten all about ME. You don't ask me to marry you because you love me; you don't ask me whether I love you or not; you only propose to me that I should quietly turn domestic housekeeper for Mrs. Ernest Le Breton. And for my part, I answer you plainly, once for all, that I'm not going to do it—no, never, never, never!'

She spoke haughtily, flashing her eyes at him in the fierce old fashion, and Ronald was almost frightened at the angry intensity of her contemptuous gestures. 'Selah,' he cried, trying to take her hand, which she tore away from him hurriedly: 'Selah, you misunderstand me. I only approached the subject that way because I didn't want to seem overweening and presumptuous. It's a very great piece of vanity, it seems to me, for any man to ask a woman whether she loves him. I'm too conscious of all my own faults and failings, Selah, to venture upon asking you ever to love me; but I do love you, Selah, I'm sure I do love you; and I hoped, I somehow fancied—it may have been mere fancy, but I DID imagine—that I detected, I can't say how, that you did really love me, too, just a very very little. Oh, Selah, it's because I really love you that I ask you whether you'll marry me, such as I am; I know I'm a poor sort of person to marry, but I ventured to hope you might love me just a little for all that.'

He looked so frail and gentle as he stood there pleading in the pale moonlight, that Selah could have taken him to her bosom then and there and fondled him as one would pet a sick child, for pure womanliness; but the devil in her blood kept her from doing it, and she answered haughtily, instead: 'Ronald, if you wanted to marry me, you ought to have asked me for my own sake. Now that you've asked me for another's, you can't expect me to give you an answer. Keep your money, my poor boy; you'll want it all for you and her hereafter; don't go sharing it and spending it on perfect strangers such as me. And don't go talking to me again about this business as long as your sister-in-law is unprovided for. I'm not going to take the bread out of her mouth, and I'm not going to marry a man who doesn't utterly and entirely love me.'

'But I do,' Ronald answered, earnestly; 'I do, Selah; I love you truly and faithfully from the very bottom of my heart.'

'Leave off, Roland,' Selah said in the same angry tone. 'If you ever talk to me of this again, I give you my word of honour about it, I'll never speak another word to you.'

And Ronald, who deeply respected the sanctity of a promise, were it only a threat, bided his time, and said no more about it for the present.

Next day, as Ronald sat reading in his own rooms, he was much surprised at hearing a well-known voice at the door, inquiring with some asperity whether Mr. Le Breton was at home. He listened to the voice in intense astonishment. It was his mother's.

'Ronald,' Lady Le Breton began, the moment she had been shown into his little sitting-room, 'I didn't think, after your undutiful, ungrateful conduct—with that abominable woman, too—that I should ever have come to see you, unless you came first, as you ought clearly to do, and begged my pardon penitently for your disgraceful behaviour. It's hard, I know, to acknowledge oneself in the wrong, but every Christian ought to be above vindictiveness and obstinate self-will; and I expect you, therefore, sooner or later, to come and ask forgiveness for your dreadful unkindness to me. Till then, as I said, I didn't expect to call upon you in any way. But I've felt compelled to-day to come and speak to you about a matter of duty, and as a matter of duty strictly I regard it, not as any relaxation of my just attitude of indignant expectancy towards yourself; no parent ought rightly to overlook such conduct as yours on the part of a son.' Ronald inclined his head respectfully. 'Well, what I've come to speak to you about to-day, Ronald, is about your poor misguided brother Ernest. He, too, as you know, has behaved very badly to me.'

'No,' Ronald answered stoutly, without further note or comment. Where the matter touched himself only he could maintain a decent silence, but where it touched poor dying Ernest he couldn't possibly restrain himself, even from a sense of filial obligation.

'Very badly to me,' Lady Le Breton went on sternly, without in any way noticing the brief interruption, 'and I can't, of course, go to see him either, especially not as I should by so doing expose myself to meeting the person whom he has chosen to make his wife. Still, as I hear that Ernest a in a very serious or even dangerous condition—'

'He's dying,' Ronald answered, the quick tears once more finding the easy road to his eyes as usual.

'I considered, as a mother, it was my duty to warn him to take a little thought about his soul.'

'His soul!' Ronald exclaimed in astonishment. 'Ernest's soul! Why, mother, dear Ernest has no need to look after his soul. He doesn't take that sordid, petty, limited view of our relations with eternity, and of our relations with the Infinite, which makes them all consist of the miserable, selfish, squalid desire to save our own poor personal little souls at all hazards. Ernest has something better and nobler to think of, I can assure you, than such a mere self-centred idea as that.'

'Ronald!' Lady Breton exclaimed, drawing herself up with much dignity; 'how on earth you, who have always pretended to be a religious person, can utter such a shocking and wicked sentiment as that, really passes my comprehension. What in the world is religion for, I should like to know, if it isn't to teach us how to save our own souls? But the particular thing I want to speak to you about is just this: couldn't you manage to induce Ernest to see the Archdeacon a little, and let the Archdeacon speak to him about his deplorable spiritual condition? I thought about you both so much at church yesterday, when the dear Archdeacon was preaching such a beautiful sermon; his text was like this, as far as I can remember it. "There is a way that seemeth right unto a man, but the end thereof are the ways of death." I couldn't help thinking all the time of my own two poor rebellious boys, and of the path that their misguided notions were leading them on. For I believe Ernest does really somehow persuade himself that he's in the right—it's inconceivable, but it's the fact; and I'm afraid the end thereof will be the ways of death; and then, as the dear Archdeacon said, "After death the judgment." Oh, Ronald, when I think of your poor dear brother Ernest's open unbelief, it makes me tremble for his future, so that I couldn't rest upon my bed until I'd been to see you and urged you to go and try to save him.'

'Mother,' Ronald said with that tone in which he was well accustomed to answering Lady Le Breton's religious harangues; 'I don't think you need feel any uneasiness whatever on dear Ernest's account, so far as all that's concerned. What does HE want with saving his soul, mother? "Whosoever will save his life shall lose it." Remember what is written: "Not every one that saith unto me, Lord, Lord, shall enter into the kingdom of heaven."'

'But, Ronald,' Lady Le Breton continued, half angrily, 'consider his unbelief, his dreadful opinions, his errors of doctrine! How on earth can we be happy about him when we think of those?'

'I don't think, Mother,' Ronald answered gently, 'that Infinite Justice and Infinite Love take much account of a man's opinions. They take account of his life and soul only, not of the correctness of his propositions in dogmatic theology; "Other sheep have I which are not of this fold—them also must I bring."'

'It seems to me, Ronald,' Lady Le Breton rejoined coldly, 'that you don't in the least care for whatever is most distinctive and characteristic in the whole of Christian doctrine. You talk so very very differently on religious subjects from that dear, good, excellent Archdeacon.'

CHAPTER XXXIII

A GLEAM OF SUNSHINE

Lady Hilda Tregellis rang the bell resolutely. 'I shall have no more nonsense about it,' she said to herself in her most decisive and determined manner. 'Whether mamma wishes it or not, I shall go and see them this very day without another word upon the subject.'

The servant answered the bell and stood waiting for his orders by the doorway.

'Harris, will you tell Jenkins at once that I shall want the carriage at half-past eleven?'

'Yes, my lady.'

'All right then. That'll do. Don't stand staring at me there like an image, but go this minute and do as I tell you.'

'Beg pardon, my lady, but her ladyship said she wanted the carriage herself at twelve puncshual.'

'She can't have it, then, Harris. That's all. Go and give my message to Jenkins at once, and I'll settle about the carriage with my lady myself.'

'She's the rummest young lady ever I come across,' the man murmured to himself in a dissatisfied fashion, as he went down the stairs again: 'but there, it's none of my business, thank goodness. The places and the people she does go and hunt up when she's got the fit on are truly ridic'lous: blest if she didn't acshally make Mr. Jenkins drive her down into Camberwell the other mornin', to see 'ow the poor lived, she said; as if it mattered tuppence to us in our circles of society 'ow the poor live. I wonder what little game she's up to now? Well, well, what the aristocracy is coming to in these days is more'n I can fathom, as sure as my name's William 'Arris.'

The little game that Lady Hilda was up to that morning was one that a gentleman in Mr. Harris's position was certainly hardly like to appreciate or sympathise with.

The evening before, she had met Arthur Berkeley once more at a small At Home, and had learned from him full particulars as to the dire straits into which the poor Le Bretons had finally fallen. Now, Hilda Tregellis was a kind-hearted girl at bottom, and when she heard all about it, she said at once to Arthur, 'I shall go and see them myself to-morrow, Mr. Berkeley, whether mamma allows me or not.'

'What good will it do?' Arthur had answered her quickly. 'You can't find work for poor Le Breton, can you? and of course if you can't do that you can be of no earthly use in any way to the poor creatures.'

'I don't know about that,' Hilda responded warmly. 'Sympathy's always something, isn't it, Mr. Berkeley? Nobody ought to know that better than you do. Besides, there's no saying when one may happen to turn up useful. Of course, I've never been of the slightest use to anybody in all my life, myself, I know, and I dare say I never shall be, but at least there's no harm in trying, is there? I'm on speaking terms with such an awful lot of people, all of them rich and many of them influential—Parliament, and Government offices, and all that sort of nonsense, you know—people who have no end of things to give away, and can't tell who on earth they'd better give them to, for fear of offending all the others, that I might

Grant Allen

possibly hear of something or other.'

'I'm afraid, Lady Hilda,' Berkeley answered smiling, 'none of those people would have anything to offer that could possibly be of the slightest use to poor Le Breton. If he's to be saved at all, he must be saved in his own time and by his own methods. For my own part, I don't see what conceivable chance of success in life there is left for him. You can't imagine a man like him making money and living comfortably. It's a tragedy—all the dramas of real life always ARE tragedies; but I'm terribly afraid there's no conceivable way out of it.'

Lady Hilda only looked at him with bold good humour. 'Nonsense,' she said bravely. 'All pure rubbishing pessimistic nonsense. (I hope pessimistic's the right word—it's a very good word, anyhow, even if it isn't in the proper place.) Well, I don't agree with you at all about this question, Mr. Berkeley. I'm very fond of Mr. Le Breton, really very fond of him; and I believe there's a corner somewhere for every man if only he can jog down properly into his own corner instead of being squeezed forcibly into somebody else's. The worst of it is, all the holes are round, and Mr. Le Breton's a square man, I allow: he wants all the angles cutting down off him.'

'But you can't cut them off; that's the very trouble,' Arthur answered, with just a faint rising suspicion that he was half jealous of the interest Hilda showed even in poor lonely Ernest Le Breton. Gracious heavens! could he be playing false at last to the long-cherished memory of little Miss Butterfly? could he be really beginning to fall just a little in love, after all, with this bold beautiful Lady Hilda Tregellis? He didn't know, and yet he somehow hardly liked himself to think it. And while Edie was still so poor too!

'No, you can't cut them off; I know that perfectly well,' Hilda rejoined quickly. 'I wouldn't care twopence for him if I thought you could. It's the angles that give him all his charming delicious originality. But you can look out a square hole for him somewhere, you know, and that of course would be a great deal better. Depend upon it, Mr. Berkeley, there are square holes up and down in the world, if only we knew where to look for them; and the mistake that everybody has made in poor Mr. Le Breton's case has been that instead of finding one to suit him, they've gone on trying to poke him down anyhow by main force into one of the round ones. That goes against the grain, you know; besides which I call it a clear waste of the very valuable solid mahogany corners.'

Arthur Berkeley looked at her silently for a moment, as if a gleam of light had burst suddenly in upon him. Then he said to her slowly and deliberately, 'Perhaps you're right, Lady Hilda, though I never thought of it quite in that light before. But one thing certainly strikes me now, and that is that you're a great deal cleverer after all than I ever thought you.'

Lady Hilda made a little mock curtsey. 'It's very good of you to say so,' she answered, half-saucily. 'Only the compliment is rather double-edged, you must confess, because it implies that up to now you've had a dreadfully low opinion of my poor little intelligence.'

So after that conversation Lady Hilda made up her mind that she would certainly go the very next day and call as soon as possible upon Edie Le Breton. Nobody could tell what good might possibly come of it; but at least there could come no harm. And so, when the carriage drew up it the door at half-past eleven, Hilda Tregellis stepped into it with a vague consciousness of an important mission, and ordered Jenkins to drive at once to the side street in Holloway, whose address Arthur Berkeley had last night given her. Jenkins touched his hat with mechanical respect, but inwardly wondered what the dickens my lady would think if only she came to know of these 'ere extrornary goin's on.

At the door of the lodgings Hilda alighted and rang the bell herself. Good Mrs. Halliss opened the door, and answered quickly that Mrs. Le Breton was at home. Her woman's eye detected at once the coronet on the carriage, and she was ready to burst with delight when the tall visitor handed her a card for Edie, bearing the name of Lady Hilda Tregellis. It was almost the first time that Edie had had any lady callers; certainly the first time she had had any of such social distinction; and Mrs. Halliss made haste to usher her up in due form, and then ran down hastily to communicate the good news to honest John, who in his capacity of past coachman was already gazing out of the area window with deep interest at the carriage and horses.

'There, John dear,' she cried, with tears of joy in her eyes, forgetting in her excitement to drat the man for not being in the back kitchen, 'to think that we should see a carriage an' pair like that there a-drawin' up in front of out own very 'ouse, and Lady 'Ilder Tergellis, or summat o' the sort, a-comin' 'ere to see that dear little lady in the parlour, why, it's enough to make one's 'eart burst, nearly, just you see now if it reelly isn't. You could a' knocked me down with a feather, a'most, when that there Lady 'Ilder 'anded me 'er curd, and asked so sweet-like if Mrs. Le Breting was at 'ome. Mr. Le Breting's people is comin' round, you may be sure of it; 'is mother's a lady of title, that much we know for certing; and she wouldn't go and let 'er own flesh an' blood die 'ere of downright poverty, as they're like to do and won't let us 'elp it, pore dears, without sendin' round to inquire and assist 'em. Married against 'er will, I understand, from what that dear Mr. Berkeley, bless 'is kind 'eart, do tell me; not as I can believe 'e married beneath 'im, no, not no ways; for a sweeter, dearer, nicer little lady than our Mrs. Le Breting I never did, an' that I tell you. Sweeter manners you never did see yourself, John, for all you've lived among the aristocracy: an' I always knew 'is people 'ud come round at last, and do what was right by 'im. An' you may depend upon it, John, this 'ere Lady 'Ilder's one of his relations, an' she's come round on a message from Lady Le Breting, to begin a reconciliation. And though we should be sorry to lose 'em, as 'as stood by 'em through all their troubles, I'm glad to 'ear it, John, that I am, for I can't a-bear to see that dear young fellow a-eatin' 'is life out with care and anxiety.' And Mrs. Halliss, who had always felt convinced in her own mind that Ernest must really be the unacknowledged heir to a splendid fortune, began to wipe her eyes violently in her delight at this evident realisation of her wildest fancies and wishes.

Meanwhile, upstairs in the little parlour, Edie had risen in some trepidation as Mrs. Halliss placed in her hands Lady Hilda Tregellis's card. Ernest was out, gone to walk feebly around the streets of Holloway, and she hardly knew at first what to say to so unexpected a visitor. But Lady Hilda put her almost at her ease at once by coming up to her with both her arms outstretched, as to an old friend, and saying, with one of her pleasantest smiles:

'You must forgive me, Mrs. Le Breton, for never having come to call on you before; but I have been long meaning to, and doubting whether you would care to see me or not. You know, I'm a very old friend of your husband's—he was SO kind to me always when he was down at our place in dear old Devonshire. (You're a Devonshire girl yourself, aren't you? just as I am. I thought so. I'm so glad of it. I always get on so well with the dear old Devonshire folk.) Well, I've been meaning to come for ever so long, and putting it off, and putting it off, and putting it off, as one WILL put things off, you know, when you're not quite sure about them, until last evening. And then our friend, Mr. Arthur Berkeley, who knows everybody, talked to me about your husband and you, and told me he thought you wouldn't mind my coming to see you, for he fancied you hadn't much society up here that you cared for or sympathised with: though, of course, I'm dreadfully afraid of coming to call upon you, because I know you're the sister of that very clever Mr. Oswald, whose sad death we were all so sorry to hear about in the papers; and naturally, as you've lived so much with him and with Mr. Le Breton, you must be so awfully learned and all that sort of thing, and no doubt despise ignorant people like myself dreadfully. But you really mustn't despise me, Mrs. Le Breton, because, you see, I haven't had all the advantages that you've had; indeed, the only clever people I've ever met in all my life are your husband and Mr. Arthur Berkeley, except, of course, Cabinet ministers and so forth, and they don't count, because they're political, and so very old, and solemn, and grand, and won't take any notice of us girls, except to sit upon us. So that's what's made me rather afraid to call upon you, because I thought you'd be quite too much in the higher education way for a girl like me; and I haven't got any education at all, except in rubbish, as your husband used always to tell me. And now I want you to tell me all about Mr. Le Breton, and the baby—Dot, you call her, Mr. Berkeley told me—and yourself, too; for, though I've never seen you before, I feel, of course, like an old friend of the family, having known your husband so very intimately.'

Lady Hilda designedly delivered all this long harangue straight off without a break, in her go-ahead, breathless, voluble fashion, because she felt sure Edie wouldn't feel perfectly at her ease at first, and she wanted to give her time to recover from the first foolish awe of that meaningless prefix, Lady. Moreover, Lady Hilda, in spite of her offhand manner was a good psychologist, and a true woman: and she had concocted her little speech on the spur of the moment with some cleverness, so as just to suit her instinctive reading of Edie's small personal peculiarities. She saw in a moment that that slight, pale, delicate girl was lost in London, far from her own home and surroundings; and that the passing allusion to their common Devonshire origin would please and conciliate her, as it always does with the clannish, warm-hearted, simple-minded West Country folk. Then again, the deft hints as to their friendship with Arthur Berkeley, as to Ernest's stay at Dunbude, and as to her own fear lest Edie should be too learned for her, all tended to bring out whatever points of interest they had together: while the casual touch about poor Harry's reputation, and the final mention of little Dot by name, completed the conquest of Edie's simple, gentle little woman's heart. So this was the great Lady Hilda Tregellis, she thought, of whom she had heard so much, and whom she had dreaded so greatly as a grand rival! Why, after all, she was exactly like any other Devonshire girl in Calcombe Pomeroy, except, perhaps, that she was easier to get on with, and smiled a great deal more pleasantly than ten out of a dozen.

'It's very kind indeed of you to come,' Edie answered, smiling back as well as she was able the first moment that Lady Hilda allowed her a chance to edge in a word sideways. 'Ernest will be so very very sorry that he's missed you when he comes in. He's spoken to me a great deal about you ever so many times.'

'No, has he really?' Lady Hilda asked quickly, with unmistakable interest and pleasure. 'Well, now, I'm so glad of that, for to tell you the truth, Mrs. Le Breton, though he was really always very kind to me, and so patient with all my stupidity, I more than half fancied he didn't exactly like me. In fact, I was dreadfully afraid he thought me a perfect nuisance. I'm so sorry he isn't in, because the truth is, I came partly to see him as well as to see you, and I should be awfully disappointed if I had to miss him. Where's he gone, if I may ask? Perhaps I may be able to wait and see him.'

'Oh, he's only out walking somewhere—ur—somewhere about Holloway,' Edie answered, half blushing at the nature of their neighbourhood, and glancing round the little room to see how it was likely to strike so grand a person as Lady Hilda Tregellis.

Hilda noticed the glance, and made as if she did not notice it. Her heart had begun to warm at once to this poor, pale, eager-looking little woman, who had had the doubtful happiness of winning Ernest Le Breton's love. 'Then I shall certainly wait and see him, Mrs. Le Breton.' she said cordially. 'What a dear cosy little room you've got here, to be sure. I do so love those nice bright little cottage parlours, with their pretty pots of flowers and cheerful furniture—so much warmer and more comfortable, you know, than the great dreary empty barns that most people go and do penance by living in. If ever I marry— which I don't suppose I ever shall do, for nobody'll have me, I'm sorry to say: at least, nobody but stupid people in the peerage, Algies and Berties and Monties I always call them— well, if I ever do marry, I shall have a cosy little house just like this one, with no unnecessary space to walk over every time you come in or out, and with a chance of keeping yourself warm without having to crone over the fire in order to get safely out of the horrid draughts. And Dot, now let me see, how old is she by this time? I ought to remember, I'm sure, for Mr. Berkeley told me all about her at the time; and I said should I write and ask if I might stand as godmother; and Mr. Berkeley laughed at me, and said what could I be dreaming of, and did I think you were going to make your baby liable to fine and imprisonment if it ever published works hereafter on philosophy or something of the sort. So delightfully original of all of you, really.'

Once started on that fertile theme of female conversation, Edie and Hilda got on well enough in all conscience to satisfy the most exacting mind. Dot was duly brought in and exhibited by Mrs. Halliss; and was pronounced to be the very sweetest, dearest, darlingest little duck ever seen on earth since the beginning of all things. Her various points of likeness to all her relations were duly discussed; and Hilda took particular pains to observe that she didn't in the very faintest degree resemble that old horror, Lady Le Breton. Then her whole past history was fully related, she had been fed on, and what illnesses she had had, and how many teeth she had got, and all the other delightful nothings so perennially interesting to the maternal heart. Hilda listened to the whole account with unfeigned attention, and begged leave to be allowed to dance Dot in her own strong arms, and tickled her fat cheek with her slender forefinger, and laughed with genuine delight when the baby smiled again at her and turned her face to be tickled a second time. Gradually Hilda brought the conversation round to Ernest's journalistic experiences, and at last she said very quietly, 'I'm sorry to learn from Mr. Berkeley, dear, that your husband doesn't get quite as much work to do as he would like to have.'

Edie's tender eyes filled at once with swimming tears. That one word 'dear,' said so naturally and simply, touched her heart at once with its genuine half unspoken sympathy. 'Oh, Lady Hilda,' she answered falteringly, 'please don't make me talk about that. We are so very, very, very poor. I can't bear to talk about it to you. Please, please don't make me.'

Hilda looked at her with the moisture welling up in her own eyes too, and said softly, 'I'm SO sorry: dear, dear little Mrs. Le Breton, I'm so very, very, very sorry for you! from the bottom of my heart I'm sorry for you.'

'It isn't for myself, you know,' Edie answered quickly: 'for myself, of course, I could stand anything; but it's the trouble and privations for darling Ernest. Oh, Lady Hilda, I can't bear to say it, but he's dying, he's dying.'

Hilda took the pretty small hand affectionately in hers. 'Don't, dear, don't,' she said, brushing away a tear from her own eyes at the same time. 'He isn't, believe me, he isn't. And don't call me by that horrid stiff name, dear, please don't. Call me Hilda. I should be so pleased and flattered if you would call me Hilda. And may I call you Edie? I know your husband calls you Edie, because Mr. Ronald Le Breton told me so. I want to be a friend of yours; and I feel sure, if only you will let me, that we might be very good and helpful friends indeed together.'

Edie pressed her hand softly. How very different from the imaginary Lady Hilda she had. pictured to herself in her timid, girlish fancy! How much even dear Ernest had been mistaken as to what there was of womanly really in her. 'Oh, don't speak so kindly to me,' she said imploringly; 'don't speak so kindly, or else you'll make me cry. I can't bear to hear you speak so kindly.'

'Cry, dear,' Lady Hilda whispered in a gentle tone, kissing her forehead delicately as she spoke: 'cry and relieve yourself. There'a nothing gives one so much comfort when one's heart is bursting as a regular good downright cry.' And, suiting the action to the word, forthwith Lady Hilda laid her own statu-esque head down beside Edie's, and so those two weeping women, rivals once in a vague way, and now bound to one another by a new-found tie, mingled their tears silently together for ten minutes in unuttered sympathy.

As they sat there, both tearful and speechless, with Lady Hilda soothing Edie's wan hand tenderly in hers, and leaning above her, and stroking her hair softly with a sister's fondness, the door opened very quietly, and Arthur Berkeley stood for a moment pausing in the passage, and looking in without a word upon the unexpected sight that greeted his wondering vision. He had come to call upon Ernest about some possible opening for a new writer on a paper lately started; and hearing the sound of sobs within had opened the door quietly and tentatively. He could hardly believe his own eyes when he actually saw Lady Hilda Tregellis sitting there side by side with Edie Le Breton, kissing her pale forehead a dozen times in a minute, and crying over her like a child with unwonted tears of unmistakable sympathy. For ten seconds Arthur held the door ajar in his hands, and gazed silently with the awe of chivalrous respect upon the tearful, beautiful picture. Then he shut the door again noiselessly and unperceived, and stole softly out into the street to wait alone for Ernest's return. It was not for him to intrude his unbidden presence upon the sacred sorrow of those two weeping sister-women.

He lighted a cigar outside, and walked up and down a neighbouring street feverishly till he thought it likely the call would be finished. 'Dear little Mrs. Le Breton,' he said to himself softly, 'dear little Miss Butterfly of the days that are dead; softened and sweetened still more by suffering, with the beauty of holiness glowing in your face, how I wish some good for you could unexpectedly come out of this curious visit. Though I don't see how it's possible: I don't see how it's possible. The stream carries us all down unresistingly before its senseless flood, and sweeps us at last, sooner or later, like helpless logs, into the unknown sea. Poor Ernest is drifting fast thitherwards before the current, and nothing on earth, it seems to me, can conceivably stop him!'

He paced up and down a little, with a quick, unsteady tread, and took a puff or two again at his cigar abstractedly. Then he held it thoughtfully between his fingers for a while and began to hum a few bars from his own new opera then in course of composition—a stately long-drawn air, it was. something like the rustle of Hilda Tregellis's satin train as she swept queenlike down the broad marble staircase of some great Elizabethan country palace. 'And dear Lady Hilda too,' he went on, musingly: 'dear, kind, sympathising Lady Hilda. Who on earth would ever have thought she had it in her to comfort that poor, weeping, sorrowing girl as I just now saw her doing? Dear Lady Hilda! Kind Lady Hilda! I have undervalued you and overlooked you, because of the mere accident of your titled birth, but I could have kissed you myself, for pure gratitude, that very minute, Hilda Tregellis, when I saw you stooping down and kissing that dear white forehead that looked so pale and womanly and beautiful. Yes, Hilda, I could have kissed you. I could have kissed your own grand, smooth, white marble forehead. And no very great trial of endurance, either, Arthur Berkeley, if it comes to that; for say what you will of her, she's a beautiful, stately, queenlike woman indeed; and it somehow strikes me she's a truer and better woman, too, than you have ever yet in your shallow superficiality imagined. Not like little Miss Butterfly! Oh, no, not like little Miss Butterfly! But still, there are keys and keys in music; and if every tune was pitched to the self-same key, even the tenderest, what a monotonous, dreary world it would be to live and sing in after all. Perhaps a man might make himself a little shrine not wholly without sweet savour of pure incense for beautiful, stately, queenlike Hilda Tregellis too! But no; I mustn't think of it. I have no other duty or prospect in life possible as yet while dear little Miss Butterfly still remains practically unprovided for!'

CHAPTER XXXIV

HOPE

From Edie Le Breton's lodgings, Hilda Tregellis drove straight, without stopping all the way, to Arthur Berkeley's house at Chelsea; for Arthur had long since risen to the dignity of an enfranchised householder, and had bought himself a pretty cottage near the Embankment, with room enough for himself and the Progenitor, and even for any possible future domestic contingency in the way of wife and children. It was a very unconventional thing for her to do, no doubt; but Lady Hilda was certainly not the person to be deterred from doing anything she contemplated on the bare ground of its extreme unconventionally; and so far was she from objecting personally to her visit on this score, that before she rang the Berkeleys' bell she looked quietly at her little bijou watch, and said with a bland smile to the suspicious Mr. Jenkins, 'Let me see, Jenkins; it's one o'clock. I shall lunch with my friends here this morning; so you may take the carriage home now for my lady, and I shall cab it back, or come round by Metropolitan.' Jenkins was too much accustcmed to Lady Hilda's unaccountable vagaries to express any surprise at her wildest resolutions, even if she had proposed to go home on a costermonger's barrow; so he only touched his hat respectfully, in his marionette fashion, and drove away at once without further colloquy.

'Is Mr. Berkeley at home?' Hilda asked of the pretty servant girl who opened the door to her, mentally taking note at the same time that Arthur's aesthetic tendencies evidently extended even to his human surroundings.

'Which Mr. Berkeley?' the girl asked in reply. 'Mr. Berkeley senerer, 'e's at 'ome, but Mr. Arthur, 'e's gone up this mornin' to 'Olloway.'

Hilda seized with avidity upon this unexpected and almost providential opening. 'No, is he?' she said, delighted. 'Then I'll go in and see Mr. Berkeley senior. No card, thank you: no name: tell him merely a lady would like to see him. I dare say Mr. Arthur'll be back before long from Holloway.'

The girl hesitated a moment as if in doubt, and surveyed Lady Hilda from head to foot. Hilda, whose eyes were still red from crying, couldn't help laughing outright at the obvious cause of the girl's hesitation. 'Do as I tell you,' she said in her imperious way. 'Who on earth do you take me for, my good girl? That's my card, see: but you needn't give it to Mr. Berkeley senior. Now go and tell him at once that a lady is waiting to see him.'

The innate respect of the English working classes for the kind of nobility that is supposed to be represented by the British peerage made the girl drop an instinctive curtsey as she looked at the card, and answer in a voice of hushed surprise, 'Yes, my lady.' She had heard Lady Hilda Tregellis spoken of more than once at her master's table, and she knew, of course, that so great a personage as that could do no wrong. So she merely ushered her visitor at once into Arthur Berkeley's beautiful little study, with its delicate grey pomegranate wall paper and its exquisite unpolished oak fittings, and said simply, in an overawed manner, 'A lady wishes to speak to you, sir.'

The old shoemaker looked up from the English translation of Ribot's 'Psychologie Anglaise Contemporaine,' with whose intricacies he was manfully struggling, and rose with native politeness to welcome Hilda.

'Good morning,' Hilda said, extending her hand to him with one of her beaming disarming smiles, and annihilating all that was most obtrusively democratic in him at once by her pleasant manner. 'I'm a friend of your son's, Mr. Berkeley, and I've come here to see him about very particular private business—in short, on an errand of charity. Will he be long gone, do you know?'

'Not very,' the Progenitor answered, in a somewhat embarrassed manner, surveying her curiously. 'At least, I should think not. He's gone to Holloway for an hour or two, but I fancy he'll be back for two o'clock luncheon, Miss—ur, I don't think I caught your name, did I?'

'To Holloway,' Hilda echoed, taking no notice of his suggested query. 'Oh, then he's gone to see the poor dear Le Bretons, of course. Why, that's just what I wanted to see him about. If you'll allow me then, I'll just stop and have lunch with you.'

'The dickens you will,' the Progenitor thought to himself in speechless astonishment. 'That's really awfully cool of you. However, I dare say it's usual to invite oneself in the state of life that that boy Artie has gone and hoisted himself into, most unnaturally. A fine lady, no doubt, of their modern pattern; but in my day, up in Paddington, we should have called her a brazen hussey.—Certainly, if you will,' he added aloud. 'If you've come on any errand that will do any good to the Le Bretons, I'm sure my son'll be delighted to see you. He's greatly grieved at their unhappy condition.'

'I'm afraid I've nothing much to suggest of any very practical sort,' Hilda answered, with a slight sigh; 'but at least I should like to talk with him about the matter. Something must be done for these two poor young people, you know, Mr. Berkeley. Something must really be done to help them.'

'Then you're interested in them, Miss—ur—ur—ah, yes—are you?'

'Look at my eyes,' Hilda said plumply. 'Are they very red, Mr. Berkeley?'

'Well....ur...yes, if I may venture to say so to a lady,' the old shoemaker answered hesitatingly, with unwonted gallantry. 'I should say they were a trifle, ur, just a trifle roseate, you know.'

'Quite so,' Hilda went on, seriously. 'That's it. They're red with crying. I've been crying like a baby all the morning with that poor, dear, sweet little angel of a Mrs. Le Breton.'

'Then you're a great friend of hers, I suppose,' the Progenitor suggested mildly.

'Never set eyes on her in my life before this morning, on the contrary,' Hilda continued in her garrulous fashion. 'But, oh, Mr. Berkeley, if you'd only seen that dear little woman, crying as if her heart would break, and telling me that dear Ernest was dying, actually dying; why—there—excuse me—I can't help it, you know; we women are always crying about something or other, aren't we?'

The old man laid his hand on hers quietly. 'Don't mind ME, my dear,' he said with genuine tenderness. 'Don't mind me a bit; I'm only an old shoemaker, as I dare say you've heard before now; but I know you'll be the better for crying—women always are—and tears shed on somebody else's account are never thrown away, my dear, are they?'

Hilda took his hand between hers, and wiping her eyes once more whispered softly, 'No, Mr. Berkeley, no; perhaps they're not; but oh, they're so useless; so very, very, very useless. Do you know, I never felt my own powerlessness and helplessness in all my life so much as I did at that dear, patient little Mrs. Le Breton's this very morning. There I sat, knowing she was in dire need of money for her poor husband, and wanting sufficient food and drink, perhaps, for herself, and him, and the dear darling baby; and in my hand in my muff I had my purse there with five tenners—Bank of England ten-pound uotes, you know—fifty pounds altogether, rolled up inside it; and I would have given anything if only I could have pulled them out and made them a present to her then and there; and

I couldn't, you see: and, oh, Mr. Berkeley, isn't it terrible to look at them? And then, before I left, poor Mr. Le Breton himself came in, and I was quite shocked to see him. I used to know him a few years ago, and even then he wasn't what you'd call robust by any means; but now, oh, dear me, he does look so awfully ill and haggard and miserable that it quite made me break down again, and I cried about him before his very face; and the moment I got away, I said to the coachman, "Jenkins, drive straight off to the Embankment at Chelsea;" and here I am, you see, waiting to talk with your clever son about it; for, really, Mr. Berkeley, the poor Le Bretons haven't got a single friend anywhere like your son Arthur.'

And then Lady Hilda went on to praise Arthur's music to the Progenitor, and to speak of how much admired he was everywhere, and to hint that so much genius and musical power must of course be largely hereditary. Whereat the old man, not unmoved by her gentle insinuating flattery, at last confessed to his own lifelong musical tastes, and even casually acknowledged that the motive for one or two of the minor songs in the famous operas was not entirely of Arthur's own unaided invention. And so, from one subject to another, they passed on so quickly, and hit it off with one another so exactly (for Hilda had a wonderful knack of leading up to everybody's strong points), that long before lunch was ready, the Progenitor had been quite won over by the fascinations of the brazen hussey, and was prepared to admit that she was really a very nice, kind, tender-hearted, intelligent, appreciative, and discriminating young lady. True, she had not read Mill or Fawcett, and was ignorant of the very name of Herbert Spencer; but she had a vast admiration for his dear boy Artie, and she saw that he himself knew a thing or two in his own modest way, though he was only what the grand world she moved in would doubtless call an old superannuated journeyman shoemaker.

'Ah, yes, a shoemaker! so I've heard somewhere, I fancy,' Lady Hilda remarked brightly, when for the third time in the course of their conversation he informed her with great dignity of the interesting fact; 'how very delightful and charming that is, really, now isn't it? So original, you know, to make shoes instead of going into some useless profession, especially when you're such a great reader and student and thinker as you are—for I see you're a philosopher and a psychologist already, Mr. Berkeley'—Hilda considered it rather a bold effort on her part to pronounce the word 'psychologist' at the very first trial without stumbling; but though she was a little doubtful about the exact pronunciation of that fearful vocable, she felt quite at her ease about the fact at least, because she carefully noticed him lay down Ribot on the table beside him, name upward; 'one can't help finding that much out on a very short acquaintance, can one? Though, indeed, now I come to think of it, I believe I've heard often that men of your calling generally ARE very fond of reading, and are very philosophical, and clever, and political, and all that sort of thing; and they say that's the reason, of course, why Northampton's such an exceptionally intelligent constituency, and always returns such thorough-going able logical Radicals.'

The old man's eyes beamed, as she spoke, with inexpressible pride and pleasure. 'I'm very glad indeed to hear you say so,' he answered promptly with a complacent self-satisfied smile, 'and I believe you're right too, Miss, ur—ur—ur—quite so. The practice of shoemaking undoubtedly tends to develop a very high and exceptional level of general intelligence and logical power.'

'I'm sure of it,' Hilda answered demurely, in a tone of the deepest and sincerest conviction; 'and when I heard somebody say somewhere, that your son was...—well, WAS your son, I said to myself at once, "Ah, well, there now, that quite accounts, of course, for young Mr. Berkeley's very extraordinary and unusual abilities!"'

'She's really a most sensible, well-informed young woman, whoever she is,' the Progenitor thought to himself silently; 'and it's certainly a pity that dear Artie couldn't take a fancy to some nice, appreciative, kind-hearted, practical girl like that now, instead of wearing away all the best days of his life in useless regret for that poor slender, unsubstantial nonentity of a watery little Mrs. Le Breton.'

By two o'clock lunch was ready, and just as it had been announced, Arthur Berkeley ran up the front steps, and let himself in with his proprietory latch-key. Turning straight into the dining-room, he was just in time to see his own father walking into lunch arm in arm with Lady Hilda Tregellis. As Mrs. Hallis had graphically expressed it, he felt as if you might have knocked him down with a feather! Was she absolutely ubiquitous, then, this pervasive Lady Hilda? and was he destined wherever he went to come upon her suddenly in the most unexpected and incomprehensible situations?

'Will you sit down here, my dear,' the Progenitor was saying to Hilda at the exact moment he entered, 'or would you prefer your back to the fire?'

Arthur Berkeley opened his eyes wide with unspeakable amazement. 'What, YOU here,' he exclaimed, coming forward suddenly to shake hands with Hilda; 'why, I saw you only a couple of hours since at the Le Bretons' at Holloway.'

'You did!' Hilda cried with almost equal astonishment, 'Why, how was that? I never saw YOU.'

Arthur sighed quietly. 'No,' he answered, with a curious look at the Progenitor; 'you were engaged when I opened the door, and I didn't like to disturb you. You were—you were speaking with poor little Mrs. Le Breton. But I'm so much obliged to you for your kindness to them, Lady Hilda; so very much obliged to you for your great kindness to them.'

It was the Progenitor's turn now to start in surprise. 'What! Lady Hilda!' he cried with a bewildered look. 'Lady Hilda! Did I hear you say "Lady Hilda"? Is this Lady Hilda Tregellis, then, that I've heard you talk about so often, Artie?'

'Why, of course, Father. You didn't know who it was, then,

didn't you? Lady Hilda, I'm afraid you've been stealing a march upon the poor unsuspecting hostile Progenitor.'

'Not quite that, Mr. Berkeley,' Hilda replied, laughing; 'only after the very truculent character I had heard of your father as a regular red-hot militant Radical, I thought I'd better not send in my name to him at once for fear it might prejudice him against me before first acquaintance.'

The Progenitor looked at her steadfastly from head to foot, standing before him there in her queenly beauty, as if she were some strange wild beast that he had been requested to inspect and report upon for a scientific purpose. 'Lady Hilda Tregellis!' he said slowly and deliberately; 'Lady Hilda Tregellis! So this is Lady Hilda Tregellis, is it? Well, all I can say is this, then, that as far as I can judge her, Lady Hilda Tregellis is a very sensible, modest, intelligent, well-conducted young woman, which is more than I could possibly have expected from a person of her unfortunate and distressing hereditary antecedents. But you know, my dear, it was a very mean trick of you to go and take an old man's heart by guile and stratagem in that way!'

Hilda laughed a little uneasily. The Progenitor's manner was perhaps a trifle too open and unconventional even for her. 'It wasn't for that I came, Mr. Berkeley,' she said again with one of her sunny smiles, which brought the Progenitor metaphorically to her feet again, 'but to talk over this matter of the poor Le Bretons with your son. Oh, Mr. Arthur, something must really be done to help them. I know you say there's nothing to be done; but there must be; we must find it out; we must invent it; we must compel it. When I sat there this morning with that dear little woman and saw her breaking her full heart over her husband's trouble, I said to myself, somehow, Hilda Tregellis, if you can't find a way out of this, you're not worth your salt in this world, and you'd better make haste and take a rapid through-ticket at once to the next, if there is one.'

'Which is more than doubtful, really,' the Progenitor muttered softly half under his breath; 'which, as Strauss has conclusively shown, is certainly a good deal more than doubtful.'

Arthur took no notice of the interruption, but merely answered imploringly, with a despairing gesture of his hands, 'What are we to do, Lady Hilda? What can we possibly do?'

'Why, sit down and have some lunch first,' Hilda rejoined with practical common-sense, 'and then talk it over rationally afterwards, instead of wringing our hands helplessly like a pair of Frenchmen in a street difficulty.' (Hilda had a fine old crusted English contempt, by the way, for those vastly inferior and foolish creatures known as foreigners.)

Thus adjured, Berkeley sat down promptly, and they proceeded to take counsel together in this hard matter over the cutlets and claret provided before them. 'Ernest and Mrs. Le Breton told me all about your visit,' Arthur went on, soon after; 'and they're so much obliged to you for having taken the trouble to look them up in their sore distress. Do you know, Lady Hilda, I think you've quite made a conquest of our dear little friend, Mrs. Le Breton.'

'I don't know about that,' Hilda responded with a smile, 'but I'm sure, at any rate, that the sweet little woman quite made a conquest of me, Mr. Berkeley. In fact, I can't say what you think, but for my part I'm determined an effort must be made one way or another to save them.'

'It's no use,' Arthur answered, shaking his head sadly; 'it can't be done. There's nothing for it but to let them float down helplessly with the tide, wherever it may bear them.'

'Stuff and nonsense,' Hilda replied energetically. 'All rubbish, utter rubbish, and if I were a man as you are, Mr. Berkeley, I should be ashamed to take such a desponding view of the situation. If we say it's got to be done, it will be done, and that's an end of it. Work must and can be found for him somehow or somewhere.'

'But the man's dying,' Arthur interrupted with a vehement gesture. 'There's no more work left in him. The only thing that's any use is to send him off to Madeira, or Egypt, or Catania, or somewhere of that sort, and let him die quietly among the palms and cactuses and aloes. That's Sir Antony Wraxall's opinion, and surely nobody in London can know half as well as he does about the matter.'

'Sir Antony's a fool,' Hilda responded with refreshing bluntness. 'He knows nothing on earth at all about it. He's accustomed to prescribing for a lot of us idle good-for-nothing rich people'—('Very true,' the Progenitor assented parenthetically;) 'and he's got into a fixed habit of prescribing a Nile voyage, just as he's got into a fixed habit of prescribing old wine, and carriage exercise, and ten thousand a year to all his patients. What Mr. Le Breton really wants is not Egypt, or old wine, or Sir Antony, or anything of the sort, but relief from this pressing load of anxiety and responsibility. Put him in my hands for six months, and I'll back myself at a hundred to six against Sir Antony to cure him for a monkey.'

'For a what!' the Progenitor asked with a puzzled expression of countenance.

'Back myself for a monkey, you know,' Hilda answered, without perceiving the cause of the old man's innocent confusion.

The Progenitor was evidently none the wiser still for Hilda's answer, though he forbore to pursue the subject any farther, lest he should betray his obvious ignorance of aristocratic manners and dialect.

But Arthur looked up at Lady Hilda with something like the gleam of a new-born hope on his distressed features. 'Lady Hilda,' he said almost cheerfully, 'you really speak as if you had some practicable plan actually in prospect. It seems to me, if anybody can pull them through, you can, because you've got such a grand reserve of faith and energy. What is it, now, you think of doing?'

'Well,' Hilda answered, taken a little aback at this practical question, 'I've hardly got my plan matured yet; but I've got a plan; and I thought it all out as far as it went as I came along here just now in the carriage. The great thing is, we must inspire Mr. Le Breton with a new confidence; we must begin by showing him we believe in him, and letting him see that he may still manage in some way or other to retrieve himself. He has lost all hope: we must begin with him over again. I've got an idea, but it'll take money. Now, I can give up half my allowance for the next year—the Le Bretons need never know anything about it—that'll be something: you're a rich man now, I believe, Mr. Berkeley; will you make up as much as I do, if my plan seems a feasible one to you for retrieving the position?'

The Progenitor answered quickly for him: 'Miss Tregellis,' he said, with a little tremor in his voice, '—you'll excuse me, my dear, but it's against my principles to call anybody my lady:— he will, I know he will; and if he wouldn't, why, my dear, I'd go back to my cobbling and earn it myself rather than that you or your friends should go without it for a single minute.'

Arthur said nothing, but he bowed his head silently. What a lot of good there was really in that splendid woman, and what a commanding, energetic, masterful way she had about her! To a feckless, undecided, faltering man like Arthur Berkeley there was something wonderfully attractive and magnificent, after all, in such an imperious resolute woman as Lady Hilda.

'Then this is my plan,' Hilda went on hastily. 'We must do something that'll take Mr. Le Breton out of himself for a short time entirely—that'll give him occupation of a kind he thinks right, and at the same time put money in his pocket. Now, he's always talking about this socialistic business of his; but why doesn't he tell us what he has actually seen about the life and habits of the really poor? Mrs. Le Breton tells me he knows the East End well: why doesn't he sit down and give us a good rattling, rousing, frightening description of all that's in it? Of course, I don't care twopence about the poor myself—not in the lump, I mean—I beg your pardon, Mr. Berkeley,'—for the Progenitor gave a start of surprise and astonishment—'you know we women are nothing if not concrete; we never care for anything in the abstract, Mr. Le Breton used to tell me; we want the particular case brought home to our sympathies before we can interest ourselves about it. After all, even YOU who are men don't feel very much for all the miserable wretched people there are in China, you know; they're too far away for even you to bother your heads about. But I DO care about the Le Bretons, and it strikes me we might help them a little in this way. I know a lot of artists, Mr. Berkeley; and I know one who I think would just do for the very work I want to set him. (He's poor, too, by the way, and I don't mind giving him a lift at the same time and killing two birds with one stone.) Very well, then; I go to him, and say, "Mr. Verney," I say,—there now, I didn't mean to tell you his name, but no matter; "Mr. Verney," I shall say, "a friend of mine in the writing line is going to pay some visits to the very poor quarters in the East End, and write about it, which will make a great noise in the world as sure as midday."'

'But how do you know it will?' asked the Progenitor, simply.

Hilda turned round upon him with an unfeigned look of startled astonishment. 'How do I know it will?' she said confidently. 'Why, because I mean it to, Mr. Berkeley. Because I say it shall. Because I choose to make it. Two Cabinet ministers shall quote it in the House, and a duke shall write letters to the "Times" denouncing it as an intensely wicked and revolutionary publication. If I choose to float it, I WILL float it.—Well, "Mr. Verney," I say for example, "will you undertake to accompany him and make sketches? It'll be unpleasant work, I know, because I've been there myself to see, and the places don't smell nice at all—worse than Genoa or the old town at Nice even, I can tell you: but it'll make you a name; and in any case the publisher who's getting it up'll pay you well for it." Of course, Mr. Verney says "Yes." Then we go on to Mr. Le

Grant Allen

Breton and say, "A young artist of my acquaintance is making a pilgrimage into the East End to see for himself how the people live, and to make pictures of them to stir up the sluggish consciences of the lazy aristocrats"—that's me and my people, of course: that'll be the way to work it. Play upon Mr. Le Breton's tenderest feelings. Make him feel he's fighting for the Cause; and he'll be ready to throw himself, heart and soul, into the spirit of the project. I don't care twopence about the Cause myself, of course, so that's flat, and I don't pretend to, either, Mr. Berkeley; but I care a great deal for the misery of that poor, dear, pale little woman, sitting there with me this morning and regularly sobbing her heart out; and if I can do anything to help her, why, I shall be only too delighted.'

'Le Breton's a well-meaning young fellow, certainly,' the Progenitor murmured gently in a voice of graceful concession; 'and I believe his heart's really in the Cause, as you call it; but you know, my dear, he's very far from being sound in his economical views as to the relations of capital and labour. Far from sound, as John Stuart Mill would have judged the question, I can solemnly assure you.'

'Very well,' Hilda went on, almost without noticing the interruption. 'We shall say to him, or rather we shall get our publisher to say to him, that as he's interested in the matter, and knows the East End well, he has been selected—shall we put it on somebody's recommendation?—to accompany the artist, and to supply the reading matter, the letter-press I think you call it; in fact, to write up to our illustrator's pictures; and that he is to be decently paid for his trouble. He must do something graphic, something stirring, something to wake up lazy people in the West End to a passing sense of what he calls their responsibilities. That'll seem like real work to Mr. Le Breton. It'll put new heart into him; he'll take up the matter vigorously; he'll do it well; he'll write a splendid book; and I shall guarantee its making a stir in the world this very dull season. What's the use of knowing half the odiously common-place bores and prigs in all London if you can't float a single little heterodox pamphlet for a particular purpose? What do you think of it, Mr. Berkeley?'

Arthur sighed again. 'It seems to me, Lady Hilda,' he said, regretfully, 'a very slender straw indeed to hang Ernest Le Breton's life on: but any straw is better than nothing to a drowning man. And you have so much faith yourself, and mean to fling yourself into it so earnestly, that I shouldn't be wholly surprised if you were somehow to pull it through. If you do, Lady Hilda—if you manage to save these two poor young people from the verge of starvation—you'll have done a very great good work in your day, and you'll have made me personally eternally your debtor.'

Was it mere fancy, the Progenitor wondered, or did Hilda cast her eyes down a little and half blush as she answered in a lower and more tremulous tone than usual, 'I hope I shall, Mr. Berkeley; for their sakes, I hope I shall.' The Progenitor didn't feel quite certain about it, but somehow, more than once that evening, as he sat reading Spencer's 'Data of Ethics' in his easy-chair, a curious vision of Lady Hilda as a future daughter-in-law floated vaguely with singular persistence before the old shoemaker's bewildered eyes. 'It'd be a shocking falling away on Artie's part from his father's principles,' he muttered inarticulately to himself several times over; 'and yet, on the other hand, I can't deny that this bit of a Tregellis girl is really a very tidy, good-looking, respectable, well-meaning, intelligent, and appreciative sort of a young woman, who'd, maybe, make Artie as good a wife as anybody else he'd be likely to pitch on.'

Grant Allen

CHAPTER XXXV

THE TIDE TURNS

When Ernest Le Breton got a letter from the business house of a well-known publishing firm, asking him whether he would consent to supply appropriate letterpress for an illustrated work on the poor of London, then in course of preparation, his delight and relief were positively unbounded. That anyone should come and ask him for work, instead of his asking them, was in itself a singular matter for surprise and congratulation; that the request should be based on the avowed ground of his known political and social opinions was almost incredible. Ernest felt that it was a triumph, not only for him, but for his dearly-loved principles and beliefs as well. For the first time in his life, he was going to undertake a piece of work which he not only thought not wrong, but even considered hopeful and praise-worthy. Arthur Berkeley, who called round as if by accident the same morning, saw with delight that Lady Hilda's prognostication seemed likely to be fulfilled, and that if only Ernest could be given some congenial occupation there was still a chance, after all, for his permanent recovery; for it was clear enough that as there was hope, there must be a little life yet left in him.

It was Lady Hilda who, as she herself expressively phrased it, had squared the publishers. She had called upon the head of the well-known house in person, and had told him fully and frankly exactly what was the nature of the interest she took in the poor of London. At first the publisher was scandalised and obdurate: the thing was not regular, he said—not in the ordinary way of business; his firm couldn't go writing letters of that sort to unknown young authors and artists. If she wanted the work done, she must let them give her own name as the promoter of the undertaking. But Hilda persevered, as she always did; she smiled, pleaded, cajoled, threatened, and made desperate love to the publisher to gain his acquiescence in her benevolent scheme. After all, even publishers are only human (though authors have been frequently known to deny the fact); and human nature, especially in England, is apt to be very little proof against the entreaties of a pretty girl who happens also to be an earl's daughter. So in the end, when Lady Hilda said most bewitchingly, 'I put it upon the grounds of a personal favour, Mr. Percival,' the obdurate publisher gave way at last, and consented to do her bidding gladly.

For six weeks Ernest went daily with Ronald and the young artist into the familiar slums of Bethnal Green, and Bermondsey, and Lambeth, whose ins and outs he was beginning to know with painful accuracy; and every night he came back, and wrote down with a glowing pen all that he had seen and heard of distressing and terrible during his day's peregrination. It was an awful task from one point of view, for the scenes he had to visit and describe were often heart-rending; and Arthur feared more than once that the air of so many loathsome and noxious dens might still further accelerate the progress of Ernest's disease; but Lady Hilda said emphatically, No; and somehow Arthur was beginning now to conceive an immense respect for the practical value of Lady Hilda's vehement opinions. As a matter of fact, indeed, Ernest did not visibly suffer at all either from the unwonted hard work or from the strain upon mind and body to which he had been so little accustomed. Distressing as it all was, it was change, it was variety, it was occupation, it was relief from that terrible killing round of perpetual personal responsibility. Above all, Ernest really believed that here at last was an opportunity of doing some practical good in his generation, and he threw himself into it with all the passionate ardour of a naturally eager and vivid nature. The enthusiasm of humanity was upon him, and it kept him going at high-pressure rate, with no apparent loss of strength and vigour throughout the whole ordeal. To Arthur Berkeley's intense delight, he was even visibly fatter to the naked eye at the end of his six weeks' exploration of the most dreary and desolate slums in all London.

The book was written at white heat, as the best of such books always are, and it was engraved and printed at the very shortest possible notice. Terrible and ghastly it certainly was at last—instinct with all the grim local colouring of those narrow, squalid, fever-stricken dens, where misfortune and crime huddle together indiscriminately in dirt and misery—a book to make one's blood run cold with awe and disgust, and to stir up even the callous apathy of the great rich capitalist West End to a passing moment's ineffective remorse; but very clever and very graphic after its own sort beyond the shadow of a question, for all its horror. When Arthur Berkeley turned over the first proof-sheets of 'London's Shame,' with its simple yet thrilling recital of true tales taken down from the very lips of outcast children or stranded women, with its awful woodcuts and still more awful descriptions—word-pictures reeking with the vice and filth and degradation of the most pestilent, overcrowded, undrained tenements—he felt instinctively that Ernest Le Breton's book would not need the artificial aid of Lady Hilda's influential friends in order to make it successful and even famous. The Cabinet ministers might be as silent as they chose, the indignant duke might confine his denunciations to the attentive and sympathetic ear of his friend Lord Connemara; but nothing on earth could prevent Ernest Le Breton's fiery and scathing diatribe from immediately enthralling the public attention. Lady Hilda had hit upon the exact subject which best suited his peculiar character and temperament, and he had done himself full justice in it. Not that Ernest had ever thought of himself, or even of his style, or the effect he was producing by his narrative; it was just the very non-self-consciousness of the thing that gave it its power. He wrote down the simple thoughts that came up into his own eager mind at the sight of so much inequality and injustice; and the motto that Arthur prefixed upon the title-page, 'Facit indignatio versum,' aptly described the key-note of that fierce and angry final denunciation. 'Yes, Lady Hilda had certainly hit the right nail on the head,' Arthur Berkeley said to himself more than once: 'A wonderful woman, truly, that beautiful, stately, uncompromising, brilliant, and still really tender Hilda Tregellis.'

Hilda, on her part, worked hard and well for the success of Ernest's book as soon as it appeared. Nay, she even condescended (not being what Ernest himself would have described as an ethical unit) to practise a little gentle hypocrisy in suiting her recommendations of 'London's Shame' to the tastes and feelings of her various acquaintances. To her Radical Cabinet minister friend, she openly praised its outspoken zeal for the cause of the people, and its value as a wonderful storehouse of useful facts at first hand for political purposes in the increasingly important outlying Metropolitan boroughs. 'Just think, Sir Edmund,' she said, persuasively, 'how you could crush any Conservative candidate for Hackney or the Tower Hamlets out of that awful chapter on the East End match-makers;' while with the Duke, to whom she presented a marked copy as a sample of what our revolutionary thinkers were really coming to, she insisted rather upon its wicked interference with the natural rights of landlords, and its abominable insinuation (so subversive of all truly English ideas as to liberty and property) that they were bound not to poison their tenants by total neglect of sanitary precautions. 'If I were you, now,' she said to the Duke in the most seemingly simple-minded manner possible, 'I'd just quote those passages I've marked in pencil in the House to-night on the Small Urban Holdings Bill, and point out how the wave of Continental Socialism is at last invading England with its devastating flood.' And the Duke, who was a complacent, thick-headed, obstinate old gentleman, congenitally incapable of looking at any question from any other point of view whatsoever except that of his own order, fell headlong passively into Lady Hilda's cruel little trap, and murmured to himself as he rolled down luxuriously to the august society of his peers that evening, 'Tremendous clever girl, Hilda Tregellis, really. "Wave of Continental Socialism at last invading England with its what-you-may-call-it flood," she said, if I remember rightly. Capital sentence to end off one's speech with, I declare. Devizes'll positively wonder where I got it from. I'd no idea before that girl took such an intelligent interest in political questions. So they want their cottages whitewashed, do they? What'll they ask for next, I wonder? Do they think we're to be content at last with one and a-half per cent, upon the fee-simple value of our estates, I should like to know? Why, some of the places this writer-fellow talks about are on my own property in The Rookery—"one of the most noisome court-yards in all London," he actually calls it. Whitewash their cottages, indeed! The lazy improvident creatures! They'll be asking us to put down encaustic tiles upon the floors next, and to paper their walls with Japanese leather or fashionable dados. Really, the general ignorance that prevails among the working classes as to the clearest principles of political economy is something absolutely appalling, absolutely appalling.' And his Grace scribbled a note in his memorandum-book of Hilda's ready-made peroration, for fear he should forget its precise wording before he began to give the House the benefit of his views that night upon the political economy of Small Urban Holdings.

Next morning, all London was talking of the curious coincidence by which a book from the pen of an unknown author, published only one day previously, had been quoted and debated upon simultaneously in both Houses of Parliament on a single evening. In the Commons, Sir Edmund Calverley, the distinguished Radical minister, had read a dozen pages from the unknown work in his declamatory theatrical fashion, and had so electrified the House with its graphic and horrible details that even Mr. Fitzgerald-Grenville, the well-known member for the Baroness Drummond-Lloyd (whose rotten or at least decomposing borough of Cherbury Minor he faithfully represented in three successive Parliaments), had mumbled out a few half-inaudible apologetic sentences about this state of things being truly deplorable, and about the necessity for meeting such a distressing social crisis by the prompt and vigorous application of that excellent specific and familiar panacea, a spirited foreign policy. In the Lords, the Duke himself, by some untoward coincidence, had been moved to make a few quotations, accompanied by a running fire of essentially ducal criticism, from the very selfsame obscure author; and to his immense surprise, even the members of his own party moved uneasily in their seats during the course of his speech; while later in the evening, Lord Devizes muttered to him angrily in the robing-room, 'Look here, Duke, you've been and put your foot in it, I assure you, about that Radical book you were ill-advised enough to quote from. You ought never to have treated the Small Urban Holdings Bill in the way you did; and just you mark my words, the papers'll all be down upon you to-morrow morning, as sure as daylight. You've given the "Bystander" such an opening against you as you'll never forget till your dying day, I can tell you.' And as the Duke drove back again after his arduous legislative efforts that evening, he said to himself between the puffs at his Havana, 'This comes, now, of allowing oneself to be made a fool of by a handsome woman. How the dooce I could ever have gone and taken Hilda Tregellis's advice on a political question is really more than I can fathom:—and at my time of life too! And yet, all the same, there's no denying that she's a devilish fine woman, by Jove, if ever there was one.'

Of course, everybody asked themselves next day what this book 'London's Shame' was like, and who on earth its author could be; so much so, indeed, that a large edition was completely exhausted within a fortnight. It was the great sensational success of that London season. Everybody read it, discussed it, dissected it, corroborated it, refuted it, fought over it, and wrote lengthy letters to all the daily papers about its faults and its merits. Imitators added their sincerest flattery: rivals proclaimed themselves the original discoverers of 'London's Shame': one enterprising author even thought of going to law about it as a question of copyright. Owners of noisome lanes in the East End trembled in their shoes, and sent their agents to inquire into the precise degree of squalor to be found in the filthy courts and alleys where they didn't care to trust their own sensitive aristocratic noses. It even seemed as if a little real good was going to come at last out of Ernest Le Breton's impassioned pleading—as if the sensation were going to fall not quite flat at the end of its short run in the clubs and drawing-rooms of London as a nine days' wonder.

And Ernest Le Breton? and Edie? In the little lodgings at Holloway, they sat first trembling for the result, and ready to burst with excitement when Lady Hilda, up at the unwonted hour of six in the morning, tore into their rooms with an early copy of the 'Times' to show them the Duke's speech, and Sir Edmund's quotations, and the editorial leader in which even that most dignified and reticent of British journals condescended to speak with studiously moderated praise of the immense collection of facts so ably strung together by Mr. Ernest Le Breton (in all the legible glory of small capitals, too,) as to the undoubtedly disgraceful condition of some at least among our London alleys. How Edie clung around Lady Hilda and kissed her! and how Lady Hilda kissed her back and cried over her with tears of happier augury! and how they both kissed and cried over unconscious wondering little Dot! And how Lady Hilda could almost have fallen upon Ernest, too, as he sat gazing in blank astonishment and delight at his own name in the magnificent small capitals of a 'Times' leader. Between crying and laughing, with much efficient aid in both from good Mrs. Halliss, they hardly knew how they ever got through the long delightful hours of that memorable epoch-making morning.

And then there came the gradual awakening to the fact that this was really fame—fame, and perhaps also competence. First in the field, of course, was the editor of the 'Cosmopolitan Review,' with a polite request that Ernest would give the readers of that intensely hot-and-hot and thoughtful periodical the opportunity of reading his valuable views on the East End outcast question, before they had had time to be worth nothing for journalistic purposes, through the natural and inevitable cooling of the public interest in this new sensation. Then his old friends of the 'Morning Intelligence' once more begged that he would be good enough to contribute a series of signed and headed articles to their columns, on the slums and fever dens of poverty-stricken London. Next, an illustrated weekly asked him to join with his artist friend in getting up another pilgrimage into yet undiscovered metropolitan plague-spots. And so, before the end of a month, Ernest Le Breton, for the first time in his life, had really got more work to do than he could easily manage, and work, too, that he felt he could throw his whole life and soul into with perfect honesty.

When the first edition of 'London's Shame' was exhausted, there was already a handsome balance to go to Ernest and his artist coadjutor, who, by the terms of the agreement, were to divide between them half the profits. The other half, for appearance' sake, Lady Hilda and Arthur had been naturally compelled to reserve for themselves: for of course it would not have been probable that any publisher would have undertaken the work without any hope of profit in any way. Arthur called upon Hilda at Lord Exmoor's house in Wilton Place to show her the first balance-sheet and accompanying cheque. 'What on earth can we do with it?' he asked seriously. 'We can't divide it between us: and yet we can't give it to the poor Le Bretons. I don't see how we're to manage.'

'Why, of course,' Hilda answered promptly. 'Put it into the Consols or whatever you call it, for the benefit of little Dot.'

'The very thing!' Arthur answered in a tone of obvious admiration. 'What a wonderfully practical person you really are, Lady Hilda.'

As to Ernest and Edie, when they got their own cheque for their quarter of the proceeds, they gazed in awe and astonishment at the bigness of the figure; and then they sat down and cried together like two children, with their hands locked in one another's.

'And you'll get well, now, Ernest dear,' Edie whispered gently. 'Why, you're ever so much fatter, darling, already. I'm sure you'll get well in no time, now, Ernest.'

Grant Allen

'Upon my word, Edie,' Ernest answered, kissing her white forehead tenderly, 'I really and truly believe I shall. It's my opinion that Sir Antony Wraxall's an unmitigated ignorant humbug.'

A few weeks later, when Ernest's remarkable article on 'How to Improve the Homes of the Poor' appeared in one of the leading magazines, Mr. Herbert Le Breton of the Education Office looked up from his cup of post-prandial coffee in his comfortable dining-room at South Kensington, and said musingly to his young wife, 'Do you know, Ethel, it seems to me that my brother Ernest's going to score a success at last with this slum-hunting business that he's lately invented. There's an awful lot about it now in all the papers and reviews. Perhaps it might be as well, after all, to scrape an acquaintance with him again, especially as he's my own brother. There's no knowing, really, when a man of his peculiar ill-regulated mercurial temperament may be going to turn out famous. Don't you think you'd better find out where they're living now—they've left Holloway, no doubt, since this turn of the tide—and go and call upon Mrs. Ernest?'

Whereto Mrs. Herbert Le Breton, raising her eyes for a moment from the pages of her last new novel, answered languidly: 'Don't you think, Herbert, it'd be better to wait a little while and see how things turn out with them in the long run, you know, before we commit ourselves by going to call upon them? One swallow, you see, doesn't make a summer, does it, dear, ever?' Whence the acute and intelligent reader will doubtless conclude that Mrs. Herbert Le Breton was a very prudent sensible young woman, and that perhaps even Herbert himself had met at last with his fitting Nemesis. For what worse purgatory could his bitterest foe wish for a selfishly prudent and cold-hearted man, than that he should pass his whole lifetime in congenial intercourse with a selfishly prudent and cold-hearted wife, exactly after his own pattern?

CHAPTER XXXVI

OUT OF THE HAND OP THE PHILISTINES

Ernest's unexpected success with 'London's Shame' was not, as Arthur Berkeley at first feared it might be, the mere last dying flicker of a weak and failing life. Arthur was quite right, indeed, when he said one day to Lady Hilda that its very brilliancy and fervour had the hectic glow about it, as of a man who was burning himself out too fiercely and rapidly; you could read the feverish eagerness of the writer in every line; but still, Lady Hilda answered with her ordinary calm assurance that it was all going well, and that Ernest only needed the sense of security to pull him round again; and as usual, Lady Hilda's practical sagacity was not at fault. The big pamphlet—for it was hardly more than that—soon proved an opening for further work, in procuring which Hilda and Arthur were again partially instrumental. An advanced Radical member of Parliament, famous for his declamations against the capitalist faction, and his enormous holding of English railway stock, was induced to come forward as the founder of a new weekly paper, 'in the interest of social reform.' Of course the thing was got up solely with an idea to utilising Ernest as editor, for, said the great anti-capitalist with his usual charming frankness, 'the young fellow has a positive money-value, now, if he's taken in hand at once before the sensation's over, and there can be no harm in turning an honest penny by exploiting him, you know, and starting a popular paper.' When Ernest was offered the post of editor to the new periodical, at a salary which almost alarmed him by its plutocratic magnificence (for it was positively no less than six hundred a year), he felt for a moment some conscientious scruples about accepting so splendid a post. And when Lady Hilda in her emphatic fashion promptly over-ruled these nascent scruples by the application of the very simple solvent formula, 'Bosh!' he felt bound at least to stipulate that he should be at perfect liberty to say whatever he liked in the new paper, without interference or supervision from the capitalist proprietor. To which the Radical member, in his business capacity, immediately responded, 'Why, certainly. What we want to pay you for is just your power of startling people, which, in its proper place, is a very useful marketable commodity. Every pig has its value—if only you sell it in the best market.'

'The Social Reformer, a Weekly Advocate of the New Economy,' achieved at once an immense success among the working classes, and grew before long to be one of the most popular journals of the second rank in all London. The interest that Ernest had aroused by his big pamphlet was carried on to his new venture, which soon managed to gain many readers by its own intrinsic merits. 'Seen your brother's revolutionary broadsheet, Le Breton?' asked a friend at the club of Herbert not many weeks later—he was the same person who had found it 'so very embarrassing' to recognise Ernest—in his shabby days when walking with a Q.C.—'It's a dreadful tissue of the reddest French communism, I believe, but still, it's scored the biggest success of its sort in journalism, I'm told, since the days of Kenealy's "Englishman." Bradbury, who's found the money to start it—deuced clever fellow in his way, Bradbury!—is making an awful lot out of the speculation, they say. What do you think of the paper, eh?'

Herbert drew himself up grimly. 'To tell you the truth,' he said in his stiffest style, 'I haven't yet had time to look at a copy. Ernest Le Breton's not a man in whose affairs I feel called upon to take any special interest; and I haven't put myself to the trouble of reading his second-hand political lucubrations. Faint echoes of Max Schurz, all of it, no doubt; and having read and disposed of Schurz himself long ago, I don't feel inclined now to go in for a second supplementary course of Schurz and water.'

'Well, well, that may be so,' the friend answered, turning over the pages of the peccant periodical carelessly; 'but all the same I'm afraid your brother's really going to do an awful lot of mischief in the way of setting class against class, and stirring up the dangerous orders to recognise their own power. You see, Le Breton, the real danger of this sort of thing lies in the fact that your brother Ernest's a more or less educated and cultivated person. I don't say he's really got any genuine depth of culture—would you believe it, he told me once he'd never read Rabelais, and didn't want to?—and of course a man of true culture in the grain, like you and me now, my dear fellow, would never dream of going and mistaking these will-o'-the-wisps of socialism for the real guiding light of regenerated humanity—of course not. But the dangerous symptom at the present day lies just in the fact that while the papers written for the mob used to be written by vulgar, noisy, self-made, half-educated demagogues, they're sent out now with all the authority and specious respectability of decently instructed and comparatively literary English gentlemen. Now, nobody can deny that that's a thing very seriously to be regretted; and for my part I'm extremely sorry your brother has been ill-advised enough to join the mob that's trying to pull down our comfortably built and after all eminently respectable, even if somewhat patched up, old British constitution.'

'The subject's one,' Herbert answered curtly, 'in which I for my part cannot pretend to feel the remotest personal interest.'

Ernest and Edie, however, in the little lodgings up at Holloway, which they couldn't bear to desert even now in this sudden burst of incredible prosperity, went their own way as self-containedly as usual, wholly unconcerned by the non-arrival of Mrs. Herbert on a visit of ceremony, or the failure of the 'Social Reformer' to pierce the lofty ethereal regions of abstract contemplation where Herbert himself sat throned like an Epicurean god in the pure halo of cultivated pococurantism. Every day, as that eminent medical authority, Hilda Tregellis, had truly prophesied, Ernest's cheeks grew less and less sunken, and a little colour returned slowly to their midst; while Edie's face was less pale than of old, and her smile began to recover something of its old-fashioned girlish joyousness. She danced about once more as of old, and Arthur Berkeley, when he dropped in of a Sunday afternoon for a chat with Ernest, noticed with pleasure that little Miss Butterfly was beginning to flit round again almost as naturally as in the old days when he first saw her light little form among the grey old pillars of Magdalen Cloisters. Yet he couldn't help observing, too, that his feeling towards her was more one of mere benevolence now, and less of tender regret, than it used to be even a few short months before, in the darkest days of Edie's troubles. Could it be, he asked himself more than once, that the tall stately picture of Hilda Tregellis was overshadowing in his heart the natural photograph of that unwedded Edie Oswald that he once imagined was so firmly imprinted there? Ah well, ah well, it may be true that a man can love really but once in his whole lifetime; and yet, the second spurious imitation is positively sometimes a very good facsimile of the genuine first impression, for all that.

As the months went slowly round, too, the time came in the end for good Herr Max to be released at last from his long imprisonment. On the day that he came out, there was a public banquet at the Marylebone dancing saloon; and all the socialists and communards were there, and all the Russian nihilists, and all the other wicked revolutionary plotters in all London: and in the chair sat Ernest Le Breton, now the editor of an important social paper, while at his left hand, to balance the guest of the evening, sat Arthur Berkeley, the well-known dramatic author, who was himself more than suspected of being the timid Nicodemus of the new faith. And when Ernest announced that Herr Schurz had consented to aid him on the 'Social Reformer,' and to add the wisdom of age to the impetuosity of youth in conducting its future, the simple enthusiasm of the wicked revolutionists knew no bounds. And they cried 'Hoch!' and 'Viva!' and 'Hooray!' and many other like inarticulate shouts in many varieties of interjectional dialect all the evening; and everybody agreed that after all Herr Max was VERY little grayer than before the trial, in spite of his long and terrible term of imprisonment.

He WAS a little embittered by his troubles, no doubt;—what can you expect if you clap men in prison for the expression of their honest political convictions?—but Ernest tried to keep his eye steadily rather on the future than on the past; and with greater ease and unwonted comforts the old man's cheerfulness as well as his enthusiasm gradually returned. 'I'm too old now to do anything more worth doing myself before I die,' he used to say, holding Ernest's arm tightly in his vice-like grip: 'but I have great hopes in spite of everything for friend Ernest; I have very great hopes indeed for friend Ernest here. There's no knowing yet what he may accomplish.'

Ernest only smiled a trifle sadly, and murmured half to himself that this was a hard world, and he began himself to fear there was no fitting feeling for a social reformer except one of a brave despair. 'We can do little or nothing, after all,' he said slowly; 'and our only consolation must be that even that little is perhaps just worth doing.'

Grant Allen

CHAPTER XXXVII

LAND AT LAST: BUT WHAT LAND?

Long before the 'Social Reformer' had fully made its mark in
the world, another event had happened of no less importance
to some of the chief actors in the little drama whose natural
termination it seemed to form. While the pamphlet and the
paper were in course of maturation, Arthur Berkeley had been
running daily in and out of the house in Wilton Place in what
Lady Exmoor several times described as a positively disgraceful
and unseemly manner. ('What Hilda can mean,' her ladyship
observed to her husband more than once, 'by encouraging that
odd young man's extraordinary advances in the way she does is
really more than I can understand even in her.') But when the
Le Bretons were fairly launched at last on the favourable flood
of full prosperity, both Hilda and Arthur began to feel as
though they had suddenly been deprived of a very pleasant
common interest. After all, benevolent counsel on behalf of
other people is not so entirely innocent and impersonal in
certain cases as it seems to be at first sight. 'Do you know,
Lady Hilda,' Berkeley said one afternoon, when he had come
to pay, as it were, a sort of farewell visit, on the final comple-
tion of their joint schemes for restoring happiness to the home
of the Le Bretons, 'our intercourse together has been very
delightful, and I'm quite sorry to think that in future we must
see so much less of one another than we've been in the habit of
doing for the last month or so.'

Hilda looked at him straight and said in her own frank

unaffected fashion, 'So am I, Mr. Berkeley, very sorry, very sorry indeed.'

Arthur looked back at her once more, and their eyes met. His look was full of admiration, and Hilda saw it. She moved a little uneasily upon the ottoman, waiting apparently as though she expected Arthur to say something else. But Arthur looked at her long and steadfastly, and said nothing.

At last he seemed to wake from his reverie, and make up his mind for a desperate venture. Could he be mistaken? Could he have read either record wrong—his own heart, or Hilda's eyes? No, no, both of them spoke to him too plainly and evidently. His heart was fluttering like a wind-shaken aspen-leaf; and Hilda's eyes were dimming visibly with a tender moisture. Yes, yes, yes, there was no misreading possible. He knew he loved her! he knew she loved him!

Bending over towards where Hilda sat, he took her hand in his dreamily: and Hilda let him take it without a movement. Then he looked deeply into her eyes, and felt a curious speechlessness coming over him, deep down in the ball of his throat.

'Lady Hilda,' he began at last with an effort, in a low voice, not wholly untinged with natural timidity, 'Lady Hilda, is a working man's son—'

Hilda looked back at him with a sudden look of earnest deprecation. 'Not that way, Mr. Berkeley,' she said quietly: 'not that way, please: you'll hurt me if you do: you know that's not the way *I* look at the matter. Why not simply "Hilda"?'

Berkeley clasped her hand eagerly and raised it to his lips. 'Hilda, then,' he said, kissing it twice over. 'It SHALL be Hilda.'

Hilda rose and stood before him erect in all her queenlike beauty. 'So now that's settled,' she said, with a vain endeavour to control her tears of joy. 'Don't let's talk about it any more, now; I can't bear to talk about it: there's nothing to arrange, Arthur. Whenever you like will suit me. But, oh, I'm so happy, so happy, so happy—I never thought I could be so happy.'

'Nor I,' Arthur answered, holding her hand a moment in his tenderly.

'How strange,' Hilda said again, after a minute's delicious silence; 'it's the poor Le Bretons who have brought us two thus together. And yet, they were both once our dearest rivals. YOU were in love with Edie Le Breton: I was half in love with Ernest Le Breton: and now—why, now, Arthur, I DO believe we're both utterly in love with one another. What a curious little comedy of errors!'

'And yet only a few months ago it came very near being a tragedy, rather,' Arthur put in softly.

'Never mind!' Hilda answered in her brightest and most joyous tone, as she wiped the joyful tears from her eyes. 'It isn't a tragedy, now, after all, Arthur, and all's well that ends well!'

When the Countess heard of Hilda's determination—Hilda didn't pretend to go through the domestic farce of asking her mother's consent to her approaching marriage—she said that so far as she was concerned a more shocking or un-Christian piece of conduct on the part of a well-brought-up girl had never yet been brought to her knowledge. To refuse Lord Connemara, and then go and marry the son of a common cobbler! But the Earl only puffed away vigorously at his cheroot, and observed philosophically that for his part he just considered himself jolly well out of it. This young fellow Berkeley mightn't be a man of the sort of family Hilda would naturally expect to marry into, but he was decently educated and in good society, and above all, a gentleman, you know, don't you know: and, hang it all, in these days that's really everything. Besides, Berkeley was making a pot of money out of these operas of his, the Earl understood, and as he had always expected that Hilda'd marry some penniless painter or somebody of that sort, and be a perpetual drag upon the family exchequer, he really didn't see why they need trouble their heads very much about it. By George, if it came to that, he rather congratulated himself that the girl hadn't taken it into her nonsensical head to run away with the groom or the stable-boy! As to Lynmouth, he merely remarked succinctly in his own dialect, 'Go it, Hilda, go it, my beauty! You always were a one-er, you know, and it's my belief you always will be.'

It was somewhere about the same time that Ronald Le Breton, coming back gladdened in soul from a cheerful talk with Ernest, called round of an evening in somewhat unwonted exultation at Selah's lodgings. 'Selah,' he said to her calmly, as she met him at the door to let him in herself, 'I want to have a little talk with you.'

'What is it about, Ronald?' Selah asked, with a perfect consciousness in her own mind of what the subject he wished to discourse about was likely to be.

'Why, Selah,' Ronald went on in his quiet, matter-of-fact, unobtrusive manner, 'do you know, I think we may fairly consider Ernest and Edie out of danger now.'

'I hope so, Ronald,' Selah answered imperturbably. 'I've no doubt your brother'll get along all right in future, and I'm sure at least that he's getting stronger, for he looks ten per cent. better than he did three months ago.'

'Well, Selah!'

'Well, Ronald!'

'Why, in that case, you see, your objection falls to the ground. There can be no possible reason on either side why you should any longer put off marrying me. We needn't consider Edie now; and you can't have any reasonable doubt that I want to marry you for your own sake this time.'

'What a nuisance the man is!' Selah cried impetuously. 'Always bothering a body out of her nine senses to go and marry him. Have you never read what Paul says, that it's good for the unmarried and widows to abide? He was always dead against the advisability of marriage, Paul was.'

'Brother Paul was an able and earnest preacher,' Ronald murmured gravely, 'from whose authority I should be sorry to dissent except for sufficient and weighty reason; but you must admit that on this particular question he was prejudiced, Selah, decidedly prejudiced, and that the balance of the best opinion goes distinctly the other way.'

Selah laughed lightly. 'Oh, does it?' she said, in her provoking, mocking manner. 'Then you propose to marry me, I suppose, on the balance of the best Scriptural opinion.'

'Not at all, Selah,' Ronald replied without a touch of anything but grave earnestness in his tone—it must be admitted Ronald was distinctly lacking in the sense of humour. 'Not at all, I assure you. I propose to marry you because I love you, and I believe in your heart of hearts you love me, too, you provoking girl, though you're too proud or too incomprehensible ever to acknowledge it.'

'And even if I do?' Selah asked. 'What then?'

'Why, then, Selah,' Ronald answered confidently, taking her hand boldly in his own and actually kissing her—yes, kissing her; 'why, then, Selah, suppose we say Monday fortnight?'

'It's awfully soon,' Selah replied, half grumbling. 'You don't give a body time to think it over.'

'Certainly not,' Ronald responded, quickly, taking the hand-some face firmly between his two spare hands, and kissing her lips half a dozen times over in rapid succession.

'Let me go, Ronald,' Selah cried, struggling to be free, and trying in vain to tear down his thin wiry arms with her own strong shapely hands. 'Let me go at once,—there's a good boy, and I'll marry you on Monday fortnight, or do anything else you like, just to keep you quiet. After all, you're a kind-hearted fellow enough, and you want looking after and taking care of, and if you insist upon it, I don't mind giving way to you in this small matter.'

Ronald stepped back a pace or two, and stood looking at her a little sadly with his hands folded. 'Oh, Selah,' he cried in a tone of bitter disappointment, 'don't speak like that to me, don't, please. Don't, don't tell me that you don't really love me—that you're going to marry me for nothing else but out of mere compassion for my weakness and helplessness!'

Selah burst at once into a wild flood of uncontrollable tears: 'Oh, Ronald,' she cried in her old almost fiercely passionate manner, flinging her arms around his neck and covering him with kisses; 'Oh, Ronald, how can you ever ask me whether I really really love you! You know I love you! You know I love you! You've given me back life and everything that's dear in it, and I never want to live for anything any longer except to love you, and wait upon you, and make you happy. I'm stronger than you, Ronald, and I shall be able to do a little to make you happy, I do believe. My ways are not your ways, nor my thoughts your thoughts, my darling; but I love you all the better for that, Ronald, I love you all the better for that; and if you were to kick me, beat me, trample on me now, Ronald, I should love you, love you, love you for ever still.'

So they two were quietly married, with no audience save Ernest and Edie, on that very Monday fortnight.

When Herbert Le Breton heard of it from his mother a few days later, he went home at once to his own eminently cultured home and told Mrs. Le Breton the news, of course without much detailed allusion to Selah's earlier antecedents. 'And do you know, Ethel,' he added significantly, 'I think it was an excellent thing that you decided not to call after all upon Ernest's wife, for I'm sure it'll be a great deal safer for you and me to have nothing to say in any way to the whole faction of them. A greengrocer's daughter, you know—quite unpresentable. They'll be all mixed up together in future, which'll make it quite impossible to know the one without at the same time knowing the other. Now, it'd be just practicable for you to call upon Mrs. Ernest, I must admit, but to call upon Mrs. Ronald would be really and truly too inconceivable.'

At the end of the first year of the 'Social Reformer,' the annual balance was duly audited, and it showed a very considerable and solid surplus to go into the pocket of the enterprising Radical proprietor. Ernest and Herr Max scanned it closely together, and even Ernest could not refrain from a smile of pleasure when he saw how thoroughly successful the doubtful venture had finally turned out. 'And yet,' he said regretfully, as he looked at the heavy balance-sheet, 'what a strange occupation after all for the author of "Gold and the Proletariate," to be looking carefully over the sum-total of a capitalist's final balance! To think, too, that all that money has come out of the hard-earned scraped-up pennies of the toiling poor! I often wish, Herr Max, that even so I had been brought up an honest shoemaker! But whether I'm really earning my salt at the hands of humanity now or not is a deep problem I often have many an uncomfortable internal sigh over to this day.'

'There is work and work, friend Ernest,' Herr Max answered, as gently as had been his wont in older years; 'and for my part it seems to me you are better here writing your Social Reformers than making shoes for a single generation. One man builds for to-day, another man builds for to-morrow; and he that plants a fruit tree for his children to eat of is doing as much good work in the world as he that sows the corn in spring to be reaped and eaten at this autumn's harvest.'

'Perhaps so,' Ernest answered softly. 'I wish I could think so. But after all I'm not quite sure whether, if we had all starved eighteen months ago together, as seemed so likely then, it wouldn't have been the most right thing in the end that could possibly have happened to all of us. As things are constituted now, there seems only one life that's really worth living for an honest man, and that's a martyr's. A martyr's or else a worker's. And I, I greatly fear, have managed somehow to miss being either. The wind carries us this way and that, and when we would do that which is right, it drifts us away incontinently into that which is only profitable.'

'Dear Ernest,' Edie cried in her bright old-fashioned manner from the ofice door, 'Dot has come in her new frock to bring Daddy home for her birthday dinner as she was promised. Come quick, or your little daughter'll be very angry with you. And Lady Hilda Berkeley has come, too, to drive us back in her own brougham. Now don't be a silly, there's a dear, or say that you can't drive away from the office of the "Social Reformer" in Lady Hilda's brougham!'